PENGUIN BOOKS

THE CHARMER

Patrick Hamilton, universally known as the author of *Rope, Gaslight,* and *Hangover Square,* was one of the most gifted and admired writers of his generation. Born in Hassocks, Sussex, England, during the first decade of this century, he and his parents moved shortly afterwards to Hove, where he passed his formative years. He published his first novel in 1926 and within a few years had established a wide readership for himself. It seemed as though his reputation was assured, but personal setbacks and an increasing problem with drink overshadowed this certainty. Yet in spite of these pressures he was able to produce some of his best work, the seeds of his own despair almost feeding his vision, sense of loss and isolation underlying his tragi-comic creations. He died in 1962.

PATRICK HAMILTON

THE CHARMER

PENGUIN BOOKS

PENGUIN BOOKS
Published by the Penguin Group
Viking Penguin Inc., 40 West 23rd Street,
New York, New York, 10010, U.S.A.
Penguin Books Ltd, 27 Wrights Lane,
London W8 5TZ, England
Penguin Books Australia Ltd, Ringwood,
Victoria, Australia
Penguin Books Canada Ltd, 2801 John Street,
Markham, Ontario, Canada L3R 1B4
Penguin Books (N.Z.) Ltd, 182–190 Wairau Road,
Auckland 10, New Zealand

Penguin Books Ltd, Registered Offices:
Harmondsworth, Middlesex, England

First published in Great Britain as
Mr. Stimpson and Mr. Gorse by Constable & Co. 1953
Published in Penguin Books 1989

1 3 5 7 9 10 8 6 4 2

LIBRARY OF CONGRESS CATALOGING IN PUBLICATION DATA
Hamilton, Patrick, 1904-1962.
The charmer.
Originally published as: Mr. Stimpson and Mr. Gorse.
I. Title.
PR6015.A4644M55   1989   823'.912   88-28915
ISBN 0 14 01.2043 2 (pbk.)

Printed in the United States of America
Set in Sabon (Lasercomp)

CONTENTS

All the characters in this book are entirely imaginary. So also are Mr Stimpson's Crossword Puzzles, the clues to which the reader is advised not to be beguiled into attempting to solve.

PART ONE

WIDOW OF A COLONEL

CHAPTER ONE

I

THERE are, clearly, in England and all over the world, countless Colonels with hard-working, valiant and enchanting characters. Why, then, is the thought or mention of a 'Colonel', purely in the abstract, faintly laughable, or even faintly displeasing, in some people's minds?

Why, for instance, did the eminent cartoonist, Low, make Colonel Blimp a Colonel, rather than a Captain, say, or an officer holding a different rank?

Colonel Blimp, of course, though laughable, was to a very large extent lovable. Many people, however, do not think of Colonels as being in any way lovable. Such people, on the contrary, can only picture Colonels either as moustached bullies bawling at men on parade grounds, or as uttering idiotic, outmoded and reactionary sentiments from the armchairs of Clubs. A progressive Colonel, to such people, is practically inconceivable.

Colonels are also famous for being 'retired'.

An ordinary man is permitted to retire in an aura of dignity and, often, of distinction – but such is not quite the case with Colonels.

'Retired' Colonels have, perhaps, brought about the faint ignominy attached to their retirement upon themselves. So many of them, for instance, have become seedy, inactive men committing the grave social error of permitting or encouraging themselves to be addressed as 'Colonel' long after they have left the Service in which they were never regular soldiers. Others – the rather self-consciously 'peppery', 'fiery' or 'choleric' type – attempt to use these attributes against servants or old ladies in the boarding-house in which they usually end their days.

There are obviously, however, innumerable meek, and possibly saintly retired Colonels in boarding-houses, and these have to suffer, in the general reputation of the world, for the folly of the others.

What, then, about Colonels' Wives? What about Mrs Plumleigh-Bruce?

2

It may be said that the popular prejudice against Colonels' Wives far exceeds that which is attached to their husbands: and it may be further said that this prejudice, amounting, often, to great dislike, is much more reasonable and easily understood than in the case of their husbands.

To begin with, the very conception of a Colonel's Wife brings waves of absurd thoughts about 'Tiffin', 'Pukka Sahibs', 'Chota Hasri', 'Indyah' and 'The Natives' surging into the mind.

This, of course, is grossly unfair; for Colonels' Wives are not, as is vaguely supposed, all 'Anglo-Indian'. Nevertheless, despite many noble, admirable or pathetic examples, Colonels' Wives form, on the whole, a very mixed class, and there are undoubtedly very many very objectionable Colonels' Wives.

3

Mrs Plumleigh-Bruce missed hardly a single characteristic appertaining to the worst sort of Colonel's wife. In fact, she was so true to this type that an author could hardly put her into fiction. She had only just enough wit to avoid naked, flaming 'Poonaism'.

She was outwardly rather stout, and inwardly beyond measure arrogant. She was rude to her servants, insensitive, vain, and a social snob. She talked (it is hard to believe) about people who did not 'come quite out of the top drawer'. She talked (but this goes without saying) about 'Pukka Sahibs', 'The Natives', etc., and this without ever having been within a thousand miles of India. She talked about *Wallahs* – appending this word to members of the middle-class respectable professions – as in 'Solicitor-Wallah', 'Doctor-Wallah', 'Parson-Wallah', and so forth – but never, let it be noted, speaking of a Grocer-Wallah, Duke-Wallah, Draper-Wallah, or Earl-Wallah.

This Anglo-Indian word 'Wallah' was wonderfully suited both to her accent and voice. Into it she was able to project all the thick, drawling fruitiness of her affectedly indolent manner of utterance.

Mrs Plumleigh-Bruce's voice and accent were not by any means peculiar to herself, though in her these were probably slightly accentuated. They were, and still are, shared by an enormous class of women – what may be called the Plumleigh-Bruce class, or, more simply, the Plumleigh-Bruces. Another Galsworthy may one day write a Plumleigh-Bruce saga. Only the briefest sketch of them can be given here.

The Plumleigh-Bruces live, usually, in rather large and rather nice houses just outside villages or towns. Their lawns and tennis-courts are amazingly well-kept, and they keep dogs.

The Plumleigh-Bruces are always connected with the Army – though not necessarily with the Indian Army. Above all things it can be guaranteed that there is a *General* somewhere in the family. The General may be obscure or famous, a remote or close connection, but there he is. One cannot conceivably be a Plumleigh-Bruce without a General in the family.

The Plumleigh-Bruces of life are not exactly ostentatious, but, rather, quietly sure of themselves to quite a repulsive degree.

The Plumleigh-Bruce boys go to Public Schools and the daughters are usually somehow 'presented at Court'.

The men of this tribe (in which, of course, there are innumerable grades) are generally much less offensive than the women, and less easy to identify. The women can be spotted at once by an astute social botanist – and this, almost always, because of their voices and accent.

It has already been said that the Mrs Plumleigh-Bruce of this story spoke in a thick, drawling, fruity, affectedly indolent way – but this does not fully describe the flavour of her mode of speech, which was, really excessively genteel.

The word 'genteel', in regard to speech, is normally associated with the thin, quick, clipped accent of the foolish, but perhaps struggling, West End shop assistant. Mrs Plumleigh-Bruce's accent, while remaining genteel, was exactly the opposite. It was rich, slow, and deliberate, and came forth from a mouth which moved much too much in an attempt to enunciate correctly every letter, vowel and syllable.

She put (like nearly all the Plumleigh-Bruces herein named after her) too much emphasis upon her 'H's'. If the servant shouted up to her that the man about the electric-light in the bedroom had called, she would not have replied rapidly and casually, as would the average 'educated' person, 'Oh – will you ask him if he'll come upstairs?' – the 'H's' here being almost completely dropped. She would have breathed the H's – saying, thoughtfully, lethargically, 'Oh – will you ask *Him* if *He'll* come upstairs?'

In other words, her accent, like that of the foolish shop assistant, was genteel because she was trying too hard.

If anyone had told Mrs Plumleigh-Bruce that she left anything in her accent to be desired or corrected she would either have laughed or been wild with anger – the first openly and when in company, the second secretly when alone.

Her pride in her knowledge of the grammar and correct usage of the English language almost equalled that which she took in her manner of pronouncing it. But here again she often made quite serious errors. She would talk, for instance, of things or people being 'aggravating' when her meaning was clearly 'irritating', and she would speak of demanding 'explicit' obedience from her servants.

As she alluded so often to people who did not come 'quite out of the top drawer', it is interesting to speculate as to what sort of drawer she thought she herself came out of. The top, surely, one would immediately imagine. But this would be to over-simplify matters. The Plumleigh-Bruce chest-of-drawers is a highly intricate one. In it the proletariat, or the tradesman class, occupy no drawer at all. But the 'genuine aristocracy' certainly does. Would Mrs Plumleigh-Bruce concede that she was in any lower drawer than the latter? She probably would – if and when she ever thought about the matter. And here, she was, for once, perhaps slightly underestimating herself, for the 'genuine aristocracy' has nowadays become by marriage so Plumleigh-Bruced as to be no longer fully itself.

As a faint extenuation of Mrs Plumleigh-Bruce's character it should be mentioned that she had had a very tricky upbringing. In addition to being a Colonel's Wife she was a Colonel's Daughter. Moreover both Colonels had been foolish, and both had been in the Indian Army.

She was, in point of fact, now a Colonel's Widow. Her husband, to whom she had been married only five years, had died shortly after the First World War. Her father and mother were also dead.

She was now forty-one, and, although rather plump, she looked frequently much younger. She was not totally unattractive. Indeed, by a businessman fresh from a Masonic Dinner, she was often thought ravishing.

She had tow-coloured hair, nice blue eyes, and a lascivious mouth. Her good teeth were slightly rabbity. The mouth and the teeth assisted her in, and accentuated, her mode of speech.

In 1928 she was living in a small house in Reading. One does not think of Colonels' Wives (or Widows) as living in Reading: there is hardly any more unlikely or unsuitable town.

She lived there, however, because she had little money, and because her deceased and only sister had bequeathed to her a small house there. She called this house a *pied-à-terre*.

The odd thing was that Mrs Plumleigh-Bruce did not at all dislike living in Reading. But this was to be accounted for by her intense absorption in the 'drawer' system.

No one, in Reading, in Mrs Plumleigh-Bruce's estimation, could imaginably come quite, or even at all, out of the 'top drawer'. She was therefore in a top drawer all by herself, and this pleased her insatiable vanity immeasurably. She looked upon herself as the eminent 'Lady' of Reading – and many residents took her at her own valuation. Businessmen in the town often alluded to her, without a trace of sarcasm as 'The Lady of Reading' – or 'Our Reading Lady'.

Mrs Plumleigh-Bruce mixed with the more prosperous businessmen of the town.

She had, like so many Colonels' Wives or Widows, a great fondness for the company and flattery of men, and for the sake of these things she even went into Saloon Bars of public houses with such men.

She 'detested snobbery', and thought public houses 'great fun'.

Also, without being in any way a heavy drinker, Mrs Plumleigh-Bruce did not find drinking a distasteful pastime – particularly as the drinks were always paid for by the men.

But she was fastidious in her taste about public houses, and the one she most frequented was The Friar. This was because its walls had recently been ye-olde panelled, and because there was a nook in it in which she could sit almost unespied by the populace, while holding a sort of Court for the prosperous businessmen.

It was in The Friar, in the year 1928, that she met and formed a friendship with the reddish-haired, reddish-moustached Ernest Ralph Gorse.

Anyone knowing the true character of Mrs Plumleigh-Bruce, and, at the same time, the true character of Ernest Ralph Gorse, would have decided that this friendship must prove an emphatically interesting one – indeed, a most exciting combination.

CHAPTER TWO

I

FOR the benefit of those unacquainted with Ernest Ralph Gorse, it is now necessary to give a brief description of his character generally, his early background, and his youthful adventures and ventures. This will also be of assistance to those who already know about him.

Ernest Ralph Gorse, who was born in 1903, and whose mother died shortly after he was born, was the son of a rather successful commercial artist who, not very long after his wife's death, married an ex-barmaid – an extremely pleasant fat woman, who in her heart detested her stepson, but treated him not only fairly but indulgently.

Ernest Ralph Gorse belonged to a very seriously criminal type, and showed as much as a boy at his preparatory school.

At this school, which was in Hove and at which he was a dayboy, he was continually creating evil mischief purely for its own sake – and this was not only amongst his fellow school-boys. He had the habit, for instance, when returning home from school on winter nights, of sticking pins into the tyres of any bicycles he could find in dark places.

He was also, at the age of twelve, suspected of having – on a summer's evening in the County Ground, Hove – tied a small girl to a cricket roller in an obscure shed, and of having robbed her of her money, a few coppers which she had in her purse.

A policeman in plain clothes called upon Gorse's headmaster about this matter. The headmaster was, for the sake of the reputation of his school, evasive with the policeman: but, like the policeman, he was, at the back of his mind, absolutely certain that Gorse was the culprit. Both were correct in the belief they held in common. Nevertheless, Gorse did not suffer in any way for this misdemeanour.

After this Gorse went to St Paul's School in London. Here he again created mischief, though not of a technically criminal kind. And here, also, he developed a remarkable taste for, and knowledge about, the Motor-Car. He had, at as early an age as that of sixteen, shady dealings with car dealers of dubious character in Hammersmith, which is very near to St Paul's School.

In 1921 he was once more in Hove on his 'holidays'. Here he mixed with two young men who had been at his own preparatory school – Peter Ryan and George Bell, and here he met Esther Downes, who was an unusually lovely and well-dressed girl who lived in a Brighton slum.

Esther Downes was picked up by the three young men on the West Pier. Ryan, a simple, good-natured, well-mannered boy – fell desperately in love with her. Gorse had no feeling for her, but found her beauty and good clothes social assets. He was then trying his wings in the art of frequenting opulent hotels, and he took her to drink cocktails at the Metropole.

In order to do this it was necessary to cut out Ryan. He succeeded in doing this by writing filthy anonymous letters, and by other abominable methods.

He discovered at a fairly early stage on this 'holiday' that Esther Downes had savings – enormous ones for a girl of her class. She had sixty-eight pounds fifteen shillings, which her industrious and ailing mother had given her, and which was kept in an old tin safe in an old tin trunk in her bedroom.

By employing the most astute trickery, which involved the use of a very smart red sports-car, he managed to deprive Esther Downes of every penny of her savings.

This was Gorse's second technically criminal offence, and he again escaped punishment.

In addition to robbing the wretched Esther Downes, Gorse sold, in London, the red sports-car at nearly double the price he had paid for it.

Since 1921 he had not actually done anything further for which the police could have arrested him. He had had no need to, for he had made a wonderful amount of money in reasonably honest speculation in cars. But the matter of necessity is really beside the point. Gorse loved trickery and evil for their own sakes, and, even if fabulously rich, would have indulged in both had he been taken by the whim to do so.

The motives of such a criminal as Ernest Ralph Gorse are only partially commercial, and their criminal behaviour comes and goes in waves – waves which, nearly always, increase in volume and power.

In years long after the events related in this book, people often argued as to whether Gorse (who was by then a famous figure) had 'any good' in him.

He had not any sort of good in him. He might have been just conceivably, and in a manner, insane – but evilly so – not pitiably. In spite of his worldly astuteness, he may have lived, perhaps, like so many outstanding criminals, a sort of dream-life. But, even if this were so, the dream was evil.

Moreover there was certainly nothing in his upbringing which could possibly account for his attitude towards life and his fellow-men.

He would have served, indeed, as a perfect model for, or archetype of, all the pitiless and not-to-be-pitied criminals who have been discovered and exposed in the last hundred years or so in Great Britain.

He had a touch of Burke and Hare of Edinburgh (though he was never a very heavy drinker); he had a touch of Dr Pritchard of Glasgow; a touch of the multitudinously poisoning Palmer; of the strangely acquitted Miss Madeleine Smith; of Neal Creame, the Lambeth harlot-prisoner, of George Smith, the bath-murderer; of Frederick Bywaters, Ronald True, Sydney Fox, Frederick Mahon, Neville Heath and George Haigh.

And, added to this, he had a pronounced touch of one who thought never of murder but incessantly of money – the false and foolish claimant to the Tichborne Estate.

It was on a cold January night in 1928, at The Friar, Reading, that Ernest Ralph Gorse first met Mrs Plumleigh-Bruce.

Mrs Plumleigh-Bruce did not at once 'take' to him.

PART TWO

GORSE THE WATCHER

CHAPTER ONE

I

THE Friar, as has been said, had only recently been ye-olded, and this had been lavishly done. It had also been enlarged, and it was one of the talks of Reading, where, in the main, it was looked upon with some awe by the public house amateur.

It occupied considerable space in Friar Street, Reading, which runs parallel to the main street, Broad Street.

Its principal feature was, of course, its dark-stained wooden panelling, with which the walls of all its bars were lined.

In its very long and large Saloon Bar was its *pièce de résistance*. This was an enormous 'Devonshire' fireplace, enveloping which was an enormous surround made of material resembling Portland Stone. Above this there were three shields upon which were brightly painted coats-of-arms.

This fireplace, which was in the centre of the long room and facing the bar itself, created, along with the panelling, a 'baronial' effect of the most painfully false character. But the Reading business barons in no way disliked it.

During the lunch-hour (lunches were given upstairs) the businessmen did not think much about their surroundings. They were too busy talking business, or telling dirty stories, or waiting with ill-concealed impatience or anger for other men to finish theirs so that they could tell their own. But in the evening, when the place was more empty, and lit with a coal-and-log fire, the businessman would look around him and be gravely pleased by the atmosphere.

The Friar was what, in those days, would have been called a 'posh' place.

The nook mostly occupied by Mrs Plumleigh-Bruce was at the end of the Saloon Bar furthest from the door, and was made a nook by a jutting partition, again of the dark-stained wooden panelling. There was another such nook nearer to the door, but this was more draughty and less intimate.

2

On the night upon which she first met Ernest Ralph Gorse, Mrs Plumleigh-Bruce was not in her usual place. Her nook had been occupied by a strange couple, and she was sitting on a high stool at the bar alone.

She was waiting for Mr Donald Stimpson, who was, most unaccountably, late. Naturally, she greatly disliked having to sit at the bar alone.

Her appointment with Mr Stimpson had been for six o'clock. She had arrived five minutes late. Ernest Ralph Gorse came into the bar at ten minutes past six, and sat on a stool rather near to Mrs Plumleigh-Bruce.

Apart from the strange couple, and the barmaid, there was no one else in the bar.

Gorse ordered a glass of beer and began to read an evening newspaper. While he did so Mrs Plumleigh-Bruce, who was sure she had never seen him before in Reading, observed him with interest.

Gorse was only twenty-five at this period, but he liked, for commercial and other reasons, to look considerably older. He pretended that he was thirty-one, and people believed that he was.

He had improved, both in his looks and his style of dressing, since his earlier days. At his preparatory school he had been a slim boy, with ginger silken hair which came in a large bang over his forehead, thin lips, a slouching gait, some freckles, an aquiline nose which always seemed to be smelling something nasty, and a nasal voice.

Now his nose only seldom, and when seen from certain angles, seemed to smell anything nasty. This was because he had managed to cultivate quite a powerful moustache.

His reddish hair was now of a thicker texture, and brushed backwards and kept in place by the discreet use of hair oil.

His moustache was, roughly speaking, of a 'tooth-brush' kind, and helped to give him the 'Army' appearance he was anxious to cultivate.

In certain carefully chosen quarters he passed as one who had been on active service in the 1914–18 War. He had awarded himself the rank of Lieutenant in this war – a Lieutenant in the Royal Horse Artillery. In the quarters in which he put forth (and elaborated upon) this falsehood, he was believed.

He wore in these days a fawn-coloured 'trilby' hat, and, for the most part, dark blue suits which were well made. His shoes were expensive and always immaculately clean. So also were his shirts and ties.

He carried a rimless monocle attached to no string in his waistcoat pocket, and this he stuck in his eye when he read in public, and on certain other occasions when people were present.

When he was younger his monocle had been made of plain glass. Now he had had the sense to have a lens made, one suitable to a person with slightly short sight.

On his left little finger he wore a gold ring with a cornelian stone upon which was engraved the crest of a family to which he did not belong.

Mrs Plumleigh-Bruce, watching him, could not make him out at all – could find no 'drawer' to put him into. The 'top' she would certainly not concede to him, but, it seemed to her, he probably belonged to a higher class than that of the businessmen with whom she mixed – Mr Stimpson for instance.

She felt instinctively that, if she made his acquaintance, she would not be able to take the slightly or strongly patronizing attitude which she took always with other men in Reading.

And so, because of this, and because she was unable to place him, and because he was a stranger, her feelings towards him were on the whole hostile.

While Mrs Plumleigh-Bruce was watching Ernest Ralph Gorse, the latter was at the same time keenly examining Mrs Plumleigh-Bruce, and by more subtle methods than her own. While giving an imitation of reading his newspaper, he was looking at her reflection in the mirror behind the bar.

He found himself as interested in Mrs Plumleigh-Bruce as she was in himself; but this was not on account of any of those slightly mature physical attractions she had for certain men. He was too young for this, and, in any case, Gorse, as a rule, had little feeling for women in that way. Though he certainly at periods knew the meaning of sexual desire he was never in love with a woman during his entire life.

What interested Ernest Ralph Gorse were Mrs Plumleigh-Bruce's bearing and clothes. Her clothes were some sort of clue to her class, and her class, possibly, to her financial status.

The precocious young man at once perceived that she did not quite belong to Reading; and he surmised that she had been married and was no longer so. He quickly took in her wonderful complacency as a being generally, and he was sure that she was, because of this, gloriously susceptible to the right kind of flattery.

Mrs Plumleigh-Bruce seemed, in short, what Ernest Ralph Gorse would have called 'right up his street'. He decided to talk to her.

Like so many women with a strong liking for the company of men, Mrs Plumleigh-Bruce kept a dog, which was usually on a lead.

A dog on a lead is an instrument for coquetry of all kinds – particularly the more nauseating kinds. A dog, also, in public haunts, is often useful in causing an introduction to men.

Having made up his mind to speak to her, Gorse decided to make use of Mrs Plumleigh-Bruce's dog. He asked the barmaid for a packet of cheese-biscuits, which he had seen amongst the bottles behind the bar.

These were given to him. Then, still pretending to read his newspaper, which lay flattened out on the bar, he opened the packet of biscuits, and began to munch one of them.

Then, making as much of a crackling noise as he could with the paper of the packet, he began to munch another.

The desired result was quickly achieved. Mrs Plumleigh-Bruce's dog – a liver-coloured spaniel – began to strain at its lead in the direction of Gorse, who feigned at first not to notice this, while making further luscious crackling sounds.

At last the dog's efforts to reach him became so obvious that they could hardly, in courtesy, be ignored. Gorse spoke both to the dog and its owner.

'Ah – I thought so . . .' he said, looking first mockingly at the spaniel, and then, amiably, at Mrs Plumleigh-Bruce. 'May I give him one – or is such a thing strictly "taboo"?'

Gorse's use and faint stressing, at this moment, of the word 'taboo', revealed his practically sixth-sensitive cleverness in the handling of certain women. 'Taboo' was, to Mrs Plumleigh-Bruce, a 'native' word, and Gorse, merely from looking at her for a few moments in a mirror, had suspected that such a word would please her. He almost knew already that she was connected with Colonels who had been in India.

Mrs Plumleigh-Bruce's opinion of Gorse at once improved because of his use of this word.

'Well,' she said, in her fruity, off-hand way. 'It is, actually . . . But I suppose one has to make an exception every once in a way.'

'Oh yes,' said Gorse. 'One can't abide by the strict Rules and Regulations all the time.'

Talking of Rules and Regulations, in the precise way he did, because it summoned up a picture of army discipline, was another clever touch, and one which further attracted Mrs Plumleigh-Bruce's friendly instincts.

Gorse now went up to the dog and gave it a biscuit.

'He'll make a dreadful mess on the floor, I'm afraid,' said Mrs Plumleigh-Bruce. 'And one's not supposed to bring a dog in here, anyway.'

'Ah yes,' said Gorse, looking ruminatively at the dog as it ate the biscuit. 'But then I imagine that he's especially favoured – isn't he? Or rather that you are?'

'Oh well – I don't know . . .' said Mrs Plumleigh-Bruce. 'Perhaps I *do* get rather special treatment in some ways . . .'

There was a pause during which Gorse gave the dog another biscuit.

'Are you a "regular frequenter", as they say, then?' asked Gorse, still looking dreamily at the dog. He had a motive in asking this. He was not going to waste any time on this woman if she did not live in Reading – if she were only staying in the town for a night or two.

'Oh yes,' she said. 'This is my favourite haunt, really. In fact very nearly my only haunt – when one comes to think about it.'

'You're a resident in this metropolis, then?' said Gorse, making assurance doubly sure. He was an extremely thorough young man in matters of this sort.

'Yes, I am,' said Mrs Plumleigh-Bruce. 'For my sins. I had a sister who left me a little house here, and somehow I never seem to have got out of it.'

'Why? Is it such a hateful place?' asked Gorse. 'I've only been here a few days myself, and I haven't had much time to look around.'

'Oh well – it has its advantages, I suppose. It's very easy to get to Town, for one thing.'

Mrs Plumleigh-Bruce had her own, markedly 'Plumleigh-Bruce' way of pronouncing 'Town'. She rounded her lips a little too much for the 'ow', and lingered a little too long on the 'n'. This did not pass Gorse by.

'But it's not really in my line,' she said, 'at all.'

'No,' said Gorse, now picking up his drink, and in the most natural way sitting on the stool next to Mrs Plumleigh-Bruce. 'I can understand that. No doubt it's a very excellent place – but the moment I saw you I thought that you must be – well – what shall I say? – not quite fitting in – rather a cut above it – if one's allowed to put it that way these days.' And, slightly lifting his chin, he looked at Mrs Plumleigh-Bruce through his monocle, at once appraisingly and approvingly.

Mrs Plumleigh-Bruce was in two minds about Gorse's approach. She liked his immediate recognition of her superior social standing in Reading. But, not being a complete fool in every way, she sensed a faint effrontery in his demeanour, his look, and his monocle. His as yet unidentified 'drawer' probably went further down in the chest. There was a pause.

'Do you go to Town a lot?' Gorse then asked.

'Oh yes. Quite a good bit. On business, and for a Show every now and again. The train service is simply wonderful in that way.'

(The Plumleigh-Bruces of life incessantly talk about 'Shows', and by this they mean theatrical performances in London – not in the provinces, where the word 'Theatre' suffices. There are, moreover, no other 'Shows' save theatrical ones.)

'Yes. I've heard the trains are very good,' said Gorse. 'Not that that bothers me very much, because I always get around everywhere by car – myself.'

Gorse here had gone too far. Mrs Plumleigh-Bruce at once felt that he was boasting about his car. If he had not thrown in the casual 'myself' like that it might have been better. Gorse, all his life, was unable to cure this sort of fault in manners.

'Well – you're very lucky to have a car,' said Mrs Plumleigh-Bruce. 'I wish *I* had one.'

Gorse was aware that he had almost been snubbed, and hastened to rectify his error.

'Well, you wouldn't like mine,' he said. 'It's just about the most gimcrack affair you could find anywhere. However, it served its purpose in the recent little outbreak.'

He was alluding to the General Strike of 1926.

'What outbreak?' asked Mrs Plumleigh-Bruce, suspecting, without being absolutely certain of, his meaning.

'Oh – the outbreak of the Great Unwashed. The General Strike. I was able to give a lot of people lifts, and all that, and to help in other sundry ways. In fact it was probably that that broke the little bus down. She was never worked harder in her life. Nor was I, if it comes to that.'

Gorse had now recovered all the ground he had lost. Mrs Plumleigh-Bruce had not enough sense or decency to have any feeling against the expression 'The Great Unwashed'. In fact, she used it frequently herself. Nor did she object to people calling their cars 'little buses'. And his attitude towards the General Strike not only pleased her; it very nearly excited her. Just as Gorse was incapable of sentimental love, so Mrs Plumleigh-Bruce was, in the ordinary way, incapable of any sort of intellectual passion. But the General Strike had had, and still had, the power to stimulate her intellect violently. She was not, as may be guessed, a friend of the working class.

'Oh – so you helped in the General Strike – did you?' she said, looking at him very much more warmly than before. 'Well – I'm glad to hear that.'

'Oh yes, I did my little bit,' said Gorse. 'I think nearly everybody did, really. I expect you did, too – didn't you?'

'Yes. I did,' said Mrs Plumleigh-Bruce. 'Though nothing very spectacular. Just secretarial work. Recruiting volunteers and all that. And it was wonderful how everybody rallied round.'

'Yes. It was – wasn't it?' said Gorse. 'And the old Bolshie certainly got what was going to him, for once.'

'Yes. He certainly did.'

There was now a silence, during which Gorse meditated as to whether or not it would be advisable to have fought in the 1914–18 War. Finally he decided to have done so. He was unknown in Reading, to which he had never been before, and in which he proposed (or had proposed), to stay only for a few weeks. He felt, therefore, quite secure from exposure.

'Yes,' he said. 'It was wonderful how everyone came up to scratch. But then, that's the Britisher all over – isn't it? He's as lazy as the devil until a real crisis comes, when it does come he's quicker off the mark than anyone on earth – whatever the inconvenience or trouble. Apart from all the bother, I know it cost *me* a pretty penny – hunting out the old uniform and all that.'

Gorse now hoped that Mrs Plumleigh-Bruce would inquire as to the nature of this uniform, but instead of this she only replied; 'Yes, it must.' And so he had to go on further.

'Reminded one,' he said, 'of the queer old days in France.'

'Why – were you in France?' said Mrs Plumleigh-Bruce, looking at him.

'I was,' said Gorse, sententiously and thoughtfully, and looking into the distance.

'Really?' said Mrs Plumleigh-Bruce. 'In the War?'

'Yes. I volunteered to play my little rôle in that little misunderstanding between ourselves and the Boche ...' Gorse now put on a faintly smiling and reminiscent, as well as thoughtful expression.

'Well, I must say that surprises me,' said Mrs Plumleigh-Bruce, who was now gazing intently at Gorse, who knew that she was doing this. 'I should have thought you were too young.'

'Yes ... I was. Definitely ...' said Gorse. 'But these things *can* be wangled – can't they? I'm not a wangler as a rule, but I think I was justified on that occasion ... In fact I managed to be on His Majesty's Service at the very immature age of sixteen ... and in France at seventeen. I suppose it was very naughty of me ...'

'Oh no – not naughty,' said Mrs Plumleigh-Bruce. 'Far from it.'

'What, then?' Gorse asked.

'Well – jolly sporty – I should say,' said Mrs Plumleigh-Bruce.

'Well – I suppose it was a fault on the right side,' said Gorse, and he again looked into the distance, as if weighing up the past.

But he was not really doing this. He was weighing up Mrs Plumleigh-Bruce generally, and his own present age as one who had gallantly tricked his way into the 1914–18 War at the age of sixteen.

He liked Mrs Plumleigh-Bruce's use of the word 'sporty'. If she had said 'sporting' he would not have been quite so pleased. By the use of the former word instead of the latter, she had shown that she had exactly that sort of vulgarity upon which he could play. Gorse was, in his soul, incredibly vulgar. He could, however, mysteriously just distinguish the difference between one sort of cheapness and another – as in these two words. All this was part of his peculiar genius.

Gorse now believed that he had fully eradicated that slight feeling of hostility towards him which he had sensed in Mrs Plumleigh-Bruce. He even thought that he was well on the way to captivating her. He was right in both cases.

She had nearly finished her drink, and he was thinking of inviting her to have another at his expense. But at this moment Mr Donald Stimpson, the Estate Agent, entered.

CHAPTER TWO

I

'A H – our Lady Joan,' said Mr Stimpson, hurrying up to Mrs Plumleigh-Bruce, whose Christian name was Joan. 'A thousand apologies for my remissness, madame.'

Mr Stimpson was a thick-set, moustached, virile, middle-aged man, of medium height, with a red face (redder now because of the cold outside), tortoiseshell-rimmed spectacles, false teeth, a heavy overcoat, a woollen scarf, gloves and a bowler hat.

Above all things Mr Stimpson was middle-aged. Merely to look at him was to think of middle age. Few other men in the world, of his years, which amounted to fifty-one, could have given forth this impression so strongly and quickly. He bounced with middle age; he had clearly been born, and would die, middle-aged, and, furthermore, he somehow seemed to glory in all this.

It is not easy to say exactly why or how he gave forth this overwhelming impression. One simply does not think of the age of countless other men of fifty-one. Perhaps it was because he was so intensely and overbearingly middle-class – in his social origins, in his profession, in his thoughts, and in his utterances. He was vehemently, formidably, almost dangerously 'middle' in every way.

'Well, you're certainly very late,' said Mrs Plumleigh-Bruce and, because of the presence of Ernest Ralph Gorse, there was an awkward silence, which Mrs Plumleigh-Bruce broke.

'Oh,' she said, 'I don't think you two know each other, do you? . . . This is Mr Donald Stimpson – and I don't really know *your* name – do I?'

She looked at Gorse, who replied 'No, I don't think you do. It's Gorse, as a matter of fact. Ralph Gorse.'

'Oh – how-do-you-do, Mr Gorse,' said Mr Stimpson, and he

snatched off his glove in order to shake hands with the stranger. He was a terrific and most adroit glove-snatcher-offer when being introduced to anyone, and his handshake was always warm to the extent of physical cruelty. He could tell the character of a man, he always said, by the way he shook hands with you: and nothing but near-violence suited his taste.

Gorse, who knew this type of handshaker, used almost as much strength with his own hand: but this did not, as had been hoped, please Mr Stimpson. Mr Stimpson loathed both the presence and the aspect of Ernest Ralph Gorse.

This was not because Mr Stimpson had enough wit even faintly to suspect that he was shaking hands with a criminal, or even with a dubious character. He detested Gorse merely because he was where he was – that is to say, in the immediate vicinity of Mrs Plumleigh-Bruce. He was afraid of a new candidate for her affections.

It would not be correct to say that Mr Stimpson loved Mrs Plumleigh-Bruce; although he often, particularly after business dinners, made love to her – either by verbal innuendo or in attempts to kiss her. He was, however, anxious to marry her.

As a widower of three years' standing, a snob, a social climber, a businessman, a boaster, and a subterraneously lecherous man, Mr Stimpson had every reason for seeking Mrs Plumleigh-Bruce's hand in marriage. The widower (as widowers so often do) wanted to marry again, the snob and social climber hankered for the outstanding 'Lady' of his circle in the town, the businessman thought she would be useful for his business as such, the boaster wanted her for both of the last two reasons, and the subterraneously lecherous man, after food and drink, found her by no means physically undesirable.

Mr Stimpson, in addition to all this, liked her small house – for its atmosphere, for its business possibilities, and for its maid's cooking. He rather liked the maid, too. He liked everything about Mrs Plumleigh-Bruce.

2

Gorse perceived that Mr Stimpson, in spite of the stupendous handshake, was displeased by his presence.

'Well,' he said, 'as you two had an appointment, I'm afraid

I'm rather butting in – aren't I? So I'll go back to my newspaper, I think, if you'll forgive me.' He smiled at Mrs Plumleigh-Bruce, and moved as if about to return to the stool upon which he had originally been sitting.

'Oh no. Please don't go,' said Mrs Plumleigh-Bruce. 'We'd nothing private to talk about – or anything like that – had we, Donald?'

Mrs Plumleigh-Bruce gave forth this invitation to stay with more warmth than she might have used or than Mr Stimpson liked. There were four reasons for this. Firstly, she was anxious to annoy Mr Stimpson for being late. Secondly, she was flattered at having undoubtedly gained the attention of a decidedly 'young' man who did not even look what must be his age, and whose youthfulness must further annoy Mr Stimpson. Thirdly, she in no way disliked making Mr Stimpson jealous; for she at times seriously entertained the idea of marrying him, and therefore wanted to keep him as much at her feet as a man like Mr Stimpson was capable of being. Finally, she was genuinely interested in Gorse himself. Doubtful as she still was about the exact drawer he occupied, he was presentable and interesting, and he held the right ideas about serious matters, such as those of the General Strike and premature enlistment in the Army. And so she conveyed strongly to Gorse that she did not want him to leave them.

'No. Nothing private,' said Mr Stimpson, in an embarrassed way. 'Nothing private at all . . . Well – what are we all drinking? . . .' And he looked at Gorse as well as Mrs Plumleigh-Bruce, as if urging both to drink with him.

Gorse now saw that Mrs Plumleigh-Bruce would respect him, and desire his company in the future much more, if he withdrew. Also he was bored beyond measure by the notion of having to remain in the company of Mr Stimpson.

'No,' he said, therefore. 'I really won't stay, if you don't mind. I'll get back to my newspaper, if you don't mind. I'm not reading it just for pleasure. I've got quite a lot of work to do to-night.'

'Work?' said Mrs Plumleigh-Bruce. 'With a newspaper?'

'Yes,' said Gorse. 'Or rather study. I take great interest in the form and activities of a famous type of fast-moving quadruped, you see.'

'Oh,' said Mrs Plumleigh-Bruce. 'Horse-racing, you mean?'

'That's right,' said Gorse. 'And I have great schemes afoot just at the moment. So do you mind if I return to my researches?'

It happened that, as Gorse said this, the couple who had been occupying the nook in which Mrs Plumleigh-Bruce usually sat, rose and left the bar. Mr Stimpson saw his chance.

'Well – if you've got *really* serious work to do – like *that*,' he said, facetiously, 'I suppose it wouldn't be *fair* to interrupt you. I also observe,' he added quietly to Mrs Plumleigh-Bruce, 'that our accustomed pew has been vacated . . . So what about sitting down properly, anyway?'

'Yes. You go and sit down,' said Gorse. 'I'll be quite happy here, concentrating for a bit.'

'Well, then,' said Mr Stimpson, looking hesitantly, first at Gorse, and then at Mrs Plumleigh-Bruce. 'What about it, Joan? If you go over I'll bring you fresh regalement.'

'Very well. It's certainly nicer over there,' she replied. 'Quite sure you won't join us?'

'No. I really won't,' said Gorse. 'Thank you very much all the same.'

'Very well, then,' she said, smiling at Gorse in a way which seemed almost to wink at him about Mr Stimpson generally. 'Well – *au revoir*, Mr – Gorse – wasn't it?'

'Yes. That's right. *Au revoir*, then.'

'*Au revoir*.' She went over to the nook, and there were now about thirty rather awkward seconds at the bar, during which Mr Stimpson ordered drinks for Mrs Plumleigh-Bruce and himself. Gorse helped out by pretending to look at his newspaper.

The drinks having been obtained and paid for, Mr Stimpson walked over in silence with them to Mrs Plumleigh-Bruce, and sat down next to her. Still no one else had entered the bar, and so, in the silence, Gorse could hear every word that passed between the other two.

'Well – where *have* you been?' he heard Mrs Plumleigh-Bruce say. 'I hope you've got a good excuse.'

'Oh,' said Mr Stimpson. 'Just Brushing Shoulders with the Nobility – as seems to be my wont these days.'

This remark gave Gorse such a start that he nearly lifted his eyes from his newspaper and looked over at Mr Stimpson. He succeeded in not doing this, but a close observer would have noticed that his head shifted a fraction of an inch upwards, as if he desired to read an item higher up on the page.

Gorse had not yet guessed, or even properly tried to guess, Mr Stimpson's profession, and he could not imagine how a man of this sort could conceivably 'brush shoulders' with the 'nobility'. Was it a joke, or piece of sarcasm, on Mr Stimpson's part? For some reason Gorse rather fancied not. He beat around in his mind for a clue to the mystery, and listened more intently than ever.

'Oh, really?' said Mrs Plumleigh-Bruce. 'You mean Lord Bulford again?'

'No. Old Carsloe, this time,' said Mr Stimpson, with that droop of the mouth, and air of indifference, or even disdain, which a certain low-thinking type of man always adopts when alluding to a member of the peerage – particularly when he has recently met one of these. 'And then the old boy insisted on me having a cup of tea and a chat afterwards – and it's a long way away, as you know, and so I got late. So I hope that's a good enough excuse. It's business, after all, and very good business. So am I forgiven?'

'Yes. I suppose you must be,' said Mrs Plumleigh-Bruce. 'Business is business, after all.'

Gorse now experienced a sense of relief. He had greatly disliked the idea of someone he disliked 'brushing shoulders' with the 'nobility'. But now it had been made clear that it was merely a matter of business and that Mr Stimpson only got his shoulders brushed in this way in some kind of menial capacity. Gorse felt, too, that he had got nearer to placing Mr Stimpson's profession and social standing: and Gorse liked to place everybody. He guessed now that Mr Stimpson was some sort of Valuer, or Auctioneer, or Agent of some sort.

All the same, a nobility-shoulder-brusher was a nobility-shoulder-brusher, and, as such, not to be dismissed too lightly. Gorse realized that, if his friendship with Mrs Plumleigh-Bruce ripened, he had a more formidable rival in Mr Stimpson than he had at first imagined. And this thought, in its turn, made Mrs Plumleigh-Bruce a more formidable and attractive proposition, and strengthened Gorse in his resolution, hitherto rather vague, to become more fully acquainted with her.

He had seen at once, of course, that Mr Stimpson either consorted with, or desired to consort with, or desired to marry Mrs Plumleigh-Bruce. Even one much less brilliant at this sort of thing than Ernest Ralph Gorse would have seen as much.

Gorse now, while staring at his newspaper, made up his mind to listen to every word exchanged between these two. But here he met with bad luck, for, all at once, the Saloon Bar of The Friar became, it seemed, full of people.

This is the way of bars of public houses during the first half-hour or so of opening time. They will remain in a state of desultory, almost deadly quiet for a long while, and then, all of a sudden, burst into life. It is almost as though a small crowd of people has been loitering outside eagerly awaiting permission to enter. And then, directly permission has been granted, they come in, one after the other, with brightened spirits, eager to drink and highly loquacious.

Three busily talking men entered first, and these, merely by themselves, disabled Gorse from hearing more than an isolated word or so spoken by Mrs Plumleigh-Bruce and Mr Donald Stimpson. And a minute or so later, because of the influx of people, they were totally beyond Gorse's audible reach. Though he was still in a position to watch them, they were as remote from him as if they had been in another house – another city.

This remoteness from him – this sudden disappearance they had made, as it were, into another orbit – at once annoyed and enticed Gorse. For the orbit into which they had moved was now somehow a higher one than his own. Whereas they were together in a familiar place, he was entirely alone in an unfamiliar one. He was now, in fact, a solitary outsider. Five minutes ago he had been very much on the inside with an interesting woman.

These feelings were made even more acute by his noticing, about five minutes later, that Mrs Plumleigh-Bruce and Mr Stimpson had been joined by another man, who had sat down beside them.

This man was, like Mr Stimpson, middle-aged – but in no way overwhelmingly so. He was fair, and stoutish, and he wore a moustache. He looked like a 'gentleman', which displeased Gorse. Worse still, he looked like an ex-military man.

For the first time it occurred to Gorse that Mrs Plumleigh-Bruce might be married. All his instincts had told him, until this moment, that she was not, but now he had to give the matter thought. Could this military-looking man conceivably be her husband?

If such were the case, he reflected, he would probably abandon the pursuit of Mrs Plumleigh-Bruce. Women with husbands were never, for some reason, in Gorse's line, and a woman with an ex-military husband was practically out of the question, for, since he had, in this case, posed as an ex-military man himself, the danger of exposure would clearly be too great.

All the same, this man might easily be neither an ex-military man nor her husband. And so Gorse decided to remain in The Friar and see what happened, 'which way the cat jumped' as he would have put it.

3

When Mrs Plumleigh-Bruce had been talking to the two men for about ten minutes, Gorse, who had been aware that Mrs Plumleigh-Bruce had been looking over at him occasionally, decided that his pretence of looking at a newspaper was becoming hollow. He therefore, having ordered another beer, took a small notebook and a pencil from his pocket and pretended to be making notes of an elaborate character. These, it was to be presumed, were racing notes, for Gorse continued, every now and again, to refer to his newspaper.

He was aware that this performance would not carry conviction for more than about twenty minutes, and he wondered how long Mrs Plumleigh-Bruce was going to stay at The Friar. It was his intention to follow her to her home, or to wherever she went next, when she left.

He decided that, if she did not leave soon, he would engage himself in conversation with someone.

Twenty minutes passed. The bar had now become very full, and Mrs Plumleigh-Bruce was still in the same place.

Next to Gorse, at the bar, and also drinking beer, there was now a young man of about thirty-six. This young man, who was between Gorse and the Plumleigh-Bruce nook, had, Gorse had noticed, on entering waved to Mrs Plumleigh-Bruce, who had waved back cordially. Gorse decided to engage him in conversation.

This was easily done, and soon the two were talking in a seemingly friendly way.

The young man was of medium height, hatless, emphatically good-looking, not at all well-dressed, and bearing the despondent air of one who works hard but fruitlessly. He did not look at all like an actor, but this he was. His name was Miles Standish, and he was running, at a loss so far, a small Repertory Theatre in Reading.

Gorse, who had a gift for rapidly discovering a person's profession, soon did so in this case, and he was much impressed.

Gorse, all his life, had a curious passion for the theatre, and a longing to be connected with it. This was to a certain extent because he greatly fancied himself as an actor.

Gorse was, of course, in the restricted and rather foolish sense of the term, a very fine 'actor'. That is to say, he could, in private, and particularly in private with women, put on an act, deceive, and create wonderfully the impression he desired to create. As an actor on the stage, however, he was something worse than hopeless – he was embarrassing beyond measure.

He fancied himself as a light comedian, as an adept in 'Silly Ass' parts in which there was a lot of 'By Gad!' 'What?', 'Bai Jove!', 'Weallay!' and all that sort of thing.

But Ralph Gorse was no Ralph Lynn, and, in the few appearances he had succeeded in making upon the amateur stage he had been very far from successful. Once he had entered for a competition for acting in a provincial town – one in which he had to come upon the stage for ten minutes by himself. The audience was indeed provincial, and, as such, willing warmly to welcome the poorest exhibition. Nevertheless, Gorse was but feebly applauded, and most of the members of the audience blushed profoundly in their souls. But Gorse did not realize the type of reception given to him, and continued to believe vigorously in his capacities in this direction.

This belief was, perhaps, Gorse's sole concession to extreme vanity and exhibitionism – a funny Achilles' heel.

He was, too, attracted by the theatre for other reasons. At an early age he had become aware of its peculiar financial, social and psychological advantages. He knew that an enormous proportion of mankind feels, weirdly but indisputably, a stronger awe for the theatre than almost any other art or activity on earth. He knew that to get in on the inside, to be 'behind scenes' in the theatre, was to achieve a glamour completely out of proportion to that attached to almost any other profession. He knew that to give to the average person free seats for the theatre (while pretending that such a thing was easy because one was intimately connected with it) gratified such a person a dozen times more than to give him the money for the seats. When anxious to flatter, cajole, or bribe people in the past, he had often himself bought seats at a theatre and then given them away with the pretence that he had come by them through inside influence and that they were of no use to himself.

He knew, in addition, that to be seen in the company of an actress was to acquire prestige, or to be envied, or both. He knew, therefore, that it was wise to cultivate the company of an actor, for an actor might easily lead the way to an actress.

Accordingly, having discovered the profession of Miles Standish, Gorse became a very different sort of young man than he would have been with the type of stranger he usually encountered in a public house. He braced himself to exercise whatever charm he possessed – and this, with undiscriminating people, was often very considerable. Another motive for his doing this was his knowledge that Miles Standish was acquainted with Mrs Plumleigh-Bruce.

He completely failed, though, to charm Miles Standish. This hard-working young man – at once actor, producer, promoter, manager, and businessman – had a remarkable sense of people, and so far from being captivated by Gorse, he took an immediate dislike to him. He saw at once that Gorse was trying to flatter and please him, and he suspected that Gorse's motive in doing so was not at all straightforward.

Then Gorse did nothing to improve matters by beginning to talk about theatrical things in a much too easy, too confident, and too appallingly ignorant way. Miles Standish was inured to philistinism from strangers in this matter, but Gorse's philistinism – because of its boastfulness and false sophistication – got under his skin.

Finally Gorse offended the young actor by suddenly and most ungraciously drinking up a half-full glass of beer and leaving him with a polite excuse.

Gorse had done this because he had suddenly observed Mrs Plumleigh-Bruce and Mr Stimpson leaving the house.

Miles Standish had observed the same thing, and he felt certain that Gorse was, for some reason, following those two.

What the reason could possibly be was, of course, beyond him. But he was certain that it was in some way a base one — that Gorse was up to no good.

Miles Standish was, in fact, one of the select few first to suspect that Gorse was up to no good in life generally — that he was, possibly, destined to see the inside of prison bars.

4

Following people without being detected by the followed is, even in the dark, no easy business. Private (and even police) detectives more often than not make complete idiots of themselves at this task. Gorse, however, was one of the most gifted followers in existence.

When outside in Friar Street he saw Mrs Plumleigh-Bruce and Mr Stimpson, at about a hundred and fifty yards distance, moving towards the eastern part of the town.

His fears were either that they would go into another public house or that they would take a bus. Without being exposed as a follower he could hardly enter one or the other after them.

But they did not do this. Instead they went, at a medium pace, and by ways which to Gorse seemed devious (but then he had not as yet found his bearings in the town) to a small dark road of what seemed to be recently built, semi-detached houses about eight minutes walk away from The Friar. There were low double gates and small front gardens in front of these houses.

Mrs Plumleigh-Bruce stopped outside one of these houses, and then, after a pause, went with Mr Stimpson through the gate.

Then they both went to the porch of the house, whose hall and ground-floor room were lit.

Gorse had a feeling that Mr Stimpson would not go inside the house, and he was right. After less than a minute's apparently rather intimate conversation in the shadow of the porch, Mrs

Plumleigh-Bruce went into the house and Mr Stimpson came brusquely back again through the double gate into the road and began to walk in the direction whence he had come. His air of brusquerie suggested, somehow, that he had kissed Mrs Plumleigh-Bruce.

Gorse succeeded, not without difficulty, in not being seen by Mr Stimpson, whom he continued to follow.

It soon became clear to Gorse that Mr Stimpson was returning to The Friar for another drink, and it is difficult to say exactly why he followed Mr Stimpson. Perhaps it was because he was a born follower, or perhaps he hoped to gain some further knowledge of Mr Stimpson's character by watching his back. Backs, even in the lamp-lit dark, give a good deal of information in regard to character.

Mr Stimpson walked less brusquely as he drew nearer to The Friar: and his shoulders, which had less than three hours ago been brushing against those of the nobility, began slightly to droop.

Gorse began to brood again upon Mr Stimpson's relations with the nobility, and he decided that, because of these relations, however slender or menial they might be, he would endeavour to make Mr Stimpson his friend.

One thing, he reflected, might well lead to another, if one was enterprising enough.

Both of these lamp-lit men in Reading – the followed and the follower – were social snobs. But whereas Mr Stimpson was a foolish, more or less superficial and light-hearted social snob, Ernest Ralph Gorse was a clever, profound, savage, bitter one.

Having watched Mr Stimpson re-entering The Friar, Gorse went into the Saloon Bar of a small public house in the same street. Here it was very much more quiet, and, sitting alone over another glass of beer, Gorse gave himself up to calm, level musings – musings upon Mrs Plumleigh-Bruce, Mr Stimpson, the military-looking man, the repertory actor, and the problem of his possible dealings with any one or all of these during his stay in Reading.

It would have been impossible for one who knew Gorse only in his debonair and talkative moods (and in company he was seldom in any other) to conceive how long and deep a thinker the red-haired, slightly freckled young monocle-wearer was when he was alone.

PART THREE

PEBBLES, BRASS, SILK, VERSES AND ANECDOTES

CHAPTER ONE

I

GORSE, that night, had surmised that Mrs Plumleigh-Bruce's house was a recently-built and semi-detached one; and he walked past it next morning, at about ten o'clock, in order to verify his impression.

He had, last night, marked the exact house by counting lamp-posts.

His overnight impressions were entirely correct. Sispara Road, which branched off, to the left, from the main road leading to Oxford, was one containing nothing but semi-detached houses, all of which were built in roughly the same architectural style.

These houses were squat, two-storied affairs, round-looking because of their bow-windows on the ground floor, and with red-tiled or green-tiled roofs.

Their fronts had all been most oddly treated. It looked as though the builder had had some sort of infantile sea-side mania for shingled beaches, and that, to indulge this passion, he had, having covered the external walls with thick glue, used some extraordinary machine with which to spray them densely with small pebbles.

Gorse, passing quickly by on the other side of the road, noticed that there were brass plates on the pillars which supported the double gates in front of both of the houses immediately adjoining Mrs Plumleigh-Bruce's. He could not, of course, this morning, see what was inscribed upon these plates. Later he learned that one of them proclaimed that a seemingly very highly qualified Chiropodist practised within during certain hours, and that the other announced the residence of a Commissioner for Oaths.

In the front gardens of most of these houses there were, in addition to sundials, countless images of Gnomes, Dwarfs, Fairies, Goblins, and Peter Pans – the inhabitants of Sispara Road having, it seemed, a strong turn of mind for the whimsical, the grotesque, and the beautiful, as well as for Oaths, Chiropody, Veterinary Surgery, Massage, Dentistry, and similar learned and healing professions.

2

Such, externally, was Mrs Plumleigh-Bruce's *pied-à-terre*, which bore the pleasing name of Glen Alan. (One of the houses next door bore the imposing name of 'Rossmore' – the other the lighthearted name of 'Deil-ma-Care'.)

Internally Glen Alan bore a strong aesthetic kinship (as did all the other houses in the road) to what was exhibited outside.

It was, to begin with, littered with pieces of brass, which had been moulded into almost every conceivable form of the whimsical, the grotesque, and the beautiful. Multitudinously sprayed pebbles outside a house nearly always indicate multitudinous pieces of brass inside.

There were brass trays, brass ornaments, and brass bells; there were brass pokers, brass shovels, brass tongs, brass coal scuttles, and brass toasting forks – all of these surrounded, of course, by brass fenders. There were brass ashtrays, brass candlesticks, brass paperweights, and brass jugs. Meals were announced by means of a brass gong.

In a clean and orderly household, such as Glen Alan certainly was, brass has to be cleaned, and only the cleaner, Mrs Plumleigh-Bruce's Irish maid, Mary McGinnis, could have given a full catalogue of all that went on in the way of brass inside this house. Mary – an extremely subdued but, in some ways, not at all unintelligent or unobservant girl in her twenties – would have been able to name the remotest brass cow, dragon, elephant, god, monkey, crocodile, lion, or snake in any room in the house.

Mrs Plumleigh-Bruce's sitting-room, in which she lunched, dined, and entertained, was, as may be guessed, the brassiest of all. The least brassy room was her bedroom.

This was exotic in quite another manner. Brass, indeed, had been almost completely banished from it, and whimsy and grotesquerie had been almost forsaken. Instead, sheer feminine beauty had been aimed at. In Mrs Plumleigh-Bruce's bedroom Silk, not Brass, reigned.

Mrs Plumleigh-Bruce's large bed (when it had been laboriously made by Mary), had an enormous rose-coloured silk coverlet which was surmounted at the bottom with a silk eiderdown, and at the top with a selection of round silk cushions. The dressing table (in front of which was a silk-covered stool) was draped with silk on runners, which were concealed by a pelmet made of the same material. There were silk lampshades, and the curtains were made of silky material. On Mrs Plumleigh-Bruce's silk-matted bedside table there was a telephone. This ugly black instrument had been most adroitly, fancifully, and enchantingly concealed by silk – that is to say by a silken doll. This doll had a miniature china bosom, neck and head (the last being adorned with a wig of silver silk), and a vast silk crinolin, which covered the telephone. This crinoline, of course, did anything but assist Mrs Plumleigh-Bruce either in answering her telephone or in getting at it to use it. But for the sake of beauty it is necessary to suffer, and the crude, mechanical twentieth century was kept at bay.

Mrs Plumleigh-Bruce's silken bedroom was, undoubtedly, a room for dalliance – silken dalliance, indeed. Mr Stimpson, who had on a few occasions been permitted to enter it, but certainly not, as yet, to dally, found it (as he was meant to do) impressive beyond measure, opulently intoxicating, heady, dangerous, thrilling, unmanning.

Mr Stimpson liked being unmanned.

3

Mrs Plumleigh-Bruce considered that her maid-of-all-work, Mary McGinnis, had a much too easy life, as 'they all do nowadays': and it is not, really, a simple matter to understand how one woman, whose sole business in the day is to attend to the wants of no more than one other, could have anything but an easy life. Nevertheless, Mary's twelve or more hours of work a day, at a salary of twelve shillings a week, was far from being easy. For Mrs Plumleigh-Bruce, who prided herself upon being a 'martinet', and who demanded what she so unhappily but so frequently called 'explicit' obedience from her servants, made, in her deceptively lethargic, slow, and fruity-voiced way, ferocious use of Mary.

Mary's life was, in fact, a sort of unending corridor in a hideous, thick dream she could not shake off – a thick dream of brass, of silk, of cooking, of laying, clearing away, washing up, log-chopping, coal-getting, fireplace-preparing, fireplace-cleaning, clothes-washing, clothes-ironing, dusting rooms, turning out rooms, turning down beds, getting hot-water bottles, making beds, making midmorning coffee, making tea, making cakes and sandwiches and thin bread and butter, making herself look seemly in her uniform (provided) in the afternoon, external and internal bell-answering, and so on and so forth. And, stalking behind her in this corridor was always Mrs Plumleigh-Bruce, with her indolent, quiet, yet steamroller-like insistence upon 'thoroughness' and 'explicit' obedience. If Mary, for instance, having made the bed, put a single round cushion at the distance of more than an inch from its correct place at the head of the bed, she would be made aware of Mrs Plumleigh-Bruce's displeasure, and any sign of such displeasure terrified Mary – for it made her feel that she might lose her employment, and be thrown upon the world.

And yet Mary did not look upon her work as a hideous corridor in a thick dream. She had the profoundest respect, one might say veneration, for Mrs Plumleigh-Bruce – as well as for her methods of discipline, which she regarded as being entirely correct.

The shrewd, sensible, humane Mary was, perhaps, not totally sane about matters of this sort: her darkly poverty-stricken upbringing in County Galway in Ireland had at an early age stunned her, distorted her idea of humane behaviour as applied to the human race as a whole. She did not really look upon herself as one meriting, or as one who would be a fitting recipient of, compassionate treatment – though she never never thought about such things on a fully conscious level.

Mary did not think that she could conceivably find a better 'place' than the one she had with Mrs Plumleigh-Bruce. She regarded her wages as excellent, and, like the Reading business-men, she took pride in her mistress as the 'Lady' of the neigh-bourhood.

Also Mary was strong, and, in a slim, rather gawky way, decidedly attractive. Naturally she looked about ten years older than her age; and her Irish teeth, of course, were in a bad way. Nevertheless the teeth which could be seen when she smiled were as yet presentable: her dark brown hair, eyes and face seemed, at moments, to be almost lovely; and, on her two afternoons off each week, which she spent with friends, she was often made aware of her charms.

These afternoons off, together with her attractiveness and the pride she took in working for an outstanding, a practically famous, local 'Lady', made her look upon her life as an enviable one.

4

Each day of Mary's enviable and unenvying life began at six o'clock.

At eight-thirty she entered Mrs Plumleigh-Bruce's silken sanctuary with a cup of tea, drawing back the silken curtains, causing the linen blinds to shoot upwards, and lighting the gas fire.

At nine-fifteen Mary again entered the room carrying Mrs Plumleigh-Bruce's breakfast on a tray.

At eight-thirty, when her tea was brought to her, Mrs Plum-leigh-Bruce was usually sleepy, and sometimes irritable. But when her breakfast came in at nine-fifteen she was often in a strong mood for amiable conversation, or even playful wit, with her Irish maid.

Mrs Plumleigh-Bruce's notion of wit suited to an Irish maid would have been, to any sensitive listener outside, extremely agonizing, for she talked in what she believed to be an Irish accent, and Irish idiom, to Mary.

She amused herself, in fact, by talking *Oirish*.

Oirish may be considered as a language in itself, and Mrs Plumleigh-Bruce's *Oirish* was, in a way, perfect – for it lacked nothing. It did not omit 'Bedad', 'Begorrah', 'Faith', 'Sure', or 'Entoirely'. She would ask Mary if it was 'afther' being, doing, or getting something that she was ('that ye are'), and she often used the greeting 'Top av the morning' to Mary. She pronounced the word darling as 'darlint', delighted as 'deloighted', indeed as 'indade', what as 'phwat', and the words 'It is' as ' 'Tis'. She used such words as 'Colleen', 'Mavourneen', 'Paddy' and 'Macushla'. It was incredible.

Was the use of this abominably facetious *Oirish* an attempt, on Mrs Plumleigh-Bruce's part, to please, to ease the lot of her poverty-exiled Irish maid? No – it was not. It was, on the other hand, a means either of patronizing Mary, or of making a fool of her. It was also a form of self-indulgence, and of Narcissism – self-indulgence because she greatly enjoyed displaying her virtuosity in *Oirish*, and Narcissism because, while talking it, she was all the time looking at herself, metaphorically, in a mirror, and profoundly admiring what she saw. While looking at Mary mockingly, quizzingly, a shocking sort of flirtatious, would-be-captivating *Oirish* twinkle came into her eye.

Mary herself did not notice this twinkle and did not really know what was happening. She did not get the impression that her mistress had gone practically mad, or even that she was making a fool of herself. She did not even know that Mrs Plumleigh-Bruce was imitating the accent and idiom of the land from which she, Mary, came. She took it all merely as one of the mysterious modes of behaviour of a class whose every deed and utterance were mysterious – almost beyond comprehension, but to be roughly identified and submitted to.

All the same Mary, on these occasions, was somehow aware that Mrs Plumleigh-Bruce was in a good humour – a better one than she was at any other time of the day. And this knowledge made her heart lighter, and show externally that it was.

Consequently Mrs Plumleigh-Bruce was given the impression that she was pleasing Mary beyond measure; and it was the remembrance of these almost daily little *Oirish* sessions with Mary which enabled Mrs Plumleigh-Bruce to boast, to her acquaintances, that she was 'great friends' with Mary, that she 'talked her own language', and that she treated her 'practically as an equal' (along with that demand for 'explicitness' in the matter of obedience).

5

This stoutish, silken Venus (as well as Lady) of Sispara Road, Reading, Berkshire, arose from bed at about eleven in the morning.

The time intervening between breakfast and this rising was spent in telephoning friends and tradespeople, and in reading.

Mrs Plumleigh-Bruce was a great reader. She called herself a 'voracious' one. (The word 'voracious' is applied almost solely to reading by the Plumleigh-Bruce class.)

But 'voracious' as she was, Mrs Plumleigh-Bruce was scholarly and highly fastidious here. No 'modern trash' for Mrs Plumleigh-Bruce, and scarcely any fiction. Mrs Plumleigh-Bruce specialized in History – French History, mostly.

'Glen Alan' French History was rather limited. It began and ended with Marie Antoinette.

In the character, life, death, looks and adventures of Marie Antoinette Mrs Plumleigh-Bruce was immeasurably interested. Mrs Plumleigh-Bruce, as has been said, was no friend of the People, so her attitude towards Marie Antoinette may be easily imagined. It was, in fact, one of admiration amounting to emotional adoration.

Mrs Plumleigh-Bruce fed this emotion by reading every popular, illustrated, and hysterically laudatory book about Marie Antoinette upon which she could lay hands. Mrs Plumleigh-Bruce was certainly not, by nature, a book-buyer, but Marie Antoinette had almost made her one. She would order from London, and pay as much as fifteen shillings for, a book about her heroine.

As an authority upon Marie Antoinette she was, naturally, almost equally well versed in the French Revolution. And this caused her also to read any popular denigrations of such characters as Robespierre or Marat that came her way. And when she alighted upon a book about the Reign of Terror her feelings both for the *macabre* and for sentimental pity were given full reign at one and the same time.

At times Mrs Plumleigh-Bruce, day-dreaming in bed, almost imagined herself to be Marie Antoinette in person – the crinolined, white-wigged, 'eighteenth-century' doll (with a patch on its cheek) covering the telephone on her bedside table being of considerable assistance in creating this illusion.

Marie Antoinette, in fact, furnished whatever there was of poetry in Mrs Plumleigh-Bruce's soul. But Marie Antoinette had more mundane uses as well. By virtue of the extensive knowledge of History she had accidentally bestowed upon Mrs Plumleigh-Bruce, the guillotined queen was extremely useful in enlarging the vanity, the complacency, and even the sharply material calculations of the pseudo-Anglo-Indian woman.

Knowledge is power. So, also, is an assumed knowledge of Knowledge. To Mr Stimpson (as well as to other men) the latter was highly exhilarating and potent in its effect. Mrs Plumleigh-Bruce, it seemed to Mr Stimpson, was something more than a Lady. She read, she understood, she 'knew' History – an important branch of Knowledge. Therefore she was 'clever'. She read History because she was 'clever', and she was 'clever' because she read History. She had a 'brain'. She was, then, for a woman, most unusual – in one way at least fascinatingly above Mr Stimpson's head.

Mr Stimpson often boasted about Mrs Plumleigh-Bruce's 'brain' – to himself and to others.

Mrs Plumleigh-Bruce was fully conscious of Mr Stimpson's feeling of veneration towards her in this direction, and she exploited it to the full. She frequently gave him lectures – lengthy and to him quite intoxicatingly recondite – upon History.

Mr Stimpson had not as yet cottoned on to the fact that History began and ended with Marie Antoinette.

6

Having dragged herself away from her researches each morning, and having forced herself to rise, Mrs Plumleigh-Bruce put on a very provokingly exotic garment.

This, also, was silken, and was, in those days, called a 'Kimono'.

Mrs Plumleigh-Bruce's Kimono was made of pale blue silk, and, after the manner of Kimonos, it was covered with dragons, chrysanthemums, and other interesting and intricate matters.

In her Kimono Mrs Plumleigh-Bruce went gracefully to the bathroom, and had her morning bath. Then she returned to her bedroom and dressed.

She was downstairs by about twelve o'clock.

She did not, at this time of day, use the sitting-dining-room, but a smaller room, which, next to her bedroom, she fancied most in the house. This room also, apart from the bedroom, was Mr Stimpson's favourite, and he fancied himself, in the event of his marrying Mrs Plumleigh-Bruce, using it a good deal.

It was, first and foremost, a room for a Man. It was 'tucked away': it contained a most serviceable roll-top desk, and it was mannish in other ways.

Mrs Plumleigh-Bruce cultivated, and in devious ways advertised to Mr Stimpson, the atmosphere of this room as one suited to the masculine spirit and habit. She alluded to it as a 'Study', as a 'Den', as a 'Snuggery', and as a 'Hidey-Hole'.

Some men, alas, are highly flattered by the notion of being provided with studies, dens, snuggeries or hidey-holes. It makes them feel that they are scholars, smokers, recluses, and clumsy lions.

This small room had a bow window facing the street, and two very small unopenable windows facing the side of the house next door. The two small windows gave little light, for, apart from their smallness, they were made of leaded stained glass which romantically depicted wave-and-foam-surrounded ships at sea.

In Glen Alan there were almost as many ships as there were pieces of brass. Nearly all of the parchment lampshades were ornamented with ships – or with ships' charts upon which ships were depicted. There were pictures of ships, including a reproduction of the seriously hackneyed 'Off Valparaiso', and there were two large models of ships – 'galleons' or 'caravels', of the sort that might be obtained from the firm of Liberty in Regent Street. Even some of the pieces of brass were ships.

There was only one reasonably pleasant ship in the house – a ship in a green bottle. But this had been relegated to the rubbish-heap – that is to say, to Mary's bedroom. And Mary herself did not think it particularly pleasing.

When she was in her 'Snuggery' Mrs Plumleigh-Bruce was brought coffee and digestive biscuits by Mary. These were put upon the desk – in front of which Mrs Plumleigh-Bruce sat upon a cushion in a swivel chair.

With her coffee Mrs Plumleigh-Bruce smoked her first cigarette of the day, and began to contend with the business thereof. She wrote letters, paid bills, or examined tradesmen's books – the last with extreme care in order to see that she had not been cheated either by the tradesmen or by Mary. Sometimes, she would ring a brass bell and question Mary closely about various items.

7

This morning, however, there was practically nothing to do, and Mrs Plumleigh-Bruce, over her cigarette, gave herself up to reflections of a mixed character.

The memory of Ernest Ralph Gorse soon entered, and at last almost completely dominated, her thoughts. In her mind's eye she saw him very vividly, and her mind's ear recaptured as clearly both his voice and the things he had said last night.

She wondered what he was doing in Reading, whether he would enter The Friar again, whether he would be staying long in the town, and, if so, where he was living or would live.

Thinking about him thus, in many different ways, and in relation to herself, one thing certainly did not enter her mind. She did not think of herself as his possible prey, or victim.

If anything, on the contrary, she thought of Ernest Ralph Gorse as her own possible victim – if not exactly prey.

CHAPTER TWO

I

WHILE Mrs Plumleigh-Bruce was thinking about Ernest Ralph Gorse, Ernest Ralph Gorse was thinking about Mrs Plumleigh-Bruce.

He was relieved from the necessity of wondering where she lived, for he had seen her house both by lamp-lit night and by day. And, having done so, he would have been glad to have given Mrs Plumleigh-Bruce information about his own present residence in Reading, for this was of a larger and more imposing kind than her own.

Ernest Ralph Gorse was now living in a three-storied house in Gilroy Road, Reading. Gilroy Road branched off from the Newbury Road, and, without being ostentatious, was much more imposing and delightful than Sispara Road. Its houses had been built in the late Georgian era, and had been reticently and decently numbered – not whimsically or impressively named as in Sispara Road – and there were no gardens or gnomes in front of them. Instead there were pleasant (and totally gnomeless) gardens at the back.

Gorse did not like the Georgian architecture of the house, for sprayed pebbles, front gardens and gnomes were actually more pleasing to his aesthetic tastes, and he looked upon Gilroy Road as being 'old-fashioned' in style.

Nevertheless, he realized that a very much higher social and economic grade of citizen dwelt in Gilroy Road than in Sispara Road.

Gorse neither owned nor rented this house, which he was occupying more or less by accident, for no particular reason, and rather reluctantly. It had been lent to him, along with its housekeeper, by an acquaintance of his – Ronald Shooter.

Ronald Shooter was, if in any business, in the car-business, and it was through this that the two had met, about two years ago. But Ronald Shooter, who was a little moustached man of about thirty-three, was not, truly, in any business; for, without ever being noticeably drunk, he drank from morning to night, and he had a good deal of inherited money of his own. For both of these reasons Gorse had made and cultivated the friendship. A friend with money, with people like Gorse, is naturally regarded as valuable, and one who drinks heavily is potentially more valuable still.

Gorse did not like Ronald Shooter at all. But then Gorse did not like anybody, and, actually, few people liked Ronald Shooter. The little man, in the drink in which he nearly always was, was bumptious, loquacious, an interminable teller of lewd anecdotes, a sordid womanizer, plainly conscious of the power of his money, and, all in all, a very serious bore. Gorse was his closest friend.

Only a few months ago Gorse and Ronald Shooter ('Ronnie') had taken together a fortnight's trip to Paris. Ronnie had insisted upon paying most of the expenses (he always embarrassingly insisted on paying for everything) and they had stayed at the Grand Hotel.

From this luxurious base they would emerge, each evening, to drink at *cafés*, and, afterwards, with the aid of guides, to visit brothels.

This trip had been, for the most part, exceptionally tedious to Gorse. For Gorse was not interested in Paris as a city; he did not like, and could only take little, drink; and, though he was by no means sexless, the level-headed young man did not like women in brothels.

However, he consoled himself with the thought that it was 'all in a good cause' – that is to say he was, by acting as companion, listener, and adviser, getting himself further and further into the good graces of the well-to-do, the lavish Ronnie.

On the trips to brothels Gorse, who acted as manager and negotiator, could, had he wished to do so, have pocketed for himself a lot of Ronnie's money. But he elected to do precisely the opposite. He had used his level head to save Ronnie's money – to preserve him from exploitation. He haggled about terms on Ronnie's behalf, and, in the sober mornings, would often present Ronnie with francs which he had either secreted or retrieved – thus greatly impressing his friend. Gorse always had both the wisdom and the self-restraint to look far ahead in cases of this sort.

On this trip Ronnie had met, and had been captivated by, a Canadian prostitute, and he had made promises to live in an apartment in Paris with her.

Gorse had thought that Ronnie, on his return to England, would not fulfil these promises; but he was wrong. Ronnie was already back in Paris and was living in an apartment, which he had rented for three months, with the Canadian girl.

Before returning to Paris Ronnie had been confronted with the problem of what to do with his house and housekeeper in Reading. He had, therefore, suggested to Gorse that he should live there – free of any charge unless Gorse cared to pay the housekeeper's wages.

Gorse had not particularly liked the idea, but, still with an eye to the future, had simulated great pleasure and gratitude.

And there were, in fact, many things to be said in favour of this exile in Reading. In the first place it was difficult to object to living in a house with a housekeeper already provided. Then Reading was very near London, and Ronnie had made it plain that Gorse was under no obligation to remain in Reading all the time – that he could spend almost as much time in London as he wished.

Then Gorse had a feeling that Reading might be a happy hunting-ground for a car-speculator – new and interesting territory. And on top of this the house in Gilroy Road was impressive – the first that Gorse, who had hitherto only lived in lodgings, had ever occupied. And an impressive house is not without its uses in the selling of cars.

Gorse had, however, as yet kept on his room in London, intending to see the lie of the land in Reading before deciding how much time he would spend there.

Having spent a few days of loneliness in Gilroy Road, Gorse had begun to hanker to return to London, and had even made up his mind to return and remain there for periods as long as were permissible during Ronnie's absence in France.

But, having met Mrs Plumleigh-Bruce, and the interesting set by which she seemed to be surrounded, and having seen her house, he was now strongly inclined to make Reading his base for a month or two.

2

As he walked this morning – he was a great walker and did most of his thinking while he walked – Gorse wondered whether Mrs Plumleigh-Bruce would be in The Friar again this evening. He rather suspected that she would not, and he decided that, even if she were there, it would not be advisable to go into the place himself.

He had, he fancied, made quite a strong impression upon the woman last night, and he believed that the right moment had already arrived, if not actually to display indifference, at least not to show any too great enthusiasm in the matter of meeting her again.

That evening, however, he was tempted to reconsider his decision. For, happening to pass The Friar on his way to a cinema, at about six o'clock, he observed the fair-moustached military-looking man of the night before entering; and this somehow gave him the impression that Mrs Plumleigh-Bruce was, or would be, in there also.

He was still not certain as to whether the military-looking man was her husband, and his anxiety to solve this problem once and for all was, he now found, very strong.

He therefore, did not go to the cinema, but to the small public house in which he had ruminated at such length last night. Here he ordered a glass of beer, and, sitting down, tried to make up his mind about his correct tactics in the next half hour.

CHAPTER THREE

I

THE military-looking man had in fact been a military man. He had joined the army during the 1914–1918 War and had risen to the rank of Major. He was known, and liked to be known, as Major Parry.

Major Parry was fifty-five, and, like Gorse's friend Ronnie, he drank and talked and thought about women in a silly way too much.

This was largely because, unknown to himself or to anyone, he was undergoing a change of life – what is now well known as menopause. This agitating condition was then, and by an enormous amount of people still is, supposed to be confined to women; but nothing in fact is further from the case. Though the physical and mental symptoms are less obvious, men are victimized by this disorder as much as women, and often with as serious, or more serious, consequences. Men constantly run away from their long-married and virtuous wives under the influence of this disorder.

In moral character and intellect Major Parry would have been, in a normal state, almost certainly Mr Stimpson's superior: but just at present he was not. He was a good deal lower in his thoughts and utterances, and thus lost favour with Mrs Plumleigh-Bruce, upon whom, despite the fact that he was married, he had eager designs.

He was, tonight, the first of Mrs Plumleigh-Bruce's court to enter The Friar. He ordered a large whisky and took it over to the vacant Plumleigh-Bruce nook. Then, having glanced briefly at his newspaper, he took out a pencil and a piece of paper from his overcoat pocket and began to scribble and think deeply, and then scribble, and think deeply again.

2

Major Parry was the victim of another misfortune besides the one already mentioned. Three years ago he had had the bad luck of having an Armistice Day Poem accepted, and spectacularly printed, on the front page and in a black frame, by a Reading newspaper.

This had made him almost a local celebrity, and he was deeply anxious to maintain his fame (and earn another three guineas) by writing another November the Eleventh poem in honour of the glorious dead.

Another poem, sent in the year before last, had been rejected: but he had had a most polite letter from the editor of the paper encouraging him to try his hand at the glorious dead next year: and by now the thing had become at once a hobby and a small obsession with him.

Diffident of his powers, and fearing the humility of another rejection, he had submitted nothing last November; but he had set his mind to the task of perfecting, during the winter and summer months, something for 1928.

Major Parry, who had somehow as a boy developed a small talent for rhyming, prosody, and even poetry of a sort, had several opening lines for his poem in his mind. His favourite, for the last three weeks or so, had been the mournful but simple:

'They are gone, they are gone, they are gone'

which was to be followed, probably, by a half-austere, half-ironical:

'Is it worth, then, thinking on'

But here the Major was in doubt. Did this line scan, and, if so, did it express the sort of tragic lilt he was aiming at? It would be all right if the reader would pause before and after the 'then', but the commas did not properly intimate that he should do this, and one could hardly use dashes. ('Is it worth – then – thinking on.') For this reason the Major favoured:

'Is the matter worth, then, thinking on.'

He liked this, but unfortunately, the solution of one difficulty only raised another. For his third line was pretty well decided on. It would be:

'Those who anguished as they shone'

or something like it. But talking about 'the matter' threw everything out. 'Is it worth, then, thinking on Those who anguished as they shone' was perfectly in order, but 'Is the matter worth then, thinking on Those who anguished as they shone,' certainly was not.

What about (Major Parry wondered, as he gazed at his piece of paper in the Plumleigh-Bruce nook in The Friar), 'Is it worth then thinking, thinking on?' Rather a nice, dreary and sort of Irish lilt, perhaps?

He would have to think about it and decide later. Of one thing he was fairly certain – the fourth and last line of the first stanza – that which followed 'Those who anguished as they shone.' This must, almost certainly, be:

'On Flanders Field?'

Major Parry was not particularly pleased by this line in itself. It was, he felt, a trifle banal and hackneyed. But its one great advantage outweighed any considerations of this sort. The Major was determined to make the last line of each stanza rhyme with the last line of each of the others, and the rhymes for the word 'Field' were not only magnificently plentiful, but richly appropriate, suggestive, and helpful to the poet.

There was, for instance, 'yield' ('Yet did they yield?'). Then there was 'sealed' ('Whose Fate was sealed.') Then there was 'healed' ('Whose wounds now healed'). And then there was 'steeled' ('To battle steeled').

Four absolute beauties you could simply conjure with. But there were, if necessary, many more. There was 'appealed' (to God . . .), 'revealed' (Light was . . .), 'shield' (Their safest . . .), and 'reeled' and 'wheeled'. You could depict Battle as having done either of the last two.

There were, even, if the worst came to the worst, 'peeled', and 'congealed'.

'Peeled' didn't seem to be much good to the Major, who simply couldn't think of anything more dramatic or stately to peel than apples, oranges, or bananas. But 'congealed' might do. One might suddenly go all realistic and congeal blood. Or, if that was going too far, mud.

Then if one came to think about it, there was 'pealed' spelt with an 'a' as opposed to an 'e'. Bells, of course. And 'heeled' was not completely to be dismissed. The heeled boot of the Hun and all that. 'Boots harsh (grim? crude?) and heeled'.

And what about 'Weald'? Sussex Weald. All earthy — and where the simple sort of ploughman chaps came from. 'From Wold and Weald' for instance.

You could, really, go on for ever, of course. And the real point was that 'On Flanders Field?', though slightly cheap, was the only possible last line for the first stanza.

It also had another advantage apart from that of providing such a fine crop of rhymes. It introduced a locality — the name of a place — Flanders — and the Major was anxious to use other names of specific places. Particularly, if it were possible, Passchendaele.

Mention of Passchendaele, he felt, would be most inspiring. It was not only a sonorous, slow, grim and romantic word in itself. It furnished almost as many rhymes as 'Field'. There was 'fail' ('Shall we then . . .?'). There was 'bewail' (Who shall . . .?). There was 'gale' (Midst War's great . . .). And 'pale', and 'dale', and 'veil', and 'hail', and 'quail' and 'flail', and 'nightingale', and 'grail' (holy, naturally) and 'vale', and innumerable other smashing ones.

But *not*, of course, 'jail', or 'male', or 'rail', or 'sail', or 'stale', or 'tail', or 'nail', or 'pail', or 'ale'. Although you *might* perhaps use 'nail', if you wanted to go all religious and do something about The Crucifixion. That involved nails, and, so as to get them into the singular, you could talk about 'Each and every nail' or 'Each piercing nail', or something like that.

Next to Passchendaele, the Major was tremendously anxious to use Ypres. But here, when it came to rhyming, he was totally stumped. In fact all he could think of, miserably, was Pepys. But the name of the famous diarist was neither a true rhyme to Ypres, nor, if you came to think about it, in the smallest way suited to the subject being dealt with.

The Major suddenly perceived that his mind was wandering, and that he must stick to essentials. He had got quite a good rough sketch of his first stanza: now he must get on to his second.

He wanted this to begin in the same mournful, repetitive way as the first, and he had already invented a first line for it which, he thought, could hardly be bettered. This was:

'They are fallen, they are fallen, they are fallen!'

But here again the rhyme problem was hideous. It was, in fact – or so it seemed to the Major at the moment – worse than hideous: it was insurmountable.

Come now, there must be something, thought the Major: and, as he went on wretchedly searching his mind, the most impractical and fantastic notions entered the Major's head.

There *was*, for instance (if you could only *somehow* break into an old-fashioned, foolish, foppish accent), 'appallin'' or, even, 'appallen', using an 'e' to make the rhyme more perfect.

The Major, who was tired, and whose whisky (his fourth this evening) had slightly affected his brain, now dreamily – and, because dreamily most ludicrously – began to extemporise.

'They are fallen, they are fallen, they are fallen,
It really was most, *most*, most, *most* appalin''.

Or:

'The slaughter, really *was* you know, appallin''.

Then there was 'mauling'.

'They got an absolutely *awful* maulin''.

Or:

'Those lads – good God – they got a frightful maulin''.

And, of course, there was 'callin''.

'Can't you hear yet, their voices callin', callin'?'

Or:

'Their sacrifice to Heaven high was callin''.

There was, even, a treatment of 'stone-walling'.

'Grit, *grit*, pluck, *grit*! They *stuck* at it – *stonewallin'*!'

Or:

'On sticky wicket – there they were – stonewallin'!'

Or:

'By Jove, *one* art they knew, those boys, *stonewallin'* '

And then there was 'crawling'. ('No whine from them, no whimperin', no crawlin' '), and 'bawling' ('Just listen! Hear the Sergeant Major bawlin'!'), and 'stalling'. ('No engine *there* was coughin', kickin', stallin' ').

To say nothing of 'galling' ('The situation really was most gallin' ').

Because of his intense anxiety and seriousness about his poem, the tired Major, in this whiskyfied rhyme-and-line reverie, had, as yet, completely failed to notice that he had entered the realms of pure idiocy, and it is really doubtful whether he would ever have done this – at any rate this evening.

But unfortunately, at this moment, Mr Stimpson entered the Saloon Bar, and, while ordering a beer at the bar from the barmaid, brusquely interrupted the Major's distressed trance with a hearty greeting.

'Evening, Major!' cried Mr Stimpson, and the composer replied 'Hullo, Stimpson', and put his pencil and piece of paper back into his pocket.

CHAPTER FOUR

1

HAVING been given his beer, and having taken a sip at it, so that it would not spill as he walked, Mr Stimpson went over to Major Parry, and sat down beside him.

'Well, Major,' he said, with great cheerfulness. 'What's the news with you?'

'Not a thing. Dull as ditch-water. What about you?' replied the Major, and there was a pause.

2

Businessmen – all over the world, in the remotest provinces and the mightiest capitals – do not, on the whole, like each other at all.

Major Parry did not like Mr Stimpson, and Mr Stimpson did not like Major Parry.

Major Parry was not, of course, strictly speaking a businessman. He was enormously and doggedly military. Nevertheless, like so many ex-officers, he mixed almost exclusively with businessmen, and, in general habit and manner of thought, he certainly was one at heart. His little, rather pathetic, school-acquired gift for versifying need not be taken into account. When Major Parry met Mr Stimpson businessman met businessman, and there was mutual dislike.

Why, then, do provincial businessmen constantly 'foregather', as they would put it, in their leisure hours?

The reason is that they are too useful spiritually to each other to refrain from doing so: they cannot do without each other. The very law of their being compels them to find someone upon whom they can unload their funny stories – the 'latest', the 'One About the . . .'

Just as *Oirish* is a language in itself, so what may be called 'One-Aboutism' is an art in itself – perhaps the only one which really stimulates people like Mr Stimpson and Major Parry.

The art of One-Aboutism, however, does not consist, as might be thought, mainly in the discovery and clever narration of the stories. These are hardly listened to, and are only perfunctorily laughed at, by the other One-Aboutist. The real art lies in succeeding in not being *out*-One-Abouted – in beating down, by astuteness, quickness, personality, and, if necessary, sheer vocal power, your rival One-Aboutist – in telling, in short, more and longer stories within a given time than anyone else present.

In those days of 1928 the now out-dated Limerick was still much used, and, before Mr Stimpson had been sitting more than two minutes with Major Parry, he had asked the latter whether he had heard the one about the Young Lady of Leicester.

Major Parry was in the unfortunate position of being unable to say that he had, and so he had patiently to listen to, and at the end manage to heave out a fairly presentable laugh at, the singular and, indeed, nauseating predicament of the Young Lady of Leicester.

Then the Major smartly counter-attacked with a Young Parson (about whom he had only heard that morning in another public house), from Brixham.

(Parsons, Vicars, Rectors, Old Ladies, Young Ladies, Old Men and Young Men are almost the only prominent or active citizens in Limerick-land.)

This amazingly quick *riposte* from the Major naturally displeased Mr Stimpson, but he also managed something quite reasonable in the way of a laugh. Then, in order rapidly to subdue his opponent, he said, 'Yes. That's a good one. And that reminds me of the story of the policeman in the tram. Know it?'

The expression 'And that reminds me', is constantly employed by the more ruthless One-Aboutist, and it is, on nearly every occasion, an absolutely lying expression – a flagrant device. The Young Parson from Brixham bore not the faintest resemblance, either in his character or his unusual experience, to the Policeman in the Tram. Therefore it was quite impossible for the one to have reminded Mr Stimpson of the other: and Mr Stimpson was hitting below the belt. Such technical fouls are, however, regarded by these *racconteurs* as more or less part of the game, for which no sort of Queensberry Rules has yet been invented.

The Major knew nothing about the Policeman, and so had to listen to Mr Stimpson describe his adventures in the tram – which, being extremely intricate, took at least three minutes in the telling.

The story of the policeman's adventure, as well as being involved, was of a sexual nature. Nearly all such stories are. Those which are not either deal with the processes of bodily elimination, or, felicitously killing two birds with one stone, deal with these processes and sex at the same time.

Major Parry listened for the three minutes with feigned pleasure, sniggering appreciatively at the indicated moments, and laughing aloud at the climax.

He found the story almost insufferably lengthy, tedious, and, because he did not really see the point of the climax, practically incomprehensible. Indeed, had not Mr Stimpson employed a certain look, certain gestures, and a certain rising and as it were goodbye-saying tone of voice – all of which could be easily recognized as showing that the end of the story had come – the Major would not have known that this had happened and that his cue for laughter had been given him.

The story of the Policeman 'reminded' Mr Stimpson of yet another story, which he related.

Of this the Major did at least see the point, but he did not think it in the smallest way funny. To his mind, it was, if such a thing were possible, as boring as the previous one.

Nevertheless Major Parry did not fail to take a mental note of this story. This was because stories of this kind, with people like Major Parry and Mr Stimpson, are capable of undergoing strange – it would not be going too far to say mystical – metamorphoses. When listened to, they are hideously dull. But if, having been heard, they are borne in mind for a few days by the sufferer, and, if, after a few days, the opportunity arises of his relating them in different company, then they are no longer dull. On the contrary, they are now quite, or very, or even uproariously or hilariously funny to the narrator, who is wounded bitterly if their richness – the last drop of the cream of the jest – is not appreciated to the utmost. The Major, almost certainly, would before long be telling this story of Mr Stimpson's elsewhere.

3

After a while the flow of story-telling – or rather Mr Stimpson's flow, for he was easily the Major's master in this art, and succeeded in finishing three stories and two Limericks up – came to an end.

They talked of other matters, including that of the weather, which was remarkably warm and muggy for the time of year.

The Major then complained that he was too warm at the moment, and he rose to take off his overcoat. As he did this, he asked:

'And is our Lady Joan gracing this hostelry tonight?'

'Yes,' said Mr Stimpson, with a rather funny look in his eye. 'I think she is . . . At least she *said* she was . . .'

'In which case,' said the Major, 'the atmosphere will be somewhat warmer still, I fancy. What?'

'Yes. I suppose it will . . .' said Mr Stimpson, and the look in his eyes became even funnier, and more evasive, than before.

Mr Stimpson's look must be explained.

Some months ago, before the Major had begun seriously to nurse and nourish designs upon Mrs Plumleigh-Bruce, and before Mr Stimpson had begun to entertain the idea of marrying her, Mrs Plumleigh-Bruce had not been treated at all respectfully in conversation between Mr Stimpson, Major Parry and other men.

Although acknowedged as the Reading businessman's outstanding Lady, she had, at that time, in fact been the subject of many joking, suggestive or lascivious remarks and innuendoes. She had been alluded to, to quote the less vulgar expressions used, as a bit of goods, the goods, a nice (or scrumptious) piece of skirt, hot stuff, and 'nice work if you can get it'. It had even been suggested that such work might not be at all difficult to get, and facetious bets had been made as to who would get it first.

But the days of such talk were, for Mr Stimpson at any rate, very much in the past. One's possible future wife cannot be spoken of in this way.

Therefore, when Major Parry, thinking of her as hot stuff, had suggested that the atmosphere would be warmer still when Mrs Plumleigh-Bruce entered, Mr Stimpson had been both embarrassed and displeased.

The Major had, in fact, in the existing circumstances, practically 'spoken Lightly of a Woman's name': and to do such a thing as this is one of the worst possible social crimes in the delicate minds of limerick-and-story tellers of Mr Stimpson's type.

Such people are exquisitely fastidious, and, therefore easily shocked in matters of this sort. (To tell a dirty, or even only slightly *risqué* story, in the presence of what they so often call 'The Sex', is only next, in caddishness and bestiality, to speaking Lightly of a Woman's name.)

The Major, being already married and having never even thought of marrying Mrs Plumleigh-Bruce, had, of course, no notion that she had recently become a Woman to Mr Stimpson – least of all one whose name could not be spoken lightly of. And so, in no way conscious of what he was doing, he continued to torment and embarrass Mr Stimpson.

'Yes,' he went on. 'As hot as jolly old Hades, in fact. At least them's *my* sentiments. I don't know about yours. What?'

'No, I don't know either really, I suppose,' was all that Mr Stimpson could manage to reply.

'Well, you ought to,' said Major Parry. 'I noticed you managed to obtain the privilege of escorting her home last night. And that's not the first time, either – unless my senses have deceived me. Or *have* they deceived me?'

'No,' said Mr Stimpson. 'I suppose they haven't – really.'

'No. So I thought,' said the Major. 'And how did *that* go?'

The Major, although he had not as yet any conception of the fact that, in Mr Stimpson's eyes, Mrs Plumleigh-Bruce had almost become a woman about whose name it was highly improper to speak lightly, was all the same aware that something of some sort was going on between these two; and he was highly interested in the exact character of the relationship. As he himself in his own way strong desired Mrs Plumleigh-Bruce, this was only natural.

He had noticed that Mr Stimpson had lately been more and more frequently given the privilege of escorting Mrs Plumleigh-Bruce home from The Friar, and one or two remarks and conversations between these two in his presence had revealed quite clearly that Mr Stimpson had more than once entered Mrs Plumleigh-Bruce's house.

As to the matters of the length of such visits, and the exact depths of Glen Alan into which Mr Stimpson had penetrated, and the capacity in which he had been received therein – these were matters of conjecture to the Major.

Was it possible that Mr Stimpson had already secretly managed to acquire that nice work which, it had been agreed, it might not be at all difficult to get?

The Major thought this unlikely, but he was determined to probe the matter, and so he had now said, in reference to Mr Stimpson's confessed escorting-home of Mrs Plumleigh-Bruce: 'And how did *that* go?'

'How do you mean – how did that "go"?' said Mr Stimpson, after a slight pause, and looking keenly at the Major through his thick-lensed spectacles.

'Well, how did it go?'

' "Go?" How?'

'I mean *Go*,' said the Major, doggedly, and, after a brief pause added, 'I mean for instance, did our Lady Joan issue an invitation to enter her abode?'

'No, I just left her at the front door – that's all.'

'Really,' said the Major. 'You didn't go further than that?'

'No,' said Mr Stimpson. 'No further than that . . .'

There was a pause in which the two men looked at each other – Mr Stimpson resentfully, the Major, in his innocence of the real situation, jovially, rallyingly, yet inquisitively. The thick lenses of Mr Stimpson's spectacles disguised his resentment, and so the Major had no qualms in proceeding with his light-hearted yet increasingly suggestive cross-examination.

'When I said "further",' he said, 'I didn't mean Geographically further.'

'What, then?' said the nettled Mr Stimpson. 'Historically?'

'Yes,' said the Major. 'Historically, if you like. I thought perhaps you'd been making History with our Lady Joan – our Lady Joan of Arc.'

'What sort of History?' said Mr Stimpson. 'I don't follow you.'

'Oh – a little amorous history, perchance,' said Major Parry, who, because he was talking about History, dropped into 'historical' language. 'Thou hast not, peradventure, made successful suit, or attempted such, with our illustrious Maid of Orleans?'

'Oh, no, nothing of that sort,' said Mr Stimpson. 'Believe me.'

'If Maid she may be termed,' said Major Parry. 'It seemeth to me very mightily otherwise. Doth it not so with you – after our now somewhat lengthy acquaintanceship with her?'

'I don't know . . .'

'Nay?' said the Major, whose whisky was now noticeably affecting him. 'I wot then, that thou'rt but little acquainted with the Sex, after all. In fact, to employ common parlance, I should say she's crying out loud for it.'

Really, thought Mr Stimpson, this is absolutely insufferable. But what could he do? He knew that the Major intended no offence, and that he himself had brought this misfortune upon himself by, at an earlier date, speaking in just the same way about Mrs Plumleigh-Bruce. He decided that he must somehow change the subject: but, for the life of him, at the moment, he could think of no subject to change to, and so he just murmured 'Do you? . . .' and the Major marched inexorably and terribly on.

'I do,' he said. 'In fact yelling the place down for it.'

'Oh – come now . . .' said Mr Stimpson.

'Well,' said the Major. 'Such are my views, at any rate . . . However – it seems that I'm mistaken about your own relations with the brave and noble girl from Orleans. Thou hast not, so thou assurest me, as yet waged amorous battle with her?'

'No. I haven't . . .'

'Nor pierced her valiant armour? What?'

'No,' said Mr Stimpson, still beating around in his mind for another topic of conversation. 'Certainly not . . .'

' 'Twould be without much difficulty pierced, methinks,' said Major Parry with mock sententiousness.

The situation had now reached a point at which the exasperated Mr Stimpson was nearly out of his mind, and, possibly, he would not have been able to control himself if, at this moment, a young man had not entered the bar and ordered a bitter from the barmaid.

The young man was Ernest Ralph Gorse. His curiosity about the Major's relationship with Mrs Plumleigh-Bruce had won the day.

4

Mr Stimpson, who, as we know, had the night before hated both the presence and aspect of Ernest Ralph Gorse, now found both pleasing.

Normally he would have either cut the young man or given him a curt greeting from a distance. Now, because of the intense suffering Major Parry was inflicting upon him, he took a totally different line. He caught Gorse's eye, and waved to him, and said, or rather shouted, cordially, 'Hullo! . . . Good evening!'

Gorse returned the greeting in the same words, and in the same spirit, and sat down on a stool to read his newspaper. But Mr Stimpson would endure no such unsociability.

'Come and drink it over here,' he said, employing the same half-shout. 'And let me pay for it.' (Gorse was at this moment paying the barmaid.)

'Well,' said Gorse, picking up his glass of bitter and walking towards Mr Stimpson and the Major. 'I'll bring it over, but I've paid for it already. How are you?'

'How are *you*?' said Mr Stimpson, warmly, and he introduced Gorse to the Major, and Gorse sat down with both of them.

PART FOUR

GORSE THE FORTUNE TELLER

CHAPTER ONE

I

THE enormously imperturbable Gorse was not always immune from fear, and he now found himself decidedly afraid of the Major, who might be Mrs Plumleigh-Bruce's husband, and who, if he were the ex-military man he seemed to be, might easily expose as false his pretensions, made last night to Mrs Plumleigh-Bruce, to having served in France during the 1914–18 War.

This fear of the Major was not lessened by the fact that the latter, as soon as Gorse was seated, began to look at him in a keen and protracted way.

In fact the Major, who was rather uncouth in the matter of staring at people, was only wondering, quite naturally, who the hell this reddish-haired young stranger was, and why Mr Stimpson had so eagerly summoned him over to the practically sacred Plumleigh-Bruce nook. But Gorse, equally naturally, did not interpret the Major's look correctly; and it even occurred to him that Mrs Plumleigh-Bruce had told her husband (the Major) about the young man she had met last night who had got into the army at the age of sixteen, and that the Major, having seen him, did not believe a word of it, and meant to examine him closely about the matter.

For all these reasons there was now a long and uneasy silence between all three. Gorse, being least at ease of all three, at last found this silence so unendurable that he was spurred into

breaking it, and he banally resorted to the weather. He said that
he thought that the evening was warmer.

'Warmer?' said the Major. 'It certainly is. In fact it's damned
muggy and unseasonable. In fact I've just taken off my overcoat,
with that blazing fire and all ... I don't know why you two
don't take off yours. I know my old friend Stimpson always
sticks to his like a leech, but I should've thought you're young
enough to be more Spartan, Mr – Gorse – was it?'

Gorse still did not like the way the Major was looking at him.
Nor did he like the suggestion that he should remove his overcoat.
Nor did he like the rather brusque and military '– Gorse – was
it?' All three made him feel that the Major was inviting, if not
almost ordering him, to enter the witness-box and undergo
examination.

'Yes. That's right. Gorse,' he said, and added, feebly employing
a small joke which he normally, when asked about his name,
brought forth with a certain gusto. 'Not Furze. Or Broom. Or
Bracken – or Heather, or anything like that ... And I think I *will*
take your advice, and doff the dear old outer garment, cloak or
mantle.'

He rose, and took off his overcoat in yet another silence. Now
his nerve was returning. This was probably because there had
luckily come into his mouth the words 'doff the dear old outer
garment, cloak, or mantle', and they had given him confidence.
Gorse, all his life, was in the habit of employing, in speech as
well as in writing, a style which was a hideous, wretchedly imitative mixture between those of Jeffery Farnol and P. G.
Wodehouse. His monocle encouraged this style. And the style
encouraged the wearing of his monocle. It was all part of that
'Silly Ass' act in which he took such pride.

He also employed, at times, the ridiculous pseudo-Elizabethan
or 'historical' style of speech which the Mr Stimpsons and Major
Parrys of life so often employed – a style of speech closely
related to his own Jeffery Farnolism.

He was now almost completely himself again. If the Major
meant to put him through it, he felt, he was ready for it.

Having briskly and neatly folded his overcoat, he put it on the
seat beside him, and, sitting down, faced the two middle-aged
men, who were still silent, but no longer, to Gorse, formidably
so.

'Well,' he said, hitching his trousers cleverly in the manner of a monocle-wearing Wodehouse character. 'I seem to be somewhat making myself at home – don't I? Aren't I butting in a bit? Haven't I interrupted some momentous confab betwixt my grave and venerable masters? What?'

He looked, first at the Major, and then at Mr Stimpson.

2

'No,' said the thickly-lensed Mr Stimpson rather shiftily. 'We had no subject in hand meriting further discussion, I fancy. You're most welcome – I assure you.'

'What?' said Gorse. 'No ponderous matters concerning the affairs of this, our state – our realm?'

At this he snatched out a high-powered gold cigarette case from his hip pocket, and without a word offered a cigarette to both – Mr Stimpson politely rejecting the offer, and the Major accepting it, thus further easing Gorse's mind.

There was a cheap mode, in those days (even more popular than in these) never to say 'Thank you' when accepting a cigarette. The Major did not say 'Thank you', and this friendly and knowing lack of courteous gesture pleased Gorse even further still.

'Well,' said the Major, tapping his cigarette on the table, while Gorse tapped his own upon his gold cigarette case. 'I don't know about affairs of state. It was more a question of a state of affairs, if anything.'

'And may I ask the purport of such question?' asked Gorse. 'Or would that be intruding? Wilt thou not tell me the matter engrossing thee?'

He went on tapping his cigarette, and so did the Major. Gorse did this rather nervously – the Major ponderously.

Then Gorse produced a brilliant silver cigarette-lighter from his waistcoat pocket, and flicked on a light for the Major.

Both cigarettes having been lit, Gorse took the initiative.

'A state of affairs, you said?' he said. 'Come now – wilt thou not disclose thy story, e'en unto a stranger?'

'Well,' said the Major, puffing at his cigarette. 'It's a very old story – a very old story indeed. In fact it's the oldest story in the world.'

'Ah,' said Gorse. 'Then I think I can guess. You're alluding – I take it – to what our friends across the English Channel, which I myself have only so recently crossed, would term *L'Amour*. Correct?'

'Yes. Quite correct,' said the Major. 'So you've just come back from France, have you?'

'Yes. Only a few weeks ago.'

'Really? ... Where did you go?'

'Nowhere,' said Gorse, 'but Gay Paree. And gay enough I found it, in all conscience.'

'You did – did you? It's such a long time since I've been there myself that I wouldn't know.' Here the Major again showed curiosity on his face as he looked at the bold and puzzling young stranger. 'What were you there for – business of pleasure?'

'Pleasure,' said Gorse. 'Three weeks undiluted pleasure – such as only Paris, as no doubt you're aware, can provide.'

Gorse, as we know, had had, in fact, an almost intolerably wearisome fortnight with his friend Ronnie in Paris. But he had been sharp enough to observe that the Major's eyes had lit up at the mention of 'Gay Paree' – and that to talk of pleasure, in the 'Parisian' sense, would both stimulate and impress the man.

'So you strolled along the Bois de Boulogne,' said the Major, quoting the old music-hall song, 'with an independent air – did you?'

'*Most* independently,' said Gorse. 'And not solely along the Bois de Boulogne – either. In fact I indulged my fancy in several other places – believe it or not.'

'The Music Halls? ... The *Folies Bergères*, and all that? ...' suggested the Major.

'Yes. The *Folies Bergères*, and a good deal *more* than that,' said Gorse. 'I'm sure I needn't tell *you*, sir, that in that gay city there are many other Halls, and haunts, in which even more enticing things than Music are provided. Or does Music come first with you in life?'

'No,' said the Major. 'Music's an also-ran, as far as I'm concerned, and particularly when I'm in Paris. And you certainly needn't tell *me*. But didn't it cost you a pretty packet of money?'

'Yes. It did indeed cut into the good old wad a bit,' said Gorse. 'It has to, if you do things properly – and I'm sure you'll agree it's wise to do things properly on such occasions, and in such a wicked city as Gay Paree. Isn't that your experience?'

Gorse was playing up this 'Gay Paree' business for two reasons. In the first place he was certain that he was obscurely exciting, as well as plainly impressing, the Major. In the second, he felt that, by keeping the conversation on this topic he would soon solve the problem about the Major which concerned himself and his possible future dealings with Mrs Plumleigh-Bruce. In fact, he rather fancied that he had solved it already. If the Major were Mrs Plumleigh-Bruce's husband he would not, Gorse fancied, talk (at any rate in a public house which his wife entered) in so eager and easy a way about the pleasures of brothels in Paris. ('And you certainly needn't tell *me*' the Major had said only a moment ago.)

However, Gorse knew that there are hardly any limits to which certain married men will not go when drinking in public houses in male company; and so he was still in doubt about the Major's relationship with Mrs Plumleigh-Bruce.

'Yes . . .' said the Major. 'You've certainly got to do things properly, or you're asking for trouble. Though perhaps you're safer in Paris than anywhere else.'

This did not help Gorse with his problem. It might merely be that a middle-aged man was giving a young man advice. Gorse decided to try a more direct, local attack.

'However,' he said, 'where were we? Weren't you saying that you were discussing a state of affairs – a state of affairs concerning the old, old story. And wasn't I inquiring what the story was?'

'Were you? . . .' said the Major, vaguely – vaguely because in his thoughts about Paris he had lost the main thread of the conversation.

'Why yes. Surely. Wasn't I, sir?' said Gorse, now appealing to Mr Stimpson, who had been sitting all this time in silence and with a glum and fishy look on his face.

Mr Stimpson, now forced into the conversation by Gorse, had been looking silently glum and fishy because he had not been liking the conversation between Gorse and the Major.

Mr Stimpson, without ever having visited Paris, had never taken to the idea of it at all. He thought of it, of course, only as a city of sin – and, though he had more than once sinned, both in thought and deed, in England, he was envious of that sort of sin, abstruse, elaborate, yet facile, which (so he had gathered) went on in Paris.

And this upright, fastidious and patriotic man, naturally did not have any fancy for those people who ate frogs, and to whom he alluded, mostly, as 'The Frogs'.

Over and above all this, Mr Stimpson was, just at this period, in a strongly puritanical mood.

Provincial businessmen contempleating marriage are more often than not in such a mood. Purity suddenly overwhelms them. The women they are about to marry must, in the course of nature, be immeasurably pure, and meaning to remain so for the rest of their lives. Therefore they, the businessmen, are under an obligation to go in for purity themselves. Impure behaviour must not be indulged in, and impure thoughts must not be thought, and impure utterances must not be made. Even other people must not speak in the smallest way impurely. (There is, of course, a sort of Special Treaty, or Dispensation, in regard to the narration of impure anecdotes or limericks.)

However, Mr Stimpson had now been directly questioned by Gorse about the main thread of the conversation, and he had perforce to answer.

'Why – yes,' he said. 'I believe you were . . .'

'Well, then,' said Gorse, looking at the Major again. 'Can't you tell me something about this particular example of the old, old story? Or would it make my juvenile ears blush?'

'No. I don't think so,' said the Major. 'We were only discussing a Certain Lady, that's all. And she's not even one you'd know about, unless I'm wrong. I mean you wouldn't unless you're a resident of Reading and a frequenter of this hostelry. And you're not either, are you?'

'Well,' said Gorse. 'Yes and no. I'm probably only what you'd call a bird of passage in Reading – but I've already frequented this pub. In fact I did so last night. Didn't I, sir?' He again appealed to Mr Stimpson.

'Yes,' said Mr Stimpson. 'Quite correct.'

'And as for ladies, "certain" or otherwise,' the audacious

Gorse continued, 'let me see now. I don't know that any have come my way at all . . .' He affected to pause, search his memory, and suddenly remember. 'Oh yes! I have met one. Only last night, and in here. That's again correct, isn't it, sir?'

'Yes,' said Mr Stimpson, now deeply regretting having, to save himself torture from the Major, spoken to Gorse this evening. 'That's right.'

'And very charming she was,' said Gorse. 'Not at all "certain", as I saw it. Or "uncertain" one might say. In fact she seemed to me a lady, in the true sense of the word, from top to toe.'

The bold, shrewd Gorse was now both pumping and flattering the two men – mitigating, or disguising, the pumping by the flattery. Mr Stimpson – to him clearly either Mrs Plumleigh-Bruce's pursuer or paramour – could not be anything but pleased by what he had just said. Nor could the Major who, in Gorse's mind, still might conceivably be her husband.

'Why,' said the Major, addressing Mr Stimpson. 'Has our young friend here met our Lady Joan?'

'Yes,' said Mr Stimpson, and looked at Gorse. 'We had a little chat at the bar last night – didn't we?'

'Really,' said the Major. 'How interesting . . . And what did *you* make of her, Mr Gorse?'

This query from the Major enabled Gorse to make up his mind once and for all that Mrs Plumleigh-Bruce was not the Major's wife. Further, the way in which the Major had put the question – his underlining of the word 'you' combined with a faintly amused and disdainful expression in his eye – made Gorse suspect that the Major in no way put Mrs Plumleigh-Bruce on a pedestal of any sort – rather the contrary in fact. And so he now hedged with both men.

'Well, I didn't really have time to make anything of her,' he said, and went on to another matter which had slightly puzzled him. 'By the way, I notice you alluded to her just now as "Lady" Joan. Is she in truth an entitled lady of quality – or did you speak in jest? I don't even know her name – with a handle attached to it or otherwise.'

'No, it's only a little joke,' said the Major, 'and her name's Plumleigh-Bruce – Mrs Plumleigh-Bruce.'

'Married, or widowed?'

'Widowed,' said the Major. '*Long* widowed.'

He was again somehow suggestive in the way he stressed the length of her widowhood, and Gorse did not fail to notice this.

'We always call her our Lady Joan, for some reason,' the Major continued. ' "Our Lady Joan of Arc" is my own usual appellation.'

'Oh yes?' said Gorse. 'But surely the widowed Mrs Plumleigh-Bruce, your Lady Joan of Arc – could not be the same Certain Lady who was under discussion when I appeared on the scenes?'

'That's all *you* know,' said the Major. 'In fact I think we were discussing a little question of her armour – weren't we, Stimpson?'

'Her armour?' said Gorse. 'Now I'm afraid I don't follow you.' (But he did.)

'Well, we were just wondering whether it could be pierced, that's all,' replied the (to Mr Stimpson) vilely vulgar and ostentatiously lewd Major. 'And, if so, how easily.'

'Oh yes?' said Gorse, quickly glancing from one to the other. 'And what conclusions did you come to – if any?'

'Well, *I've* got *extremely* decided views,' said the Major. 'But my friend Mr Stimpson here seems to be in doubt. Don't you, Donald, my boy?' (Mr Stimpson's Christian name, it will be remembered, was Donald.)

Mr Stimpson, who would now willingly have physically wounded the Major, could only reply: 'Yes. I am. Certainly.'

Gorse perceived that the man would have liked physically to wound his friend. He hesitated as to whose side he should take, and, in order to satisfy his curiosity by the light of the sparks he might make fly, he decided to encourage the Major.

'Well,' he said. 'The proof of the pudding is in the eating – isn't it?'

'Yes,' said the Major, going from worse to worst. 'And what we all want to know is whether anybody's *eaten* the pudding yet, and, if so, who it is that's done the eating.'

'Yes. I see ...' said Gorse. 'Though I suppose it's a little impolite to allude to so charming a lady as a pudding – isn't it?'

The Major now achieved the miracle of going from worst to worse than worst.

'Well, I don't know about that,' he said. 'She is a bit puddingy, if you look her all over and come to think about it ... Didn't *you* notice certain traces of avoirdupois, Mr Gorse?'

'Well, my meeting was so brief that I hardly noticed,' said

Gorse, deciding to make the sparks fly further and faster. 'But she certain struck me as no skeleton, shall I say?'

'Not,' said the Major, 'that I have any particular objection to puddings. In fact puddings are rather in my line, on the whole . . . But perhaps I've got curious tastes.'

'Well,' said Gorse, in a detached way, 'I don't really know . . .'

'You *will*, young man,' said the Major, 'when you're older. The older you get the more puddingy you like them. I was like you when I was young. But when you're more advanced it's the extra pound of flesh you want – believe me. What think you, my silent friend, Mr Stimpson?'

There was a pause.

'By the way,' said Mr Stimpson. 'You know that Mrs Plumleigh-Bruce is coming in here tonight. In fact any moment now.'

Mr Stimpson seemed to think that the announcement that Mrs Plumleigh-Bruce was soon to appear in their midst, was near, would somehow scare the Major, make him drop the subject. But he was mistaken. Nor did the Major (though his whisky had now gone violently to his head) miss Mr Stimpson's pompous use of 'Mrs Plumleigh-Bruce' instead of the easy and familiar 'Our Lady Joan'.

'Oh – so "Mrs Plumleigh-Bruce" is – is she? So much the better. We can then more closely scrutinize the pudding – see exactly how puddingy Mrs Plumleigh-Bruce is. Plumleigh's rather a good word, by the way. Makes you *think* of puddings. Plum Puddings. *Delicious* plum puddings – what?'

The Major drank off the little whisky which remained in his glass. 'Well – what about all of us having another drink while we await the serving of the pudding – what?'

At this moment, most alarmingly to the Major, the pudding was within less than three yards of himself.

Mrs Plumleigh-Bruce, though arrogant in manner, was an exceedingly quiet and unobtrusive intruder into rooms or into company. Mr Stimpson, even, had not observed her entrance into the bar. This soft, supremely dignified unobtrusiveness was, perhaps, part of the woman's inner arrogance.

'What *are* you men talking about?' said Mrs Plumleigh-Bruce, with gracious humour. 'Puddings? What on earth do you know about puddings?'

CHAPTER TWO

THE three men rose – the Major giving a brisk military salute to the woman who had so recently figured in his imagination as a plum pudding.

Mrs Plumleigh-Bruce. who had not heard enough of the conversation to know that she had been compared to something you stick holly into at Christmas, all the same sensed that there was something slightly funny in the reception she was now given by Mr Stimpson, Major Parry and Gorse.

She was inclined to put this down, however, to shyness – shyness caused by the presence of the stranger, Gorse. And, in any case, she quickly dismissed any such suspicious thoughts, for she was, though she would never have admitted it to herself, delighted beyond measure to see Gorse. She had thought, during the day, that the interesting young man had possibly gone out of her life for ever. Now he was in her very own nook – her web, as it were.

Mr Stimpson, Major Parry, and to a certain extent Gorse, were, needless to say, in a state of grave embarrassment, which they tried to conceal as well as they could.

Mrs Plumleigh-Bruce had brought her 'bloody dog' (as both Mr Stimpson and Major Parry, for once in agreement, always secretly thought of her spaniel) with her, and the settling-down and insincere flattery of this animal delayed for a few moments at least, the tactful management of the pudding question.

But soon enough the dog was settled, and the pudding was there again.

What on earth was to be said, and how was it to be explained away? Everything depended, of course, upon how much of the conversation Mrs Plumleigh-Bruce had heard, and this was completely unknown.

The whole matter, perhaps, might be tactfully dropped. But

this was risky. Moreover, Mrs Plumleigh-Bruce did not herself permit this.

'Well. Do go on,' she said, having sat down. 'What were you saying about puddings? And what do you think you know about them?'

Gorse came to the rescue.

'No,' he said. 'We weren't professing to *know* anything about them. We were just talking about them. We were, in fact, mundane as it may seem, having a lengthy discussion, as to what would be our favourite meal, if we were given *carte blanche*. And we were going through it course by course. The Major here had arrived at plum pudding – hadn't you, sir?'

'That's right,' said the Major. 'I'm all for it.'

'Every day?' said Mrs Plumleigh-Bruce. 'Or just at Christmas time?'

'Oh – every day,' said the Major. 'In fact three times a day if necessary.'

'Oh – you detestably coarse man,' said Mrs Plumleigh-Bruce, employing, as she so often did, what she imagined to be a sort of Marie Antoinettish flirtatiousness. 'It's *just* what I'd've thought of you.'

She was not usually flirtatious with the Major, who, she considered, did not deserve such a compliment. But flirtatiousness, though directed apparently towards one man, may be in fact aimed at another. She was, in reality, at this moment, flirting with Ernest Ralph Gorse.

'Well,' said Gorse. 'We weren't only talking about eating – we were talking about drinking – having another spot, in fact. Yours is a whisky, I think, Major – and yours is a beer, I think, sir, isn't it?' He then, as he rose, turned from Mr Stimpson to Mrs Plumleigh-Bruce. 'And yours, I fancy – unless there's any variation from last night, is a Gin and It – No?'

There were now the usual claims from the men as to whose 'turn' it was to pay for the round, and Gorse succeeded in establishing his own.

'There's plenty of time after this,' he said. 'Besides, the situation simply demands a drink all round on me tonight. My researches, last night, into the form and qualities of the equine quadruped richly rewarded me – believe it or not. So if you'll all remain seated I shall now play the rôle of *garçon* and bring you the sustenance as specified.'

At this he went over to the bar and ordered drinks from the barmaid.

While waiting for these he wondered what sort of impression he had made upon Mrs Plumleigh-Bruce with the shots he had fired. He had shown himself as one casually lavish in the matter of paying for drinks; he had (lyingly, of course) intimated that he had won a good deal of money on today's Racing; he had done this in what he considered a most gracious and well-worded little speech which included the French word *garçon* (he had used *carte blanche* earlier on, and he intended to use his recent trip to France as much as possible when he had rejoined her); and, best of all, he had flattered Mrs Plumleigh-Bruce by remembering what she had been drinking last night.

Gorse fancied that at least one of these shots must have gone home.

In fact, all of them had.

Gorse ordered a large Gin and Italian for Mrs Plumleigh-Bruce and himself, a pint of bitter for Mr Stimpson, and a large whisky for the Major. He carried them over, in two journeys, to the Plumleigh-Bruce nook.

When he was seated again, Mrs Plumleigh-Bruce protested against his having ordered a double, as opposed to a single, Gin and Italian: but Gorse said 'Well, you know, I really don't think it'll bring you to ruin,' and then, after he had been thanked by all for the drinks, and there had been a rather awkward pause, he said, 'Well – here's jolly old How, and all that. And what have you all been discussing in my absence? The problem of the perfect repast – as before?'

The others – all of whom were now looking, almost staring, with great curiosity at this perhaps over-bold and overgenerous young stranger – replied that they had not.

'Not that it's not a most fascinating subject,' said Mrs Plumleigh-Bruce. 'May I ask your ideas?'

'Well – it's difficult to say,' said Gorse. 'But of one thing I'm certain. I certainly wouldn't go to England for it.'

'Where, then?' said Mr Stimpson. He spoke rather sharply, for, whereas Mrs Plumleigh-Bruce was emphatically intrigued by Gorse's personality, and the Major found it puzzling but by no means intolerable, Mr Stimpson was liking it less and less. This was largely because he had already sensed that his possible future wife was decidedly interested in the young man. He was also quite certain that Gorse was yet again going to allude to the unvisited yet deeply envied and hated France.

'Oh,' said Gorse. 'France. Where else? I'm afraid English cooking isn't at all in my line. Is it in yours?' He looked at Mrs Plumleigh-Bruce, amusedly and knowingly.

'No,' said Mrs Plumleigh-Bruce. 'It certainly isn't – if I had my way. But don't tell my Irish maid that. She does try so hard – poor thing.'

'The deadly secret shall not be revealed,' said Gorse. 'However, I'm sure you'll agree that French cooking is really the only possible thing. Don't you?'

Before Mrs Plumleigh-Bruce could reply, Mr Stimpson cut in quickly.

'Including,' said Mr Stimpson, 'frogs?'

The jaws of the man suffering so acutely from Gallophobia were now set hard, and his tone was quite savage. Gorse took advantage of this by adopting a particularly urbane, and therefore gently reproachful tone.

'Why, yes, I can't say I exclude the frog – though it's not a delicacy I go in for regularly. May I ask *your* opinion on that much discussed matter?' said Gorse, again addressing Mrs Plumleigh-Bruce.

'No,' she replied. 'I entirely agree with you. There's a lot to be said for the frog.'

Mrs Plumleigh-Bruce had never actually eaten a frog. Indeed the idea of doing so nauseated her. But she was aware that those who would seem sophisticated must profess delight, or at any rate not disgust, in frog-eating, and so, in order to hold her own with Gorse, she had as good as said that she had indulged in this experiment.

Major Parry, who himself had never eaten a frog, was now more candid than Mrs Plumleigh-Bruce, and admitted that he had not, but that he would not have any objection to doing so. He then made the well-known, agonizingly stale remark about the resemblance between the flavour of a frog and that of a chicken.

Mr Stimpson had now been made a fool of, and his spectacles did not prevent him from showing as much on his red, moustached face.

Mrs Plumleigh-Bruce who, it must be remembered, often entertained the notion of marrying this man, saw that frogs must not be rubbed into Mr Stimpson, and that she must help him out.

'However – one can't survive on frogs only – can one?' she

said. 'And we still haven't come to your perfect meal – have we? What would you begin with – anyway?'

'Well – if I had my way, I'd begin with nothing but the best,' said Gorse. 'But then, if I had my way, which I haven't, I'd have nothing but the best all round – food, cars, clothes, everything. It's an economy in the long run – don't you agree?'

'Yes,' said Mrs Plumleigh-Bruce. 'I certainly do . . . But how would you start this meal of yours?'

'Oh – paté, prawns, oysters, and all that,' said Gorse. 'And I'm on remarkably friendly terms with lobster soup – if correctly made.'

'Yes. I adore lobster soup, I must say,' said Mrs Plumleigh-Bruce.

'Oh – and then I was forgetting caviare,' said Gorse. 'Caviare, above all.'

Mrs Plumleigh-Bruce felt that it was permissible to dispute the merits of caviare. Her husband once, in the presence of, and with the support of, a senior officer, had done so. She therefore decided to do the same thing with Gorse. She was now in the position of finding it quite difficult to hold her own with this young man – a type of experience she had not encountered for a long while anywhere – least of all in Reading.

'Well – I'm not so certain about caviare,' she said. 'I'm afraid I rather waver in that direction.'

'Oh – do you?' said Gorse, and Mr Stimpson, having himself eaten caviare, and encouraged by Mrs Plumleigh-Bruce's seeming hesitation, saw a chance of recovering lost ground.

'Tastes like cart-grease to me,' he said, grimly. 'Ball-bearings soaked in cart-grease.'

'Oh, Donald,' exclaimed Mrs Plumleigh-Bruce. 'Do not be so horribly vivid and lurid. You're worse than Leonard.' (Leonard was Major Parry's Christian name.)

The words 'horribly', 'vivid' and 'lurid' (in addition to suiting Mrs Plumleigh-Bruce's low-toned, studiously mouth-projected and fruity voice to perfection) were, she felt, taken together and used one after the other, impressive, clever, and charming – charming in her own particular manner. She had even practised, in the privacy of her bedroom – both mentally and vocally – the use of these three words in combination, as a girl of another era might have practised 'Stewed prunes and prisms'. She was very satisfied by the rendering she had just given, and wondered whether Gorse had been charmed.

Gorse had not. Women, in any case, never charmed Gorse – at any rate conversationally – and, in this case, he perceived that Mrs Plumleigh-Bruce was being abominably affected. He decided, in the near future, to play upon, by seeming to be ravished by, any further affectations of the same kind. And he observed, among other things, that both Mr Stimpson and Major Parry had been captivated by her words and voice at this moment. Gorse was advancing rapidly with what now seemed almost certainly to be his Reading holiday-task – Mrs Plumleigh-Bruce.

'Yes,' Mrs Plumleigh-Bruce went on. 'I must say I *am* in two minds about caviare ... However – what would you choose to follow?'

'Well,' said Gorse. 'We mustn't overlook our dear old friend the omelette – particularly our friend when cooked in France and nearly always our enemy when cooked over here – don't you agree?'

'I certainly do,' said Mrs Plumleigh-Bruce. 'The French are absolutely superb at omelettes – aren't they? ... But do go on. You're simply making my mouth water with all these delicacies.'

'I'm sorry,' said Gorse. 'I suppose I've been spoiled by my recent sojourn in Paris.'

'Oh. Really?' said Mrs Plumleigh-Bruce. 'Have you been to Paris lately, then?'

'I have indeed,' said Gorse. 'And very reluctant I was to return to my native land – I can tell you – though I hope I'm being in no wise unpatriotic.'

'No. You must find it a very dismal contrast – between Reading and Paris,' said Mrs Plumleigh-Bruce, looking at him. 'And from what you told me about yourself yesterday evening, one could hardly call you unpatriotic.'

Gorse knew exactly to what she was referring. She had in mind his (imaginary) service in France during the 1914–18 War and his (actual) activities among the ranks of those opposing the working class in the General Strike of 1926. But he feigned complete ignorance.

'Well, I hope I'm not,' he said. 'But what makes you so certain, after my remarks concerning my country's culinary efforts, about my patriotism?'

'Oh – only what you were telling me last night.'

'Oh. Really? What was that?'

Gorse was aware, of course, that the tricky moment had come. Now he was in danger, possibly, of being exposed as an impostor by the military man sitting opposite to him. (He had no fear of Mr Stimpson.) However, he had worked out a long while ago, and had again gone over in his mind only this morning, the details of his regiment and general record in his invented military experiences in France. Gorse, who as a boy at school had had a tremendous predilection for uniforms and war, knew almost as much about Army matters as he did about cars. Also he had pumped, and by pumping flattered, his loquacious friend Ronnie Shooter, about his military adventures in France, and he had decided, that, if ever questioned too closely about his own spurious career as a soldier, he would impersonate, in retrospect, Ronnie. Now, too, he was conscious of being in a good mood, and felt that he could hold his own with the Major, or, if that became too difficult, cunningly dodge the subject.

'Well – your joining up and all that,' said Mrs Plumleigh-Bruce. 'I hope I'm not revealing a secret. *You* told it to me, anyway.'

'Oh,' said Gorse. *'That . . .'*

'What?' said the still aggressive Mr Stimpson. 'Did you join up? When?'

'Yes,' said Mrs Plumleigh-Bruce. 'And he managed to do it at the age of sixteen. That's right, isn't it, Mr Gorse?'

'Yes. Correct enough,' said Gorse, and here, as Gorse had expected, the Major cut in.

'Good Heavens,' he said, 'you weren't old enough for that – were you? I mean even if you got in at sixteen – were you?'

Gorse noticed, with pleasure, that the Major's look and tone, so far from being suspicious and hostile, were credulous and flattering.

'I was, though,' said Gorse. 'Of course, I looked a lot older than my age in those days. Just as, so it seems, I look a lot younger than my age nowadays. How old would *you* take me to be at the moment?'

The Major looked at him.

'Oh,' he said, 'Twenty-two – three – four. Just possibly five.'

'And you?' Gorse asked Mrs Plumleigh-Bruce.

Mrs Plumleigh-Bruce did not know whether Gorse wanted to look older or younger than his years. She thought older, probably.

'Well – possibly twenty-five,' she said. 'But I certainly wouldn't like to bet on it.'

'And you, sir?' said Gorse to Mr Stimpson.

'Yes,' said the crudely spleenful Mr Stimpson. 'I'd say you're a good twenty-five.'

'Well – you're nearest,' said Gorse, 'but you're all hopelessly out. I'll be thirty within a matter of weeks.'

'Well – I certainly'd never have thought that,' said the Major.

'No. Nobody does. And I can never make up my mind whether it's an advantage or not. I suppose it's very nice to be thought so extremely juvenile. On the other hand, when it comes to business matters, I often fail to be treated with the respect which I consider due to my years.'

'Well,' said Mrs Plumleigh-Bruce. 'I certainly think you ought to be treated with respect. Anyone who wangles his way into the army at the age of sixteen should be treated with the profoundest respect, I should say. And you were in France, too, weren't you?'

'I was,' said Gorse, sententiously, ruminatively, and retrospectively, looking into the distance. Things were now getting decidedly warmer, and this distant look served to conceal the fact that he was thinking quickly in preparation for the cross-examination which he felt certain was coming.

'Really,' said Mr Stimpson. 'Were you in France? Where?'

Mr Stimpson was proving much more suspicious and difficult than the Major, but Gorse still was not in the least afraid of him.

'In many and varied places,' he replied.

'And in an active capacity?' the Major, who had only served in an administrative capacity and had not been to France during the war, now asked.

'Well,' said Gorse. 'For long periods not at all as active as one could wish. But extremely lively – I can assure you. However, I came out completely unscathed.'

'And what outfit were you associated with?' The Major certainly was now looking quite keenly at Gorse, but, Gorse surmised, in a respectful and marvelling rather than doubting way.

'The Gunners,' said Gorse. 'The Royal Horse Artillery – to be precise.'

'And did you get a commission?' asked Mrs Plumleigh-Bruce. 'You certainly must have deserved it.'

'Yes,' said Gorse. 'I did finally achieve the rank of Lieutenant.'

'And were you in any of the big shows?' asked the Major.

'Yes. I was present at more than one – I must say.'

'Do tell us,' said Mrs Plumleigh-Bruce.

'Now – I really mustn't become reminiscent, you know,' said Gorse. 'If there's any reminiscing to be done, I'm sure that's up to the Major.

'No,' said the Major. 'I had an extremely dull time. In fact, hard as I tried, I never actually crossed the Channel. So it's for you to hold forth – if anyone.'

'Well, *I* think it'd be better if no one did,' said Gorse. 'To *begin* with these stories are always extremely boring to everybody – except the participant . . .'

'And to go on with?' said Mr Stimpson, who simply could not control his rage.

'And to go on with,' said Gorse, imperturbably, 'one doesn't really like – at least *I* don't – digging up these things. There are some things one wants to forget – and most of all when drinking in cheerful company. I know some people simply can't resist pouring forth their war experiences – but that's not my line at all. And I know a lot of other fellows – particularly those who went through the worst of it – who feel just the same. I'm sure *you* can understand that – can't you – Mrs Plumleigh-Bruce?'

'How on earth did you know my name?' Mrs Plumleigh-Bruce was surprised into asking.

'Well – I have to admit that I was making inquiries about it before you came in. I hope you don't think it impudence. It was really a compliment – I assure you.'

'And taken as such,' said Mrs Plumleigh-Bruce. 'I assure *you*.'

'Well, I'm glad to hear that.'

Gorse now saw that this rather stupid, rather plump woman, was falling for him, hook, line, and sinker, and that he must not, at present, go too far – particularly in front of the two men who were so clearly enslaved by her.

He looked at her, seeking the cause of this enslavement, and wondering whether he himself could be attracted by her physically in any way in the future. Such a thing, he now thought, was not absolutely inconceivable. Plumpish she certainly was, but the Major, inspired by whisky, had certainly gone too far even in facetiously comparing her to a plum-pudding. She had very nice, friendly, sparkling eyes, a good skin, and a lascivious mouth, which was, to Gorse, not spoiled by the rather rabbity teeth. Gorse, like many other men, had a liking for rabbity teeth. Also, affected as they were, and as he knew they were, he did not altogether dislike her low, 'musical' voice and fruity accent.

Gorse was not, it must be remembered, seeing the Mrs Plumleigh-Bruce whom her maid Mary saw during most of the day. With Mary the eyes were narrower and meaner, the mouth was sulky and malicious rather than lascivious, and the voice, while remaining affected, was coolly commanding in a most objectionable way.

But now Mrs Plumleigh-Bruce was dressed in her very best clothes, and 'got up to kill' – to kill Ernest Ralph Gorse, actually – though, while dressing this evening, she certainly would not have admitted this. Nor did Gorse suspect any such thing.

'Well,' said Mrs Plumleigh-Bruce. 'You certainly seem to have crowded a lot into your twenty-nine – or as you say nearly thirty – years.'

'Yes. I think I've managed to see a bit of the world – one way and another, and in its various aspects.'

'And what on earth brought you to Reading?' asked Mrs Plumleigh-Bruce. 'Surely *that's* not a very desirable aspect of life to want to see?'

'What's wrong with Reading?' said Mr Stimpson.

'Now, then, don't be foolish, Donald,' said Mrs Plumleigh-Bruce. 'You're not at your best when you're pretending to be so violently provincial.'

Once again, in her queenly, low-voiced snubbing of Mr Stimpson, Mrs Plumleigh-Bruce was flirting with Gorse.

'Well, I *am* provincial,' said Mr Stimpson. 'I don't go gadding about on the Continent and all that. I'm too busy. And even if I weren't I doubt if I would. It's not in my line, as it happens.'

'Don't mind him, Mr Gorse,' said Mrs Plumleigh-Bruce. 'But tell me – how did you manage to land up in Reading?'

'Yes,' said the Major. 'It's certainly a pretty awful hole – taken all in all.'

'Well,' said Gorse. 'It was purely by chance, as a matter of fact. I have a friend – he was doing Paris with me, by the way – and he's lent me his house here, along with his housekeeper.'

'That sounds very generous of him,' said Mrs Plumleigh-Bruce.

'It is,' said Gorse. 'But then he's absolutely rolling, wallowing in money – and so I suppose he can afford to be generous.'

Here Gorse, having greatly exaggerated the wealth of his friend in Paris purely for the sake of impressing Mrs Plumleigh-Bruce, had a sudden inspiration.

'And there's a little more to it than that,' he added. 'He's bored stiff with the house himself – he's got a lot of property and houses all over the place – and he wants me to buy it from him – lock, stock, and barrel. Whether I shall or not remains, of course, to be seen . . . However, that's why this bird of passage has alighted in Reading, and proposes to stay here until he's made up his mind.'

Gorse, all his life, had, when lying, the gift of sudden inventions and inspirations of this sort. It was largely because of this gift that, when he was ultimately a nationally famous figure, people often said that he had a 'genius' of a perverted and evil kind. Such people were, perhaps, right.

This particular little fiction about his friend wanting to sell the house in Gilroy Road, which had entered his mind seemingly purely by accident, was destined to have most serious and interesting consequences in his dealings with Mrs Plumleigh-Bruce.

CHAPTER THREE

'WHEN you say,' said Mr Stimpson, still in a bellicose and cross-examining mood, 'that your friend's got property all over the place – do you mean all over the place in Reading, or just all over the place everywhere?'

Knowing as much about house property in Reading as, perhaps, anyone else in the town, Mr Stimpson had a faint hope of catching Gorse out, or, at any rate, of showing his superiority in at least one branch of knowledge or sophistication.

'No, not "all over the place in Reading", – just all over the place – all over this island – this "precious isle set in a silver sea", or whatever Shakespeare calls it.'

'And where's the house – if it's not a rude question?' said Mr Stimpson, asking a rude question.

'Gilroy Road,' said Gorse. 'Know it?'

This made Mr Stimpson sit up. It gave him, indeed, almost as much of a shock as he had inflicted upon Gorse last night when he had alluded to the brushing of his shoulders against those of the nobility. For Gilroy Road was, Mr Stimpson knew, possibly the most distinguished road in Reading. In Gilroy Road dwelt the most affluent, the most old-fashioned, and the most gently born residents of the town.

Mr Stimpson, like Gorse, did not at all like the 'old-fashioned' Georgian architecture of Gilroy Road: but it was, all the same, a road which had to be taken very seriously by an Estate Agent.

'Really,' he said, hardly endeavouring to conceal that he was astonished. 'Gilroy Road? Yes . . . I certainly know it.'

The Estate Agent had now displaced the snubbed and envious man.

'Yes, I know Gilroy Road all right,' he went on. 'And a very interesting little bit of Reading it is.'

'Why so interesting?' said Gorse. 'They seem to be asking a pretty stiff price for the houses there, and I haven't quite been able to find out why – as yet, at any rate. They're nice and spacious and large and all that, but they seem to be a bit too old-fashioned to me – both outside and inside.'

'Oh,' said Mr Stimpson, now almost completely forgetting his animosity towards Gorse in his interest in the subject in hand. 'That's the mystery. They *are* old-fashioned – you're right. In fact I doubt if I'd want to live in one if you paid me. But our view isn't shared by everyone, I can tell you. In fact, they're asking for more money for a house in Gilroy Road than you'd believe – believe me.'

'I certainly do believe you,' said Gorse. 'In fact I have every reason to – from personal experience.'

Gorse had noticed the change in Mr Stimpson's mood, and decided to make friends with him.

'Tell me – what sort of price would *you* say was reasonable?' he asked.

'Well. I wouldn't say it was reasonable,' said Mr Stimpson. 'But I can give you a rough idea of the price . . . You certainly wouldn't get one, freehold, under two thousand five hundred, and three thousand pounds'd be nearer the mark.'

'That,' said Gorse, 'is exactly what I've found – somewhat to my surprise. In fact that is just about where I am at the moment, in my present negotiations – or rather contemplated negotiations.'

'Well,' said Mr Stimpson. 'If you got one for twenty-five hundred you wouldn't be a loser, I can assure you.'

'Again you reflect my own sentiments, and what I've gathered elsewhere. But it still remains a bit of a mystery.' He turned to Mrs Plumleigh-Bruce. 'Do *you* know Gilroy Road?'

'No,' she replied. 'I've never heard of it, as a matter of fact . . .'

'Oh, come now, surely you have, Joan,' said Mr Stimpson. 'You must know it. It's where Sir Charles Wharton lives. In fact I've pointed it out to you.'

'Oh, yes,' said Mrs Plumleigh-Bruce. '*I* remember . . . I remember the road at any rate. I just didn't know it was called Gilroy.'

'Sir Charles Wharton?' said Gorse. 'Now – who is he? . . . My friend Ronnie never told me about him . . . Knight, or Bart?'

'*Bart*, believe it or not!' exclaimed Mr Stimpson. 'Of course he's got a house in London as well, but he was born in Gilroy Road, and he's stuck on to the place. Sentimental, I suppose. He's pretty old. How he got born there I wouldn't know. But there's a lot more to Reading than you'd think – I mean anyone who'd just seen Broad Street and Huntley & Palmer's, and just that . . . Yes. We Boast a Baronet in our Midst – believe it or not.'

Gorse was, secretly, as delighted by the Baronet as Mr Stimpson was. For, as he was at present occupying a house in Gilroy Road, he could now himself Boast a Baronet, not only in a vague Midst, but as a near neighbour. Everything seemed to be falling into his hands.

'I wouldn't be surprised,' said Mr Stimpson, 'if Sir Charles hadn't helped to put the prices up. A Bart – and he's none of your new creations – he goes back pretty well to the Conqueror, as far as I can gather – gives a sort of *cachet* to the place, I suppose. Now I'm breaking into French myself. But that's the word I want, isn't it?'

'Yes. That's the word all right,' said Gorse, as if politely attempting not to be too patronizing to Mr Stimpson in front of Mrs Plumleigh-Bruce. 'It's incredible, isn't it – the length to which snobbery goes – even in these days. So I'm living within a stone's throw of a Baronet! I must see that I behave myself! But, joking apart, you don't think twenty-five hundred too much to pay for a house in Gilroy Road?'

'I certainly don't,' said Mr Stimpson. 'In fact I think you'd be extremely lucky if you got away with it at that.'

'Well, I'm very grateful for your advice, and I'll think about it, and very likely act upon it.'

Gorse now thought the time was ripe for the further subduing of Mrs Plumleigh-Bruce by asking about her own small dwelling-place. He again turned to her.

'And where do *you* live?' he asked her. 'Are you in as august a position as myself, or more humble – or perhaps very much more august?'

'Oh,' said Mrs Plumleigh-Bruce, 'Very much more humble.'

'I find that hard to believe,' said Gorse. 'But stranger things than that happen in life nowadays. May I ask where it is?'

'Oh – it's off the Oxford Road,' said Mrs Plumleigh-Bruce. 'Just a quiet little row of semi-detached houses. My chief reason for living in it is that it was "bequeathed" to me by my sister. It bears the remarkable name of Sispara Gardens.'

'What-ara?' said Gorse.

'Sis,' said Mr Stimpson. 'Sispara. It's a funny name.'

'It certainly *is* funny,' said the Major. 'Funny in two ways. It always makes *me* think of *Cas*cara – in fact.'

'Oh, Leonard,' said Mrs Plumleigh-Bruce, rebuking (half in order still to flirt with Gorse) the Major for this allusion to the then enormously popular aperient. 'You really are abominable. What am I to do with you – you atrocious man? And you've made that particular little joke at least a dozen times before.'

'Have I?' said the Major, meekly. 'I'm sorry . . .'

'However,' said Gorse. 'What's in a name? The point is whether Sispara Road's comfortable and convenient. Is it?'

'Well – it's not too bad – in its own way, of course,' said Mrs Plumleigh-Bruce. 'But I've never looked upon it as anything more than some sort of temporary *pied-à-terre*, really.'

'Well – I trust it's not so old-world in style as Gilroy Road. And that all, or nearly all, modern conveniences are supplied – running h. and c. – reasonable amount of min's walk to Station or bus. And telephone, and all that?'

The last-named convenience – the telephone – was the one in which Gorse was interested.

'Yes. Running h. and c.,' said Mrs Plumleigh-Bruce. 'But I'm afraid my maid Mary frequently allows it to run cold just at the wrong moments. And it's quite ten minutes' walk to the Station.'

'And the telephone?' asked Gorse, permitting himself to look in a rather suggestive way at Mrs Plumleigh-Bruce – as if he might telephone her himself in the near future. He had meant not to go any further with this sort of thing in front of her two admirers. But he had to find out whether the woman was on the telephone. Meetings in The Friar would, if he meant seriously to tackle and pursue Mrs Plumleigh-Bruce, clearly not be enough.

'Oh yes,' said Mrs Plumleigh-Bruce. 'I've got a telephone.'

'And are you in the book?' asked Gorse, with the same look, 'or do you keep it secret from the world?'

'No,' said Mrs Plumleigh-Bruce, interpreting his look exactly as Gorse had wished she should, and giving him a by no means uninviting glance in return. 'It's open to the public gaze.'

There was now, almost, a secret understanding between the two – the subtle but familiar telephone-pact which is revealed in the eyes of those who desire to become more privately or intimately acquainted with each other.

Gorse saw that his two rivals had both smelt the possible existence of such an eye-pact, and he hastened to do his best to destroy their suspicions.

'I asked you,' he said, 'because I'm not in the book myself as yet – naturally. And if I'm *going* to take the house I'll certainly have to be. Tell me – can it be done fairly quickly, or do you have to wait for months and months?' He was addressing all three – but particularly the now almost tamed and friendly Mr Stimpson.

'Oh no,' said Mr Stimpson. 'It shouldn't be long. It's a question of luck, really – whether you're inserting it at just the right time. But you ought to get to work as soon as possible, if you *are* going to stay here.'

'And the question is,' said Gorse, ponderously. '*Am* I? Would *you*?'

'Well,' said Mr Stimpson. 'It really all depends on –'

But Mr Stimpson was prevented from finishing what he wanted to say.

For at this moment, Mrs Plumleigh-Bruce, meaning to get a handkerchief out of her bag, accidentally spilt her glass of Gin and Italian with the sleeve of her coat. The drink went over the table, on to her hand, and on to her skirt.

Just as Gorse's unpremeditated lie about his contemplated purchase of a house in Gilroy Road was to have a serious and intricate effect upon his future dealings with Mrs Plumleigh-Bruce – so was Mrs Plumleigh-Bruce's accidental upsetting of her drink, at this moment, also fated to have considerable influence upon these dealings. They were, at any rate, expedited by the small accident.

CHAPTER FOUR

I

'O H – how appallingly clumsy of me!' said Mrs Plumleigh-Bruce, but, before she had got the words out of her mouth Gorse had snatched the handkerchief displayed in his front pocket, and was himself wiping her skirt.

Gorse's handkerchief was immaculately clean and made of the finest Irish linen. Mrs Plumleigh-Bruce noticed this.

'Oh – thank you so much,' she said. 'And you really shouldn't spoil your handkerchief.'

'Never mind about the handkerchief,' said Gorse soothingly, as he dabbed at her skirt in a modest yet expert and very thorough way. 'It's sticky stuff – Gin and It – and particularly sticky when taken externally. Also quick measures are advisable in such a case . . . There . . . I don't think there'll be much of a stain now – or at least nothing that a little petrol won't remove . . . And I see your hand's wet. Come along now. Let's deal with that, and then we'll replenish your glass . . .'

Gorse took her hand and began to wipe it.

'I feel just like a nursemaid,' he said.

'And I feel just like a very naughty little girl,' said Mrs Plumleigh-Bruce.

Gorse was, for the second time, breaking his resolution not to proceed with his enticing of Mrs Plumleigh-Bruce in front of the two men. But Gorse seldom let a gift-opportunity simply handed to him on a plate, as this had been, go by – and he was determined not to do so in this case. His flirtation with Mrs Plumleigh-Bruce (particularly after her 'little girl' stuff) was now flagrant, but he did not care. He meant, indeed, to press it further.

Having wiped the palm of Mrs Plumleigh-Bruce's hand, he went on to wipe the table, saying, while doing this:

'That's a very interesting hand, by the way. Or palm, rather.

But then I suppose you don't believe in the science of the palm. I personally do – believe it or not.'

He was now putting his soiled handkerchief into his overcoat pocket.

'What do you mean?' said Mrs Plumleigh-Bruce. 'Fortune-telling?'

'Yes. If you like to put it that way. Character reading, anyway. Perhaps it's the same thing.'

'You mean you think you could read my character by looking at my palm?' said Mrs Plumleigh-Bruce.

'I certainly do. And I *will*, if you like, moreover . . . However, the immediate business in hand is to replace your drink. You had hardly any of that one – so shall it be the same again?'

'No,' said Major Parry, rising. 'This is my turn. What are you all going to have?'

Mr Stimpson said he would 'stay out'. Mrs Plumleigh-Bruce said that, well, she *would* have a *small* Gin and It. Gorse said that he would go over to beer again – a half of bitter.

The Major went to the bar to get the drinks, and Mr Stimpson, taking another sip at his beer, looked intently at his possible future wife and Gorse. This look did not bother Gorse at all. He was on top of his form.

'Well,' he said. 'What about this hand of yours. Shall I have a try?'

'Well, you can have a try,' said Mrs Plumleigh-Bruce. 'Though I don't really believe in a word of it, myself.'

'Very well, then, let's try – shall we?'

He took her hand without any sort of hesitation, and there was a pause, as he gazed at it.

'Well,' said Mrs Plumleigh-Bruce, who, particularly because of Mr Stimpson's look was by no means at her ease, 'Can you discern my future? . . .'

'Well,' said Gorse. 'Your *immediate* future, at any rate. You are going to be brought, by a soldierly man, a small Gin and Italian . . . But we must go deeper than that – mustn't we?' And he gave a very fine imitation of one who is really quite serious about what he is doing.

Gorse, when he ultimately achieved great fame, had many stories told about his 'fortune-telling'. Journalists, as well as more serious writers, nearly always mentioned it.

The cheaper journalists enlarged upon this alleged gift. One of them said that it was 'a pity he couldn't tell his own'. And his alleged 'Hypnotic eyes' were nearly always mentioned along with his power of deceiving women by pretending to look into their future.

Gorse had neither the gift of hypnotism nor that of looking into the future. In regard to fortune-telling, all he had was common sense, shrewdness and bravado.

To one who has these qualities, nothing is easier than making women (and men) believe that their characters, pasts and possible futures are being explained and exposed with almost uncanny intuition. Treated properly, sceptics often become near converts about 'fortune-telling' – in which art Gorse was, though spurious, certainly very capable indeed.

Gorse had discovered that this art was, like all arts, though difficult in a way, enormously simple – that it really relied mostly upon simplicity.

He had a few simple rules.

Having roughly summed up the character of the one who is having her or his hand held, you first of all very deftly pretend that you are much more interested than you thought you were going to be. Then, after a pause of the right length, you say 'You're disappointed in some way,' or 'You haven't got from life *just* the thing you wanted,' or both. Men, as well as women, always agree with both of these hypotheses.

Then you seem to be even more interested still. Also puzzled. And then you say: 'Yes – there's some *frustration* somewhere – I can't quite *get* at it . . .'

This also is universally agreed with.

Then, when you are dealing with a woman, you say, with a little giggle: 'Well – I'm afraid there's been a *man* in your life – in fact very much *more* than one . . .' (The most hideous, jealous, malicious and neglected spinster will unfailingly rise to this.)

Then you say: 'I may be wrong, but I'd say you're in *slight* money troubles – or at any rate money complications . . .' (Agreed again by all.)

Then, having said: 'Of course this is the most fascinating thing *ever* . . .' you say: 'Not only have there *been* a lot of men in your life – there's one coming *into* it, before many moons – unless I'm gravely mistaken.'

Such were Gorse's usual openings – all of which he now, and in the order named, employed upon Mrs Plumleigh-Bruce, who, while holding on to as much as she could of her scepticism, became very fascinated indeed.

2

The Major returned with the drinks.

'Oh, you've started, have you?' he said, alluding to the couple who were holding hands. 'Has he already disclosed the mysteries of your future?'

'No,' said Mrs Plumleigh-Bruce. 'He's really only more or less dealt with things as they are, so far, and I must say he hasn't been far out. Now let's get to the future – shall we? What about this "man" who's coming into my life, for instance?'

'No,' said Gorse, as if this did not at the moment interest him. 'I'll come to him in due course. Let's stick to generalizations for a little – shall we?'

'Very well,' said Mrs Plumleigh-Bruce, with half-mocking, half-serious meekness.

'Well,' said Gorse. 'One thing's extremely clear ... You're an easy-going person on the whole – *very* easy and long suffering – but when you're taken advantage of you're an extremely formidable opponent. In fact, I certainly wouldn't like to be up against you, myself.'

'Wouldn't you? ...'

'No. Definitely not.'

Gorse for a moment wondered whether he was going too far with this drivelling flattery, but then decided that he was not. He was, after all, in exceptionally foolish company, and both the Major and Mr Stimpson seemed to be pleased by, rather than jealous of, this gross praise of the woman by whom they were both so enchanted.

'Well? ...' said Mrs Plumleigh-Bruce.

'Well – although you like taking things easily, you're extremely fastidious.'

'In what way?'

'Oh – about the house ... I mean I wouldn't like to be a servant of yours. I mean I wouldn't like to be one unless I did the work very thoroughly indeed. I should say that everything has to be very much "just so". Am I correct?'

Gorse knew he was on doubtful ground here. But he would have been willing to bet that Mrs Plumleigh-Bruce fancied herself as a 'martinet', and the suggestion could do no harm, anyway.

'Yes,' said Mrs Plumleigh-Bruce. 'I rather think you are. I think my maid Mary would be slightly inclined to agree with you, anyway.'

'Yes. So I thought,' said Gorse, who thought it would be wise, at this moment, to mix just a little bitterness with this odiously sweet treacle. 'And I'm not sure it's a virtue, really.'

'Oh – really? . . . Why?'

'Well – it's quite clear that you like all the best things in life – food, clothes, drink, etcetera . . .'

'Well – why shouldn't I? Don't we all?'

'Yes – but that's beside the point, really. The point really is,' said Gorse, again pretending to giggle, 'that you're very much like me, and a lot of other people, if it comes to that. In fact, to put it bluntly you're just a tiny, *tiny* bit lazy.'

'Well, I suppose I am,' said Mrs Plumleigh-Bruce. 'But then again – aren't we all, if we have the opportunity?'

'Certainly. That goes without saying. But has one the right to demand everything perfect from those who attend upon us, if we're lazy ourselves? Personally, I'm absurdly easy-going with servants. I err on the other side, probably.'

'Well, you may be right,' said Mrs Plumleigh-Bruce, 'but I don't think my Mary would really agree with you. In fact she and I are tremendous friends – aren't we, Donald?'

'Yes,' said Mr Stimpson. 'I certainly haven't noticed any dissatisfaction in that quarter.'

'But all the same,' said Gorse, 'I expect she knows all about it when things aren't done properly.'

'Yes,' the low-voiced Mrs Plumleigh-Bruce conceded. 'That's true enough. But it's all done just by delicate hinting. I've never had to have her really on the mat ever since she's been with me. Of course she's a very good girl. But go on. What about this future? What about this "man" who's coming into my life?'

'Ah – the man . . . Yes . . . Now let's see . . . Well – I'm not sure he's not already *in* your life. Or, again, he may be someone who's going to take a much more serious part in your life than he has hitherto.'

Mr Stimpson fell for this like a load of bricks.

'Young – or old?' asked Mr Stimpson.

Gorse now had to decide quickly whether he should make himself, Gorse, the man, or further flatter Mr Stimpson by suggesting that it was he who was being mystically discussed. He compromised.

'Neither . . .' he said. 'Of course, it depends upon what you consider young or old.'

'Well,' said the almost savagely middle-aged Mr Stimpson. 'Middle-aged, perhaps?'

Here Gorse thought that a good time had come for him to produce his monocle. Doing this also gave him time to think.

'Ah – we must go more deeply into this,' he said, and, still keeping Mrs Plumleigh-Bruce's hand in his own, he took a sip at his drink, brought his monocle forth from his waistcoat pocket, neatly stuck it into his eye, and said 'Now – let's see . . . Yes – conceivably middle-aged . . .'

'Dark or fair?' said Mr Stimpson, who was dark.

'Just a moment,' said Gorse. 'Now I look more closely, I think I can perceive *two* men. I hope I'm not seeing double. I haven't drunk enough for that . . . One's dark and verging on middle age – the other's fair and a bit younger.'

'And who's going to win the day with the lady?' asked the Major, who, as Gorse had intended, thought that the fair and slightly younger man might be himself.

'Ah – I'm afraid that's beyond my powers of divination. And I don't even know for certain that either of them are actually going to *try* to win the day,' said Gorse. 'And I expect you think that all this is nonsense – don't you? I do myself – sometimes. Anyway, I think we've had enough – haven't we?' He looked at Mrs Plumleigh-Bruce, smiled at her, released her hand, took another sip at his beer, and put his monocle into his waistcoat pocket.

'When you say you think it's all nonsense "sometimes",' said the Major, 'do you mean that at other times you don't?'

'Yes. That's exactly where I stand, really. There are times when I think it's anything but nonsense. I've been almost forced to.'

'And who taught you this magic art?' asked Mr Stimpson.

'Well – that was rather odd. It was in France, actually – during the war – when I was on leave in Paris. I ran into a most extraordinary little man in a café. I don't know how it was, but we somehow became friends, and he initiated me into the secrets. I think he was half spoof and half genuine. I've never made up my mind. All I know is that he made absolutely weirdly true predictions about myself, and that since I've tried to practise his art I've made astonishing forecasts about people – I mean astonishing to the people, and astonishing to myself.'

The extraordinary little man whom Gorse had met in Paris was nearly always used by Gorse when he looked at women's palms. He existed only in Gorse's elaborately inventive mind.

'Well,' said Mrs Plumleigh-Bruce. 'You haven't really made any "forecast" about me – have you? Apart from two rather vague men who are going to enter my life . . . All you've done is to tell me something about my character – and I must say you've got remarkably near the truth . . . What I want to know is whether I'm going to be *happy* or not? Am I?'

'Yes, of course you are.' Gorse looked at her again. 'Or as happy as anyone can be. And one hasn't got to look at your hand to tell you that.'

'Really? . . . Why not?'

'Because you simply radiate happiness, in your own way.'

There are few people in the world, Gorse knew, who take violent objection to being told that they radiate happiness.

'Well,' said Mrs Plumleigh-Bruce, modestly, 'that sounds very nice – but I certainly never thought of myself in that light.'

'Or rather you radiate happiness for other people. And that means that in the long run it radiates back upon yourself – doesn't it? Don't forget I used the words "in the long run".'

'Well – I only hope you're right,' said Mrs Plumleigh-Bruce, and there was a pause in which she was so pleased that she was unable to conceal from her face the look of a cat who has less than a minute ago eaten a canary.

The perfect moment had arrived, Gorse perceived, to leave. He had not only pleased Mrs Plumleigh-Bruce. He had, he fancied, by no means displeased either of her middle-aged admirers.

And he was entirely correct. Major Parry was looking forward, in a rather coarse way, to basking quite gloriously in the rays of

Mrs Plumleigh-Bruce's happiness. Mr Stimpson, more purely, had practically made up his mind to marry the woman on the spot.

It was Gorse who, in effect, had radiated happiness.

And so, Mrs Plumleigh-Bruce being in the telephone book, it was time to go – to radiate an air of indifference or aloofness – to radiate doubt, in the minds of his listeners – particularly Mrs Plumleigh-Bruce's, of course – as to whether the radiator would ever be met again.

Gorse looked at his wrist-watch and was most surprised by the time.

'Good Heavens,' he said. 'I must be going.'

'Oh – for Heaven's sake don't do that,' said Mr Stimpson, who was, just at present, at the young criminal's feet. 'I owe you a drink, anyway.'

'Well – perhaps that matter can be adjusted at a later date,' said Gorse, as he rose, and drank off the remains of his beer quickly. 'But go I must. I certainly won't radiate happiness with my present housekeeper, Mrs Burford, if I'm late for the meal she's preparing for me with such scrupulous care at Gilroy Road. So I must buzz off. Will you forgive me?'

'Yes,' said Mrs Plumleigh-Bruce. 'We'll forgive you. But we hope we're going to see you again sometime.'

'Well, so do I,' said Gorse. 'But I suppose that's rather in the lap of the gods. In fact *everything* seems to be rather in the lap of the gods with me, just at present ... However, I do hope we meet ... Cheerio!'

He looked and smiled at all three, waved, and left them.

When he had gone into the street all three began to talk about Gorse. When he was in the street Gorse began to think about all three.

PART FIVE

KIMONO

CHAPTER ONE

I

'A<small>N</small>' sure,' said Mr Stimpson, ''tis a greatly pretty girl you're after lookin' this mighty evening.'

Mr Stimpson was speaking to Mary McGinnis, Mrs Plumleigh-Bruce's maid, in Mrs Plumleigh-Bruce's brassy hallway, at about nine-forty-five, three evenings after the evening upon which Gorse had told Mrs Plumleigh-Bruce's fortune. He had dined at 'Glen Alan' and was just leaving.

Mr Stimpson, who had himself often dabbled in *Oirish* on his own account, had lately, because he had listened to Mrs Plumleigh-Bruce using it on Mary, himself been spurred into trying to brush it up.

But Mr Stimpson was by no means fully at home with this language. The word 'greatly', for instance (in his sentence ''Tis a greatly pretty girl you're afther lookin' this mighty evening'), does not really belong to *Oirish* at all. Nor does the word 'mighty' as used in his 'this mighty evening'. They were both pure inventions of his own – innovations which no serious student of *Oirish* would permit.

Mary, who had just helped Mr Stimpson on with his coat, was as puzzled as she was when submitting to her mistress's *Oirish*, but did at least understand that she had been called pretty.

'Thank you very much, sir,' she therefore said, modestly.

'*Noth* at *Arl*!' said, or rather cried, Mr Stimpson, who was genially translating, for Mary's sake, the English 'Not at all'. And then he gaily and gently pinched Mary's cheek.

The man had had too much to drink, and he had always had a dim notion that pinching young girls' cheeks was somehow all part of being *Oirish*.

'Top av the evening to you,' he added. 'Well, it's going that I must be afther – entoirely.'

Mrs Plumleigh-Bruce, who was in the hallway watching all this, did not at all like what was going on.

She was aware that Mr Stimpson's *Oirish* was not only grossly incorrect but imitative of her own: she was aware that her imitator had drunk too much, and that Mary was probably aware of the same thing: and she did not like his pinching Mary's cheek.

She put the last down to his having taken too much to drink. But here she was mistaken. Mr Stimpson, apart from wanting to be *Oirish*, had certain other motives, as will be seen.

'Well, then, it's top av the evening to yourself, as well, it seems,' said Mr Stimpson, taking his gloves from his overcoat pocket, and looking rather defiantly at Mrs Plumleigh-Bruce, who was here even further revolted by the hopeless ineptitude of Mr Stimpson's *Oirish*. 'Top av the *morning*' was, of course, altogether in order, but 'Top av the *evening*' was absolutely ridiculous.

Mr Stimpson, if he had been wiser, would have stuck to *Scotch* ('Wheel mon' 'I Dinna Ken' etc.) or *Welsh* ('Indeed – Gootness – Whateffer!' etc.). He was quite good at these languages, and with them did not offend either Mrs Plumleigh-Bruce or his business friends – nearly all of whom talked *Oirish*, *Scotch*, and *Welsh* – as well as a certain amount of *American* ('Aw – shucks!' 'Say Bo' etc.).

'Well – good-bye,' said Mrs Plumleigh-Bruce, in a more frigid tone than she had employed with Mr Stimpson for a long time.

Mr Stimpson, who had put on his gloves, did not notice the coldness in her voice, snatched off a glove in the finest Stimpson manner – a glove-snatcher-offer's hit for six, as it were – said 'Good-bye, madame,' kissed Mrs Plumleigh-Bruce's hand, leered at her, and left the house.

Mrs Plumleigh-Bruce returned to her sitting-room, which was

filled with Mr Stimpson's cigar smoke – and sat down on her sofa to think.

Unlike Ernest Ralph Gorse, Mrs Plumleigh-Bruce very seldom thought intently for any length of time. But tonight Mr Stimpson (as well as, oddly enough, Ernest Ralph Gorse) made it seem necessary. She put a cigarette into her long, black cigarette-holder, and lit the cigarette, in order to assist herself in rising to the occasion for thought.

2

Because Mr Stimpson had been so recently with her, and for so long a time, and because he had behaved so uncouthly, she thought first about him. She could come to Gorse, whom she had still not seen since the fortune-telling episode, later.

Mr Stimpson, this evening, on the sofa on which she was now sitting, had made love to her.

There was, of course, nothing unusual about his doing this. But this evening he had been much bolder in his approach. He had kissed her and leered and talked at her at much greater length and with much greater strength than ever before.

She had, in one way, been considerably interested in and gratified by the comparatively prosperous Estate Agent's more audacious attitude. But there was a debit as well as a credit to what had gone on.

On the credit side were, mostly, the things he had said rather than done. He had, she believed, come nearer this evening to a straightforward verbal proposal of marriage than he ever had in the past. She tried to recall his exact words.

'You and I were made for each other – *are* made for each other, Joan,' he had said, either breathlessly or passionately (she could not tell which) after a protracted kiss. And to this she had replied ' "Were"? or "are"?'

'Are' somehow suggested the notion of marriage much more than 'were', and she had wanted to make sure that he had corrected himself.

'Are!' he had said, vehemently. 'You know it.'

'In what way?' she had then tried. 'Tell me . . .'

'In *every* way,' he had said. 'You *must* know. I mean the whole *hog*.'

Mrs Plumleigh-Bruce had been (and still was) mystified as to the exact nature of Mr Stimpson's Whole Hog, which, for some weeks now, had been appearing in his conversation.

How whole was this puzzlingly allegorical animal? And, even if it were wholly whole, where did it lead to in life? To marriage – or to sordid sin in Sispara Road, Reading?

And so she had then braced herself to force Mr Stimpson to give a much clearer picture of his own conception of his own Hog.

'When you say "whole" hog,' she had said, 'what do you mean, exactly?'

'You *must* know what I mean,' said the agitated leerer.

'I don't, you know . . . I really don't . . .' said Mrs Plumleigh-Bruce. 'Do you mean you want to "live" – with me . . .?'

'Of course I do. To all eternity – as far as I'm concerned.'

But there are different ways of dwelling in eternity.

'But in what way?' she persisted. 'I mean in what capacity?'

'In *every* capacity,' said Mr Stimpson.

'Yes – but in *what capacity*?' said Mrs Plumleigh-Bruce.

Mr Stimpson – the cautious Mr Stimpson, nearly always as cautious when he had taken drink as when he had not – here hesitated. He had spotted that Mrs Plumleigh-Bruce had spotted that there were all sorts of whole hogs, and many different ways of inhabiting eternity, and he was not willing to commit himself to any greater accuracy.

'Oh – *every* capacity,' he said.

But 'every' is a word which may be used elastically.

'Yes – but such *as*? . . .'

'Such as *everything*,' said Mr Stimpson, attempting to use his vehemence to disguise his ambiguity, but, of course, not succeeding, and hardly hoping to do so.

'Yes – but what does "everything" mean?' said Mrs Plumleigh-Bruce. 'And what do you mean when you say "live"?'

'Why – LIVE!' said Mr Stimpson, feigning a sort of impatience. 'What else should I mean?'

But impatience did not serve Mr Stimpson's purpose any better than vehemence.

Mrs Plumleigh-Bruce realized that she would get no more out of Mr Stimpson by the more or less delicate methods she had used so far. Now she must either drop the matter or come completely out into the open with 'Do you mean live as man and wife – or what?' or something like that.

She very nearly took this course, but something held her back.

She felt, really, that she could not possibly humiliate herself so far.

It must be remembered that Mrs Plumleigh-Bruce, the daughter of a Colonel, and the widow of one, despite her often entertaining the notion of marrying him, looked upon the Reading Estate Agent with considerable contempt – contempt generally, but most of all social contempt.

Mr Stimpson was removed very far indeed from the top drawer. Furthermore, he could not even be classed as 'One of Nature's Gentlemen'. Nature had neglected to polish Mr Stimpson in any way – and, in the event of marriage, no such excuse could possibly be used with any of those remaining acquaintances of Mrs Plumleigh-Bruce who were on the Colonel level. Harsh, self-seeking, bustling Estate Agency – not kind, disinterested and placid Nature – had moulded Mr Stimpson's character and manners. He was not at all the sort of man to introduce in those circles from which Mrs Plumleigh-Bruce considered she had, on account of her exile in Reading, almost fallen, and to which she was anxious to return.

Therefore, Mrs Plumleigh-Bruce felt that she could not conceivably lower herself by being the first to hint at marriage. And, of course, if she did so and received any sort of rebuff, the situation would be unbearable.

However, she decided to have one more shot at delicacy.

'I do wish you'd explain yourself properly,' she said. 'I really don't understand you.'

At this Mr Stimpson decided to hide behind facetious flirtatiousness combined with further physical approaches. The two usually went together in Mr Stimpson's theory and practice of love-making.

'Don't you – you damned fascinating little devil?' said Mr Stimpson, leering more horribly than ever. 'I'll bet you do . . . I understand *you*, at any rate. I can read every little thought that goes on in that fascinating little head of yours. I even know what's going on in it just at this moment.'

'Do you?' said the actually rather large-headed Mrs Plumleigh-

Bruce, momentarily hating Mr Stimpson intensely, but non-plussed. 'What?'

'*This*,' said Mr Stimpson, and he lunged at her to kiss her in a very much more clumsy and revolting manner than usual.

At this Mrs Plumleigh-Bruce was as near to losing her temper violently as so smug and complacent a woman could be.

She thrust him away from her, and he said in a surprised way 'What's the matter?'

'Nothing's the matter,' said Mrs Plumleigh-Bruce, regaining her composure. 'But don't you think it's time you went home? It's after half past nine.'

'Well – you often let me stay till ten – or after – don't you?'

'Yes. But I'm tired tonight, and I want you to go. It's not as though we were talking sense of any sort.'

'*I* thought we were talking great sense. I don't follow you.'

'Well – don't *try* to follow me. Just do as I tell you and go, will you, Donald?'

There was a look in Mrs Plumleigh-Bruce's eye which Mr Stimpson had never seen before, and which he did not like. Also his physical advances had never been repelled in exactly the way they had a moment ago, and he did not like this, either.

Normally he would certainly have been cowed or made uneasy by this change in her manner – but tonight he was in a different sort of temper generally – one which requires explanation.

3

The odd thing was that, had Mr Stimpson not been in this altered mood, this evening's session with Mrs Plumleigh-Bruce might well have ended in a proposal of marriage, and its immediate or tactfully delayed acceptance. But Mr Stimpson was not, in regard to Mrs Plumleigh-Bruce, at all the same man he had been three nights ago.

Mr Stimpson had, in fact, got above himself. Or he had at any rate got above his previous more timid self. And this had been brought about, paradoxically enough, by that conversation about Mrs Plumleigh-Bruce – which he had at the time so blackly hated and despised – with Major Parry.

The Major, by speaking so coarsely and cheaply about Mrs

Plumleigh-Bruce and by suggesting that Mr Stimpson had possibly won her favours in the fullest way, had, after Mr Stimpson had had time for reflection, put ideas into his head.

A piece of impudence on the Major's part had, indeed, been transformed magically into a piece of flattery.

What, thought Mr Stimpson, if Mrs Plumleigh-Bruce were, after all, a woman about whose name it was permissible, or even correct, to speak lightly?

And, if such were the case, did it not follow that it was permissible, or even correct, to treat her lightly – amorously trifle with her?

And had not Major Parry clearly intimated that he imagined that Mr Stimpson, if he had not already trifled with her in such a way, was clearly the principal man in the running for such a thing? And was there not an enormous amount of truth in the Major's suggestion?

Brooding upon the matter, Mr Stimpson had suddenly been visited by a vision of a glorious feather in his cap.

In his life hitherto he had seen himself, had taken pride and almost revelled in himself, as a hard-working, average human being. He was very fond of calling himself 'just a simple plodder'.

Now, out of the blue, had come a startling, violent picture of himself as anything but a plodder. Instead he saw himself as a potential dog – a lad – a lady-killer – a *dasher*. Without ever having heard of Casanova he almost pictured himself as the possible Casanova of Reading. He imagined an event which would simply ring through Reading. What if the Lady of Reading became, not his wife, but his acknowledged mistress?

Mr Stimpson – the snob, the social climber, the boaster and subterraneously lecherous man – had all at once perceived that he might satisfy his snobbery, his social climbing, his boasting and his subterraneous lechery in a much easier and more magnificent way than he had dreamed of before. And on top of all this he would be saving *money*.

He was awe-inspired by, he trembled before, the audacity of his own vision; but the very fact that he was so afraid in a manner fortified rather than softened the businessman's determination to pursue his design.

Thus it was that Mr Stimpson had, this evening, adopted,

towards Mrs Plumleigh-Bruce, a very different manner from the usual one.

Mr Stimpson was, of course, very easily influenced by popular expressions. And if they served his purpose they practically hypnotized him.

Mr Stimpson was now closely mentally wrapped up in the matters of marriage, love and seduction – and two famous slogans governed his mind. These were 'Love 'em and Leave 'em' and 'Treat 'em Rough'.

And so, on being rebuked and almost dismissed by Mrs Plumleigh-Bruce tonight, he had decided to treat her rough, and at any rate give the appearance of perhaps loving and leaving her.

And so when Mrs Plumleigh-Bruce had told him to go, he had at once obeyed her, and, in drink and defiance, spoken a tremendous amount of *Oirish* to, and pinched the cheek of, the maid Mary McGinnis.

4

Mrs Plumleigh-Bruce, not having the faintest idea that she was being treated rough and loved and left, was, naturally, bewildered, and, in order to assist herself in the solution of the puzzle, put yet another cigarette into her black cigarette-holder and lit the cigarette and puffed away in that nauseatingly affected way she always did in the presence of men. No man was present, but Mrs Plumleigh-Bruce was seldom able to drop her affectations even when alone.

As she smoked and thought in front of the embers of her densely brass-surrounded fire, Mrs Plumleigh-Bruce gradually began to entertain thoughts that Mr Stimpson would not do – would not do at all.

At the moment she hated him physically more than she had ever hated any other man. And this was saying a lot.

Mrs Plumleigh-Bruce disliked men physically almost as much as she disliked the working-class spiritually.

Money, this nasty woman decided, wasn't everything.

5

Thinking of Mr Stimpson led Mrs Plumleigh-Bruce into thinking about Ernest Ralph Gorse.

This young man had not turned up again at The Friar. Nor had he fulfilled the eye-telephone-pact he had made with her when she last saw him there.

In fact it seemed to her that Gorse must be written off. He had probably gone back to London. Or dashed off to Paris. He clearly had money.

And so perhaps money (Mr Stimpson's) was, after all, something.

She had no sooner had this thought than she heard her telephone ringing.

She had an extraordinary feeling that Gorse was telephoning her.

Though no runner, Mrs Plumleigh-Bruce almost contrived to run up to her bedroom to answer the telephone.

She snatched off the Marie Antoinette doll and said 'Hullo?'

A nasal voice replied, slowly, 'Hullo . . .'

She wondered whether this voice belonged to Ernest Ralph Gorse.

It did.

CHAPTER TWO

GORSE, when dealing in a predatory way with men or women, always liked to telephone them late at night, or at any rate as late at night as he thought advisable.

It was, he found, likely to frighten them – or, failing that, to catch them unawares, if only because of their sleepy or fatigued condition.

And women were often intrigued. They would be surprised but excited – pleasantly shocked. Gorse would often telephone women as late as or later than midnight.

With Mrs Plumleigh-Bruce, Gorse had struck one of his finest successes in this direction. He could not have caught her at a better moment. She was surprised, excited, pleasantly shocked, and tremendously relieved to know that the odd but highly inter-esting young man had not left Reading, or forsaken the eye-telephone-pact made at The Friar.

In addition to this Mr Stimpson's recent revolting behaviour gave the reddish-haired head of Gorse a kind of golden halo.

'Hullo. Who's that?' she said.

'Oh, is Mrs Plumleigh-Bruce there, by any chance?' said Gorse.

'Yes. Speaking . . .'

'Ah,' said Gorse, 'I thought I recognized your voice . . . But I don't expect you can recognize mine – can you?'

'I'm not sure,' said Mrs Plumleigh-Bruce, who was by now absolutely sure. 'But I have just a vague idea . . .'

'Well – do you want me to give you a hint? Or shall I save time by telling you outright?'

'I think you'd better tell me outright – hadn't you?'

'Very well, then, the name's Gorse. Ralph Gorse. Ralph or Rafe – whichever you prefer. And I think we met in An Certain Hostelry, not so long ago.'

Mrs Plumleigh-Bruce took no exception to Gorse's foolish and vulgar way of describing The Friar. She rather liked it.

'Oh – yes,' she said. 'I remember it very well.'

'Oh, well, I'm glad of that . . . However, the point is, do you prefer Rafe or Ralph? I'm sure you'll have to use one or the other, sooner or later.'

It suddenly occurred to Mrs Plumleigh-Bruce that Gorse, like Mr Stimpson, had had too much to drink.

'You sound very gay tonight,' she therefore said. 'And it's very late to phone – isn't it? I hope you haven't been hitting it up – painting the town red, or anything like that.'

Gorse's whole tone changed.

'No. Believe me not. No gaiety. Anything but. That was all bluff,' he said, as if utterly exhausted, but bravely fighting his own condition. 'In fact I'm absolutely worn out. And as for being gay I can only tell you I'm absolutely miserable. And that's why I've telephoned you. I know it's horribly late at night, but I felt I simply had to.'

'But what's the matter?'

'Well, the point is, really, what *isn't* the matter . . . I'm just off the train after the most appalling day in London any man's ever had, and I rang you up to ask you if you could help me.'

'But what's the trouble?' asked Mrs Plumleigh-Bruce. 'And how on earth can I help you?'

'Well – the trouble's business trouble. But I'll get over that all right. In fact I'm pretty certain I'll come out on top in the long run. But the run's been a very long one today and I'm feeling depressed and completely done in.' Gorse's voice now became, in a restrained way, quite piteous. 'And that's where you can help me, if you will, and if you can. Will you?'

There was a pause.

'Yes. Of course I will. If I can . . . But how?'

'Oh, just let me come round and talk to you – let me spill out a few of my woes. Hold my hand for a little.' Gorse's tone became that of one wearily attempting humour. 'I mean figuratively, of course – or metaphorically or whatever the word is.'

There was another pause in which Mrs Plumleigh-Bruce half doubted, and half believed in, the sincerity of Gorse's voice and intentions.

'Yes. I'd like you to,' she said. 'But when?'

'Now,' said Gorse, with noble simplicity and directness. 'I expect it's impossible. In fact I expect you've gone to bed or that you've got people there. But I thought there'd be no harm in asking. I never did find any harm in asking for anything. *Have* you gone to bed, and *have* you got people there?'

'No,' said Mrs Plumleigh-Bruce dubiously, and added, slightly defensively, 'Except for my maid, Mary.'

'Well, then. If you're still up, and if your maid's still up, would there be any impropriety in my looking in just for a little while? Or is it all too much of a crashing bore?'

'No. Of course it wouldn't be a bore. But I don't know that *I'd* be of much help.'

'Well, then. You don't know enough about yourself.'

'In what way? I don't follow you.'

'Well, I told you about yourself when I read your hand. Didn't I tell you that you radiate happiness – for *other* people at any rate?'

'Why, yes. I believe you did . . .'

Mrs Plumleigh-Bruce, who, in fact, envied or loathed practically every member of the human race with whom she did or did not come into contact, had, nevertheless, been fancying herself as a radiator of universal happiness ever since Gorse had endowed her with this gift. She had been much nicer to Mary (who had had to listen to more *Oirish* than ever) and she had put on a playful, tolerant tone even with tradespeople.

'Well,' said Gorse. 'I'm afraid it's a bit like begging – but after the day I've just had I'd like to bask – for however short a time – in the good old beams I mentioned the other night. You radiate comfort, too – although I suppose comfort and happiness are roughly the same thing – on the spiritual level anyway. And comfort's what I want. So may I come round for a bit?'

'You're being very flattering, you know,' said Mrs Plumleigh-Bruce, now having a strong notion that the young man was making love to her, and not disliking the notion at all.

'I *am* being flattering,' said Gorse, firmly. 'But that doesn't mean I'm being insincere. I know I've many faults, but insincerity isn't one of them. It isn't, really. Anyway, the point is that I can hardly wait to see you again. So may I come round now? Just give me judgment, oh wise – and fair – Portia. I promise you I won't take it ill, like Shylock, if you refuse.'

Being called a fair, as well as a wise Portia, went to Mrs Plumleigh-Bruce's head. She had no doubts now that Gorse was making love of some sort to her, and she found herself almost delighting in his love-making.

'Very well. I pronounce sentence,' she said. 'You may come. But not for long. Because I'm rather tired, and I can't keep Mary up much longer. Do you know where I live?'

Mrs Plumleigh-Bruce brought out these words in the most glorious 'Plumleigh-Bruce' manner. Her 'You may come' was superb. It was lady-like, fruity, and regally indolent beyond measure. Mrs Plumleigh-Bruce was endeavouring to use every ounce of 'charm' she believed she had. An intelligent outsider would have found this 'charm' quite nauseating. Gorse was not nauseated. He was merely pleased – for he knew that things were going very much his way with this easily flattered woman. For him she was, at the moment, a sitting bird – sitting almost idiotically.

'Yes,' he said. 'I know where you live all right. I've found *that* out.'

'Really? . . . How? . . .'

The charmer laboriously and seductively breathed the 'H' of the word 'How' and pronounced its 'w' with fantastically rounded and luscious lips.

'Well,' said Gorse. 'You told me you were in the telephone book, and so I looked you up without very much delay. You live at Glen Alan, Sispara Road – don't you? And I've found out where Sispara Road is.'

'Have you? . . . HoW? . . .' sighed the delicious Portia.

'Well – just by asking people . . . However – that's beside the point. The point is that you've given me permission to call – isn't it? So may I? I can do it in about ten minutes – or even less, I think. So may I come round?'

Mrs Plumleigh-Bruce told Ernest Ralph Gorse that he might come rOWnd, and they rang off.

Then Mrs Plumleigh-Bruce at once found Mary, and asked her, hurriedly and apologetically, to make fresh coffee and tidy the sitting-room as much as possible. She explained to Mary that she had had an important telephone call, and that she had to see a man on a matter of urgent business at once.

This deceptive woman was, for some reason, never very good

at lying, and Mary saw something in her mistress's eye which made her guess that she was not telling the truth. However, Mary did not show that any such suspicion had crossed her mind, and she immediately did what she had been told to do.

Then Mrs Plumleigh-Bruce went up to her bedroom again in order to make herself look as attractive as she possibly could.

She had not taken much trouble with Mr Stimpson tonight, and she did not think that the dress she was wearing was adequately or correctly enticing. She wondered whether she had time to change it – and, if so, into what she should change.

She had, all at once, a startling but most exciting inspiration.

Her *Kimono*! What if she entertained her late visitor in her Kimono?

Did not his lateness justify such a thing? And would not the wearing of a Kimono make the hour seem later than it was, and therefore more alluring, bewitching, intriguingly 'fast'?

And she could change much more rapidly into a Kimono than into another dress, and thus, probably, be given time to arrange the sitting-room (the 'scene', she was really thinking), exactly to her liking.

Yes – she would wear her Kimomo – and that was *that*!

2

Mrs Plumleigh-Bruce was downstairs, in her Kimono, five minutes before Gorse arrived.

She arranged the sitting-room with great care – improving upon Mary's work. She removed every sign of her recent entertainment of Mr Stimpson. She brought forth, from the cupboard, brandy, whisky, and port, in decanters. (Mr Stimpson had been drinking beer.) She poked and tidied the fire and beat and changed the places of the cushions.

Mary, meanwhile, was making fresh coffee in the kitchen. Mary was considerably interested in what was going on. Her mistress had had, perforce, to let her see the Kimono, and Mary knew that this garment had never before purposely been worn when a man called. The lateness of the hour – combined with the Kimono – slightly scandalized Mary. A Kimono somehow did not go with what Mrs Plumleigh-Bruce had called urgent business.

Mrs Plumleigh-Bruce, waiting in the sitting-room for the ringing of the bell, was fully as scandalized as Mary – possibly more so. She was now afraid of what she had done.

Was she losing 'caste'?

She was also a little bit afraid of Gorse himself. Indeed, it even crossed her mind, because of the lateness of the hour, her Kimono, and the fact that she had only met Gorse twice, that he might be in some way slightly dangerous, and she was glad that Mary was in the house.

Then she asked herself 'In what way dangerous?'

Then it crossed her mind that she might be entertaining a thief, a raper, or swindler. Or even a potential slayer!

She then dismissed, or tried to dismiss, these thoughts as absurd. She had, she decided, been reading the sensational newspapers too much recently.

The door-bell rang, and she heard Mary go to the door.

A few moments later Gorse entered the room.

The moment she had greeted and shaken hands with Gorse she was completely reassured.

Any thoughts of him as a thief, a raper, a swindler, or a potential slayer fled from her mind.

Mrs Plumleigh-Bruce, however, was shaking hands with one who was all these things.

Furthermore Gorse was to be, in reality, a slayer.

CHAPTER THREE

I

THE future slayer's manner, as he sat down in the armchair offered him, was charmingly exhausted, wistfully grateful. Mrs Plumleigh-Bruce fell a hundred per cent, or more, for his exhaustion and gratitude. She almost bustlingly offered him whisky, brandy, port and coffee.

He accepted coffee and brandy. He thought it wise to take the most expensive drink. It showed that he was 'used' to things, and it flatteringly implied that his hostess was equally so. The neat brandy and black coffee, taken at the same time, gave forth, he thought, an air of worldliness.

He said nothing, of course, about her wearing of her Kimono. He took it easily for granted. Nevertheless he saw that she fancied herself enormously in it, and he made a point of looking at it as though he shared her enthusiasm. (Actually his first thought about it had been 'My God!' Though his own taste was far from being good, Gorse disliked dragons and chrysanthemums surrounded and grown all over with fusses on blue silk.)

'Ah –' he said, when his coffee and brandy had been put on a small table behind him. 'Just what the doctor ordered. *Un café et une fine.*'

Thus Gorse reminded Mrs Plumleigh-Bruce of his recent trip to France and displayed his knowledge of the French language.

But Gorse was a poor linguist, and he pronounced the '*et*' as 'eight'. Thus, as students of French will know, he had not said, as he had wished, 'A coffee and liqueur brandy' but 'A coffee *is* a liqueur brandy'.

Mrs Plumleigh-Bruce, whose knowledge of French was worse than Gorse's, had no knowledge that she had been given the bewildering information that a coffee is in reality a liqueur brandy – and the Marie Antoinette in her was delighted to have heard French spoken in her presence.

'Well, now. Tell me. How can I help you?' she said, crossing her legs and putting one arm over the back of the sofa on which she sat. 'You certainly look very tired, poor thing. Tell me. What's all the trouble?'

She was astonished by the effrontery of her own 'poor thing'. But the whole atmosphere – the late hour – the Kimono – the charm, the dejection, the brandy-drinking and French-speaking of her guest – had simply forced it from her. Also it must be remembered that just at this period she was radiating universal happiness and comfort. Nothing could keep her off it.

'Oh – what I told you over the phone,' said Gorse, looking sadly into the fire. 'Business, business, business ... But I'll get over it all right, I can assure you. It's the incessant wrangling that gets you down – wrangling with people who don't keep their word. But I suppose that *is* business. Do *you* know anything about business?'

'Not the *first* thing,' said Mrs Plumleigh-Bruce, gaily. 'I'm a complete ignoramus in that way, I'm afraid.'

Gorse's eyes left the fire and were turned sharply – but not with noticeable sharpness – upon Mrs Plumleigh-Bruce.

Was the woman speaking the truth? There could, of course, be no better news if such was the case. And, looking at her, he very much inclined to the view that it was. He had always suspected that she was, generally speaking, a dupe of the first water for someone like himself, but he had feared that she might have some sort of 'head' for business matters.

'Really? . . . .' he said. 'I should have thought you were pretty shrewd in that way. I shouldn't have thought you'd be easy to do down.'

'Oh, no. I'm not easily done down,' said Mrs Plumleigh-Bruce. 'In fact anybody who tries to do me down always finds, I think I can say without fail, they're very much done down themselves.'

That (Gorse's thoughts were, as he looked at her) is all *you* know, and we shall see what we shall see.

'But I don't know anything about business details and all that,' said Mrs Plumleigh-Bruce. 'In fact you could call me, in that way and perhaps every other way, a complete fool, really.'

Gorse did not say 'It seems to me as though you certainly could do both', but this was his thought.

'Well,' he said. 'Perhaps you're very well out of it. Money-making's a sordid, grabbing affair on the whole. But money's got to be made.'

'And are *you* good at making it?'

Gorse pretended to look back on his past as a money-maker. Then he smiled faintly, and tapped the table beside him with his forefinger.

'Touch wood. Yes,' he said. 'Very much so. In fact you could almost say that everything I touch, in a small way, seems to turn to gold. Or a lot of silver and coppers at any rate.'

'Well. I wish *I* had the gift,' said Mrs Plumleigh-Bruce, looking at him and almost completely believing him. 'Or that you could bestow it on me.'

'I'm certain I could bestow it on you. But it's not really a gift. It's only common-sense and hard work. Hard work, and, on the whole, very silly work. I'm not particularly keen on money, really – are you?'

'Well,' said Mrs Plumleigh-Bruce. 'I wouldn't go as far as that. It has very important uses, hasn't it?'

'Yes. But I mean money in *itself*. Some people just chase it for its own sake – not for the realities it helps you to get. Money isn't really a reality – is it?'

'Well – I'm not so sure. What would you call a real reality?'

'Oh ... Health, and love, and fresh air, and freedom, and a clean conscience, and a thousand other things that bring genuine happiness.'

Gorse, speaking slowly, had, with the most adroit indifference, slipped in love between health and fresh air, but, as he suspected, Mrs Plumleigh-Bruce had done anything but miss the inserted word.

'Yes, I suppose you're right,' she said. 'And which would you call the most valuable of the realities you've mentioned?'

'Oh health, of course, first. Because without that you can't do or enjoy anything. And next, I suppose, love. In fact all *I* want to do is to settle down peacefully with the woman of my choice ...'

There was a pause, in which Mrs Plumleigh-Bruce wondered whether she dared to be so bold, and then decided to be.

'And have *you* found the woman of your choice?' she asked.

There was another pause in which Gorse again seemed to be looking into his past, and also his present. It would not be advisable, he thought, to hand her what she was asking for – the acknowledgment that he was not committed – on a plate, and so he held the pause for as long as he could, and when he at last spoke, his tone was slightly dubious and enigmatical – perhaps just denying the literal sense of his words.

'No,' he said. 'Still searching – searching . . . And I think you'll admit it's a pretty difficult search. And a pretty difficult choice.'

'It is indeed,' said Mrs Plumleigh-Bruce.

'And how do you stand in that direction?' asked Gorse. 'If it's not a rude question, have you brought yourself to making any choice?'

'No,' said Mrs Plumleigh-Bruce. 'I'm quite fancy free, just at the moment.'

'But not without a great deal of fanciers, I fancy?' said Gorse, smiling charmingly.

'Oh – I don't know about that . . .' the Lady and Venus of Sispara Road modestly replied.

'Oh – come now . . . Now I believe you're fishing for compliments. You mustn't forget I've observed your hand.'

'Well, you've said that's probably all nonsense, haven't you?' Gorse ignored this.

'And I've observed *you*, too . . . And I've also had the opportunity of observing you in the company of men.'

'Well? And what did that tell you?'

'It told me very plainly that you're very far from being unattractive to men – very far indeed. I have eyes in my head, you know.'

'Well – even if you're right,' said Mrs Plumleigh-Bruce, remembering the odious behaviour of Mr Stimpson less than an hour ago, 'it's really more a question of whether I'm attracted to them – isn't it?'

'Oh, yes. Of course. *Cela va sans dire.* All the same I can still tell you that though you may have other troubles you'll have no trouble in *that* direction.'

'Well – you're very flattering about me,' said Mrs Plumleigh-Bruce. 'But you didn't come round here to talk about me – did you? We're here to talk about you and your troubles – aren't we?'

'Oh – they're so sordid – I don't really want to talk about them,' said Gorse. 'At any rate *now*. You know, it's so peaceful here, I've completely forgotten them. That's really why I wanted to come round. I told you you radiate happiness and peace. And somehow, looking at you now, I feel you're not at all the person to talk about filthy lucre to. It'd be rather like counting out your silver in a cathedral – if you see what I mean . . .'

Gorse glanced at her to see if he had succeeded in making a woman swallow a cathedral. He believed that she had almost digested it already.

'Well,' she said. 'You're still very flattering . . . But I do agree that money matters are very sordid. I've always found them so, at any rate – little as I know about them.'

'And the more you know about them, the more you'd find out about it, believe me . . . You know, I suppose it's a weird and rather awful thing to say – but do you know what I sometimes feel . . ?'

'No . . . What?'

'Well, I sometimes feel that I'm fed up with civil life – with all its damned pettiness. I feel that I'd – well – I'd like to be back in the Army again. I certainly don't want another war, and I'm certainly not a blood-thirsty person – but all the same that's what I sometimes feel. Can you understand it?'

'Indeed I can,' said Mrs Plumleigh-Bruce. 'And I know a lot of other men who feel the same way.'

'Yes. I believe there are . . . I can't personally say I had a nice time "over there". In fact it was very unpleasant and very peril-ous. But one's got to realize that people degenerate, and that there're the perils of peace as well as the perils of war.'

'Yes. I see what you mean,' said Mrs Plumleigh-Bruce, very much impressed by his epigram.

'At least,' Gorse continued, 'one was doing something, *serving* something, over there. Now one's only doing things for oneself and serving oneself. Helping oneself to what one can get of little bits of metal . . . Well, I suppose it's got to be done, but I've got a bit of metal that wouldn't fetch anything on the market, but it's worth more to me than all the King's coinage – all the coin of the realm.'

'Oh. What's that?' said Mrs Plumleigh-Bruce, looking at him, and guessing what was coming.

'Oh – a little trinket for services rendered to the King. Rendered, not taken.'

'You mean a medal?'

'Yes. A Military Cross, actually,' said Gorse, still looking into the fire. 'But as I said, it has very little value on the money market.'

'Good Heavens!' Mrs Plumleigh-Bruce was stunned, but not incredulous. 'Did you get an M C?'

'Yes . . . Why do you seem so surprised?'

'Well – it's a pretty high honour – isn't it? What did you get it for?'

'I don't know why on earth I'm telling you about all this, you know . . .'

'No. Go on. Do tell me.'

'Well, for certain very obvious reasons,' said Gorse with a sly, yet winning smile, 'we were, I regret to say, retreating from certain positions, and I managed to carry an extremely badly wounded man for about a quarter of a mile to a place of greater safety. Thank Heavens he was a small man and a pretty light weight, or I couldn't have done it. But he was fearfully shot up – poor fellow . . .'

'Well, I think that's wonderful, and that you ought to be very proud.'

'Oh – I don't know . . . These things are tremendously a question of luck, you know. Thousands of other fellows did the same sort of thing, and much better, but didn't get any award . . . It's a crude thing to say but the whole point is that you've got to be *seen* doing things like that – and that's where the luck comes in. I can assure you there were many unnoticed deeds of valour which have been lost in oblivion. So perhaps there's not so much in the medal itself. I often think I get more satisfaction from the letters of gratitude I get from the man and his parents. They're very humble folk, and they live in Middlesbrough, of all places. I go up and see them sometimes – they're too poor to come down here – and I'm regarded as a sort of hero. It's all very touching, but an awful bore to have to go up to Middlesbrough. That *is* heroic!' The tired Gorse again smiled.

'Well, I think it's absolutely wonderful,' said Mrs Plumleigh-Bruce. '*Wonderful* . . .'

2

Gorse had not previously awarded himself a Military Cross, but his richly inventive imagination had often caused him to long to do so, and he had ready the full story of his method of acquiring it.

He was aware of the dangers entailed – of the fact that the matter could be checked up on by anyone hostile or suspicious. That was why he had until now abstained from this luxury. But Mrs Plumleigh-Bruce simply asked for it, and he had found the temptation wholly irresistible.

Also, should any enemy get to work, he had, he believed, all the answers ready.

He was not, however, willing to let the story go any further than Mrs Plumleigh-Bruce, and so he now hastened to insure himself against such a thing.

'I can't conceive why I'm telling you all this,' he said. 'And you won't let it go any further, will you?'

'But why not? I should've thought you'd've been proud of it. I don't see any sense in being *too* modest.'

'No. You don't understand. People're odd. They think you're boasting or something. As I said, I can't imagine why I told *you* – except that you're the sort of person who simply invites confessions, somehow. But you realize it *is* a confession – that what I've told you is in the confessional – don't you? You realize that you're bound by vows not to disclose it to another soul – don't you?'

Mrs Plumleigh-Bruce had by this time not only swallowed and digested the cathedral. She had become a cathedral – with all its holiness, hangings, and furniture. She was, therefore, necessarily a confessional-box as well.

'No,' she said. 'If you want it that way, you can certainly rely upon *me*.'

'Yes. You haven't got to tell me that,' said Gorse, and there was a silence in which he thought that the time had approached at which it would be advisable to withhold any further stimulation of Mrs Plumleigh-Bruce's vanity. It would now be wise, he decided, to stimulate, instead, her financial greed.

3

'Anyway, I can assure you I'm not *really* a hero in any sense of the word,' he said. 'In fact I'm not sure that I'm not a bit of a crook, on the whole – believe it or not.'

'Well – I don't find it easy to believe.'

'Well – I'm what they call a "fast worker" anyway. And I'm not at all averse to the material things of life, as you know. And in spite of all the things I've said against money I've absolutely no objection at all to raking it in – and using all my wits in the raking. I've got quite a strong gambling streak, too. Have you?'

'No,' said Mrs Plumleigh-Bruce, quite truthfully. 'I can't say I have, really . . . And in what way do you like to gamble?'

'Oh – horses, mostly – as I've told you. I suppose I do it mostly for the fun of the thing – but I've found it very profitable fun. Don't you ever put money on a horse?'

'No,' said Mrs Plumleigh-Bruce, again truthfully. 'Hardly ever, except on the Derby and things like that. And then I always have to get somebody to do it for me. And I generally lose. I don't know the first thing about racing, but personally I'm a believer in the old saying that you can't beat the book. Aren't you?'

Gorse once more looked into the fire to think. 'No. I'm not,' he said. 'I think the book *can* be quite easily beaten – but I think you've got to know how to set about it.'

'And how do you do that?'

'By knowing the right people,' said Gorse. 'I don't believe in any of these silly "systems" or anything like that. But if you know the right people and put in a few hours of intelligent study every other day – you saw me doing it the other night, by the way – I believe the book, or the bookmakers – not a crowd I like – are quite easy to beat. Anyway, I did it in a big way the other night, and I've every intention of doing the same thing tomorrow. By the way, do *you* want to be put on to something good? I'll do it for you, if you like.'

'Something good. Do you mean what they call a "dead certainty"?'

'No. There's no such thing as a *dead* certainty . . . Well – just think about it. There wouldn't be any betting on a race if there was. But there's such a thing that's as near a dead certainty that

it makes practically no difference. If you know the right people –
that is.'

'What do you mean by the "right" people?'

'Well – some of them are very high up, and some of them, I
regret to say, are very low down. I've got a foot in both worlds.'

'And you think you know this nearly dead certainty tomorrow?'

'I don't *think* I know – I *know* I know – or *will* know tomorrow.'

'What's the name of the horse? And where's it running?'

'It's the Bramford meeting,' said Gorse, 'and the first race.
Two o'clock. But I can't give you the name of the horse just at
the moment. It might be one of two – *Lazy Boy*, or *Stucco*. And
it might be yet another. And just *conceivably* I won't bet at all
That'll all be ascertained by yours truly early tomorrow morning.'

'And you're so sure, if you do bet, that it's going to win?'

'So sure that I'm willing to put money on it for you, and to
guarantee now, if it loses, to pay you back the money myself.
That's fair enough – isn't it?'

'No – it's absurd. It's heads I win tails you lose. In fact I
couldn't do it. And, really, you know, I don't like betting.'

'Oh come now. Have a little flutter – although this could
hardly be called a "flutter". It's just a way of making easy
money.'

Mrs Plumleigh-Bruce was silent as she reflected.

'Well, I don't know what to say . . .' she said.

'Well – perhaps I shouldn't persuade you if you don't like that
sort of thing. But you'll regret it tomorrow evening when you
read the newspaper.' Gorse broke off to laugh at himself. 'You
see I *am* a crook, after all, as I said! Or at any rate a tipster.
Aren't I?'

'Don't be absurd . . .'

'But I am, you know. Because racing, on the whole, is a
crooked business, and I've got to admit that I'm employing,
more or less, crooked means, or rather dealing with more or less
crooked people. On the other hand I'm only removing money
from even more crooked people, and that pleases me a lot. It also
puts my conscience almost completely to rest. Wouldn't it
yours?'

'Yes. Of course it would. But all this is simply Greek to me. I don't know how you set about it all.'

'Yes – I can understand that. And it's all much too long and complicated and silly to go into, really.'

Gorse was speaking the truth. What he had been talking about, suggesting, was certainly much too long and complicated and silly to go into – above all silly – and would not have borne any sort of critical examination. Gorse was merely throwing forth a wordy mist of horsey wisdom with which to deceive an ignorant woman.

'Very well,' said Mrs Plumleigh-Bruce. 'I'm game for a little flutter. How much shall I put on? Two and six – five shillings, or something like that?'

'*Five shillings!*' Gorse exlaimed. 'Good Heavens, no. If you're not going to go further than that it's not worth anyone's while. I'm not expecting big odds, you know. In fact I don't expect more than three to one – if that . . . You don't want to rope in seven and sixpence or something like that do you? . . . Oh, no. Let's say five pounds – or leave it alone.'

'Five *pounds!*' said Mrs Plumleigh-Bruce. 'But I can't afford to risk five pounds. I'm not a rich woman you know.'

'All the more reason for enriching yourself. And it's not really a risk, and, as I've said, I'm willing to insure you against any loss.'

'And, as *I've* said before, I couldn't possibly let you do that . . . No. Really. Five pounds is too much for me. Really it is.'

'Oh, come now. Now you're not speaking like yourself. Unless I've mistaken you – and I'm quite sure I haven't. In this world one's got to do things in the right way – and that means the big way – or not at all, hasn't one? If one does things in the small way – in the Reading way, if I may say so – one never gets anywhere. And, although chance has brought you temporarily to Reading, I know you're not the type of person who does things in the Reading way, the silly, fiddling, petty little middle-class way.'

Gorse, when defrauding women, all his life took this line about doing things in the big way. (He had used it most successfully with the wretchedly ambitious slum-beauty, Esther Downes, at Brighton.) It was a line which shamed and flattered his victims at the same time, and was therefore almost irresistible.

Mrs Plumleigh-Bruce, though much older than Esther Downes, was, nevertheless, like her, both shamed and flattered. All the same, she still tried to hold out.

'Yes. You're right there, certainly,' she said. 'But I still say five pounds is too much for me. And I haven't got all that ready cash in the house, anyway.'

'Nobody's asking for ready cash,' said Gorse. 'As I've said, I'll put the money on for you, and take the rap myself if you lose.'

'And I've said I certainly wouldn't allow it. It's absurd.'

'Very well,' said Gorse, looking at her in a quizzing way. 'Let's make a compromise. You write me an I O U now for five pounds – and if the horse goes down, I'll come on you like an extortionate money-lender for my due.'

'Well – that'd be *slightly* more reasonable.'

'Not "slightly more" reasonable. Absolutely reasonable ... Very well, then, let's settle for that. Shall we? Come along now. Be a sport. I know you are one at heart, but be one now. I'll think very poorly of you if you're not. Actually it's not a very "sporting" thing to say, but I swear to you that in this case you've simply got nothing to *lose*. In fact it hardly *is* sport.'

Mrs Plumleigh-Bruce was again silent, as she turned the proposition over in her mind. She saw that there was indeed, not such an awful amount to lose – particularly as Gorse had suggested an I O U. She had not liked the idea of parting with five pounds in cash. It had, indeed, crossed her mind that Gorse might disappear with it into the blue. But an I O U was a different matter – and the more so because Gorse had said he would not, and to her mind obviously would not, insist upon its being honoured.

Over and above this she fundamentally trusted Gorse, and believed that his horse would almost certainly win. Had he not won last night? And when he had said he would think very poorly of her if she was not a 'sport' Gorse had got at her in two ways. It had filled her with an intense longing to show that she was something more than fully a 'sport'; and it had filled her with the fear that, if she did not show herself one in front of this affluent visitor to Paris (who had joined the Army at the age of sixteen, won the Military Cross, been active with his car against the enemy in 1926, and was now dwelling in an imposing house in Reading) he might think so poorly of her that he would drop her altogether. In spite of his fortune-telling and eye-telephone-pact he had already shown a curious coolness and indifference towards her by making no further effort to meet her for a matter of three days, and he might do the same thing again – only this time permanently.

And would not an arrangement about betting prevent such a thing? Would it not, on the contrary, assure his quick return to her – cement their friendship?

All these thoughts, taken in conjunction with his slightly wearied charm, and the cosy, Kimono lateness of the hour, made her suddenly make up her mind to take the risk.

'Well – I must say it all sounds very tempting,' she said.

'It is, indeed, very tempting,' said Gorse, who saw clearly that he had achieved what he wanted, and so feigned half to withdraw. 'But for Heaven's sake don't let *me* persuade you. If you've got a real hatred of betting, you stick to your guns. One should never go against one's own instincts. That's *one* of the things I've learnt from life, at least. Well – which shall it be? "To bet or not to bet, that is the question" as our friend Hamlet might have said.'

'To bet,' said Mrs Plumleigh-Bruce. 'Definitely. But you've got to let me give you the IOU.'

'Oh – *must* we go through that formality?'

'Yes. We certainly must. And I'd like to do it now.'

'Very well, then. If you must you must, I suppose. But don't let's make a fuss about it.' Gorse began to fumble in his breast-pocket and brought out some letters. 'Here you are. Just jot it down on the back of one of these. Here we are.' He had selected a letter and was glancing at its contents. 'Yes. This'll do ... Have you got a pen? Here's one if you haven't.' He produced an extremely expensive fountain pen from the same pocket, and rose and went over to her, folding the letter. 'Now – you just write it on the back of that, and all's in order. And while you're doing it I'd like to go and wash my hands if I may – to be excused, as we used to say at school. May I be excused?'

'Yes. You may be excused,' said Mrs Plumleigh-Bruce, in her own rich regal way. 'The bathroom's just at the top of the stairs ... There's a light on up there, I think. But I've no idea how you write out these things.'

'Now – surely you do,' said Gorse leaning over her, and putting the pen into her hand in a way which, like his earlier fortune-telling, established direct physical contact. 'All you've got to do is write "I O U" in capital letters, and then five pounds in numerals, and then again words. And then sign it. Haven't you ever seen an I O U?'

'Yes. I have, as a matter of fact, but I've somehow forgotten the exact thing you do. Never mind. I think I can manage . . .'

'Very well, then you do your best, while I leave you for a moment or two. And if you've done it wrong I'll tell you when I come back. *Au revoir*.' And Gorse left the room.

Gorse had two objects in making this excuse to leave her alone.

CHAPTER FOUR

GORSE, it may have been noticed, had a remarkable gift for killing two, or even three, birds with one stone. One of the birds he had in mind at the moment was a quick exploration of as much of 'Glen Alan' as he could; the other was his desire to leave Mrs Plumleigh-Bruce alone, so that she should have time to unfold and read the letter on the back of which she was to write the I O U. He had not the faintest doubt that she would do this, and the letter, used before for roughly similar purposes, had been seeming casually but in fact most carefully, selected from his pocket.

One of Gorse's settled habits was to steal any sort of headed notepaper which he thought might be useful to him – notepaper from private houses, from business and solicitors' firms (the bigger and better-known the house and firms the better) – and from West End clubs. The notepaper he had just left in Mrs Plumleigh-Bruce's hands came from the Bath Club, Dover Street. He had managed to gain an invitation to enter this club by means of a prospective deal with a car (imagined by himself) with one of its members – and, by telling a hasty lie, he had managed to gain access to and pocket the notepaper without any difficulty.

On the headed sheet which he had given to Mrs Plumleigh-Bruce he had written a letter in a disguised hand. Gorse never attempted to be a great, but was always a competent, forger.

The letter began with 'My dear Ralph', ended with 'Yrs. ever', and was throughout of a jovial and intimate nature. Thus Gorse was demonstrating to Mrs Plumleigh-Bruce that he was on jovial and intimate terms with a member of the Bath Club.

2

On leaving the sitting-room and mounting the stairs, Gorse had no difficulty in spotting which room was the bathroom. But he played to himself the rôle of an absent-minded or undiscerning young man, and made straight for what he felt certain was Mrs Plumleigh-Bruce's bedroom.

Here the wool-gatherer switched on the light, boldly because innocently. Then, seeing that the room was in fact Mrs Plumleigh-Bruce's bedroom, and unoccupied, he had a good look round. He was highly pleased by the silken opulence and femininity of the room – pleased, of course, commercially, not artistically or amorously.

He then boldly switched off the light and went to the bathroom. This also was to his satisfaction from a commercial point of view. About half a minute later he returned downstairs to the sitting-room.

'Well,' he said, 'Done your homework?'

'Yes. I think that's all right – isn't it?' said Mrs Plumleigh-Bruce, handing him back his fountain pen and his refolded letter.

Gorse glanced at the IOU.

'Yes. Perfect,' he said. 'We'll make a sharp business woman of you yet.' He sat down again in the armchair, putting the Bath Club letter casually back into his pocket, and speaking humourously. 'And now you're in my clutches – aren't you? I've only got to pretend I've backed the wrong horse – and I can come round and claim five pounds.'

Mrs Plumleigh-Bruce giggled. 'Yes,' she said. 'I never thought of that . . .'

'You should think of everything when dealing with a crook like me . . . You obviously don't know the ways of crooks at all . . .'

'No. I must say I don't . . .'

Gorse became serious again.

'Well – I've been more or less forced to myself. You see, there're enough of them about these days – everywhere. It's the aftermath of the war, I suppose . . . However, I hope you're confident about your own safety in the little transaction we've just made – provided the horse comes in – that is.'

'Oh, yes. *I'm* satisfied enough. But I don't think that my bank manager would approve. He's very much against speculations of any kind.'

'Oh – so you're on friendly terms with your bank manager? Is he in Reading or London?'

'Reading ... Yes. We're on very good terms. He's a funny little man but I quite like him. He gives me advice about my investments. He's very nice, really.'

'Well – if you've got a credit balance – *all* Bank Managers are nice, really. It's their job. The trouble about Bank Managers is that they're usually too conservative.'

'How do you mean – conservative?'

'Oh – I don't mean conservative politically. I wouldn't mind that. In fact I'm a dyed-in-the-wool Conservative myself from that point of view. And am I right in suspecting that you are, too?'

'Yes. I certainly am.'

'Yes. So I thought. But I meant conservative in another way – from a money point of view. I know it's their business to give absolutely safe and sound advice – but some of them carry it too far – particularly in the provinces. They get stuck in the mud, and won't give advice against the most reasonable changes or shiftings of investments. Thus losing a considerable amount of completely sound and honest profit to the holder. No. He's trustworthy enough, your provincial bank manager – but he's as dead as mutton, usually. Personally, I bank in the City – where I think one should bank – at Coutts. And I'm also a friend of the Manager there, like you. And he's a very live wire, for a bank manager anyway. None of them could be called *really* live wires, of course. You've got to go to the Stock Exchange for that – and I've got an extremely sound man in that direction.'

'A stockbroker, you mean?'

'Yes. I'm afraid to say I dabble a good bit on the Stock Exchange. It's rather like horses with me. But I don't know why I say I'm "afraid". I've done extremely well out of it up to date.'

'Well – I'd certainly be "afraid". All that sort of thing's beyond me, and I leave it strictly alone,' said Mrs Plumleigh-Bruce.

Gorse had been both pleased and displeased on learning about Mrs Plumleigh-Bruce's investments. On the one hand it seemed to prove for certain that she had a certain amount of money behind her; on the other hand investments, with a bank manager of her own guarding them, might be difficult to dig out of her.

He had thought it wise to plant a seed in her mind by at once disparaging her provincial bank manager, and speaking of the City and the Stock Exchange: but here, he thought, the matter had better be completely dropped for a little.

'Yes,' he said. 'And I think you're wise to leave it alone. You've got to know your way around if you go in for that sort of thing. Putting five pounds on a horse is a very different thing from playing with large sums on the market. One's a bit of fun – a bit of sport – the other's quite a serious business – believe me.'

'Yes. I'm sure it is . . .'

There was now a long silence in which both, finding nothing to say, looked into the fire. Gorse looked at his watch.

'Well,' he said. 'I suppose I must be going. It's quite late and you said you were tired.'

'Oh no. Do stay and have another drink, or cigarette or something – won't you? I'm feeling quite lively now.'

'And I'm feeling quite soothed,' said Gorse, looking at her. 'As I predicted I would. But all the same, I do think I'd better go. I don't know what your maid Mary'll be thinking.'

He rose, and warmed his hands at the fire.

'I wouldn't bother about Mary,' said Mrs Plumleigh-Bruce. 'She doesn't think at all. I'm afraid she wasn't trained for thinking, poor girl.'

'All the better for her,' said Gorse, turning from the fire, and looking at her. 'But I must go. Really I must. And I can't thank you enough for letting me come round. As I said, I'm feeling completely soothed, and all my troubles seem to have vanished into thin air.'

'But you haven't really *told* me about your troubles,' said Mrs Plumleigh-Bruce, rising, and looking, with a shyness which was half genuine and half flirtatious, at her visitor.

'No. I know I haven't,' said Gorse, putting his hands behind his back with an air of one using will-power in order to refrain from flirting with her, or, even from attempting to kiss her. 'In fact all I've done is talk about myself – and a bit of my past – and a lot about racing – and to give you a tip, which you've taken, and to get an IOU from you, which *I've* most ungraciously taken . . . All the same, as far as I'm concerned, I've got even more than I hoped for.' He was walking towards the door. 'It'd be funny if the horse falls down, after all, and you lose your money, wouldn't it? And horses do fall down, you know – particularly over the sticks.'

He opened the door, indicating that she should join him in the hall.

'Well,' said Mrs Plumleigh-Bruce, joining him in the hall. 'I'll just have to keep my fingers crossed. By the way – how and when will I know what's happened? I don't even know the name of the horse – do I?'

Gorse began to put on his overcoat in a leisurely way.

'Do you take an evening paper?' he asked.

'Yes. The *Evening News*. . .'

'And what time does it come?'

'Oh – about five-thirty to six.'

'Well, I'll know what we're on a long while before that – so I can telephone you or send you a message in the morning – or at any rate early in the afternoon. Then you'll have to wait breathlessly for the *Evening News*. It's rather fun – don't you think – waiting breathlessly?'

'Mm . . . I'm not so sure about that,' said Mrs Plumleigh-Bruce, and went on to ask the question which now interested her most. 'But if all goes well, or ill, how will I meet you again, anyway? I've either got to pay you five pounds or collect my winnings, haven't I?'

'Yes. You've certainly got to collect your winnings, anyway.' Gorse was slowly putting on his scarf. 'And if it's a question of winnings we ought to celebrate a little. So what about meeting at the good old Friar at about six-thirty? Then we can drown our sorrows in drink, at any rate, if we've lost. I may tell you I'm putting on a great deal more than five pounds myself. So what about it? About six-thirty at The Friar?'

'Yes. That'd suit me.'

'Very well. The Friar it shall be . . . Six-thirty . . . Well – I must be off. And I really can't thank you enough for having me round. I only wish I could do something for you in return – I don't mean just by putting you on to a winner.'

Gorse was putting on his gloves.

'Well – if the horse wins,' said Mrs Plumleigh-Bruce, 'it'll be a question of me having to think of doing something for *you* in return – won't it? And I can't think of anything at the moment. Can you?'

Gorse fiddled with the button of his glove, and pretended to be thinking for a moment.

'Well,' he said, 'as a matter of fact, you can. It's only provided the horse wins of course. If it doesn't, you must cast me out.' He smiled at her. 'But I think you *could* help me – give me your advice – about a small matter.'

'Yes. What is it? Do tell me. What small matter?'

'I should have really said quite a large matter,' said Gorse, flicking his wrist, thoughtfully, and gently, with his other glove. 'And one I know pretty well nothing about. I've just been telling you about a lot of things I *do* know about. But it might be possible to change parts, and for you to tell me something I feel certain *you* know about.'

'Yes? What is it?'

'Oh. About houses . . . One house in particular, really. I mean that house in Gilroy Road. I simply can't make up my mind about it. I can't make out whether it's really a property – whether I'm on to a really good thing or not.'

'But *I* don't know the first thing about the value of houses,' said Mrs Plumleigh-Bruce.

'Yes. That may be – about their value in money – from just a crude masculine point of view. But what I'm wanting is a *woman's* angle. Because that's the only thing that counts in the long run. Women are the only people who know how to run a house, and if a house *can* be run comfortably. I have a feeling that this one can't – although it may be going for a song. But I don't want to sing a song for a white elephant, and that's where you could help me. *Would* you?' Gorse looked at her appealingly.

'Of course. But how, exactly?'

'Oh – just by coming round and looking at it – going over it thoroughly, and casting around that deadly searching eye that only a woman has – employing that awful instinct that belongs to the female sex alone. I have an idea you'd be able to spot all the snags, and then make up my mind about it once and for all. So will you? Couldn't you come to tea or something one day? It'd be perfectly respectable. Old Mrs Burford – that's my housekeeper – she'd be there. And she makes, I may say by way of tempting you, just about the most heavenly scones you've ever tasted. So do come one day, will you?'

'Yes. Of course I will. Whenever you like.'

'Well – I'd like to say tomorrow – but actually tomorrow's Mrs Burford's afternoon off. And anyway we've fixed up six-thirty at The Friar – either to drown our sorrow or celebrate. But what about the day after? Anyway we can discuss it when we meet tomorrow. It's really very good of you . . . Oh – and by the way, about tomorrow . . .'

'Yes. What?' . . .

'Well, is this rather – er – unorthodox visit of mine to you, so late in the evening, supposed to be official? I mean – is it to be mentioned in front of anyone else we might meet in The Friar?'

Mrs Plumleigh-Bruce thought for a second or two, and then, remembering Mr Stimpson's alcoholically defiant air earlier, decided to be defiant herself.

'Yes,' she said. 'Of course. Anybody can know. There's been nothing wrong about it – has there?'

'Certainly not. In fact I hope, if the horse wins, there'll be everything very much right. I only asked you because you know how people gossip in these provincial towns – don't you? But I might have known you're above even thinking of such things, as I am . . . Well – now I really must be off. Good-bye, and thank you again."

Gorse, who unlike Mr Stimpson earlier in the evening, had put no glove on his right hand to snatch off (as Mrs Plumleigh-Bruce noticed), shook hands gracefully with Mrs Plumleigh-Bruce, and a few moments later had left the house – a silent house in which Mary had gone to bed, and in which Mrs Plumleigh-Bruce, returning to the sitting-room, had a lot to think about – Mr Stimpson, Gorse, Military Crosses, being a Cathedral, and the possibility of having lost five pounds.

She could hardly believe she was likely to win any money, and she was still, somehow, dimly suspicious and afraid of Gorse – or at any rate of the, to her mind, slightly too dashing and monied way he did things.

PART SIX

GORSE THE TEMPTER

CHAPTER ONE

I

THE next evening Mr Stimpson was the first to occupy the Plumleigh-Bruce nook at The Friar.

Owing to his having been partially inebriated as well as defiant last night, Mr Stimpson had made no appointment to meet Mrs Plumleigh-Bruce. He had been tempted, during the day, to telephone her, but, as a lustily thriving lover and leaver and treater of them rough, he had resisted the temptation.

2

Mr Stimpson, like Major Parry, had suffered a small misfortune about a year ago – a misfortune, very much like Major Parry's, derived from unexpected success. He had solved a crossword puzzle set by a well-known national evening newspaper, which had presented him with a guinea and mentioned his name. This had been, rather feebly, used in defence against Major Parry's front-page, black-framed Armistice Day Poem, and had rather upset his life. Like Major Parry, Mr Stimpson desperately wanted to repeat his performance. He had a faint suspicion that Major Parry was secretly having another go at the glorious dead, but he was not certain of this. At any rate Major Parry had obviously not had any luck for the last two years, and so he might, Mr Stimpson thought, have decided to retire from the ring – from the black frame. In which case, if Mr Stimpson could only solve

another crossword puzzle, he would be on equal terms with the
Major. In Mr Stimpson's reckoning, two solved crossword
puzzles in a national paper were well worth one Armistice Day
Poem in a local one.

Unhappily, Mr Stimpson was no good at all at crossword
puzzles. He was, in fact, much worse at them than the Major
was at his poems. He had solved the one he had by dogged
patience, luck, and, mostly, by obtaining the assistance of acquaintances in public houses and elsewhere. But he had grimly determined not to surrender, and whenever he had the time, he had a
go at one of the beastly things.

What faced him tonight was even more beastly than usual,
and he had got practically nowhere with it. He was faced by a
few black and a lot of white squares, underneath which had been
printed the following objectionable, sly, whimsical gibberish:

Across	*Down*
1. Cartographer's business.	1. Shy girls do this.
8. Lowland reels perhaps.	2. Extremely small.
9. Diverges.	3. Rigid.
10. Flies at sea.	4. Not permitted.
11. False.	5. Latin for scales.
14. Boredom.	6. Plant leaps (Anag.).
15. Many of these make one.	7. Lonely talk.
18. Jenny – me when we met.	13. Unrealized.
(Leigh Hunt)	14. 19 across would like this.
19. Mean Lady (Anag.).	16. Fruitful.
21. Of course.	17. Perhaps.
23. Northern 'lights'.	18. Beginning.
24. Both ways.	20. Rough justice.
25. Illuminated.	22. More than edible to unbelievers.

Well, some of these seemed to be more or less in the bag.
Take 1 Down for instance: 'Shy girls do this'. That must be
'blush' . . .

But no – it *wasn't*! 'Blush' was only five letters, and six were
required. Shy girls do this . . . Shy girls do *this* . . . Blush. What
was another word for 'blush'? What *was* blushing? It was going

red in the face. Red. Hullo! What about 'Redden'? How many letters in 'redden'? One, two, three, four, five, *six*!

But be careful, now. Don't mess up the white squares with pencil until you're certain. What *else* did shy girls do. Smirk. Simper. Oh God – 'simper' was six letters, too. Better leave it for the moment, and try something else.

'Cartographer's business', 'Lowland reels', 'Diverges'. All beyond him at the moment. (He didn't even know what a Cartographer was, but he could look it up in his Cassell's when he got home.)

'Flies at sea' – a long one – nine or ten letters. Flies at sea, Flies at sea, Flies at *sea* . . . Hullo! *Hydroplane*! Surely he was home here. Hurrah! Brilliant! Check up on the number of letters. Hydroplane. One, two, three, four, five, six, seven, eight, nine, *ten*. It looked as though it would fit. Now check on the number of white squares. One, two, three, four, five, six (things were looking good), seven, eight, *nine* – blast it!

Check again on squares and hydroplane . . . No. No good . . . What on earth sort of thing, then, flew at sea? There were millions of flies on the river – there was fly-fishing – but what about the sea?

Wait a minute! What about flying fish?

What about *porpoises*? Didn't porpoises fly out of the water, or sort of jump out of it at any rate? It could be *called* flying, and porpoises looked about ten letters . . .

No. No good. Caught again. Even if porpoises flew the clue was 'flies', not 'fly', and so only one porpoise would be flying. And one porpoise would never run to be ten letters, surely.

Mr Stimpson checked up (in a purely academic spirit, for he knew now that he was getting nowhere) on his lonely porpoise . . . Yes. Two letters short.

What about trying the Anags. Sometimes he got these in a flash.

'Mean Lady' . . . Mean Lady, Neam Ydal, Dylad Name . . . Dynamo? No. Dynamaled? No such word, but you must try out everything. Named Yal? Named Lay . . . *Damnedly*? Yes, surely! . . . No. Too many 'd's and not enough 'a's. And anyway there probably wasn't such a word. 'Damnably' there certainly was, but 'Damnedly' would almost certainly not be in Cassell's.

The other Anag., then – 'Plant leaps'.

Pleasant? No. Pleasance? Unpleasant? No . . . Slant-something? Nap-something? *Pale*-something. *Ape*-something.

No. 'Plant leaps' was worse than 'Flies at sea'.

Perhaps 'Flies at sea' was a pun. Flies. Things you swatted. See. Vision. Flies obstructing the view. See. Holy See – flies in a church or something, or on a Bishop or something . . . Top C. A soprano trying to hit the top C. – flying at it. *Soprano*!

No. Caught again! Soprano was only seven.

This was getting absurd. 'Simper' and 'redden' were as yet his only hopes. Better go for the *really* easy ones.

After much morose mental lurking around Rough justice, Perhaps, Beginning, Many of these make one, Rigid, Extremely small, Both ways, and Fruitful, Mr Stimpson at last alighted upon what he thought were two dead certainties. These were 'lit' for a three-letter 'Illuminated', and 'untrue' for a six-letter 'False'.

He was pencilling these in, with a feeling of frustration and compromise rather than elation, when he was joined by Mrs Plumleigh-Bruce.

As he rose to greet her he hastily put away the newspaper and pencil into his overcoat pocket. He was as anxious to hide his continued preoccupation with crossword puzzles from Mrs Plumleigh-Bruce, as he was anxious to hide it from the poem-writing Major. Until he was again successful with one, he wanted to hide it from all the world. That was why he never now sought advice on clues from any kind of acquaintance, and, as a consequence, never got within even a reasonable distance of solving a problem.

3

Mr Stimpson had been so absorbed by hydroplanes and blushing girls that he had completely forgotten Mrs Plumleigh-Bruce, and the situation in regard to her. He was not, therefore, for a moment, particularly surprised or pleased to see her. He simply welcomed her politely, ushered her into her usual seat (her throne one might say), and went over to the bar to get a Gin and It, together with another beer for himself.

When he was at the bar, however, and waiting for the drinks, he came to his senses and realized that a remarkable, and remarkably gratifying, thing had happened.

Last night he had given her no invitation to join him in The Friar. She never, so far as he knew, went into The Friar without an invitation. And yet here she was, seemingly following him in, seeking his company.

What could this indicate but a triumph for himself? Was it not evident that his tactic last night had succeeded brilliantly – that loving and leaving them and treating them rough were now proved to be incomparable slogans? Good Heavens, he thought, the Lady of Reading, the famous Lady Joan, so far from having taken offence, seemed to be practically chasing him! Women, this original thinker decided, were Funny Creatures. All they needed was Handling ... As he returned with the drinks he complacently braced himself to the most agreeable task of Handling her.

But, when he had sat down beside her, he somehow had an instinct that she was for some reason not in any sort of mood to be Handled.

This was not because she was in any way disagreeable. Rather the contrary. She was, perhaps, more pleasant to him than usual, and she was, it seemed to him, in a state of internal happiness and excitement which she was not, in spite of an effort, quite able to subdue. He could not in any way account for this mood. He only knew that it was certainly not one of 'chasing' him. It looked, really, as if she had been chasing something else, and had captured it.

Mrs Plumleigh-Bruce's mood, if only Mr Stimpson had the requisite knowledge, could have been easily explained.

During the middle of the afternoon she had received a written message from Gorse, in which, among other things, he had named the horse which he had backed on her behalf – *Stucco*.

She had waited in anguish for her evening newspaper, rushing into the hall to get it, opening it dizzily, and, having seen that *Stucco* had won, at 4–1, returning to the sitting-room in a condition of dazed and almost delirious pleasure.

Those who back horses regularly have little idea of the emotion which is awakened in the breasts of those who, having in their lives hitherto only put a little money on big events (and usually lost it), all at once have the experience of winning money on an everyday race. And in this case Mrs Plumleigh-Bruce had won what seemed to her an enormous amount of money – twenty pounds. (She kept on thinking of it as twenty-five, including her stake in her winnings, as the inexperienced so often do.)

With such inexperienced people, who never even glance at Racing pages or news, the very obscurity of the race furnishes the major part of the excitement and pride they take in having found and backed its winner. To win on the Derby or the Grand National — that is nothing, mere racing froth and frivolity. Everybody around you has had a bet, and won or lost. But to have picked the winner of a race which most people have never even heard of — this is indeed getting behind the scenes, sends one soaring above the trivial class of the amateur punter.

Such people, carrying their evening newspapers announcing the news about with them (as Mrs Plumleigh-Bruce was now), somehow feel that they are themselves in the news — in the limelight of print. They almost look upon themselves as celebrities. They are in the 'know', too, which is almost as good as, or perhaps better than, being in the news.

And, because they are in the 'know' they feel enormously, enormously clever, shrewd, and far-seeing — even if, as Mrs Plumleigh-Bruce had, they have obtained their information entirely fortuitously, and have supported it reluctantly.

Delicious gratification, in fact, floods in upon them from every conceivable side. And, today, Mrs Plumleigh-Bruce had further cause for gratification.

Along with his afternoon message about the horse, Gorse had sent Mrs Plumleigh-Bruce flowers — six or seven very fine chrysanthemums. Both these and the message had been despatched from what was recognized as easily the finest florist in Reading.

4

Gorse had not, in fact, put any money on any horse, either on Mrs Plumleigh-Bruce's or his own behalf. Instead he had caused, by means of an early morning telegram, a Hammersmith friend of his, who attended every race-meeting, to telephone him and give him the result of the two o'clock race. He had then hastened to the florist.

It may be wondered why he had gone to all the trouble — why he had not waited until he had found the winner of the race by ordinary methods, and then announced to her that he had backed the winner.

This was all part of Gorse's life-long technique with women – that of submitting them to as much suspense and relief as he possibly could. Relief was his main object – but for this suspense was necessary. In a state of wild relief women would agree to almost anything he proposed.

5

Mrs Plumleigh-Bruce, then, sitting with Mr Stimpson, was not only bathing in the luxurious complacency of a successful racing expert: she was bathing in relief, and in the pleasure and vanity – which she could not, however much she tried, restrain – derived from having received such delightful flowers from so young a man.

She had entered The Friar at 6.33. Gorse had said 'about' six-thirty. She would, normally, have arrived five minutes late – but her happy impatience had made her cut off two minutes – a favour never conceded to any other man. She was disappointed, as Gorse had meant her to be, not to find him there already, but she fully consoled herself with his use of the word 'about', and was, indeed, radiating true happiness without any effort or self-consciousness.

Mr Stimpson, the Handler so fresh to Handling, found himself puzzled (and of course completely unable to do the smallest thing in the way of Handling), when confronted with this odd, agitated, but obviously joyous mood in Mrs Plumleigh-Bruce.

He hoped it would simmer down after a bit. But it did not, and when two or three minutes had passed Mr Stimpson became very seriously annoyed by it. He tried to control this annoyance, but at last could do so no longer.

'You seem to be very cheerful about something tonight,' the ungracious man, the thwarted Handler, said at last. 'What's happened? Some good news? Somebody left you a fortune or something?'

'No,' said Mrs Plumleigh-Bruce, with a sparkling, teasingly satisfied look. 'Not a fortune. But I *have* come into an extremely nice little bit of money, as a matter of fact . . .'

This scared Mr Stimpson out of his wits.

He had no idea what she meant, and it occurred to him that she might have suddenly inherited money – and done so in quite a big way. This would be awful. He knew something of her financial situation, which was not at all a good one, and, in his heart, he knew that his one hold over her was his own money, his financial soundness, acumen, and growing prosperity.

As if a switch had been suddenly turned off, in the next few moments the recently-lit but warm electric fire of Mr Stimpson's imagination – his dreams of becoming the Casanova of Reading – began to fade, go white. Even his red face became almost visibly whiter.

On the other hand, Mr Stimpson, thinking intensely, managed quickly to find the switch of some secondary lighting. If Casanova was down, Mr Stimpson reflected, the idea of marriage could come up – could be resumed. And, if she had inherited money, marriage was all the more desirable.

'Really? . . .' he said. 'And what do you mean by "quite a little"?'

'Oh – *quite* a little,' said Mrs Plumleigh-Bruce, mischievously.

'But what does "quite" mean? These things are relative, aren't they?'

'Just what I said. *Quite* a little. In fact I might say quite a *lot* – for somebody like myself at any rate.'

Mr Stimpson was more frightened than ever.

'But where did it come from?' he asked. 'Have you inherited money, or something? I mean how did you come by it?'

'Ah,' said Mrs Plumleigh-Bruce, who intended to keep him guessing as long as possible, partly because of her high spirits, and partly to revenge herself upon the man who had kept her guessing and behaved so uncouthly last night. 'That'd be telling.'

'And you won't tell me?'

'I'm not so sure. Why should I? . . . By the way,' said Mrs Plumleigh-Bruce, showing more astuteness than was usual with her, 'you seem to be looking very miserable at the thought of my having got some money. I should've thought you'd've wanted to congratulate me.'

'But of course I want to congratulate you. But how can I until I know how much it is, and how you came by it?'

'I don't see how I came by it really has anything to do with it,' said Mrs Plumleigh-Bruce. 'The point is, I've got it.'

Here she looked at the door. It had suddenly struck her that she had not as yet got the money, and that her doing so depended entirely upon Gorse. What if Gorse – the still faintly suspect young man – had decamped? What if he had decided to keep for himself the twenty pounds he had made? What if he did not want to pay up? Such a thing would, indeed, make her look foolish – idiotic.

She had looked quite a few times at the door before, and Mr Stimpson had noticed it. This last look stung the highly irritated man to comment.

'Why do you keep on looking at the door?' he asked.

'Was I? I didn't know I was.'

'Are you expecting all this wonderful money to come through the door, or something?'

He had, of course, accidentally, hit the nail on the head.

'Well,' said Mrs Plumleigh-Bruce. 'Such a thing *could* happen, you know . . .'

Mr Stimpson experienced considerable relief. Only a comparatively small sum of money, probably in cash – not an inheritance – could possibly come through the door of the Saloon Bar of The Friar.

'You know, I do wish you wouldn't be so mysterious, Joan,' he said, in a much less irritated tone. 'Do tell me. Won't you? I believe you're enjoying keeping me guessing.'

'Perhaps I am,' said Mrs Plumleigh-Bruce. 'Perhaps it's a secret.'

'Oh well, if it's a secret you'd better not tell me. Is it a secret?'

'No. It's not a secret,' Mrs Plumleigh-Bruce relented. 'Or it's a very open secret, anyway.'

'How open?'

'Well – it's free for everybody to see. It's in the newspaper, as a matter of fact.'

'The newspaper!' Mr Stimpson again had horrible forebodings of some spectacular inheritance.

'Yes. In fact, you can look at it, if you like. There you are.' She gave him her newspaper. 'You'll find it on the back page.'

As with all successful punting fledglings, the incessant looking at and showing of the evening newspaper were the peak-points of Mrs Plumleigh-Bruce's happiness.

'I don't follow you. Where am I to look?' said Mr Stimpson, happy at any rate to have observed that Mrs Plumleigh-Bruce's picture was not on the back page. 'Do help me out.'

'Look at the racing.'

'Yes. What about it?'

'And look at the winner of the two o'clock at Bramford.'

'Yes ... Yes ... *Stucco* ... What about it?'

'Well – I've backed it, that's all. And it's come in at four to one.'

'Good Heavens,' said Mr Stimpson, now perfectly happy again – so happy that he was almost happy for Mrs Plumleigh-Bruce, who, he imagined, had for some reason put two bob or something on the race. 'Well. I never knew you went in for betting, Joan. Good for you. How much did you have on?'

'Five pounds.'

'Five *pounds*! *Pounds* did you say?'

'I did.'

'Joan – have you been going mad? Five pounds on a *horse*?'

'Yes. Why not? After all,' said Mrs Plumleigh-Bruce, in her smugness almost quoting Gorse word for word, 'in this world one's got to do things in the right way – and that means the big way – doesn't it? ... And look at the result. I've won twenty pounds – instead of just a few shillings.'

'But I never dreamed you went in for this sort of thing.'

'I don't – as a rule ...'

'No. So I thought. Then somebody must have put you up to it.'

'Perhaps they did ...'

'I'm sure they did. Come along now. Who was it? Or is that a secret, too?'

'No. That's not a secret of any sort, really.'

Mrs Plumleigh-Bruce had made up her mind to be absolutely candid about Gorse's visit last night. She had had his permission to do so, and, in addition to the fact that it was the safest course to take, it would almost certainly make Mr Stimpson very jealous indeed, and so, in its turn, make herself much more desirable in his eyes. Then, fired by jealousy and desire, Mr Stimpson might, before long, become much more explicit about his Hog. It might indeed, turn out to be not only whole, but wholly estimable and matrimonial.

'Well, then, don't keep me waiting,' said Mr Stimpson. 'Who was it?'

'Only the newcomer in our midst. He certainly seems to know something about horses.'

'Oh . . . *Him* . . .' said Mr Stimpson. 'So *he* gave you the tip . . . But how on earth did you get it from him? I haven't seen him for about four days. I thought he'd vanished.'

'Yes. So did I, rather. But he's only been to London, and so far from vanishing he turned up last night as large as life.'

'Last night? When?'

'Oh – after you left.'

'How do you mean? Did he phone you or something?'

'Yes, he did phone me as a matter of fact. But after that he came round to see me.'

'Came round!'

'Yes. He was frightfully miserable, poor boy. He'd had a simply awful day in London, haggling over business. And he asked me to give him a little bit of comfort, by talking to me, and I simply didn't have the heart to refuse him.'

'And did you give him "comfort"?' said Mr Stimpson, not unsuggestively.

'I hope I did. I gave him a drink and some coffee, anyway, and although he was only with me about half an hour, he seemed to be in a much happier frame of mind when he left.'

'And he gave you a tip about a horse in among?'

'Yes. So my good deed had its reward, you see. He's a funny young man. He seems to be amazingly worldly-wise, and yet fearfully pathetic and dependent, at the same time. He sent me some flowers this afternoon. It's just a tiny bit embarrassing to tell you the truth.'

Mr Stimpson was in too stunned a state at the moment to feel jealousy.

'Well,' he said. 'Flowers and visits late at night *do* seem a bit embarrassing. You don't, by any chance, think he's "smitten", do you?'

Mrs Plumleigh-Bruce seemed to deliberate on this question.

'I sincerely *hope* not,' she said at last. 'I certainly haven't encouraged it, if he is. There's quite a considerable difference in our ages, isn't there?'

'Yes. There is. But funnier things than that happen in life, you know. And I'm sure you'll agree with me. I hope you're not going to turn into a baby-snatcher.'

Mrs Plumleigh-Bruce again deliberated.

'No. I don't think there's much danger of that,' said Mrs Plumleigh-Bruce, and then turned the screw a little further on Mr Stimpson. 'And yet, you know, although he's so young in years, he's so amazingly grown-up in everything he does. And everything he's done, too. You'd be surprised by the things he told me about himself last night.'

'Oh – what was that?'

'No,' said Mrs Plumleigh-Bruce, who had in mind Gorse's Military Cross. 'That was in the confessional.'

'What, something discreditable?'

'Oh, no. Very much the opposite. But I just happened to promise to keep it secret. I don't know why he wanted me to, and if he gives me permission I'll be only too happy to reveal it. And I'm sure he will, if I ask him . . . By the way, I'm wondering why he's not here now, to tell you the truth. We arranged to meet about 6.30, and it's much more than that, isn't it? True, he only said "about " six thirty.'

'Yes,' said Mr Stimpson. 'But here he is, if I'm not gravely mistaken.'

Gorse had entered.

Gorse went to the bar and ordered a drink with the pretence of not looking at the Plumleigh-Bruce nook.

Then he stuck his monocle into his eye, and, apparently with its aid, saw that Mrs Plumleigh-Bruce and Mr Stimpson were present.

Then, looking at Mrs Plumleigh-Bruce, he lifted his head with an air of restrained pleasure and mock 'I told you so' conceit. Then he put his monocle back into his waistcoat pocket, and paid for his drink.

Then he brought his drink over to the other two, with the mock-strutting gait of one who was highly pleased with himself, and said 'Well – how *are* we all this evening?'

'We're *extremely* well,' said Mrs Plumleigh-Bruce, 'and I think we have rather good cause to be, haven't we? You and I, at any rate.'

'Yes, I must say there isn't *too* much rotten in the state of Denmark just pro tem,' said Gorse, sitting down opposite Mrs Plumleigh-Bruce and Mr Stimpson.

'No,' said Mr Stimpson. 'You two seem to have been doing pretty well for yourselves, as far as I can gather.'

'Oh – so you've been told about our little excursion into the realms of chance, have you?' said Gorse. 'Not that it was really chance. It was as near to a dead certainty as you could get in this uncertain world.'

'I only wish *you'd* been there a little later, Donald,' said Mrs Plumleigh-Bruce. 'And then you could have been put on to it. I know you're very flourishing, but I don't expect you'd turn up your nose at getting twenty pounds – would you?'

'No, I – ' began Mr Stimpson, but Gorse cut in.

'What did you say?' he said, raising his chin and looking intently at Mrs Plumleigh-Bruce. 'Twenty pounds?'

His intent and serious look might easily be interpreted as a look of alarm: and Mrs Plumleigh-Bruce was alarmed. There was a pause.

'Well,' said Mrs Plumleigh-Bruce. 'That's right, isn't it? It *is* twenty pounds – isn't it? I put five pounds on it, and it came in at four to one. That makes twenty pounds, doesn't it?'

'Oh no,' said Gorse, maintaining his steady look. 'Not twenty pounds.'

Gorse was playing at suspense and relief again.

'But it *did* come in at four to one – didn't it?'

'Yes. It certainly did.'

'Then what's the trouble?' said Mr Stimpson. 'That's twenty pounds all right, isn't it? Unless I'm a Dutchman.'

'Then I'm afraid you *are* a Dutchman, Mr Stimpson,' said Gorse, producing his gold cigarette case, and taking out a cigarette. 'The sum's not twenty pounds, I can assure you.'

'What then?' said Mr Stimpson.

'Twenty-five,' said Gorse. 'A clear twenty-five. A quarter of a century, in fact.'

'No,' said Mr Stimpson, glad to be able to argue in a business-like way on Mrs Plumleigh-Bruce's behalf, this having been, for a long while, another of his holds over her. 'You don't mean a *clear* twenty-five – twenty-five clear profit. You're not thinking of the original stake – are you? That's not part of the profit.'

'Agreed. All the same,' said Gorse, 'I still say a clear twenty-five.'

'Well – it beats me,' said Mr Stimpson.

'It does me, too,' said Mrs Plumleigh-Bruce.

'It's very simple,' said Gorse. 'If you'll only think for a little.'

'Well,' said Mr Stimpson. 'No amount of thinking's going to make *me* see it differently. Unless I've cracked up on my simple arithmetic.'

'No. You haven't done that, but it's still very simple. I backed *Stucco* each way – that's all.'

'Oh – I see!' said Mr Stimpson. 'Why didn't you say so before?'

'Oh – I don't know. I somehow thought it was taken for granted, I suppose . . . Oh yes, I was on to *Stucco* for a place as well. I told you only last night,' said Gorse, addressing Mrs Plumleigh-Bruce, 'that you've got to do things in the big way – didn't I?'

'Yes. I believe you did,' said Mrs Plumleigh-Bruce, after a pause. 'We were certainly agreed on *that* matter.'

With these words Mrs Plumleigh-Bruce was trying desperately to cover up her tracks in front of Mr Stimpson. Only a few minutes ago she had spoken to Mr Stimpson about the necessity of doing things in a big way – and this as if she had been expressing her own life-long opinion. Now Gorse had made it seem that she had cribbed dreadfully – that her opinion, indeed, so far from being life-long, had only been acquired last night.

Mr Stimpson was not fooled by her suggestion that there had last night been a spontaneous, mutual agreement between Gorse and Mrs Plumleigh-Bruce on this method of procedure in life. He was pleased to have found her embarrassed by the accidental disclosure, and, in order to regain a little more power over her by further embarrassing her, he did not drop the matter.

'Yes,' he said, looking at her meaningly. 'That was just what you were saying a few minutes ago, wasn't it?'

Mrs Plumleigh-Bruce, aware, like Gorse, that Mr Stimpson had scored, changed, or rather returned to, the subject.

'Well, then – that's simply wonderful, isn't it?' she said. 'Twenty-five pounds! I can't believe it. And I don't really think I ought to take it from you just on the strength of that I O U . . .'

'Oh – here it is, by the way,' said Gorse, taking the piece of Bath Club notepaper, and handing it to her.

'And what do I do with this?' she asked. 'Keep it, or tear it up?'

'I wouldn't bother about anything till you've got your money,' said Gorse, facetiously.

'And when do I get that?' said Mrs Plumleigh-Bruce. 'You know you're making me most horribly greedy and commercial, and I can hardly wait to grab the money. When do I get it?'

'Ah,' said the indomitable salesman of suspense. 'That's the question. I don't actually square up accounts with my book-maker until the end of each month, and that's a long way away.'

'Oh dear,' said Mrs Plumleigh-Bruce, pouting and shaking her hands with kittenish impatience. 'Have I got to wait all that time? Oh – poor, greedy little me!'

Gorse noticed that Mrs Plumleigh-Bruce was not much good as a kitten. He felt that it would be better if she stuck to her slow, royal, fruity stuff. All the same, he managed to seem to be fascinated.

'No,' he said, in a kitten-stroking voice. 'Not all that time. But I'm afraid I can't give it to you this evening, I haven't got it on me. In fact, I'm afraid you'll probably have to wait until the day after tomorrow . . . And that brings me to another matter, by the way . . .'

Gorse's serious look and tone again frightened Mrs Plumleigh-Bruce.

'What matter?' she said.

'I'm afraid I've got to go to London,' said Gorse. 'And that right soon.'

'How soon?' asked Mrs Plumleigh-Bruce. 'And for how long?'

'As soon as this very evening that ever was, I'm afraid,' said Gorse. 'And it'll be for two nights at least. In fact I think I'll buzz off after this drink. I hate driving a car with more than one drink inside me. It's not that I can't – but if anything *did* happen in the way of an accident, the policeman smells it on your breath and draws false conclusions.'

'Oh dear. What a pity,' said Mrs Plumleigh-Bruce. 'What on earth's happened? Some further business crisis?'

'No. Just the culmination of the crises I told you about last night. And I think all's well. But I've got a nine-thirty visit tomorrow morning with a very tough customer in Kensington, and I want to be up in good time and have my head clear for it. So I'm making the journey tonight. And then, tomorrow evening, I've got yet another visit, at the King's Hotel in Piccadilly, with a much more pleasant customer – still business, but a friend. And so that means I'll be two nights away altogether.'

'Oh dear,' said Mrs Plumleigh-Bruce.

'You know, *that's* funny,' said Mr Stimpson. 'I've got to go to London myself tomorrow on business. And I'm staying up for the night, too. I'm staying with my sister, out Richmond way.'

'Well – that's a coincidence,' said Gorse, thinking quickly, 'And are you going to be *very* busy?'

'Oh – no. Not as busy as all that. In fact I ought to be through by tea-time.'

'Well,' said Gorse. 'In that case – couldn't we meet?'

'Why yes. I don't see why not. But where? And when?'

'Well – what about the King's?' said Gorse. 'I expect you know the very nice cocktail bar there – down below. And if my business goes through as expected I'll be in a mood for gaiety – even for painting the town red – or at any rate a mild pink.'

Mr Stimpson had indeed heard of the King's Hotel – which was a very large and well-to-do Hotel almost opposite the Lyons 'Pop', which Mr Stimpson mostly used when bent on gaiety or relaxation in the West End. Mr Stimpson had always regarded the King's as above his mark – financially and socially – though he had never done more than glimpse enviously through its re-volving doors.

Mr Stimpson had also heard of the downstairs cocktail bar at the King's, which was well-known for furnishing facilities for making the acquaintance of an expensive type of prostitute – too expensive and too frightening for Mr Stimpson. Mr Stimpson always went for Wardour Street.

Mr Stimpson made a trip to London about once a month, in fact doing business and staying with his sister at Richmond. But with these duties he combined, or had until recently combined, pleasure: and he had in the past seldom appeared in his sister's house, of which he had the key, until midnight or afterwards.

In his last few visits, however, he had been back in time for an evening meal with his sister. This had been because of that fierce attack of purity which had overtaken him ever since he had first seriously thought of marrying Mrs Plumleigh-Bruce.

But now, with his changed attitude towards Mrs Plumleigh-Bruce, purity was on the wane. Indeed, impurity was very much on the up and up.

Therefore, when Gorse suggested a meeting at the King's, Mr Stimpson was very interested indeed. If such a meeting came off he would not only, because of a companion, be able to enter the King's without social fear: he would be exploring fascinating avenues of improper behaviour.

This young man Gorse, he decided, certainly had something to him. He went to France, won big money on horses, and had a general air which Mr Stimpson in a way envied and in a way admired.

'But aren't you doing business at the King's?' he asked Gorse. 'And won't you have a friend there? I don't want to butt in or anything.'

'No,' said Gorse, having noticed the gleam of happy anticipation in Mr Stimpson's eye. 'I don't expect the business'll take more than half an hour at the outside. And then I'll probably be alone. And even if I'm not – who cares. The more the merrier. What about it?'

Gorse had always suspected that Mr Stimpson was the sort of man who made occasional visits to town in order secretly to pursue paid women. His aggressive middleness of age and class made it almost transparent. Gorse had also wondered whether he might, somehow, take advantage of Mr Stimpson's secret, if it existed. And the gleam in Mr Stimpson's eye now almost assured him that it did.

Gorse had formed no precise plan as to how he might exploit the Reading man's guilt in London, but that he could do so, in one way or another, he had no doubt.

Gorse, strangely enough, was never a direct blackmailer. But he was, when it suited him, a tale-teller, and a careful hoarder (or brilliant inventor) of the shameful secrets of others.

Mr Stimpson, it must be remembered, was Gorse's enemy and rival in the case of Mrs Plumleigh-Bruce. He was formidable too – for he had marriage and money to offer, a long acquaintance-ship with Mrs Plumleigh-Bruce, and a business head with which to advise and protect her. Mr Stimpson, in fact, would sooner or later have to be moved from the arena – or at any rate reduced to impotence therein.

'Well,' said Mr Stimpson. 'That sounds all right to me. In fact it sounds a *complete* bit of all right.'

Gorse's ability to make everybody and everything centre around himself was, indisputably, phenomenal. Along with Mrs Plumleigh-Bruce, Mr Stimpson himself was now seeking his favours.

Not only was Mr Stimpson enormously relishing the idea of visiting the King's Hotel, Piccadilly: he was getting his own back, taking it out of Mrs Plumleigh-Bruce. She, a few moments ago, had adopted the attitude of having the red-haired young man almost pathetically in tow. But now he had been snatched away from her, and practically belonged to Mr Stimpson. Mr Stimpson of course was not able to exercise any sort of feminine control over Gorse, but a masculine bond, in the present circumstances, was, really, considerably stronger. His meeting with Gorse at the King's introduced a wonderfully monied, 'all-boys-together', London, West End atmosphere – something which Mrs Plumleigh-Bruce might put into her pipe and smoke.

'Well, then – that's fine,' said Gorse. 'What time shall we meet? Seven o'clock? You know the bar, I take it?'

'Oh yes. I know the bar,' said Mr Stimpson, who did not, but who had learned that it was 'down below', and, confident of his ability to find it, was not going to betray his ignorance in front of Mrs Plumleigh-Bruce. 'And seven o'clock'd do fine.'

'Very well, then. Seven o'clock it shall be,' said Gorse. 'And then, the next morning, I can run you down here again in my car, if you like. Or are you motoring up?'

Gorse was certain that Mr Stimpson had no car, and, in order, Cardinal-like, to keep the balance of power, he had given a point to Mrs Plumleigh-Bruce.

'No,' said Mr Stimpson, knowing that Mrs Plumleigh-Bruce was regaining a little ground. 'I haven't got a car as a matter of fact. Not just at the moment at any rate.'

'Well, then,' said Gorse. 'You must let me run you back ... And talking of running, I ought to do a bit now, myself. I've laid on a meal with my landlady in London, and I mustn't keep her up. Also I want an early night.'

'Oh, come on,' said Mr Stimpson. 'Have another drink. I owe you one from the other night, anyway.'

'Yes. Do stay and have *one* more,' said Mrs Plumleigh-Bruce.

'No. I really won't ... And the repayment of the drink can be done tomorrow night at the King's – can't it? ... No,' said Gorse, drinking off his drink, and rising and buttoning his overcoat. 'Rules are rules. And particularly when you're driving. Thanks very much all the same ... Very well, then. Seven o'clock – King's Bar – downstairs – tomorrow evening. And the evening after that perhaps we'll *all* meet again.' He looked at Mrs Plumleigh-Bruce. 'I'll arrange to have your money by that time, at any rate ... Well – good night, both.'

He smiled and waved at Mrs Plumleigh-Bruce and Mr Stimpson, and walked, in an erect, rather hurried, military way from the Saloon Bar of The Friar.

The two he had left were, on the whole, despondent, though they had no reason for unhappiness. Mrs Plumleigh-Bruce should have still been rejoicing at her winnings; but owing to the sudden departure of Gorse, and his meeting tomorrow with Mr Stimpson, she was not. She was gloomy.

Her gloom infected Mr Stimpson, and at last damped his pleasure in the thought of his meeting with Gorse tomorrow evening.

They spent an uneasy half-hour over another drink, and then told lies in order to escape from each other.

CHAPTER TWO

I

THE next day Mr Stimpson, while going about his business in London, vacillated most uneasily between the ideals of purity and impurity.

And the problem, he knew, would, almost without doubt, confront him in a concrete form in the evening.

Had Mr Stimpson taken Gorse seriously as a rival in the pursuit of Mrs Plumleigh-Bruce, purity would have won the day. He would have 'fought' for Mrs Plumleigh-Bruce, and sustained himself in the battle with the knowledge of his own white, Galahad-like behaviour. He was sure that the France-visiting Gorse was not the type of young man who would allow purity to enter into his calculations at any time.

Mr Stimpson rather fancied the idea of 'fighting' for Mrs Plumleigh-Bruce. As a self-styled 'plodder' he took great pride in his pedestrian, indefatigable qualities – and would not at all mind a situation in which he would be able to exercise his 'grim' or 'dogged' determination.

But Mr Stimpson was quite unable to think of Gorse as a rival. Gorse was too young, to begin with – the discrepancy between his and Mrs Plumleigh-Bruce's years making the notion of an affair (or marriage) between the two seem quite absurd. Mrs Plumleigh-Bruce was, after all, too sensible to make that sort of a fool of herself.

Gorse, in addition, was too light-hearted and worldly, too much a man about town, to dream of any such thing.

Gorse, bored in Reading, might, of course, be in a small way 'smitten' by Mrs Plumleigh-Bruce, but such a thing clearly presented no danger.

Therefore, during at least half of the time he gave to reflection on the theme, it seemed to Mr Stimpson that the situation had not really been changed in any way by the appearance of Gorse at Reading. And so renewed impurity in London was entirely in order.

Mr Stimpson, when looking at things from this angle, so far from being made jealous by Gorse's interest in Mrs Plumleigh-Bruce, experienced, in anticipation, the pleasures of vanity. If Gorse was indeed a little 'smitten', then here was the possibility of yet another feather in Mr Stimpson's cap – Gorse being the feather. If the Lady of Reading became Mr Stimpson's acknowledged mistress, a highly presentable and slightly 'smitten' young man hanging around made her more enviable a capture than ever.

Thinking on these lines, Mr Stimpson permitted himself happily to indulge in a gentle, almost sentimental pity for the young man.

This, in its turn, made him like Gorse more and more, and to look forward to the Mrs Plumleigh-Bruce-ousting, 'all-boys-to-gether' meeting at the King's Hotel with very great relish.

Mr Stimpson was in the vicinity of the King's Hotel a full hour before the time of the meeting, and had two pints of beer at a public house before meeting Gorse. Mr Stimpson always drank more in London than in Reading, and, in this case, he wanted to fortify himself for the coming ordeal of passing through the portals of the large, imposing hotel.

Over his beer Mr Stimpson's attitude towards Gorse grew even more warm and deliciously patronizing. The 'old plodder' decided, if the opportunity arose, graciously to give the 'young shaver' a 'wrinkle' or two.

Mr Stimpson, in his rather excited mood failing to allow for the conventional five minutes by which the public house clock was fast, found himself outside the King's Hotel about seven minutes before seven o'clock.

He had no intention of going in too early. He meant, on the other hand, to be at least five minutes late – so that he might find Gorse already there.

Middle-aged provincial businessmen are often as shy, or shyer than, young boys. The thought of entering and being alone in the downstairs cocktail bar of the King's – the bar with the reputation it had – was too much for Mr Stimpson.

He therefore took a stroll in the neighbourhood for about

twelve minutes, interesting himself by glancing at what went on on one or two of those pavements best known at that time for bringing about encounters desired by businessmen bent on illicit and rapid pleasure.

2

What Mr Stimpson was able to see early in 1928 was very different from what he would have seen to-day – and, from his own point of view, very much more satisfying.

Prostitution, in fact, was just then approaching its heyday – the collapse of the 1926 strike having put the working class into a mood of dejection, apathy and submissiveness, which, taken in conjunction with increasing national unemployment, had thrown more dejected, apathetic and submissive women upon the West End streets than, perhaps, ever before.

Many of these women or girls were quite desperate. On the other hand many others – more beautiful, lucky, or experienced – were by no means desperate, for there was a lot of money about. Taken all in all, though, the supply of street-women far exceeded the demand, and street-women thronged certain streets of the West End.

In 1928, in fact, it was almost impossible for any sort of man to walk given streets, at given times, without being ferociously accosted, sometimes by more than one woman or girl simultaneously. And such streets rang with the cries of 'Hullo, darling', 'Where are *you* off to, darling?', 'How are you, dear?' or the 'Where you go, dar*leeng*?' of the French in Old Bond Street (Old Bond Street had long ago been conquered, and is still held, by the French).

Because it was not yet seven o'clock, and because of the rather superior nature of the area in which he was walking, Mr Stimpson was not actually accosted this evening.

Nevertheless, Mr Stimpson saw, particularly when he was in Vigo Street and in Sackville Street, much that interested him.

3

He was six minutes late for Gorse when he went timidly, hat in hand, through the revolving doors of the King's Hotel.

He was fortunate enough to see at once, in front of him at some distance, an electric-lit arrowed-sign saying 'COCKTAIL BAR' – the arrow pointing to somewhere downstairs.

He found the Bar – and Gorse waiting for him.

The Bar was practically empty, and Gorse was standing at one end of the bar by himself.

He was smoking a cigarette and wearing his monocle and an extremely impressive dark blue 'lounge' suit. He was, in this suit, noticeably and gracefully 'lounging' against the bar, and, though he waved and smiled at Mr Stimpson, this did not disturb his poised, calm, cool demeanour.

CHAPTER THREE

I

GORSE, when lounging at one end of an expensive bar, nearly always wore a monocle and looked like a curious, undistinguished mixture between Bertie Wooster and Satan.

An astute observer would have been more impressed by the moustached-satanic, rather than the monocled-Wooster, aspect of the young man, and would have realized that he was looking at a character by no means unformidable.

Mr Stimpson was not an astute observer, and at the moment even less so than usual, because of his uneasiness at his first entrance into the well-known, well-lit, glittering, thickly-carpeted bar. The fact that Gorse was there, indeed, made the young man seem quite angelic – certainly not satanic.

Nor did Mr Stimpson observe, in the first few minutes of talking to Gorse, that he had been tempted by Satan, in the person of Gorse, and had succumbed. He had, however.

For Gorse had ordered for Mr Stimpson an extremely strong cocktail. This was on the bar beside his own drink, and both had a most pleasant, green, frothy appearance. But Gorse's drink, though it resembled Mr Stimpson's externally, had practically no alcohol in it. He was, therefore, deceiving as well as tempting Mr Stimpson.

'I've taken the liberty of ordering a drink for you,' he said. 'In my view it's the very best they provide here – but if you don't like it, I'll order something else, and drink it myself . . . I often think it's a pity they don't like you drinking good old beer in places like this – don't you?'

Mr Stimpson did not like cocktails, but, by these last words of Gorse, was of course shamed into readily accepting what Gorse had provided for him. The Tempter tempts with shame very often.

'No,' said Mr Stimpson. 'That looks like just what I wanted. But now you're *two* drinks up on me. I mean I owe you *one*, already, as I said last night.'

'Plenty of time,' said Gorse, smoothly.

'Well, here's how,' said Mr Stimpson, and 'Here's how' said Gorse, and they both drank.

Gorse noticed with pleasure that the inexperienced Mr Stimpson took a large amount of his cocktail with his first mouthful.

It was Gorse's ambition to make Mr Stimpson drink too much tonight.

And, if possible, he would make him fully and uninhibitedly drunk.

If Mr Simpson drank too much he might disclose many secrets – secrets about the nature of his relationship with Mrs Plumleigh-Bruce, and his real attitude towards it. Mr Stimpson might also, if tactfully handled, disclose such secrets about his own private life as Gorse might, by repeating them deftly to Mrs Plumleigh-Bruce, use against the Estate Agent.

Then, if Mr Stimpson could be led into really serious and really uninhibited drinking, the result might be the disclosure of even more shameful secrets, and also something better still – the performance of some shameful act, which Gorse might witness.

'Your friend not here?' said Mr Stimpson.

'No,' said Gorse, whose friend was fictitious. 'He hopped off just before you came in.'

'And how did business go?'

'Fine,' said Gorse. 'Couldn't have been better. I'm through with all my difficulties and everything's fixed up beautifully. So I'm in a mood for frivolity and gaiety ... And how did *your* business go?'

'Oh – mine was just ordinary plodding routine.' Mr Stimpson took another large mouthful of his cocktail. 'I'm only a plodding sort of chap you know. Not a gay spark – like you.'

This early, personal and rather sentimental confession made Gorse suspect that Mr Stimpson had been drinking before he had entered the King's Hotel, and that drink had already slightly affected him.

'Well – I don't know that I'm much of a gay spark,' said

Gorse. 'And, by the general look of you, I should say you've done a good deal better out of straightforward plodding than I have in my line . . .'

There was a pause. Then Mr Stimpson, having taken another sip at his drink, looked at Gorse and said, 'Tell me, old man, what *is* your line, exactly? That is if it's not a rude question. If it is, don't *tell* me, but just tell me *off*!'

Because of the premature 'old man' and the premature question, Gorse was now certain that alcohol had affected Mr Stimpson's head.

'No. It's not a rude question at all,' he said. 'But it's rather a difficult one to answer, because I've got so many little lines. What I was dealing with just now – with my friend, who's given me such satisfaction – was about wireless sets – or rather parts. I've got quite a lot of money in that line. But then I hope to take a lot of money out. There *is* money there, you know. In fact I think it's still only in its infancy, and that if you can get in on the ground floor there's a packet to be made.'

'I've no doubt of it,' said Mr Stimpson.

'And then cars is another line of mine – the one I like best, I suppose. I suppose, really, you'd call me a sort of all-round speculator. Do you go in for speculation of any sort?'

'No. I just go jogging along the good old middle path. No fancy stuff for me. Not that I'm not interested in speculation. I always was. What other lines do you indulge in, may I ask?'

Gorse saw that the moment had arrived to change the conversation. His recently revealed speculation in wireless parts had been as fictitious as the friend who, having given him such satisfaction on the matter, had just 'hopped off', and Gorse had not worked out any other fictitious form of speculation.

'Oh – they're much too many and involved to go into,' he said. 'And for Heaven's sake don't let's talk about business tonight. We're on pleasure bent, I trust. I know I am, anyway. Tell me, don't *you* feel that way, when you get out of Reading for a night?'

'I certainly do,' said Mr Stimpson, his mental vision already roving back in the direction of Vigo and Sackville Streets. Gorse guessed roughly where his mind was, but did not want the man to start anything of that sort just at present. Gorse wanted first to do some solid digging – or rather unearthing – on the Plumleigh-Bruce soil.

'And what happened to *you* two last night?' he asked. 'Did you make a night of it?'

'No. Anything but. We just had another drink and both went off home like the respectable citizens that we are – or we're supposed to be.'

'Meaning you're not, really?' said Gorse, with a sly confidence-inviting twinkle in his eye.

'Well,' said Mr Stimpson, 'that's a question I'd find difficult to answer, really.'

'You mean about yourself, or Mrs Plumleigh-Bruce?' said Gorse, with the same sort of look, perhaps slightly slyer.

'Both, I'd say. It depends on what you mean by respectability, really, doesn't it?'

'You mean to say,' said Gorse, speaking ostensibly in jest, but in fact taking the bull by the horns, 'that you don't look upon Mrs Plumleigh-Bruce as the height – the very cream – of respectability?'

'Ah now,' said Mr Stimpson. 'That'd be telling, wouldn't it?'

'Yes, I suppose it would ... All the same, something in your eye tells me that there's a story to tell – and that you're the one to do the telling – if there's anybody.'

Gorse, with his wonderful sense of timing, had been watching Mr Stimpson's reactions to alcohol closely, and had hit upon the exact moment in which to put forth a suggestion which at another time might have given offence.

The plodder in Mr Stimpson had suddenly changed into the dog.

'Yes. I wouldn't be surprised if I could tell a thing or two – quite a thing or two ... Now tell me, old man (or should I say young man?) ... You're a newcomer to the scene, with a fresh eye. What're *your* impressions of our Lady Joan?'

Mr Stimpson, though speaking in beer-and-cocktail boldness, was honestly seeking the truth. He respected the sophisticated London, Paris-visiting, horse-race-winning young man's judgment, and he wanted to know whether he thought of Mrs Plumleigh-Bruce gravely, as he, Mr Stimpson, had once done, or lightly, as he had recently been trying to do.

'In what way?' said Gorse. 'Physically, intellectually, or morally?'

'All three,' said Mr Stimpson. 'Go on. Begin at the beginning. Physically, for instance?'

'Well. That's hard to say. I'd say that she was tremendously attractive – to a certain type of man. But then there're so many types of men, aren't there?'

'Yes. And so many different ages. Is she attractive to you, for instance?'

'No. Not in that way,' said Gorse, after thinking carefully. 'Not at all in that way.'

'You mean,' said Mr Stimpson, 'she's a bit too long in the tooth for the likes of a young man like you. Come on now, young man. Out with it. We're all lads together now, you know.'

'Long in the tooth? You mean she's got slightly prominent teeth? I don't mind that, and she's got a lovely mouth.'

'No. I *don't* mean that – and you ought to know it. I mean too long in the *tooth* – too old, to put it plainly. For someone of *your* age, at any rate.'

'No – I wouldn't say that. It's just that, although I can see her attractions, I just don't think of her in that way. It's funny.'

Gorse was hedging, for he knew that this conversation would almost as certainly be repeated to Mrs Plumleigh-Bruce by Mr Stimpson, as it would, in an edited or elaborated form, be repeated to her by himself. Having built up Mrs Plumleigh-Bruce as a radiator of universal happiness, a comforter, and a cathedral, it was necessary to stick to his guns. The woman must remain, somehow or other, pretty holy. And also nothing must be said against her physical attractions.

'I don't think it's funny,' said Mr Stimpson. 'I think it's only natural, in someone of your age.'

'Well, maybe it's that,' said Gorse. 'I can only say again that I never think of her that way . . . I feel – it may be a silly thing to say – that it'd be a sort of – well – sacrilege.'

This at once slightly nettled and absolutely delighted Mr Stimpson. He was slightly nettled because Mrs Plumleigh-Bruce – if truly sacred – could not, perhaps, be treated in the light way for which he had lately been making mental preparations. On the other hand he was absolutely delighted at being told she was sacred. If he married her, it suited him down to the ground. If he made her his mistress it was just as good. And then, remembering the countless deep kisses which had taken place at Glen Alan, his bosom swelled secretly with the pride of the violator – the masculine, worldly-wise snatcher of veils from the temple. If only the poor young man, the 'smitten' Gorse, knew what had gone on at Glen Alan! The thought that Gorse did not – that the neophyte merely admired, or, conceivably, worshipped, from afar – added to his delight. Indeed his heart was so filled with sudden, gushing, alcoholic pity for the now almost pathetic Gorse, that he could not refrain, having taken another sip at his drink, from gushing.

'You know, I *like* you, young man,' he said. 'I did the first moment I saw you.'

'Well,' said Gorse, 'that's a very nice thing to be told . . . But what on earth do you like in me?'

'I like the way you speak about Women,' said Mr Stimpson. 'I like the respectful way you speak about them – as you did just then.'

'But surely there's nothing particularly likeable about that,' said Gorse, assuming the charming, puzzled demeanour of one who was little more than sixteen years old. 'It's only right to respect them – or to respect the right kind – isn't it?'

'Yes. Certainly. Of course it is,' said Mr Stimpson, whose soul was growing larger and larger. 'But it was the way you did it. It was so youthful – so straightforward and youthful – that's what I liked.'

It may be thought strange that Mr Stimpson's soul could get so large, so quickly, on the strength of two pints of beer and the better part of a single strong cocktail.

Gorse, in fact, who did not know what he had been drinking, imagined that he must have had a good deal more than he had in fact had.

The explanation was, however, that Mr Stimpson had been drinking heavily with business friends at lunch-time. And it is a well-known drinking law that heavy lunch-time drinking can be extremely treacherous. Its effects, having lain seemingly more or less dormant during the late afternoon, are often suddenly resurrected, released as by the pulling of a trigger, and given a sort of fresh, augmented, wild potency, by merely a few drinks taken again in the early evening. Many a man who has drunk heavily at lunch-time will become quite absurdly, excitably, and, to his friend, inexplicably drunk over only a small amount of alcohol thrown down his throat at such a time.

'Well –' began Gorse, but Mr Stimpson would not let him go on.

'Ah, youth, youth, *youth* . . .' said Mr Stimpson, looking into the distance. 'So confused, so poetical, so *happy* . . . What wouldn't I give for *my* youth again.'

'But surely there's not all *that* difference in our ages,' said Gorse.

'Oh yes, there is, and you know there is. I'm middle-aged – nearer an old man than a younger man. I'm just a middle-aged old plodder . . . Well – I suppose it has advantages. You know your way around, and you're treated with more respect . . . And that's *another* thing I like about you, my boy.'

'Oh – what's that?'

'*Respect*,' said Mr Stimpson, finishing off his drink and looking Gorse straight in the eye. 'I like the respect you show to your elders. It came out only the other night, in the way you called me "Sir", if you want to know. You don't get much of that sort of thing nowadays, and it doesn't mean much, but I liked it.'

The sardonic Gorse was here tempted to say 'Well, I'm very glad to hear it, sir,' but decided not to go to quite such lengths, for the time being at any rate. So he said merely, 'Well, I'm very glad to hear it.'

'Not that it *means* anything,' said Mr Stimpson. 'Good Heavens, *I* don't want any of your silly "sirring". You and I are out on the spree, now – just a couple of lads together . . . And so what about another drink? Same again? I don't know what that was, but it was very nice. So shall we have the same again? You do the ordering, and I'll do the paying. Go on.'

'Right,' said Gorse, and spoke to the barmaid, who was near, and with whom he was on friendly terms. 'Can we have the same again, Pixie?' he said. 'Just exactly the same again?'

And here, unseen by Mr Stimpson, he gave the barmaid a look, which was in effect a wink, and which intimated that Mr Stimpson was to be given a powerful drink once more, while Gorse would remain content with another weak one. The barmaid fully understood Gorse. She had done things like this with him before.

'Yes . . . Respect . . . Respect,' said Mr Stimpson, almost as if he were reciting, as they waited for the drinks. 'And respect for Women, too . . . You stick to it – stick to it. Maybe you'll learn

things later that'll shatter your illusions – maybe you won't . . .
But stick to it while you've got it. There's nothing like respect for
Women – nothing. Treat every one of them as Sacredly as you'd
treat your Mother – that's my advice to you.'

Here Gorse saw that he must not overdo, or allow Mr
Stimpson to overdo, this sacred stuff. If he did he would clearly
be unable to extract any sharply material information about the
relationship between Mr Stimpson and Mrs Plumleigh-Bruce.
Nor must he allow Mr Stimpson to get too drunk too quickly.

'Do you mean you've personally had your illusions shattered?'
he said, hoping that this might lead to a more solid and earthly
level of discussion.

Mr Stimpson paused heavily, and swayed slightly.

'I fear I have,' he said at last. 'Yes. I fear I have. Yes, many's
the castle I've built in the air that's fallen about my head like a
pack of cards. *Many*.'

'But not with the right sort of woman, surely?' said Gorse.

Mr Stimpson, perhaps blinded and confused by a kind of
snow-storm, or blizzard, of cards from castles falling about his
head, suddenly switched from pure idealism to fearful cynicism.

'Is there such a thing?' he asked. 'I wonder. If there is, name
her.'

'Well,' said the audacious Gorse. 'What about Mrs Plumleigh-
Bruce, for instance?'

Mr Stimpson again paused.

'No women are goddesses, you know,' he said. 'They've all
got feet of clay, somewhere . . . I could tell you things that'd
surprise you . . .'

'Could you?'

'Yes. I could indeed . . . Pretty girl,' said Mr Stimpson, alluding
to the barmaid, who had just put the new drinks in front of
them, and gone off to serve another customer.

'Yes. She is. Very pretty,' said Gorse.

'Where's she gone to? I haven't paid,' said Mr Stimpson, fishing
in his trouser pocket.

'Oh – she'll come back. She and I usually square up at the
end.'

'Yes. Very pretty,' said Mr Stimpson, looking at the barmaid
from a distance. 'Very pretty indeed.'

'But – I suspect – with feet of clay,' said Gorse, in order to lead back Mr Stimpson to Mrs Plumleigh-Bruce. 'There I'd certainly agree with you – in fact I know it for a fact. But a barmaid in the King's Hotel isn't the same thing as a Mrs Plumleigh-Bruce, I imagine.'

'Isn't she?' said Mr Stimpson, who had now made a complete *volte-face*, and who, swelled out with new cynicism, took a large mouthful of his new drink.

'I don't know. Is she? I certainly don't think she'd be so easy-going with men as the beauty serving us yonder. In fact, I wouldn't say that she'd be easy-going at all, in that direction.'

'Really? . . . That's all you know.'

'Well,' said Gorse. 'You surprise me, I must say . . . I mean, she's an attractive woman, and no doubt a lot of men want to – well – kiss her, and all that. But I should think she's pretty adamant even about that sort of thing.'

'Would you? . . . You'd be surprised.'

'But how do you know?'

'How do you think?'

'From personal experience, you mean?'

'I do.'

'Well – there's no harm in kissing. It's an attractive woman's due after all. She looks upon it as a sort of homage. But I don't expect the lady in question – and she's obviously a lady in every sense of the term – lets matters go further than that.'

'Oh, no,' said Mr Stimpson. 'I don't mean she goes the Whole Hog, or anything like that. But she certainly kisses, I can assure you. And *how* she kisses – believe me. Oh boy! – as our American friends say. She goes the limit there all right! She goes the whole hog when it comes to kisses. And she might go the whole hog altogether, if treated in the right way. "Wimmin is funny critters" as the old countryman said . . . They only want a bit of handling, you know, my boy.'

Gorse's nature was not a delicate one, but he was slightly nauseated by Mr Stimpson's astonishingly quick leap into this sort of vulgarity and lack of reticence. Gorse, who drank, who was only able to drink, little himself, was always repelled by drunkenness.

He was happy, though, in having obtained, with such astonishing rapidity, as much as he wanted to know about Mr Stimpson and Mrs Plumleigh-Bruce, and as much conversational material to repeat to the latter as he could desire. It hardly needed editing or elaborating.

Mr Stimpson had said that she was long in the tooth, that she had feet of clay, that he could 'tell' Gorse some things about her, that he had kissed her, that she had returned such kisses in a violent 'Oh boy!' way, and that she might, if properly handled, 'go the whole hog'. What more could one want?

'Well,' he said. 'I must say you surprise me. But I should think she'd be pretty fastidious, whatever she did. It wouldn't happen just with any man who came along. After all, she's a lady.'

'Oh no . . . No Tom, Dick, or Harry for her. And she's a lady all right, from the top of her fingers to the tip of her toes. *Breeding*, old boy, that's what she's got. It sticks out a mile.'

'It certainly does.'

Gorse had now to decide on his next move with this foolish man. He had succeeded, according to plan, in getting him drunk and in making the required disclosures. But now his second plan had to be put into operation. This was, as has been said, to make Mr Stimpson even more fully and uninhibitedly drunk and so indulge in shameful behaviour.

But here Gorse had to be careful. If Mr Stimpson became too drunk he would be incapable of any sort of behaviour.

PART SEVEN

ODETTE

CHAPTER ONE

I

THE main characteristic of people like Mr Stimpson is their
extraordinary ability, mentally and morally, to eat their
cake and have it too. After which they consume it.

They will bathe gloriously, firstly in the Sacred, and then
(without any sense of inconsistency or knowledge of the transi-
tion) burst into the Profane – and will leap back from the Profane
to the Sacred in the same way.

Mr Stimpson had exemplified this splendidly tonight with
Gorse in his lightning jump from almost scout-masterly idealism
into swaggering worldliness.

In the same way, such men will turn, at a moment's notice,
from the keenly shrewd to the lusciously sentimental, and from
the grasping to the giving – though they seldom give away much
materially.

Again, they will, as rapidly, and with one and the same man,
turn from the obsequious pursuit of favours or patronage, to the
boastful giving of favours (or talk of it) and a patronizing attitude. In accusing the Jews of doing this they are very black pots
calling grey kettles black.

Tonight Mr Stimpson had nervously entered the King's Hotel
willing to seek worldly knowledge from Gorse, but only a little
time had passed before he was lavishly bestowing worldly knowledge upon the latter.

After another quarter of an hour two further drinks for both had been almost finished by both, and Gorse was still being patronized, and Mr Stimpson was now, to use his own expression to Gorse, Seeing through Gorse like a *Book*.

2

This magnificently transparent Book had appeared upon the scene because Gorse, slightly embarrassed by Mr Stimpson's loud voice, had dropped his in the hope of infecting Mr Stimpson with his own more seemly tone. But Mr Stimpson had taken this for dejection on Gorse's part, and had, with spirituous cunning, discerned its cause.

'*You're* looking very glum,' Mr Stimpson had suddenly said. 'What's the matter?'

'No. I'm not glum,' said Gorse. 'What should make you think I am?'

'Oh yes – you are. Don't try and fool me,' said Mr Stimpson. 'I can see through you like a *Book*. I can, you know.'

'And what can you see?' Gorse asked.

'The Green-Eyed God,' said Mr Stimpson. 'Ever heard of him? He's there all right. The Little Green-Eyed God.'

'You mean jealousy?' Gorse asked.

'I do,' said Mr Stimpson. 'I can see through you like a *Book*.'

'But jealousy about what?'

Gorse was trying to look as much like an easily read (and jealous) Book as was possible, for the results of Mr Stimpson's violent perspicacity, if revealed, might give him some clue as to Mr Stimpson's real thoughts about him – and it would be useful to know these.

'About a Certain Lady,' said Mr Stimpson. 'You're a bit smitten with her – aren't you? Go on. Admit it.'

'Well,' said Gorse. 'Perhaps I am a little. But in a very humble and reverent way.'

'There you are! I told you so!'

'And what do you mean by jealousy?' Gorse asked.

'Well, perhaps, I shouldn't've said jealousy,' said Mr Stimpson. 'I ought to have said disappointment. I've gone and shattered your illusions about the lady, haven't I? Don't try and deny it! I can see through you like a Book, old boy.'

Gorse was already getting rather impatient at having to look and behave like a Book, particularly as Mr Stimpson kept on looking and slightly nodding at him, through his thick-lensed spectacles, as if he were turning page after page of it with delicious comprehension. But Gorse, as usual, curbed his impatience.

'Well,' he said. 'I suppose what you said did come as a bit of a shock.'

'I know it did. I can see through you like a Book. A *Volume*, my boy!' said Mr Stimpson, as if a Volume were something very different from and much easier to read than a Book.

There was a silence in which Gorse tried to look like a Volume.

Mr Stimpson was now not only enjoying his superiority over and patronage of Gorse. He was, after the way of his type, enjoying to the full a splurging belief in his own fiction. He had now got Gorse exactly where he wanted him – a worshipper from afar of Mrs Plumleigh-Bruce. And no doubts assailed him as to whether or not Gorse in fact stood in the place assigned to him. This self-deceiving self-assurance, this psychological grabbing of everything in every way, was partially attributable to drink, but mostly to the provincial businessman mentality mentioned above.

'Yes – like a *Volume* . . .' said Mr Stimpson, swaying visibly as he ruminated. 'And perhaps I did wrong. It never does to shatter illusions. I did wrong. You're only a kid, you know, for all your cleverness. One should never shatter illusions.'

'Well,' said Gorse. 'On the other hand, it's no use living in a dream world – is it?'

'No. Never shatter illusions. Never,' said Mr Stimpson, with an air of severe admonition, as if it had been Gorse who had committed this error. 'Never *do* it.'

Gorse, without replying, nodded humble but hearty agreement, as one who, enlightened by a master, has decided never again to shatter illusions.

Mr Stimpson had, it will be seen, had his cake, eaten it, and consumed it. He went on to munch it.

'No,' he said. 'Keep your eyes on the stars.

"Two men looked out of prison bars,
One saw the earth. The other saw the stars."

That's a poem. My old Mother taught me that – God bless

her – and I've never forgotten it. See the stars, my boy! See the stars!'

At this there was a very moving Old-Motherly silence, in which both seemed to be looking upwards from a cocktail bar to the stars. Neither was, however. Gorse was wondering how he was going to keep this man from getting incapably drunk, and Mr Stimpson expressed his real thoughts by asking, in a secretive, confidential, but alarmingly sudden way 'Where's the Gents' here, old boy?'

Gorse told him what he wanted to know, and Mr Stimpson left the bar.

Gorse took advantage of his absence to put his own weak drink in place of Mr Stimpson's, and into Mr Stimpson's drink he poured powdered Aspirin from a folded piece of paper. This was taken from his waistcoat pocket. When the farseeing Gorse saw a night of drinking ahead of him he nearly always took the precaution of carrying powdered Aspirin about with him. He did this for his own sake, in the belief, derived from a conversation with a chemist's assistant, that the sedative held drunkenness at bay. But tonight the position was reversed: he was defending not himself but his companion from drunkenness.

He hoped that, when Mr Stimpson returned, he might be more sober. Mr Stimpson, however, was a good deal less sober.

He showed, on the contrary, in his gait as he moved towards Gorse, that intense upright sobriety which always indicates its polar opposite, and he at once returned to the Book, which, seemingly, was on his brain.

3

'Yes,' he said, laying his hand ponderously on Gorse's shoulder. 'A Book. I saw through you like a Book ... No one's ever saw through a Book as I've sawn through you.' He was conscious of some verbal or grammatical error in what he had just said, and he hastened to rectify it. '*I* saw through you ... *I* saw ... I'm a saw-mill, in some ways, when it comes to sawing. Not that I get *sore*. Oh *dear* me, no! ...'

'Well, I hope you're not sore with me,' said Gorse.

'Sore with you! God forbid,' said Mr Stimpson. 'I *like* you. I liked you from the moment I saw you. We're lads together tonight. We're going to be lads. Are we or aren't we?'

Though Mr Stimpson had in mind nothing particular in what he had just said, Gorse saw his chance, and leapt to it.

'Yes,' he said. 'I'm game if you are.'

'Game for what?' said Mr Stimpson, momentarily more than ever confused.

'Game for anything,' said Gorse, with a knowing look. 'Game for games – what?'

Knowing looks always strike home with inebriated men – who are, of course, the most knowing on earth, and who will often force themselves into a sort of self-restraint in order to do credit to their own knowingness.

Mr Stimpson braced himself. He saw Gorse's meaning, and his mental vision again wandered back towards Vigo and Sackville Streets.

'Games where?' he asked.

'Well – there's only one sort of game that I know of around these parts,' said Gorse. 'It's one of the oldest games in the world, and we're right bang in the middle of where it's played most.'

Here Mr Stimpson took fright. He thought that Gorse was alluding to the King's Hotel – and this was not in the Wardour Street adventurer's line at all. It was too 'flash', dangerous, and intimidating because above his head. Also Mr Stimpson was, just at that moment, rather less interested in encounters with women than in drinking and conversation – in seeing and sawing through people.

Also he did not want to give away to Gorse that he ever embarked upon such enterprises. If he decided to do so later, he would somehow shake Gorse off.

'Yes. It's old enough,' he said. 'And dangerous enough, too. *And* expensive.'

'But all nice things are dangerous and expensive, aren't they?' said Gorse.

'*You* know a thing or two, young man – don't you?' said Mr Stimpson. 'Be careful you don't know too much.'

'I certainly know my way around this part of the world, anyway,' said Gorse. 'And if *you* don't, I'll be only too happy to show you.'

'No,' said Stimpson. 'Not for me. It's all right for a young chap like you – but it's different for me . . . You're a gay young spark with all those things in front of you – and quite right too. But I'm just a silly old plodder – that's all I am.'

'Really? That's not how you strike me at all, you know,' said Gorse. 'In fact you give me exactly the opposite impression, and I bet *you* could give *me* a wrinkle or two, if you cared.'

But this piece of flattery, to Gorse's surprise, entirely failed. Mr Stimpson had stopped seeing and sawing and had gone mad about plodding. And plod he meant to.

'No,' he said. 'I'm just a plodder. I plod along. Plod, plod, plod. That's me . . . I'm nobody. I'm just a *clod*, perhaps . . .'

'Oh – don't say that,' said Gorse, but Mr Stimpson was adamant about his own cloddishness.

'Yes, just a clod. That's what I am. A clod that clods.'

Gorse here observed, with some consternation, that Mr Stimpson was entering that comatose, rhyming phase known to experts in inebriation. The man, in fact, was practically asleep on his feet, and talking in his sleep.

'A clod that plods. Nods,' said Mr Stimpson, and nodded.

Gorse was silent, wondering whether it would soon be necessary either to abandon Mr Stimpson or have him removed from the hotel.

Suddenly, however, like a snorer who wakes himself with his own snore, Mr Stimpson stood at attention and shot out a sharp observation – so sharp that it seemed almost to be trying to bring a mentally wandering Gorse to order.

'A nod's as good as a wink to a blind horse,' he said, most aggressively. 'Is it, or isn't it?'

Gorse agreed that it was, but did not like Mr Stimpson's quarter-deck voice and manner.

'Or a horse is as good as a wink to a blind whatever-it-is. Or isn't it? . . . It's all the same, isn't it?'

Gorse again concurred.

'I suppose you think I'm drunk,' said Mr Stimpson, having gazed at Gorse with glassy penetration for a long while. 'But I'm not you know. I may be a plodder, but I jog along all right. I can take my drink all right. I may be a silly old buffer – but I jog along. And sometimes I go the whole hog.'

'Do you?'

'I do. Wasn't that what we were talking about?'

'Yes. It was.'

'Yes. I knew it was. I may be just an old buffer, but I remember things all right.'

'And so you go the whole hog sometimes, do you?' said Gorse.

'I *do*. Although I'm just an Ancient old Buffer. Who *said* I didn't?'

Gorse welcomed this less comatose and much more combative mood, but realized that he must not permit Mr Stimpson to become too violent. The thing to do was to let Mr Stimpson – the vigorously, almost vindictively, self-styled old buffer – let Mr Stimpson Anciently Buff, plod, nod, jog, and be a clod to his heart's content – but to do so in the direction into which Gorse was anxious to steer him.

'Well,' said Gorse. 'It's sometimes just the old plodders who go the whole hog a good deal more than the rest – isn't it? Or that's my experience.'

'And your experience is correct,' said Mr Stimpson, mollified, but not wholly so.

Gorse realized that he was now dealing with a child (very young people bear an amazing resemblance to very drunk people) and Gorse was good with children. He certainly did not like them, but they liked him. The same thing applied to dogs, and that this should have been so was regarded as a strange paradox by those who wrote about Gorse later. There was, however, no paradox. The powers of mystical discernment popularly attributed to dogs and children are in fact practically non-existent.

'Yes. Give me the plodders,' said Gorse. 'Give me the plodders, all the time.'

Mr Stimpson, suddenly and capriciously, that is to say childishly, more sober, now saw a chance of doing what Gorse did so often and so well – killing two or three birds with one stone. He could, he thought, if he played his cards correctly, plod, jog, go the whole hog before long, and get worldly advice into the bargain.

'Yes,' he said. 'I'm a plodder all right. But sometimes we old plodders get into a bit of a rut, you know.'

'What about?'

'What we were talking about. Going the whole hog. How'd *you* set about it in these parts, for instance? You know your London better than me, perhaps. I've been jogging along in Reading for a bit too long, I sometimes think.'

Mr Stimpson still had in mind Vigo and Sackville Streets.
What he had seen there earlier in the evening had impressed
him as something a good deal better than his familiar Wardour
Street; and, in his present alcoholic audacity, he was anxious
to try out new territory. At the same time he was afraid of the
unknown.

'How do you mean – "these parts"?' said Gorse. 'Exactly?'

'Well – not so far from here. I saw some pretty spicy things
round in Sackville Street just before I came in here, as it happens.'

'Yes, Sackville Street's all right,' said Gorse. 'But one can do
better than that.'

'Really? Where? How?'

'Well – one can go farther afield without walking much further
– into foreign lands, as it were, if it suits your taste. Of course,
you must remember I've just returned from Paris.'

Mr Stimpson recoiled, both with fear and repulsion, at this,
and became more sober still. Gorse was obviously alluding to
Frenchwomen.

'Oh,' he said. 'You mean the Frogs – do you? No. No Frogs
for me. Sorry, old man. You like 'em, don't you? But Frogs
aren't up my street.'

'They aren't up mine, really,' said Gorse. 'But they have their
uses – the female of the species have, at any rate.'

'No, thanks. No fancy stuff for me. I don't go in for fancy
stuff. I've never tried it, and I don't mean to start it.'

'Really,' said Gorse. 'You mean you've never been with a
French girl?'

'No. And never mean to,' said Mr Stimpson, swilling off the
remainder of his aspirin-powdered drink. 'Come on, let's have
another of these.'

By good fortune and raising his voice he caught the attention
of the barmaid, who was now very busy, and gave the order.

'Well,' said Gorse. 'I think you're missing something. You get
better value for your money, even if you do have to pay a little
more for it.'

Gorse had a reason for pressing a French rather than an English
woman upon Mr Stimpson.

Gorse was always very popular with prostitutes, with whom
he mixed only socially, and who liked him. (In later days there

were many West-End women of the streets who hotly defended him.)

His popularity here was easily explained. His assured sense of social superiority made him very much at ease with such women, who, because of their low educational level and somewhat debased sense of humour, were pleased, or even delighted, by his dashing air, his monocle, and the 'Silly Ass' act in which with them, he was able to indulge to the full. 'Hullo, girls!' or 'Hullo, old things!' or 'Hullo, old beans!' were his cries when entering their haunts, where he was thought of as a 'card' a 'one', and, though foolish (perhaps *because* foolish) a 'gentleman'. A 'public-school' voice and a monocle are regarded as symbols of a 'gentleman' in such credulous circles. But he was also thought of as a 'real gentleman'. For he was generous with his money, made no amorous advances, and frequently went out of his way to do one of these girls or women a 'good turn' – such as lending her money (usually repaid), or giving her a lift in his car.

Gorse was not totally disinterested here, for he knew that all sorts of uses and contacts might arise from such friendships. He was also, in his precocious way, aware of that almost drivellingly sentimental loyalty and generosity which is part of the looseness of these loose livers. He knew that, should he ever be in trouble, financially or criminally, help would be gushingly forthcoming. However, it may be said that, on the whole, he liked their company for its own sake.

Recently Gorse had taken to frequenting a small café in Mayfair in which mostly Frenchwomen resorted late at night, and where he was already a popular figure.

He knew exactly where these Frenchwomen walked, and was anxious to make Mr Stimpson walk amongst them.

He might thus, not only do another 'good turn' to one of his café acquaintances: he might be able to learn the exact locality of the adventure upon which Mr Stimpson was, obviously, determined to embark. Furthermore, he might be able, afterwards, to learn the nature of the adventure in detail.

And so Gorse risked incurring the displeasure of Mr Stimpson by boldly praising the French.

4

New drinks were brought: Gorse, though severely lectured, stuck to his guns about the French, and Mr Stimpson, swallowing another furious mouthful, turned his back on Gorse to look around the crowded room, and became, in a flash, deliriously drunk again, and was in his delirium converted to the French and the whole world. He liked the world. He liked everything that was in it.

'Frogs – eh?' he said, turning again to Gorse. 'All right then – frogs it shall be. If *you* want frogs – *I* want frogs. Lead me to 'em –worthy varlet . . . Always believed in trying everything once. Lead on, sirrah! On, knave! On! "Charge, Chesters, charge, on, Stanley on!" were the last words of Marmion. Excuse my French. Poetry . . . Sir Walter Scott – the old bastard. Bart, too. Learned him at school. Bloody bore, if you ask me. However, lead on, noble lord . . .'

'Very well,' said Gorse, now aware that people were looking at and listening to his companion. 'We'll go directly we've paid. But I suppose we must do that . . . Pixie . . . How much do we owe you?' He put his hand to his hip pocket, but Mr Stimpson would have none of this.

'Oh no,' said Mr Stimpson. 'Oh *dear* me no . . . Oh *dear* me no . . . Me . . . *All* me. *Only* me . . .' He produced a wallet from his breast pocket.

'But you can't pay for all the drinks,' Gorse protested.

'Me were the words I *used*,' said Mr Stimpson. 'And Me were the words I *meant* . . . Me. Simple word. Second person singular – or plural – or accusative. It doesn't bother me. *Accusative* . . .'

Mr Stimpson then said that he wasn't Accusing anybody, and found himself in difficulties with the money in his wallet. Gorse aided him, extracting two pounds from the wallet, which he managed to get back into Mr Stimpson's pocket, and he gave the barmaid the notes.

While the barmaid got the change Mr Stimpson went on saying that he had accused nobody, and that nobody had accused anyone, that there was too much suspicion in the world. Everybody accused everybody else and what was wanted was Trust.

He then called Gorse his Trusty Companion – his Trusty

Companion of the Bath – and picked up the change from his two pounds from the counter.

Gorse, using the same methods as those which he had adopted with his friend Ronnie Shooter in Paris not long ago, allowed Mr Stimpson to pay without protest. In the morning he would remind Mr Stimpson of the debt, and insist on repaying it.

Mr Stimpson, however, did not know that, in a place of this sort, a barmaid should be tipped, and this error Gorse could not allow. He winked at his friend Pixie, and gave her two and sixpence from his own pocket.

'Well, then,' he said. 'Off we go – what?'

'Fine. Off we go. Off ... Lead on, then, good my page,' said Mr Stimpson, and, having put his arm on Gorse's shoulder, gave Gorse a chance to assist him from the bar, and up the stairs.

Mr Stimpson took the stairs in a very silent and serious spirit. With his arm around Gorse he leaned over them, looking at them intently, not like a man walking up them, but like a General (in a third-rate picture or illustration depicting military head-quarters at the most desperate moment of battle) fiercely scru-tinizing maps and making dramatic decisions.

'All right,' he said, when he had gone through all the maps, and was on the ground floor. 'All right.'

As if with these words dramatically announcing that the battle had been won, he dispensed with the assistance of Gorse's shoulder, and made for the revolving doors.

These he reached in reasonably good order, and, preceding Gorse, got through very finely. When Gorse had joined him in the street, though, he wanted assistance again, and put his arm, with an affectation of pure affection, around Gorse.

'Nobly done, good mine page,' he said. 'Now whither?'

'You just follow me,' said Gorse. 'I'll show you whither.'

'Whither thou goest I shall go too,' said Mr Stimpson, 'and thy people shall be whither thou goest ... Frogs, I fancy.'

'Yes,' said Gorse. 'But you mustn't call them that, you know, if you meet one.'

'Why not? They *are* Frogs, aren't they?'

'Well – one's got to be tactful, hasn't one?'

'Tact? Very well. Tact it shall be,' said Mr Stimpson, as they walked along in the direction of Dover Street. 'Tact with Frogs ... Tact with Frogs ...'

There was a silence, and then Mr Stimpson said 'Tact with *Logs*,' and, receiving no reply from Gorse, said 'Tact with Cogs.' He was now rhyming-drunk again, but, since he was walking reasonably steadily with Gorse's support, Gorse did not mind this.

'Tact with *Hogs* ...' said Mr Stimpson. 'Tact with *Hogs* ... Tact with *Dogs* ... Tact with *Cogs*. Cogs. We're all Cogs in a Great Machine, you know. Aren't we?'

'Yes,' said Gorse. 'That's all we are.'

'Tact with Fogs,' said Mr Stimpson, and then went, in an orderly way, through the whole alphabet from beginning to end – mentioning, laboriously, Tact with Bogs, Cogs, Dogs, Fogs, Gogs, Hogs, Jogs, Logs, Mogs, Nogs, Pogs, Quogs, Rogs, Sogs, Togs, Vogs, Wogs, Yogs, and Zogs.

Doing this took him some time, and because of the mental concentration demanded by the feat, he was again more sober when he had finished.

Indeed, by the time they had reached (and at Gorse's instigation turned up) Dover Street, Mr Stimpson was walking without Gorse's aid, and had returned to Frogs, and was compaining of their absence.

'All right – just wait a bit, and follow me,' said Gorse, but no sooner had he said this than, to Gorse's annoyance, the matter was taken out of his hands.

The familiar 'Where you go, dar*leeng*?' was heard from a door-way, and Mr Stimpson stopped.

5

Gorse was annoyed because he had not as yet got Mr Stimpson into the exact quarter he wanted, and he did not know the woman who had accosted them. He was upset in his managerial capacity. He would have liked, indeed, to have led Mr Stimpson on, but Mr Stimpson, having heard the accent of a Frenchwoman, would not be led on.

The Frenchwoman – a short, dark, rapacious-looking woman – in moving from the doorway had in fact ignored Mr Stimpson and addressed herself to Gorse. But Mr Stimpson did not realize this.

'Ah-ha!' said Mr Stimpson, and bowed low, adding 'Madame!'

'I give you a nice time?' said the Frenchwoman, now rather confused and addressing both. 'You have nice time with me?'

'No,' said Gorse. 'Not for me. Definitely not for me. And I'm afraid my friend here's a bit beyond it.'

'Beyond eet? He drink too much? Ah, poor Monsieur!' She looked at Gorse. 'Then I give him nice time and he get better – no?'

'No. Really – ' began Gorse, but now Mr Stimpson was controlling the situation.

'Drunk too much?' he said. 'Beyond it? Who said I've been drinking too much?'

'No. Of course you not drink too much. So I give you nice time? No?'

The woman, Gorse saw, was now turning against himself. So also was Mr Stimpson, whose momentary recovery was remarkable and bull-doggish. Gorse thought quickly, and decided to keep on the right side of both.

'No,' he said to the woman. 'We really are a bit beyond it, you know. But if you could take us both back for a cup of black coffee – we might get better. What about it, darling?' He winked at her, as if to call attention to his friend's state. 'Strong black coffee – that's the thing. *Café noir. Très fort.* Agree?'

The woman looked at both, trying to make up her mind.

'I'll make it worth your while,' said Gorse. 'You needn't worry about *that* side of it.'

At this Mr Stimpson suddenly lurched sideways, and assisted the street-walker in making a decision. She had seen from Gorse's wink and promise that he was sober and presumably reliable, and she had seen from Mr Stimpson's lurch that he was spectacularly drunk. The proposition, in fact, looked exceedingly promising to her. Drunk men are lavish with money, and should this one prove aggressive or parsimonious, she had a protector in Gorse. She took Gorse's side at once, winking back at him. At the same time she took a patronizing attitude towards Mr Stimpson, going up to him.

'Ah – poor old thing,' she said. 'You drink too much. You come with me. Odette – she makes you well. She gives you coffee and makes you well. She gives you nice time. She gives you what you want. The poor old thing – he drink too much wine. Odette make him well.'

As they moved on she kept up this chatter, which displeased Gorse, while apparently delighting Mr Stimpson, who was now silent. Gorse did not like the mixture, in this woman, of rapacious looks and skittish talk. But there was nothing to be done.

Odette lived quite near, and they were soon mounting the many stairs leading to her flat. Mr Stimpson again made General's maps of stairs, and at this Odette was even more offensively skittish than ever as she assisted him.

They entered her flat, which had two main rooms – a bedroom and sitting-room – and a kitchen and a bathroom.

All of these were highly characteristic, in their furnishing and atmosphere, of such a woman's flat. The kitchen was dirty and disordered: the walls of the bathroom were peeling around a rusting bath. There was a large doll on the bed of the bedroom – whose walls displayed provocative drawings of girls, along with a crucifix bearing a plaster image of a crucified Christ. In the sitting-room there were statuettes of nude girls, two more dolls, and religious pictures. In brief – the familiar rust, dolls, dirt, girls, and emblems of piety everywhere. These flats change hands incessantly, collecting the symbols of the different moods of their occupants, nearly all of whom are constant at least to religion.

Mr Stimpson was fairly easily persuaded to lie down on the bed, while Odette went into the kitchen with Gorse to make black coffee.

Here terms were discussed, and Odette found that she was dealing with a very much more sharp (yet calm and knowledgeable) antagonist than she had expected. There was, indeed, haggling – the usual weary, dreary, haggling amidst surroundings of dirt, dust, dolls, girls, and emblems of piety – in which Gorse used Mr Stimpson's drunkenness as a weapon, claiming that two pounds was reasonable compensation for a cup of black coffee and less than an hour of Odette's time.

During this contest Gorse went into the bedroom and found, to his delight, that Mr Stimpson was fast asleep. He removed Mr Stimpson's wallet from his breast pocket, and, having put it into his own, he returned to the kitchen.

Here he reported that Mr Stimpson was asleep, and said that he would fetch his own car, which was in a garage not far from where they were, and take him away.

Having been given two pounds, which Gorse extracted from

his own hip pocket, Odette allowed him to leave the flat in order to get his car.

Gorse was away less than twenty minutes.

When he returned he found that the hopeful Odette had been attempting to restore Mr Stimpson to a normal condition – arduously but ineffectually. Mr Stimpson was less than half awake on the bed, and the only word he was capable of bringing out (or apparently knew) was *Frogs* . . . He answered all queries as to his condition and capability of moving with this word.

He was at last made to rise, however, and at last left the flat with Gorse. The disgruntled Frenchwoman, who in Gorse's absence had, needless to say, searched Mr Stimpson's pockets (in vain), nearly slammed the door in their faces.

Gorse, having got Mr Stimpson into his car, managed to extract the address of his sister in Richmond, and drove him to it.

Mr Stimpson was, perhaps, fully able to enter his sister's house without assistance. But Gorse insisted upon aiding him – aiding him, most skilfully, to sway rather than to walk properly. The frightened sister – a widow of about sixty – was more than grateful to Gorse, who helped her to get Mr Stimpson to bed, and who asked her her telephone number. He wanted, he said, to telephone Mr Stimpson in the morning, to see that he was all right.

The grave, sober, sane, tolerant young man then drove back to his West Kensington lodging – in the grave, sane, sober, tolerant spirit which characterized him.

CHAPTER TWO

1

MR STIMPSON, next morning, was given a handsome breakfast in bed by his sister, but he did not want to eat it at all.

He wondered what he could do with it, and even contemplated making a plausible mess of his plates, and then enclosing eggs, bacon, porridge, toast and marmalade in some newspaper, and hiding these ingredients in his suit-case – this in order not to offend, and to preserve his dignity in front of, his sister.

But, alas, he had left his suit-case at Paddington Station yesterday morning, meaning to pick it up later in the day. He remembered this much about yesterday – but little else.

He was saved, temporarily, from much gloomy plotting of this sort by the announcement, made by his sister from outside a knocked door, that he was wanted on the telephone below.

Dressed only in the shirt and dressing-gown in which he had been put to bed last night (the dressing-gown had once belonged to his widowed sister's husband) he went, slipperless, downstairs to the telephone, and was greeted by a jovial voice.

2

'Hullo,' said Gorse. 'And how are *we* this morning?'

'Oh ... Hullo ... I'm all right,' said Mr Stimpson, who did not exactly take to Gorse's obvious 'you' implied by his underlining of the word 'we', and who decided to be defiant. 'I'm in the middle of breakfast, as a matter of fact.'

Thus a slipperless man, dressed only in his shirt and a borrowed dressing-gown, endeavoured to give a picture of an orderly, respectable citizen having breakfast, as it were, *en famille*.

'Enjoying it?' said Gorse, again with offensive jollity.

'Yes. Fine, thanks,' said Mr Stimpson. 'How are *you*?'

Mr Stimpson, because he was as yet hardly able to remember a single thing about last night, had a faint hope that Gorse might have been drunk too, in which case his underlining of the 'you' would be striking back and home.

'Fine,' said Gorse. 'In the pink. But there's a spot of bother.'

'Oh. What's that?'

'Well – I've been on the phone this morning, and it looks as though there're still some snags in my business and that I'll have to stay up another night. And that means that I can't run you down in my little bus to Reading, I'm afraid.'

'Oh ... *That's* all right,' said Mr Stimpson, overjoyed at the thought of not having to meet Gorse or being driven down to Reading. The thought of the latter almost made him vomit. 'I can get along fine.'

'But I'll tell you what,' said Gorse. 'I've got most of the morning free, and I can call for you in the car and take you to Paddington.'

'Oh, no. Don't bother. I can easily get there. It's very nice of you – but don't bother.'

'No. No bother at all. I'd like it,' said Gorse. 'And there's another more important reason for seeing you, too, if it comes to that.'

'Important? ... What? ...'

'I've got some money of yours, and I'd like to hand it back.'

'Money?' said Mr Stimpson, taken completely unawares. 'What money?'

'Well – a walletful of it. I managed to save it from the wreckage last night. Haven't you missed it yet?'

Mr Stimpson tried to think and remember quickly, but was unable to do so, and could only say feebly, 'No ...'

'Well – I didn't *think* you'd remember the episode, as a matter of fact,' said Gorse, and was silent so that this might sink in.

It did so, frightening Mr Stimpson horribly.

'Oh ...' was all he could manage, and then he decided that he must see Gorse as soon as possible in order to get information about this forgotten episode, which Gorse, by using a particular tone of voice, had made sound extremely sinister. 'Well ... Yes ... Well, if you could come over here and give me a lift to Paddington, it'd be very nice. And we could have a chat.'

'Yes,' said Gorse, mercilessly. 'Compare notes ... By the way I can't imagine why I didn't stick the wallet back into your pocket last night, when I got you home. But in states of confusion like that one forgets these things.'

'Yes,' said the sick, cold, slipperless, and almost trembling Mr Stimpson. 'I know ... What time'll you be along, then?'

'Ten-thirtyish suit you?'

'Yes. That'd do fine.'

'Fine. Cheerio, then. See you ten-thirty.'

'Cheerio.'

They rang off and Mr Stimpson went upstairs again. In the wreckage of his spirits – the wreckage, it seemed at the moment, almost of his whole life – he forgot entirely about the matter of deception in regard to his breakfast, and concentrated fiercely upon the mental reconstruction of his behaviour last night.

He took a bath, hoping that this might help him.

3

When Gorse called at ten-thirty Mr Stimpson was dressed and ready for him, had regained a certain uneasy, shifty dignity with his sister, and was a little more composed in his mind.

He now remembered a good deal about last night – but how he had lost his wallet, and in what sort of 'episode', were beyond him.

The breezy Gorse rang the bell as a telegraph boy might, and Mr Stimpson opened the door, wearing his overcoat and hat, and shut it after him.

'What?' said Gorse. 'No luggage?'

'No,' said Mr Stimpson, walking down the pathway of his sister's suburban villa. 'That's at Paddington Station.'

'Paddington Station? Why on earth there?'

'Well,' said Mr Stimpson. 'I meant to collect it last night. But things went a little awry, didn't they?'

He had not as yet made up his mind as to what attitude to take with Gorse about last night – whether he should be stubborn, light-hearted, or contrite. Gorse, similarly, though he had started off by treating Mr Stimpson pretty roughly on the telephone, was in two minds as to how far he should go with such treatment. He was certainly going to maintain and use the hold he had acquired over Mr Stimpson, but he did not want to make an enemy of the man. It might be wiser to use last night as a means of deepening the friendship. As they entered Gorse's car and drove away, both, therefore, were hedging.

'So you've got some money of mine, I gather,' said Mr Stimpson. Mr Stimpson was compelled to open the necessary discussion by the sheer force of his curiosity about the 'episode'.

'Yes. All safe and sound,' said Gorse, and was silent so as to make Mr Stimpson come to him again. Mr Stimpson did so. He now felt that confession and contrition were the best lines to take.

'You know, it's a weird thing,' he said. 'But I simply can't remember a thing about losing it. What happened?'

'Well, you wouldn't remember it,' said Gorse, after a pause. 'Because you were deep in the arms of Morpheus at the time. It was most skilfully stolen from you, actually.'

'Stolen. Who stole it?' said Mr Stimpson, his heart nearly missing a beat at the thought of having fallen amongst thieves as well as loose women last night.

'*I* did,' said Gorse.

'*You?*'

'Yes. But that was just to see that no one else did. You got yourself in with a very crooked and dangerous little lady last night, you know . . . Can't you remember "Odette"?'

'Oh – that was her name, was it? Yes I remember. But what do you mean *I* got in with her? It was you who wanted us to pick up a Frog – wasn't it? I was all against it from the beginning – wasn't I?'

'Yes. But you changed your mind. And when once you did change it, there was no stopping you, and you lost your powers of selection. One's got to be very fastidious when dealing with French dishes in the West End of London, and your choice couldn't have been worse, I'm afraid. However, I stuck with you and got you out of it, in the long run, at the cost of two pounds. Believe me, it was cheap at the price . . . I also took the precaution of pinching and concealing your wallet on my own person while you were asleep. And so, as there wasn't any money to be found on you, our charming little "Odette" let us go. Otherwise it might have been a very nasty business. She was quite ready for blackmail and intimidation of any kind. I know the type.'

Theft, blackmail, intimidation! . . . The Reading businessman became almost faint with horror.

'And, of course,' Gorse added, taking a corner sharply in order to make Mr Stimpson feel even fainter still, 'very much worse dangers than that.'

Gorse was hinting at venereal disease, and Mr Stimpson knew that he was doing so. He searched his mind frantically to remember whether he had had any sort of physical contact with the woman. He could not recall anything of that sort – in fact he was almost willing to swear that there had been none. But doubt – black, lurking, nagging doubt – sickly mistrust of one's own memory – is the main symptom of the malady of the morning after the night before, and Mr Stimpson pathetically sought assurance from a witness as to what exactly had happened.

'Well, anyway, there was no danger of *that* in *this* case, was there?' he said.

'How do you mean?' said Gorse.

'I mean – well, nothing Took Place, or anything of that sort – did it? I just went to sleep, as far as I can make out. Didn't I?'

'Well – I don't know,' said Gorse, hooting impatiently at an obstructive vehicle in front of him.

'But you were there – weren't you? You must know.'

'Yes. But I wasn't there all the time. I had to leave you for about three quarters of an hour to get the car to bring you home. When I came back you were sitting up in bed drinking coffee, attended upon by our loving "Odette".'

'Oh – no – there was nothing of that sort, I'm *sure* of it. Quite sure of *that*,' said Mr Stimpson, as if to assure himself by auto-suggestion, and there was a long silence as the car approached the thronged Chiswick High Road and Mr Stimpson continued unconsciously to attempt to employ the methods of the then still popular M. Coué.

4

Gorse, having glanced at Mr Stimpson, and having observed that he was already, as had been intended, suffering horribly from venereal disease, thought that it was time to change his attitude.

'Well,' he said. 'We had a jolly good time while it lasted. You
can't always strike it lucky all the evening. No harm done, and
no regrets – that's what *I'd* say.'

Gorse's 'No harm done' uttered in an authoritative, bracing,
doctor-like tone, at once cheered Mr Stimpson. Sufferers from
mornings after nights, in the weakness of their anxiety, are
absurdly easily susceptible to outside suggestion.

'Yes,' said Mr Stimpson. 'No harm done and no regrets. That's
always been *my* slogan . . . All the same, it'll be a very long while
before I indulge myself in *that* way again.'

'Oh – don't say that . . . One can't keep on the straight track
all the time, and a little of what you fancy does you good, *I've*
always been told.'

'Yes. Perhaps you're right. But perhaps I'm getting a bit too
old for that sort of thing.'

Mr Stimpson had now practically thrown off venereal disease,
and was concentrating on another matter – that of ensuring
absolute secrecy from Gorse about what had happened last night
– absolute secrecy, in particular, in the case of Mrs Plumleigh-
Bruce – indeed plain lying.

Needless to say, the recent sufferer from venereal disease had
swung wildly over from the ideals of impurity and adventure
to those of purity and marriage, and would, had she been present, probably have been willing to propose marriage to Mrs
Plumleigh-Bruce without delay.

'So you're not coming down tonight?' he tried. 'Our Lady
Joan'll be mighty disappointed, methinks.'

'Yes. And I owe her some money, too,' said Gorse. 'If you see
her, will you tell her I'll be down tomorrow, and that I'll give it to
her then? Will you be seeing her?'

'Yes. I expect so. I can telephone her at any rate . . . But if I
meet her, and she should ask for a description of last night's
revels – what description am I to give?'

'Well, we met and had a few drinks at the King's . . .'

'Yes. And then . . .?'

'And then, I should say, we went off quietly to our respective
homes. Wouldn't you?'

'I certainly would,' said Mr Stimpson. 'And can I rely on you
to relate the same tale?'

'You certainly can,' said Gorse. 'Women don't quite see these things as men do ... And a woman like Mrs Plumleigh-Bruce least of all ... There's nothing I detest more than lying – and particularly with someone as clean and straight as she is – but – well – I'm afraid we men are made of a rather lower mould generally, and there *is* such a thing as discretion.'

'There is. Beyond a doubt. Then I may rely on your discretion?'

'Absolutely and completely. You needn't have any trouble on that score.'

'By the way,' said Mr Stimpson. 'I seem to remember talking a lot of drivel about Joan last night.'

'Really? ... When?'

'Oh – early in the evening. Don't you remember?'

'No. Not a word of it. What did you say?' said Gorse, casually.

Mr Stimpson looked at Gorse in order to see whether his casual air was assumed. He believed that it was not. He therefore took an audacious line.

'Oh – I don't know,' he said. 'I seem to remember getting a bit sentimental, one way and another.'

'Well – I can't remember it, but there's no harm in that – is there? I'm a bit sentimental about her myself, if you want to know the truth.'

'Are you? *How* sentimental? You don't mean you're "smitten" by her – do you?'

'Why, yes,' said the candid Gorse. 'I should say that's just what I am, really.'

'Really? You don't mean you're in love with her, or anything like that – do you?'

'Good heavens, no – not in love. I wouldn't dare to be. She's much too above my head – in years and other ways. But I can pay homage from a distance, and I love talking to her and all that. Don't you?'

The credulous and greedy Mr Stimpson, not content with having thrown off an abominable malady and having obtained an oath of secrecy from Gorse, resumed his habitual trick with the cake, and began to indulge in the delicious pleasure of praising the virtues of the woman of his choice.

'You can bet I do,' he said. 'You don't know that woman, my boy. She's got everything. She's a lady through and through –

she's got what I'd call poise – she's attractive – and she's as clever as they're made. And when I say clever I mean it in the real sense. I mean she reads. Reads and thinks. In fact she's above *my* head I can tell you – when it comes to reading. You wouldn't guess the books she goes in for.'

'Really? What sort of books?'

'Oh – History, Marie Antoinette, French Revolution and all that. What she doesn't know about History's absolutely nobody's business, I can tell you. I wish I knew a quarter of it – that's all I can say. She's got *intellect*, that woman. That's what I admire in her.'

'Yes. I can well believe you,' said Gorse. 'But you're not a little "smitten" on her yourself, by any chance, are you?'

'Well – I suppose even that's not impossible,' said Mr Stimpson with a smirk in his voice.

'Well, if you are – good luck to you,' said Gorse, changing gears in the Chiswick High Road. 'You've certainly got a prize worth winning. By the way, you don't object to *my* friendship with her, do you? It's very innocent, I can assure you.'

'*Mind* it! *Mind* it! Don't be absurd, old boy. I *admire* it. She's as near a goddess as they're made – so why shouldn't you pay her obeisance? I know that *I* do.'

Gorse saw that Mr Stimpson, talking about goddesses, was just about to enter the semi-lachrymose state of one who had drunk too much the night before, and thought it advisable to stop this nonsense.

'By the way,' he said, 'I haven't given you your money back yet.'

Mr Stimpson became less lachrymose.

CHAPTER THREE

SHORTLY after six that evening Mrs Plumleigh-Bruce heard her telephone ringing. She ran to the Marie Antoinette doll, certain, for some reason, that it was Gorse who was telephoning. She was therefore bitterly disappointed when she recognized Mr Stimpson's voice, saying 'Hullo, Joan, how are you?'

'Hullo,' she said. 'How are you?'

'I'm all right,' said Mr Stimpson. 'Are you stepping forth tonight?'

'Well – I haven't really thought about it,' said Mrs Plumleigh-Bruce, who had been thinking of little else during the last hour. Practically Gorse's last words to her, the evening before last, had been 'And the evening after that perhaps we'll *all* meet again', and, though no firm arrangement had been made, Mrs Plumleigh-Bruce, often looking at the chrysanthemums she had received from Gorse, had been confident that she would receive a telephone call, if not a message, during the day.

'Well – what about it?' said Mr Stimpson.

'Where are you phoning from?' she asked.

'I'm at the good old Friar. Coming along?'

'Are you all alone, then?' she asked, seeking to discover whether Gorse was with him.

But Mr Stimpson saw through her seemingly disinterested, almost solicitous query. He knew that it was Gorse that she was after, so that she could collect the money she had won on the horse *Stucco*. And so, being anxious to see her, he was not going to give away the fact that Gorse was not, and would not, be present.

'Yes – at the moment,' he said. 'But that won't last long. I seem to have got in here very early. Anyway, the point is, will you join the merry dance?'

Mr Stimpson had been most wily in speaking of 'the merry

dance'. It suggested the presence of the gay, dashing Gorse most vividly.

'Very well,' said Mrs Plumleigh-Bruce. 'I'd like to.'

'Fine. How long will you be?'

'Oh – about half an hour. I've got to get ready and all that,' said Mrs Plumleigh-Bruce, who was entirely ready and could have been at the Friar within ten minutes.

'Fine. Hurry up, then,' said Mr Stimpson, and they said goodbye and rang off.

2

Mrs Plumleigh-Bruce had said 'about half an hour', and, if she had thought she had been going to meet Mr Stimpson alone, she would not have been at The Friar until three quarters of an hour later. But with Gorse it was a different matter. He was, she had been compelled to learn, a slightly elusive as well as forthcoming young man, and, if she was too late, he might easily have disappeared. She therefore made a compromise and was at The Friar within five and twenty minutes.

She found Mr Stimpson sitting and thinking gloomily by himself.

Since the morning Mr Stimpson had had several recurrences of venereal disease – the sharpest of these being at teatime. This had brought him in despair to The Friar as soon as its doors were open. A pint of beer, as expected, had slightly reduced both the likelihood and severity of the malady, and by the time Mrs Plumleigh-Bruce had arrived Mr Stimpson was deep in repentance as to the past, and in burning resolution as to upright behaviour in the future.

Mrs Plumleigh-Bruce was, of course, highly disappointed at not seeing Gorse with him, but hoped that he might turn up before long. She concealed her disappointment as well as she could – but not successfully – from Mr Stimpson, who went to the bar and got her a Gin and Italian.

When he returned, in order to conceal her disappointment more fully, Mrs Plumleigh-Bruce made an effort to be particularly cheerful and gracious with him.

'Well,' she said. 'And how did you get on in the great gay City? Not led astray, I hope.'

'No,' said Mr Stimpson. 'Very dull on the whole. Very much as usual.'

'What? Not lured by the gay night lights?' said Mrs Plumleigh-Bruce.

She was, of course, fishing for information about the manner in which he had spent, not his day, but his evening with Gorse.

Mr Stimpson noticed that she was doing this, and decided to keep her waiting. It would, he thought, do her good. Although, at the moment, he was in no way jealous of Gorse – was, on the contrary, feeding his own vanity of Gorse's admiration for Mrs Plumleigh-Bruce – he was slightly annoyed at her too flagrant interest in the young man.

'No. Not lurid in any way,' he said. 'The lights of Reading are good enough for me. And how have *you* been keeping?'

'Oh – just the same.'

Mrs Plumleigh-Bruce saw that Mr Stimpson was withholding information either out of obstinacy or foolishness, and that if she was to get what she wanted, she must slightly humiliate herself. She did so.

'And did you go to The King's?'

'Oh – yes. We went there . . .'

'And how did that go?'

'How do you mean "go"?'

'Well – *go*,' said Mrs Plumleigh-Bruce, now infuriated by the maddeningly obtuse, or deliberately irritating, Mr Stimpson. 'I mean what *happened*?'

'What "happened"?' said Mr Stimpson, infected by her own irritation, and – in the condition of general exhaustion and touchiness caused by his drunkenness last night, his possible disease, and his remorse – not at all inclined to take things sitting down. 'What *should* happen? Nothing *happened* that I know of. An Elephant or anything didn't walk in, if that's what you mean.'

'I didn't imagine that an Elephant walked in,' said Mrs Plumleigh-Bruce. 'I simply –'

'Well, one certainly didn't,' said Mr Stimpson, interrupting her. 'You'd've read about it in the newspapers if there had, I imagine.'

'I'm not *talking* about Elephants,' said Mrs Plumleigh-Bruce, to which Mr Stimpson quickly rejoined 'I didn't say you were. Why have we suddenly got on to Elephants?'

'Well – you *started* them,' said Mrs Plumleigh-Bruce, flicking ash irritably from the cigarette in her holder.

Mr Stimpson looked at the angry woman who had, after last night, been reinstated as his proposed wife – and, having looked at her, decided that he would certainly think twice about the project of marrying her. 'Lady' she might be, but he certainly wasn't going to get tied up with an irritable dominating bitch.

For a moment Mr Stimpson was seeing the Mrs Plumleigh-Bruce whom her maid Mary saw most of the day – the narrower and meaner eyes, the sulky and malicious rather than lascivious mouth. And he was hearing the coolly commanding rather than rich and fruitily seductive voice.

Mr Stimpson was aware that her accusation was correct – that he had indeed started Elephants – but his mood was such that he was willing to irritate her further by pretending that she had. Having captured her for the first time in a more unfavourable light than ever before, he was eager, for the sake of experiment, to make the light worse still.

'*I* started Elephants?' he therefore said. '*I* didn't start them. I'm not *interested* in Elephants.'

'Really,' said Mrs Plumleigh-Bruce. 'This is absolutely childish, Donald. If you've just dragged me out to talk about Elephants, I might just as well go home,'

'Well, let's keep our sense of humour, at any rate,' said Mr Stimpson.

'Yes. Let's. By all means,' said Mrs Plumleigh-Bruce. 'I was only asking you if you had a nice time at The King's, you know. Surely there's no harm in that.'

Her more placid and peace-making tone had been so suddenly adopted that Mr Stimpson was easily able to discern its cause. She was determined to get back to Gorse. He supposed it was about time he gave her the bad news.

'Well, I had quite a nice time,' he said. 'But nothing spectacular. Just a few drinks and we both went our ways.'

'And how was our young friend?'

'Oh – he was in very good form, as usual . . . Oh, and by the way, he asked me to give you a message.'

'Really? What about?'

'He hoped to be in tonight, but he couldn't make it. He said I was to say he was sorry – that's all.'

'Oh. Really . . .?' said Mrs Plumleigh-Bruce, and, in her acute disappointment, she swallowed nothing. This empty gulp she attempted to conceal by quickly taking a sip at her cocktail, but Mr Stimpson was not deluded.

'He's kept in London on business or something,' said Mr Stimpson. 'And I was to send his apologies.'

'Well,' said Mrs Plumleigh-Bruce. 'There was no need to apologize. There wasn't any fixed arrangement, was there? Or *was* there?'

'I can't remember,' said Mr Stimpson, who, having administered full punishment, had now completely regained his temper, and was sorry for the woman. Twenty-five pounds was twenty-five pounds, after all, and he could understand her childish feeling of frustration at this further delay in receiving so novel and glittering a prize.

'But anyway,' he said. 'He told me to tell you he'll be down tomorrow – and that he can give you the money he owes you then.'

'How do you mean by "down"? In here or where? Or what?'

'I don't know. That was left vague. In here I should think. Anyway that was the message.'

'Oh, well – it doesn't matter much, does it?' said Mrs Plumleigh-Bruce. 'No doubt he'll get into touch.'

Because he was now sorry for the rather subdued Mrs Plumleigh-Bruce, Mr Stimpson turned his thoughts to marrying her again, and, though he was neither jealous nor afraid of Gorse, he thought that it would do no harm to put in a word against him in order to enhance his own value as a candidate for her hand.

'He's a funny young man,' he said. 'Isn't he?'

'Well – I don't really know him . . . How "funny"?'

'Well. Flighty, let's say. A bit of a gad-about, wouldn't you say? That's the impression I got in London, at any rate.'

'You mean you wouldn't trust him?'

'Oh – good Heavens, no. He's all right at the bottom, I'd say. But just a bit of a butterfly, that's all. Not like yours truly, at all. Yours truly's probably a bit *too* steady. He's been pretty steady to you, anyway, hasn't he, for a pretty long time, now?'

'Yes,' said Mrs Plumleigh-Bruce after a pause. 'I suppose he has.'

Her flirtatious pause, and the flirtatiousness conveyed in her deliberate manner of speaking as she looked down her nose, put ideas into the vacillating and changeable Mr Stimpson's head. Why not have some more drinks and make love to her as usual?

'Come on, Joan my dear,' he said. 'Drink that off. I feel in the mood for a few tonight – don't you?'

Mrs Plumleigh-Bruce at once detected her companion's new mood, and as rapidly made up her mind that it was not her own tonight, and that she would have none of it.

She looked at her watch, was surprised at the time, stubbed out her cigarette and said Good Heavens no, she must fly. She had given Mary permission to go to the pictures this evening, and had arranged to be home for her meal at a quarter past seven at the latest.

Mr Stimpson then began to argue with her, making many plausible, and indeed logical suggestions that Mrs Plumleigh-Bruce should telephone Mary and dine with himself in a restaurant in Reading.

But Mrs Plumleigh-Bruce remained adamant, and this threw Mr Stimpson into a very bad temper again. This, in its turn, threw Mrs Plumleigh-Bruce into a temper, and she said No, she really must go at once – really.

Then Mr Stimpson began to fish for an invitation to dinner at Glen Alan the next evening, but Mrs Plumleigh-Bruce, feeling that she had a lot to think about and that she must keep herself free for Gorse tomorrow evening, made further excuses, which increased Mr Stimpson's rage.

'Well – I can't see you home,' he said. 'I've promised old Parry I'll be in here tonight. He ought to be in here now, in fact. And I can't very well let him down – can I?'

Mrs Plumleigh-Bruce said No of course he couldn't, and she rose. Mr Stimpson, controlling his rage, accompanied her to the door, and said goodbye to her with reasonable cordiality in the street.

Then, on re-entering The Friar he obtained a large Gin and Italian at the bar, took it over to the Plumleigh-Bruce nook, and sat sulking . . . Take the bitch home – Trust *him*!

Mr Stimpson had, in fact, no appointment with Major Parry, and was only fearful that the talkative man might appear. All he wanted to do was to sulk, and think and drink.

Such were the last gloomy effects of Mr Stimpson's hopeful journey to London. He had two more drinks, sulking and thinking deeply over them.

He then decided that he must take his mind off himself and his problems, and, getting his evening newspaper and a pencil from his pockets, he looked at the clues of the Crossword Puzzle.

He saw:

Across	*Down*
1. Mollified.	2. Displeasing to actors.
7. Follows suit.	3. Game.
9. Bean.	4. Wraith.
10. A picnic.	5. Emollient.
11. Deliver (anag.) Reviled.	6. Euphemism for theft.
13. Affirmation.	8. Rodent.
15. Spirit.	12. Shrewder than bees.
16. Slow to anger.	13. Complicated.
19. Sagging.	14. Headquarters.
22. Obviously.	17. Snakes' Paradise.
24. Only one in five escapes.	18. Celebration.
25. Recedes.	20. Sought place in sun.
26. The end.	23. '– is for remembrance'
27. Elderly female found this bare.	(Shakespeare)

But persons, words or things Mollified, Following Suit, Displeasing to Actors, Sagging, Slow to Anger, or Euphemistic for Theft, did not take Mr Stimpson's mind off himself. In fact they seemed only to drive him back upon himself.

Over his last drink, however, he managed, angrily, to solve the Anag. *Reviled* with *Deliver*. But then he became even more angry at realizing that Reviled would do as well, and then less angry because the last letter of *Deliver* was an 'r' and this fitted in with the three-letter 8 down – *Rodent* – obviously *Rat*. Then, with the last sip of his drink he solved *Elderly female found this bare* with *Cupboard*, walked out of The Friar, and made for home.

He tried to console himself with the thought that he had got three anyway. But he was not truly consoled.

For a crossword puzzle man, he knew, cannot thrive on *Deliver, Rat,* and *Cupboard* alone.

PART EIGHT

GORSE THE REVEALER

CHAPTER ONE

I

LOOKING back on it afterwards, Mrs Plumleigh-Bruce believed she could recall exactly the moment at which she decided that she might just, just conceivably succumb to Gorse's proposals of marriage – his proposals of marriage, that was to say, if they were repeated, and if they were indeed proposals of marriage.

She was sitting drinking coffee and brandy with him after dinner at Glen Alan, and they were talking about Mr Stimpson.

It was three weeks after the latter's disastrous trip to London, and, somehow or other, this journey had come up in the conversation.

Or, rather, Mrs Plumleigh-Bruce imagined that it had come up somehow or other. In fact it had been steered into by Gorse, who, having done so, had said, with a reflective sigh, 'Oh dear – it's a pity our Mr Stimpson, for all his sterling qualities, hasn't really reached the years of discretion – isn't it?'

'How do you mean?' said Mrs Plumleigh-Bruce. 'I should have thought he was the most discreet, steady-going person – too steady-going, if anything, in fact.'

'Would you?' said Gorse, looking into the fire, and his tone of scepticism, combined with that of one who could tell much if he wished so to do, interested Mrs Plumleigh-Bruce beyond measure.

2

Mrs Plumleigh-Bruce had, in fact, been for a long while interested in this trip of Mr Stimpson's to London, having a feeling that a great deal more had happened than she had been told about.

She had felt this even during her meeting with Mr Stimpson on the evening of his return: but a few evenings later the feeling had grown into a conviction.

On that evening the four of them – herself, Mr Stimpson, Major Parry, and Gorse – had all met at The Friar, and it had been Mr Stimpson who had by his own stupidity put the conviction into her head.

Having mentioned their meeting in London, since when Gorse and Mr Stimpson had not seen each other, he had said to Gorse, 'Well, it was nice to have had a nice quiet evening in the gay city the other night – wasn't it?'

The mere forced use of the word 'quiet' would have aroused Mrs Plumleigh-Bruce's suspicions in any case. But Mr Stimpson had not been content with this. He had faintly underlined the word, and, in pencil, drawn some inverted commas around it.

Worse still he had looked at Gorse with a sort of bulldoggish leer which the simplest-minded observer would have interpreted as a broad wink.

In extenuation of so much folly on Mr Stimpson's part, it may be said that he thought that it was necessary to convey to Gorse that he had already told Mrs Plumleigh-Bruce that the evening had been a quiet one – and to remind Gorse, in case he had forgotten, that there had been a pact between them that this was to be the story told by both.

But later on Mr Stimpson had gone far beyond possibly excusable folly. He had descended almost to idiocy.

'Yes,' he had said to Gorse. 'We'll have another nice quiet bachelor evening together in London one of these days.'

At this, of course, Mrs Plumleigh-Bruce lost any shred of doubt she might have maintained that Mr Stimpson had been up to nonsense of some sort. She had always suspected that Mr Stimpson, on his visits to London, indulged in furtive adventure of some sort.

But what about Gorse? Was not he also involved? This matter was, really, more interesting than that of Mr Stimpson.

For, as she sat, three weeks later, drinking coffee and brandy with him at Glen Alan, Mrs Plumleigh-Bruce was very much more interested in Ernest Ralph Gorse than Donald Stimpson.

After Gorse's sad sceptical 'Would you?' Mrs Plumleigh-Bruce was quite unable to control her curiosity.

'Why yes,' she said. 'I would. Wouldn't you? You know, you look as if you wouldn't – somehow . . .'

'Do I?'

'Yes. In fact you look as though you could say a lot of things if you wanted to.'

'Do I? . . . Well – even if I could, I wouldn't.' Gorse looked at her quizzingly. 'So I think this is where we change the subject – isn't it?'

'No. Why change it? It's extremely interesting. I mean the subject is – not Mr Stimpson. Go on. You mustn't start something and not go on with it.'

'Did I start something?'

'Yes. Of course you did. You know you did. Come along, now. What makes you think Donald Stimpson hasn't reached the "years of discretion" as you put it?'

Gorse was silent.

'No,' he said, at last. 'There are certain things one just doesn't reveal: I've no particular feelings of respect or friendship for Donald Stimpson, but he's done me no harm, and there *is* such a thing as honour amongst men – as well as amongst thieves. Particularly men out on the spree, as on *that* occasion.'

'Why? Were *you* out on the spree that night?'

'Me? Oh dear me no. Believe me – it was most dreary. Now – do let's change the subject – shall we?'

'No. You started it, and I think it's only fair that you should go on with it.' Mrs Plumleigh-Bruce here adopted her queenly, fruity, semi-joking tone. 'I shall be very angry with you if you don't, you know.'

'Well, then, I'm afraid you must be angry. Though God forbid that,' said Gorse, and then, after another long pause, added, 'It'd be different, of course, if you and I stood towards each other in the relationship I've been proposing recently . . .'

3

This, Mrs Plumleigh-Bruce realized, was probably Gorse's third proposal of marriage.

She thought quickly – her mind reviewing the almost incredible landscape of her last three weeks with Gorse, and the two proposals, if such they were, which stood out as peaks in the novel and exciting scenery.

The first proposal had been over drinks at The Friar shortly after she had been over and had tea at the house he occupied in Gilroy Road. Then he had said, talking of the house, 'Or perhaps it might be yours – as well as mine', and dropped the subject.

The second proposal had been a week or so ago, over brandy and coffee at Glen Alan. Then they had been talking about Life, and he had said 'Unless yours and mine were one, you know,' and again the subject had been dropped.

There had then been a half-proposal when he had kissed her. This he had done in a gentlemanly, reverent way (and again in the sitting-room), saying immediately afterwards, 'I'm sorry. But I don't do that sort of thing unless I'm taking things very seriously, you know,' and yet again no more had been said. Mrs Plumleigh-Bruce doubted whether this 'counted'.

Now he had just spoken of a relationship he had been 'proposing' recently. The very word 'proposing' suggested a proposal. And it was exactly at this moment (she thought afterwards) that she decided that she might, just, just conceivably succumb to his proposals of marriage if and when he renewed them.

4

Three proposals and a half, then, thought Mrs Plumleigh-Bruce, looking at Gorse looking into the fire. But none of them direct, demanding direct compliance or rejection. And so modesty demanded that she should again ignore what he had said.

Intense feelings of curiosity about Mr Stimpson (and his evening in London with Gorse), however, were at conflict with the demands of modesty, and curiosity momentarily won the day.

Therefore, in order to entice Gorse into revelations about Mr

Stimpson, she said 'How do you know that we might not come to stand in that relationship?'

After a pause Gorse threw his cigarette into the fire and looked like one who wanted to jump from his chair.

'Do you realize what you've just said?' he said.

'No . . . What?' Mrs Plumleigh-Bruce looked down her nose – an affectation she had employed a great deal with Gorse in the last three weeks.

'Do you realize you've given me some hope – or a little morsel of it, anyway?'

'Have I? . . .'

'Of course you have. You know you have. In fact if you weren't what you were, I'd say that you're leading me on. Come now, Joan, admit that you've given me a tiny morsel. I don't mind how tiny – as long as it's there.'

Curiosity should now, Mrs Plumleigh-Bruce thought, collaborate with modesty. Both (it seemed to the vain woman) would benefit.

'Well,' she said, looking even more concentratedly down her nose. 'Perhaps a teeny-weeny. And perhaps it's wrong of me. And anyway that sort of thing wants a lot of thinking about, doesn't it?'

'Of course it does.'

'So shall we go back to where we were?'

'Yes . . . Where were we? I'll do whatever you say. I'm an extremely patient person. Where were we?'

'We were talking about Mr Stimpson not having reached the years of discretion. I rather doubt whether *you* have, if it comes to that. But tell me about Mr Stimpson. Go on.'

Gorse looked at her, as if confused and almost maddened, for a long while.

'Joan,' he said, sententiously. 'Have you ever heard the story of Samson and Delilah?'

'Yes.'

'Well. I'm certainly no Samson, but it seems to me you've got a very strong touch of Delilah.'

'Why? . . .' said Mrs Plumleigh-Bruce, and because Gorse was silent, added a deliciously throaty 'Wherefore? . . .'

This silly complacent fool, thought Gorse, will develop adenoids and a permanent squint if she goes on looking down her nose and talking like this.

But this was none of his business. The point was that the late Cathedral and radiator of universal happiness was now Delilah, and extremely wicked. He strove to make her wickeder still.

'Well – you're only asking me to betray secrets,' he said. 'In other words, you're only twisting me round your little finger. But after what you've said, after that little morsel you threw me, I'm willing to do your bidding . . . Anyway, my conscience isn't very much disturbed. It's only a very silly and very absurd and sordid little secret. And I know I can trust you in every way. I know you're "Steel true and Blade-straight", as Stevenson said . . . "Steel-true and Blade-straight, The Great Artificer Made my Mate". That's what he said of his wife, you know.'

Gorse, who had accidentally come across these words only a few days ago while browsing in the Reference Room of the local Public Library, had memorized them with the dimly formulated object of using them at some time upon women. He had had a curious fleeting notion that if you could only convince women that they were Steel-true and Blade-straight, you could make them, before long, and for your own purposes, as malleable as plasticine and as crooked as hair-pins.

But just at this moment he feared he had gone a little too far. If Mrs Plumleigh-Bruce became Steel-true and Blade-straight on the spot (and he feared she had) she might forbid him to disclose the secrets concerning Mr Stimpson which she was so anxious to hear and he was so anxious to disclose. He should, perhaps, have kept her as Delilah and not tried to have forged a sword.

His Delilah, however, as her next remark revealed, was by a piece of good fortune a spectacularly clever sword-swallower.

'Well, you can certainly trust me. You know that,' she said, clearly having thrust right down her throat, and enjoyed to the utmost, the sword, without suffering the smallest internal damage or letting it in the smallest way interfere with the business of cropping the strong man's tresses. 'But if it's all so absurd and silly, I don't see why you shouldn't tell me. Go on. Tell me your silly story. I hope it's not too sordid.'

'But what do you want to know, exactly?' said Gorse.

'Oh – just what happened that night.'

'It's not so much what happened,' said Gorse. 'It's the way it happened, I suppose. There are ways and ways of doing things, aren't there?'

'You mean ways of drinking, for instance?' said Mrs Plumleigh-Bruce, who had seen Mr Stimpson foolishly drunk more than once, particularly at Christmas time.

'No. Not drinking,' said Gorse, heavily. 'Though that certainly came into it – most strongly. I mean other things really . . .'

'What things?' said Mrs Plumleigh-Bruce, now thrilled at the thought of having her darkest suspicions fulfilled.

'Oh, *things*,' said Gorse. 'The things men do . . . All the sinful lusts of the flesh, and all that. The things they do particularly when they've been drinking, and particularly when they're in the West End. I don't think I need explain myself further – do you?'

'No. I don't think you need, really . . . And so he'd been drinking heavily, and then pursued – "all the sinful lusts of the flesh", as you put it?'

'You seem to know a lot about him. It sounds almost as if you were there yourself.'

Gorse had been visited by a sudden fear that Mr Stimpson had made some sort of confession to Mrs Plumleigh-Bruce – in which case the present conversation would lose half its potency.

'Yes. I think I know a lot about him,' said Mrs Plumleigh-Bruce. 'In fact a good deal more than he thinks I know.'

'But how? He doesn't ever *talk* to you about that sort of thing – does he?'

'Oh – good Heavens, no. It's just that I've always had an instinct, that's all . . . And so there was drinking and – the other thing – that night, was there? And did you partake of these pleasures?'

'Now. Don't be absurd. Didn't I say I didn't? In fact I found it all incredibly dreary . . . Mind you, I don't want to set myself up as a plaster saint in any direction. Don't get that into your head. In fact, in my early roaring twenties I've done a lot of things that – well, I was going to say regret – but I don't know that I *do* regret them. They're all part of one's growing pains and you have to get that sort of thing out of your blood. And you'd be a prig if you didn't do what everybody else in your circle does . . . But as I said, it's the *way* you do it – that's what matters.'

'And Donald Stimpson did it all the wrong way?'

'He certainly did, in my view. In fact first of all he got objectionably drunk, and then betook himself to the most objectionable quarters to satisfy his other desires. There was no stopping him.'

'But how do you know about that part of it? Unless you joined him?'

'I *did* join him.'

'Really. Why?'

'I kept with him so that I could look after him. And it was a good thing that I did. I was able to save him a little matter of something like fifteen pounds. Although, perhaps, it'd've been better if he'd lost it. It might have taught him a lesson. Although, again, you can't really teach that sort of a man a lesson. They just never learn from experience. That's what I meant when I said he hadn't really reached the years of discretion.'

'But how on earth did you save him fifteen pounds?'

'Oh – I took the precaution of removing his wallet during a period when he was half asleep, so that an extremely low but extremely determined young lady didn't get at it.'

'But surely she wanted some money – for "services rendered", as they say.'

'Yes. And I gave her two pounds. And that was a good deal more than she was worth, I can assure you.'

'And were the "services rendered" for that amount?'

'That I can't say for certain. I'd hardly be standing by and watching it happen, would I? The only thing was that I did have to leave him alone with her for about three-quarters of an hour while I dug out my car from a garage, so that I could take him home to his sister at Richmond. And what happened in the interim I'm afraid I can't tell you.'

There was a pause, as Gorse looked at her looking into the fire.

'Yes,' said Mrs Plumleigh-Bruce. 'It's just what I always thought, you know.' And there was another pause.

'Anyway,' said Gorse, 'it's all very trivial, as I said. Men are men, and that's that. Or at any rate a certain type of man is a certain type of man, and though I certainly hope I'm not personally that type, I suppose one's got to make allowances. I really think that that little episode wasn't as bad as what went before it.'

'You mean his drinking. I've seen him drunk myself, before now.'

'No – not exactly his drinking . . . It was what he *did* in his drinking – or rather what he said . . .'

'You mean he used a lot of bad language?'

'Oh dear no. I'm used to that. It was the way he revealed himself – the things he *gave away* . . . I could hardly listen to him I was so disgusted . . . But then, of course, there's no stopping a drunken man. Especially when he's with another man. He'd be different with you . . . I mean, a man . . .'

Mrs Plumleigh-Bruce here, rather brusquely, interrupted Gorse's discourse in order to focus upon its two vital words.

'*Gave away?*' she said. 'What did he give away? Things about himself – or about other people?'

'Both,' said Gorse. 'A drunken man always gives *himself* away in any case.'

'And what did he say about other people? What sort of other people?'

'Oh – all sorts . . .' said Gorse.

'But who? Anyone in particular?'

'Yes.'

'Who?'

'You,' said Gorse. 'In fact it was you more than anyone else. That's what made the whole thing so horribly embarrassing and revolting.'

'Really,' said Mrs Plumleigh-Bruce. 'This is extremely interesting. Go on. What did he say?'

Gorse took a sip at his drink, lit a cigarette, put his elbows on to his knees, looked into the fire, and said 'Joan . . .'

To which Mrs Plumleigh-Bruce, herself nervously snatching at a cigarette from a box beside her, replied 'Yes' . . .

There was a silence while Mrs Plumleigh-Bruce lit her cigarette.

Then 'You've been asking me a lot of questions. Now I want to ask you one,' said Gorse. 'You needn't answer it if you don't want to – but may I ask it?'

'Yes. Of course you may. Go on.'

'Well – has there ever, at any time, been anything "between" you and Donald Stimpson?'

'What do you mean by "between"?'

'Well – has he – kissed – you, or anything like that?'

'Yes. He's kissed me.'

'And you've allowed it?'

'Yes. I suppose I have. I've put up with it, anyway.'

'Oh Joan,' said Gorse, still looking into the fire. 'How *could* you? ... You know you'll make me think he's right in what he said. You *have* got feet of clay.'

'Did he say that?'

'He did.'

'And what do you imagine he meant?'

'I don't know. I only know he said he could "tell" me a lot of things about you if he wanted to.'

'You don't mean he suggested – you don't mean . . .'

'Oh, no. I've got to be fair to him. Drunk as he was he didn't go as far as that. He wouldn't have dared to, for one thing.'

'Why not?'

'Well – if he had there'd've been a very unusual little scene in the most respectable precincts of The King's Hotel.'

'What scene?'

'I'm afraid Mr Stimpson would have found himself flat on his back from a blow well and truly delivered by Mr Gorse. I can stand a good amount of drunken drivel, but one has to draw the line somewhere – hasn't one? No – he didn't go quite as far as that. However, he did say that you had feet of clay, and he did say that he had kissed you. I thought it was drunken drivel at the time – but now it seems that he's right.'

'Well, you'd know he's not right, and that it was drunken drivel, if you knew the circumstances. You can't slap a silly man's face just for trying to kiss you every now and again, you know. Can you?'

'No. You can't. In fact, if you could, I'd've had my own slapped – wouldn't I? Don't think I don't know all that you must have to put up with from men all the time. I'm not a fool, you know.'

Mrs Plumleigh-Bruce, who had, in fact, not been kissed by any man, apart from Mr Stimpson, in the last four years, here looked down her nose again – seeing, beyond her nose, multitudinous kisses from multitudinous men, welcome and unwelcome.

'No. I'm not fool enough to blind myself in that way,' Gorse went on. 'All the same, one does get a bit of a shock, in the circumstances, when one knows the man – and what sort of man he is ... But I knew you'd tell the truth straight out like that. "Steel-true and Blade-straight" as I said ... You see, I'm always right about you ... Don't bother, I'll get over it.'

'There's nothing to get over in *that* case, I can assure you,' said Mrs Plumleigh-Bruce. 'But tell me, did he say anything else?'

'Oh – he drivelled on. It was half complimentary – half abusive.'

'Abusive?'

'Well – it seemed abusive to me. But then I'm prejudiced, as you know.'

'But what *did* he say?'

'Do you know, I can't remember properly? ... I wasn't really listening, of course ... Oh – yes, there *was* one thing – one fantastic expression he used ... Now what on earth was it? ... Oh yes! *I* remember! It'll make you laugh, if I tell you.'

'Go on. Tell me.'

'He said you were "long in the tooth",' said Gorse. 'For some reason I've never personally heard the expression – as applied to a human being, anyway – and I didn't even know what he was talking about at first. I thought he meant that you had slightly projecting teeth. And as a matter of fact you *have* – very slightly – haven't you? ... It's all part of the fascination ... But then I got his meaning.'

'And what did you say when he said I was "long in the tooth"?'

'I thought he meant what I was thinking of, and I agreed with him, I'm afraid. In fact I said I thought you'd got one of the loveliest mouths I've ever seen on any woman. And I meant it, needless to say. That rather took him aback, I'm afraid. But don't think I descended to gossiping about you with him. It just came from me spontaneously ... He must have seen that, because a moment afterwards he asked me whether I was "smitten" by you.'

'And what did you reply to that?'

'I replied that I wasn't – that I didn't think of you in that way. I said that I thought it would be sacrilege. And I still do. At least I do in a way. But three weeks have passed since then – haven't they? And in those three weeks maybe I've been guilty of sacrilege – both in thought and deed ... But we'd better not go into all that at the moment . . . Now, what *else* did he say? There was another weird expression . . . They do get hold of some funny words, these funny men . . . Oh yes! He said that women only wanted "handling", and that if you were properly "handled", you'd probably do *something* –now what *was* it? It meant go to extremes. Go to the limit. Go the whole – way or something – what on *earth* was it? . . .'

'Hog?' asked Mrs Plumleigh-Bruce, with a terse air.

'Hog!' said Gorse, triumphantly congratulating Mrs Plumleigh-Bruce on her capture of the word. '*Hog*. That was the word. Aren't they wonderful – these people?'

'And what did you reply to that?'

'I've forgotten. You must remember I wasn't really listening to the man. If I'd realized his implication at the time there might have been trouble. However, let's drop Mr Stimpson, shall we?' Gorse looked at his wristwatch. 'It's a very dull subject, and if I'm going to keep our pact not to scandalize Mary and go home by ten forty-five as promised, we've only a few moments left to talk about more edifying things in – haven't we?'

The time being less than five and twenty to eleven, there were actually more than ten minutes left in which to talk, but Gorse, seeing from her general look and bearing that Mrs Plumleigh-Bruce was now wholly preoccupied with rage against Mr Stimpson, had made a deliberate error when looking at his wristwatch. It would be well, he thought, to leave her alone in her present mood and with her present thoughts. By his doing this, he felt, a totally ineradicable hatred against Mr Stimpson would be almost assured. He believed he had said neither too little nor too much.

He was right, Mrs Plumleigh-Bruce furiously wanted to be left alone with her furious thoughts.

So much was this so that all the Delilah went out of her, and she said, 'Well – it *is* rather late – isn't it? And I *am* rather tired, I must say.'

Gorse jumped to his feet, with a slightly martyred, yet brave, disciplined and soldierly air.

'Very well, then,' he said. 'No edifying conversation. I'll be off. I can see you're tired.'

'For Heaven's sake don't think I'm turning you out,' said Mrs Plumleigh-Bruce. But she rose.

'No. I don't think that,' said Gorse. 'And even if I did I wouldn't mind. You've given me enough – you've said enough – for one night. You might spoil it if you said any more.'

'What have I said? What have I given you?'

'Oh – just that little morsel – that little particle of hope. You know what I mean all right. And it's really more than a morsel with someone like you. Because you're not the sort of person who leads people on – unless I'm a very bad judge of character.'

'I certainly hope I'm not. And I certainly hope I haven't led you on. But do you realize I hardly know you? Do you realize how short a time it is since we first met? It's a very short time, you know.'

'I know exactly. It's three weeks and five days, if you want it exactly. Two days off a month. Do you think I'd forget a thing like that? But what may be called a remarkable three weeks, I fancy . . . I don't expect they're as clear to you as they are to me. Now – don't say any more, and let me see myself out as usual.' He kissed her fraternally on the cheek. 'If you said any more you'd be bound to spoil it. Good-night, Joan. A ring in the morning – also as usual. I'll go to my thoughts, and I'll leave you to yours. Good-night.'

Within ten seconds Gorse was outside the room (the door of which he had closed with a semi-conspiratorial quietness all his own) and within a minute Mrs Plumleigh-Bruce had heard the last sound of his car, as it turned from Sispara Road into the Oxford Road. And within two minutes Mrs Plumleigh-Bruce, having lit another cigarette, was alone with her thoughts and thinking them with remarkable intensity.

CHAPTER TWO

1

CONTRARY to Gorse's (and her own) expectations Mrs
Plumleigh-Bruce's thoughts soon turned from Mr Stimpson
to Gorse himself, and to the 'remarkable' three weeks he had just
mentioned.

Her fury against Mr Stimpson melted in thoughts of the gentle,
protective, upright, amorous (and yet so reticently amorous)
Gorse. With such an admirer in attendance upon her Mr
Stimpson became merely crude and despicable – swinish – something beyond the pale.

The three weeks which Gorse had mentioned had indeed been
'remarkable' – to Gorse, perhaps, even more than to Mrs Plumleigh-Bruce – and a brief account should now be given of them.

2

Thinking it advisable still further to exploit, just at present, his
gift of causing and using the emotion of relief in women, Gorse
had not returned to Reading on the day promised in the message
he had given to Mrs Plumleigh-Bruce through Mr Stimpson on
the morning after Mr Stimpson's calamitous night. He let another
day – a Thursday – go by.

Nor did he communicate with Mrs Plumleigh-Bruce in any
way until Friday evening.

Then he telephoned her at about a quarter past six. Mary told
him that she was out, but would be returning to dinner at half
past seven. Gorse did not leave his name, but said that he would
ring again in about an hour's time.

Gorse rightly guessed that she was round at The Friar with Mr
Stimpson. She had intended not to see Mr Stimpson until she had
heard from Gorse, but his continued absence and silence had put

her into a small panic about the money owing to her. She now practically regarded those deliciously lucky winnings more or less in the light of solid property which she had held for years, and she had a sense of being temporarily deprived of this property – or even robbed.

She had, therefore, during the day of the evening on which Gorse telephoned, her, accepted an invitation to meet Mr Stimpson at The Friar. Mr Stimpson had telephoned her during the afternoon, and she had accepted because she had a feeling that Gorse might be also present, or that Mr Stimpson might know something about his continued absence.

Mr Stimpson was, however, as puzzled as herself, and gained renewed favour in her eyes by virtue of his constancy seen against the background of Gorse's elusiveness.

Because he was again in favour Mr Stimpson, who, as on the night before last, desired either to take her out to a restaurant or to return to Glen Alan for dinner, managed to make her drink larger quantities of Gin and Italian more quickly than usual. But he over-reached himself and did not succeed in having dinner with her. Mrs Plumleigh-Bruce suddenly felt her head swimming, and felt that she must get home – be alone at home – as soon as possible. She also had a feeling that Gorse might have telephoned her or be telephoning her. She made polite excuses.

Mr Stimpson escorted her home, kissed her in the porch, and left her. Her head was now no longer swimming.

No sooner had she entered Glen Alan than Mary informed her, in a rather frightened way, that a 'gentleman' had rung and that he had said he would ring again soon. This made Mrs Plumleigh-Bruce's head swim again, but with pleasure and excitement rather than Gin and Italian Vermouth.

A few minutes later the telephone rang, and twenty minutes later Gorse, having been invited to take 'pot luck', was in the Glen Alan sitting-room drinking champagne with Mrs Plumleigh-Bruce.

The champagne had been brought by Gorse so that they might 'celebrate' Mrs Plumleigh-Bruce's victory on the turf, and Mrs Plumleigh-Bruce, having told Mary to delay the 'pot luck' (a cold meal from which a good deal of the luck had been eliminated, and into which a good deal of discretion had been quickly thrown during the time intervening between Gorse's telephoning and

arriving) – took a glass of champagne with Gorse, half reluctantly
and half with delight.

Gorse, who saw that she had had too much to drink, nevertheless managed to make her take yet another glass before eating.
This he did by bemusing her, at exactly the right moment, with
the sight and sound of fresh pound notes taken from his pocket.
No one in England could make more delicious, fresh, crisp noises
with fresh pound notes than Gorse.

By the time the pot luck was served Mrs Plumleigh-Bruce was
hilarious – so much so that Mary (at whom more fantastic *Oirish*
was flung than had ever been heard at Glen Alan before) noticed
her hilarity, and suspected its cause. Gorse, in order to sustain
the general tempo, indulged in a little *Oirish* himself, and made
Mary take a small wine-glassful of champagne back into the
kitchen with her.

After Mary had cleared away and brought the coffee, Gorse
had persuaded Mrs Plumleigh-Bruce to drink brandy with him.
The meal had now allayed Mrs Plumleigh-Bruce's slightly too
sharp hilarity. But this had been replaced by a deep, deep elation,
and a very beautiful faith in life, and in the cleverness, kindness
and grace of her visitor.

Gorse having asked her what she was going to do with her
winnings, and Mrs Plumleigh-Bruce having told him that she had
no idea, the subject of money generally was embarked upon.
Gorse took an extremely cautious attitude towards money.

He was, indeed, in spite of the sucess they had been and still
were celebrating, severely and admonitorily cautious. It was as if
he were afraid that success might go to her head.

Mrs Plumleigh-Bruce, listening to him in a gin-champagne-
supper-coffee-brandy haze, soon became shrewdly yet sublimely
cautious. Indeed, leaning back on the settee, and looking at her
worldly-wise visitor, she bathed in caution.

While thus bathing, on Gorse's delicate prompting, she disclosed something of the nature of her own investments to Gorse,
throwing around them a sort of beautiful, rose-tinted mist of
caution.

Finally, and again at Gorse's instigation, she became so cautious that she could not resist jumping out of her caution-bath
and dragging her investments back into it in order to play with
them. In other words, she left the room and withdrew (from the

desk in her 'Hidey-hole', 'Study', 'Den', or 'Snuggery') a list of her investments, and showed them to Gorse.

Gorse, having stuck his monocle into his eye, now changed the mood of caution into one merely of serious concentration upon the document in his hands.

He then began, slowly, to be unable to refrain from giving forth a faint giggle at some of the items he was reading. Others he seemed to take more seriously.

Mrs Plumleigh-Bruce, watching the monocled but austere young man closely, was disconcerted by these giggles. Did they denote delight in her caution, or scorn at her lack of it? At last she was compelled to ask him if he thought anything was wrong.

To which Gorse replied (while he still looked in a preoccupied way at the document) that No, there was certainly nothing *Wrong*. It was all just a little bit too *Right*.

This struck fear into the soul of Mrs Plumleigh-Bruce, who, naturally, was terrified by the thought of anything which was a little bit too Right. She had visions of an evil or fearfully ignorant adviser (her Bank Manager) and pictured herself in an almost immediate state of penury.

'You know,' said Gorse. 'You really ought to have someone who knows his business to keep an eye on this sort of thing. Tell me, what sort of man is your Bank Manager? You were telling me about him the other night – weren't you?'

A sort of despairing yet resigned tone used by Gorse in putting this question threw Mrs Plumleigh-Bruce into greater panic than ever.

'I've always thought him very helpful and nice,' she said, feebly. 'Why? Does anything make you think he isn't?'

'No. But it's the helpful and nice people who land one into such trouble in this world, isn't it?' said Gorse, and then, putting his finger on another item in the document he was holding, he added, 'Good God! The man ought to be *prosecuted*.'

He flung the document upon his lap, took his monocle out of his eye, and gazed in astonishment at Mrs Plumleigh-Bruce, who said, 'What do you mean? You don't mean that everything there's not perfectly safe – do you?'

'What do you mean by "safe"?' said Gorse, realizing that he could hardly extract any further drop of anxiety, even of the minutest kind, from his hostess, and that the time had come for her to drink her draught of relief. 'Safe? Of course they are. You're as safe as houses, believe me.'

'Well – I'm glad to hear that,' said Mrs Plumleigh-Bruce. And (as if it were her draught of relief) she took a sip at her brandy.

'In fact you're so safe,' said Gorse with jovial sarcasm, 'that you're only losing about a half – or at any rate, a quarter – of what ought to be your income. However – that's your business. It's none of mine.'

During the next ten minutes Mrs Plumleigh-Bruce endeavoured to make her own business Gorse's – but he would have none of it. He didn't like, he said, advising other people about their investments. All he wanted to say was, that, if she got proper advice, she could nearly double her income – that was all.

He then feigned tiredness, seeming to suppress a yawn – a suppressed yawn which was so perfectly timed that it made Mrs Plumleigh-Bruce, who was genuinely tired, yawn as well, and in less than a quarter of an hour he had left Glen Alan in a rather indifferent, and perhaps slightly rude and abrupt way.

Mrs Plumleigh-Bruce went to bed in a disturbed frame of mind.

She was disturbed by thoughts about her investments, by Gorse's sudden slight indifference and abruptness, and by the knowledge that she had drunk too much. She hoped, as she went to sleep, that she would feel better about things in the morning.

So far from feeling better next morning, Mrs Plumleigh-Bruce, waking much earlier than usual at the hideous summons of stale gin, champagne, and brandy, felt very much worse, and Gorse, later in the morning, made use of this.

3

Waking early on the Saturday morning, Mrs Plumleigh-Bruce had, naturally, a headache, but she looked upon this as the least of her miseries. She was conscious of having made a fool of herself in front of Gorse, and a fool of herself in front of Mary. She also remembered her general indiscretion – particularly her impulsive disclosure of her investments. She remembered, too, Gorse's rather hasty and cool departure, and thought that this might have been due to his displeasure or boredom at her loose-ness of behaviour.

Mary had no *Oirish* thrown at her that morning; nor was Marie Antoinette studied in bed after breakfast. Instead of this Mrs Plumleigh-Bruce smoked three cigarettes in bed – with her an almost unknown thing – and gave herself up to melancholy brooding.

Gorse, last night, so far as she could remember, had made no mention of a future meeting, and this increased Mrs Plumleigh-Bruce's melancholy.

When, therefore, at about ten-thirty, the telephone rang, and, the doll having been snatched off it, she heard Gorse's nasal 'Hullo? . . .' she was made relieved and happy beyond measure.

She had already made up her mind as to what line she should take with Gorse about last night. She would boldly admit that she had had, or feared she had had, one 'over the eight', and had been a little 'squiffy' (the feminine Plumleigh-Bruce word for inebriation, and, pronounced as 'Squiffeh', suiting this particular feminine Plumleigh-Bruce's voice and accent to perfection).

She did this, and Gorse at once took advantage of her mistake in doing so. Instead of 'pooh-poohing' what she said, he took an 'Oh, well, we all have to sin some time' attitude, which aggra-vated Mrs Plumleigh-Bruce's distress and humiliation, and gave Gorse, temporarily, almost complete mastery over her. He told her that he knew exactly what she wanted, and asked her if he might bring it round that morning. He would not disclose the nature of his remedy, and Mrs Plumleigh-Bruce, less eager for physical alleviation of her condition than for his mere company, the chance to reinstate herself as a sober, well-bathed, well-groomed, well-dressed, disciplined, dignified woman, invited him to come round at twelve o'clock.

Gorse, accordingly, came round at twelve, and was received in the sitting-room. His remedy for Mrs Plumleigh-Bruce's con-dition was a bottle containing ready-prepared gin cocktails – the 'hair of the dog that bit you'. The pleasant-shaped bottle, with frosted-glass somehow suggesting ice and coolness of mind, was enticing without at first enticing Mrs Plumleigh-Bruce. She was shocked at the idea of drinking in the morning and might well have refused to do so had not Gorse somehow managed to put in a remark about the necessity of being able to 'take one's oats'.

To members of the Plumleigh-Bruce tribe there is, perhaps, no more horrible suggestion to be made than the one that they are unable to Take their Oats. They would be willing not to play with straight bats, not keep their chins up, let sides down, lose caste, and all the rest, rather than show this atrociously un-pukkahish weakness. Mrs Plumleigh-Bruce, therefore, was soon taking her oats, and liking it.

She was persuaded to drink two cocktails, and after that she went out to lunch with Gorse at the best restaurant in the town, where she drank wine and brandy.

In the evening they went to The Friar and drank with Mr Stimpson and Major Parry.

Mr Stimpson was told neither about the 'pot luck' they had taken last night, nor the drinks and lunch they had taken that morning. Mrs Plumleigh-Bruce, telling Gorse that she had not allowed Mr Stimpson to dinner the night before, made him promise not to reveal these things. Already, although no word had been spoken against either Mr Stimpson or Major Parry, there was a pleasant feeling of mildly conspiring against the two provincial men.

It was at this meeting in the evening at The Friar that Mr Stimpson had made those idiotic references to his 'quiet' evening in London with Gorse – thus putting violent suspicions into Mrs Plumleigh-Bruce's mind.

At this meeting, too, Gorse contrived to make Mrs Plumleigh-Bruce drink more than she thought she was drinking, and more than was good for her.

Gorse allowed Mr Stimpson to see her home, he himself being happy in the knowledge that he had a secret arrangement to call on her the next morning at twelve. Indeed he almost forced Mr Stimpson, who was in a lazy mood, to see her home – thus further charging with an electric air of conspiracy and naugh-tiness his relationship with Mrs Plumleigh-Bruce.

Gorse was round at Glen Alan next morning at twelve o'clock and both were drinking prepared gin cocktails from the frosted-glass bottle by a quarter past twelve.

Gorse felt, on this second morning of successfully tempting her to drink, that he had, as it were, really weighed anchor with this woman, and that the voyage had begun.

He was right. From that morning onwards there were few

mornings during which he did not drink cocktails at Glen Alan, and this curious combination between these two curiously ill-assorted people began to develop, in outline, signs of that finally almost weird aspect it was to assume.

CHAPTER THREE

BOTH Gorse and Mrs Plumleigh-Bruce were aware of the slight weirdness of what was happening – Mrs Plumleigh-Bruce supinely and apathetically, Gorse more consciously.

To begin with, Gorse, who was seldom at a loss with any woman, before long found himself in some ways a little out of his depth with Mrs Plumleigh-Bruce, and he decided to be cautious. He did not like being cautious with women.

His next move, with another sort of woman, would have been to exploit social and money snobbery to its utmost.

But with Mrs Plumleigh-Bruce (he sensed just in time) this move would be a bad one to play too quickly or too obviously.

Paradoxically enough, seen in a certain light the Plumleigh-Bruce tribe, though snobbish, is not snobbish – either monetarily or socially. It is too complacent to be so.

It will talk about people not coming, or (worse still) coming, out of the top drawer – it is drawer-conscious to an agonizing or revolting degree – and yet remains, in many ways, not snobbish.

Towards the industrial lower classes it is not even snobbish in any way. Its emotions towards these are those simply of bitter class-hatred. Towards the agricultural lower classes its attitude is condescending and patriarchal rather than snobbish: towards the middle trading classes it is merely disdainful: and towards the upper class – which it meets occasionally at bazaars, fêtes, flower-shows, etc. – its feelings are strangely neutral. It does not really think about the upper classes – it does not compare itself with it, and, while vaguely revering it, it makes little or no attempt to enter it or mix with it.

And the Plumleigh-Bruces are, with one exception, never social climbers.

The one exception lies in the direction of the Army. Here the mothers and daughters climb frantically, and the fathers and sons do the same thing – though less frantically because they simply regard doing so as the main business of their lives.

It has been said earlier that, with the Plumleigh-Bruces, there is always a *General* somewhere in the family. The General, it has been said, may be obscure or famous, a remote or close relation or connection, but there he is. A Plumleigh-Bruce without a General is not fully a Plumleigh-Bruce.

Our Mrs Plumleigh-Bruce herself had quite a good General within a reasonable distance. Her late husband's sister had married a man whose uncle was a General – General Sir George Matthews-Browne. Sir George, whom Mrs Plumleigh-Bruce had never met, and who was now dead, had received little publicity in the press during his life-time, but he was good enough for Mrs Plumleigh-Bruce, who, sooner or later, in any social acquaintance-ship she struck up with anyone, would drawlingly mention him. She had also acquired a photograph of this General, and put it into a silver frame on her mantelpiece.

Gorse, before long, was told about this General (who was made to seem much more nearly connected to Mrs Plumleigh-Bruce than he was), and he was considerably thrown out by him.

Gorse was thrown out because he had a General of his own up his sleeve – one whom he would, in the ordinary course of events, have played at this stage.

Gorse's General was both a false and true one – and Gorse had acquired him by a piece of wonderful good fortune. The General was false in that he was in no way related to Gorse, true in that he had in fact existed until a few years ago.

Indeed, General Sir Trevor Gorse had done more and better than exist. He had obtained, during a brief period, considerable publicity over a small but bloody civil-military encounter in India a few years after the 1914–18 War. General Gorse of Assandrava was never any rival, from a publicity point of view, to General Dyer of Amritzar, but all the same the press, during a 'silly' season, gave him a good deal of attention, and his countless foolish relations often endeavoured to put him on a level with the notorious Dyer.

Ernest Ralph Gorse, reading about him, and knowing that Gorse was by no means a common name, felt almost over-whelmed with his good luck. He decided without hesitation to unite his own family with that of the General, and he cut out from the newspapers every paragraph or photograph of the latter that he could find.

These cuttings, the most impressive of which he went to the extent of obtaining in duplicate or triplicate, he preserved carefully and cleanly, while making up his mind as to the precise nature of his kinship with the General.

Finally he decided to vary this according to the company in which he found himself, and hitherto, he had only used the General on three or four occasions, on only one of which, and then in low company, had he made the military hero his uncle. The General, he felt, was too fine a property to be expended frivolously or indiscriminately.

On his first meeting with Mrs Plumleigh-Bruce he had realized that she would be exquisitely susceptible to his General – indeed so exquisitely (and therefore inquisitively) susceptible, that the greatest caution would have to be used. He had, therefore, bided his time.

On learning, over morning cocktails at Glen Alan, of Mrs Plumleigh-Bruce's General – General Sir George Matthews-Browne – Gorse applauded himself warmly for his own reserve. He had very nearly sprung General Sir Trevor Gorse too early. Now, obviously, Sir Trevor must be held in reserve, or even abandoned. There were serious perils in throwing a General against a General, and, in any case, it would be unwise to make the atmosphere too Generally all at once. It would be infinitely shrewder to let, or cleverly make, Mrs Plumleigh-Bruce entirely exhaust her mantelpiece General – extend her mantelpiece General-communications to the fullest extent – and then hurl in his own with annihilating force.

2

And so Gorse, who at the same time was beginning to realize that Mrs Plumleigh-Bruce was not, as he had thought, an all-round social snob, decided altogether to abandon the exploitation of social snobbery just at present.

Herein lay another curious feature of the Gorse–Plumleigh-Bruce combination, for Gorse, unlike Mrs Plumleigh-Bruce, was a deep, burning, embittered social snob. Social snobbery, indeed, may conceivably have been his one true passion in life. Probably it far exceeded his love of money, which, perhaps, derived only from his ambition to appease his social aspirations.

And, next only to social snobbery, was Gorse's passion for anything to do with the 'Army'.

From early boyhood he had had a passion for military things and military uniforms, and, as the years passed, he had completely dropped his real parentage (his father had been a quite successful and in some circles quite well-known commercial artist) and turned his 'people' into 'Army People'. He had assisted himself in the task of robbing Esther Downes by impressing her with these 'Army People', and, since then, having spread the fiction so much, he had come almost mentally to accept this sort of thing himself.

He had, as has been seen, used it upon Mrs Plumleigh-Bruce on his first encounter with her, giving himself a romantic career in France in the 1914–18 War – and this (because such a thing was by now part of his being) without the slightest strain and practically believing what he was saying. (Later this passion for the 'Army' was to become almost pathological with Gorse, and to cause him to masquerade in uniform in the West End of London and elsewhere.)

And yet, here, with Mrs Plumleigh-Bruce, he was dealing with one who was paradoxically not only less snobbish generally than most women, but, disconcertingly, the genuine daughter and widow of a Colonel.

He saw that he must watch his step, and while doing so, listen to Mrs Plumleigh-Bruce and perhaps learn from her.

There was no harm, however, in continuing to play upon her cupidity, and so he now began to draw her attention to the house he occupied in Gilroy Road.

3

On the afternoon of the Tuesday following the Friday upon which she had been admittedly 'Squiffeh!', Mrs Plumleigh-Bruce went most sedately to tea with Gorse at the house lent to him at Gilroy Road.

The scones were, as he had promised at an earlier meeting at Glen Alan, indeed delicious: the housekeeper was respectable and respectful: and the house made a deep impression upon Mrs Plumleigh-Bruce.

For all her brass, maps, and ships at pebble-sprayed Glen Alan Mrs Plumleigh-Bruce knew at once that 21 Gilroy Road was, as a residence and in its furnishings, on an enormously higher and more solid level than her own.

She knew, perhaps, in her heart of hearts, that her own brass, maps, and ships were more or less defiance – whistling in the decorative dark; and the more Gorse (humbly seeking her advice in room after room, beseeching her to agree that the place was hopelessly old-fashioned, and pointing out every defect he could find or imagine) the more she was impressed. She told him as much.

After tea they walked to The Friar, and here Gorse made his first strange 'proposal' with his 'Or perhaps it might be yours – as well as mine' – quickly dropped.

Mr Stimpson had entered almost immediately after this, and Gorse had made a point of boldly and immediately disclosing the manner in which Mrs Plumleigh-Bruce and himself had spent the afternoon.

He asked Mr Stimpson if he would do him the same favour as Mrs Plumleigh-Bruce had done – that was to say, take a look over the house – and he made Mrs Plumleigh-Bruce and Mr Stimpson discuss the details of the house earnestly – Mrs Plumleigh-Bruce undertaking the describing, and Mr Stimpson undertaking the listening and nodding and abstruse commentary, and both getting rapturously above the head of the silent, pathetic seeker after knowledge – Gorse.

All three were very much annoyed when joined by Major Parry – who was talkative and not interested in house-property – decidedly mundane.

Later in the week Gorse made his second 'proposal' with his 'Unless yours and mine were one, you know' after a discussion, at Glen Alan, upon Life, and early in next week he had kissed Mrs Plumleigh-Bruce and assured her of the seriousness of his kiss.

In the week following Gorse had appeared at Glen Alan one morning in an extremely luxurious Vauxhall car which, he said, he was contemplating buying, and some days later, having covered considerable mileage in rambling and talkative drives in the country in this car, he had persuaded Mrs Plumleigh-Bruce to transfer five hundred pounds from a deposit account she held at the bank into a current account.

Finally, he had decided that the time had come to betray the secret of Mr Stimpson's night in London, and to make it absolutely clear to Mrs Plumleigh-Bruce that he desired to marry her. And, doing both at one sitting in the manner described, he had left her, in her sitting-room, to the intensity of her thoughts by the ashes of her fire.

4

The luxurious Vauxhall, the transfer of the money, the betrayal of Mr Stimpson's secret, and the proposal of marriage, were all cards played excellently and characteristically by Gorse.

But his ace of trumps, the General, had as yet been withheld.

PART NINE

THE DIARIST

CHAPTER ONE

I

THE painful fact must now be revealed that Mrs Plumleigh-Bruce kept a diary.

Worse still – in order to throw in their only true light Mrs Plumleigh-Bruce's real feelings about Gorse and his behaviour from the moment she first met him until she decided that she might, just, just conceivably, marry him, it is necessary to give extracts from this exceedingly embarrassing document.

Mrs Plumleigh-Bruce had, in fact, kept a diary most of her life – but only intermittently. Although in reality an inveterate diary-keeper, for long periods she would completely forget that she was one or even that she had ever kept one. But then, for some reason, the urge would return.

Two days after Gorse's revelations about Mr Stimpson, and his (as it seemed) firm proposal of marriage to herself, Mrs Plumleigh-Bruce's instincts subtly informed her that diary-time had come round again. And, happening to discover, in a Reading bookshop, a brown, suede-bound book containing blank pages, and upon the brown suede of which had been stamped, askew at the top and in gold, the simple but inviting words 'My Thoughts' – she had bought it with the intention both of thinking thoughts and making them endure within the brown suede.

The book had been intended, no doubt, for the use of schoolgirls – but Mrs Plumleigh-Bruce did not realize this. Nor did her style have any of the directness, pathos or simplicity of many schoolgirl diarists.

For, in the last seven years or so, Mrs Plumleigh-Bruce had begun strongly to fancy herself as a potential 'writer' (she meant, she had confided to Mr Stimpson and others, to 'write a novel one of these days') and those who acquire this fancy, without having the ability to write, are seldom either direct, pathetic or simple. Mrs Plumleigh-Bruce's more recent diaries, therefore, had been from the point of view of style, below the level of the average schoolgirl.

Also she made the mistake of adopting several different styles – sometimes as many as three in the same entry, and just as they suited her whim. In all these styles, however, four tricks were always cropping up – the use of alliteration, the use of ex-clamation marks, the use of inverted commas around words for no discernible reason, and the use of Wardour Street English gone mad. Also she was infatuated by a stupid use of the word 'very'.

The opening words of her first entry in the brown-suede diary were written in bed after Mary had brought her breakfast, and were, after she had given the date, cleverly instilled with a feeling of drama.

2

'Morning – of another day!' she wrote, in a paragraph all by itself.

The dash and the exclamation mark, of course, were what gave these words their dramatic and intriguing quality. It was as though days were rather unusual things, that days, in the normal course of life, did not necessarily follow days, and, somehow, that days did not always begin with mornings. She had made it clear, in fact, that something most interesting, if not alarming, was afoot.

'Morning,' she repeated, and then got into the narrative. 'Irish Maid Marian has left my room, leaving me with my thoughts – and my breakfast!'

(The dash and the exclamation mark here indicated not drama, but humour.)

'My thoughts! Round and round they go! In and out, to and fro, backwards and forth!

'Usually I chat with Irish Maid Marian at this time of day – chaff her and cheer her – cheat the churlish hour by asking and advising her about her childish concerns. But this morning Maid Marian was dismissed without a word, and here I am with my thoughts, committing them – seeking relief from very anguish of mind – to these pages.

'My thoughts. What shall I do? Whither shall I turn? What woman, ever, was in such woeful or wildering pass! Shall I or shall I not? Do I or do I not? Yes or no? Aye or Nay?

'I am loved. Yes, it seems that I am truly loved. But do I love? "Ay – there's the rub". And, did I love, have I the *right* to *love*?

'"He" is so young. "He" seems, at times, hardly more than a boy. And yet, at others, so worldly and mature.

'How has it all happened? It is less than a month ago since I first met him. I "took" to him at once, and he (as I now know to my very cost) indeed "took" to me!

'How shall I describe him? He is tall, fair, slim, and has a well-groomed, well-tubbed appearance. He wears a small moustache – the relict, no doubt, of his days in the Army. (He "wangled" his way in at the age of sixteen, by the way, and was endowed with the Military Cross for his services!)

'He has a cultured voice, an easy manner, tact, humour, and an "air" – all the things so sadly missing in the "gentlemen" I meet in Reading. He is a man of the world, too. When I first met him he had just returned from Paris, and he speaks French fluently.'

Mrs Plumleigh-Bruce, who had heard Gorse use only a few French expressions, who did not know anything whatsoever about his abilities in this direction (and knew that she did not), nevertheless could not resist making Gorse speak French fluently. There is a sort of woman who is intoxicated by the word 'fluently' in regard to their friends' skill in languages: it gives them, themselves, a vicarious, warm, superior, fluent feeling.

'He has money,' Mrs Plumleigh-Bruce went on, 'and he obviously knows how to handle it. Indeed – this "boy" is already handling mine! (He won me, by the way, twenty-five pounds by putting me on to a "good thing" at the races soon after I had met him, and now he is "keeping an eye" on my investments.)

'He runs a large Vauxhall car, and, on his own admission, "likes the good things of life".'

Mrs Plumleigh-Bruce, as in the case of Gorse's fluent French, could not refrain from making him 'run' a 'large Vauxhall car', although she knew, from his own lips, that he had only been driving it for about a week, that he had not paid for it, and was merely contemplating buying it.

Mrs Plumleigh-Bruce, of course, like most diary-writers of her kind, although seemingly making a detached statement, was in fact doing something else as well. She was writing a letter to an imaginary woman friend – a friend who was, occasionally, so disagreeable as to be almost an enemy – and with whom, therefore, it was necessary to hold one's own. With Gorse's fluent French and large car Mrs Plumleigh-Bruce was, as it were, tossing her head disdainfully at this friend, at whom, throughout, she was making incessant 'digs'.

'And do not I?' she continued, alluding to the good things of life. 'Alas, I know only too well that I do. I am, I often think, quite hopelessly spoiled, and I know full well that "he" would fain spoil me. There would, if I did what he asked – come now, let's be blunt and say if I "married" him – certainly be no lack of "the good things of life".

'Am I "commercial"? Am I a "gold-digger"? Have ever such thoughts ever entered my mind since first I knew, for certain, that he would, if he could, make me "his own". I sometimes think so.

'"Nay – out o' the thought! I am, at least, something of what he thinks I am. "Steel-true and blade-straight" he called me only the other night. For all his worldly wisdom my "boy" has strange "flashes" of poetry.

'Are we not, then, perfectly matched? Am I not worthy of him as he is of me? Sometimes I think that nothing shall stand in my way.

'And yet, and yet, and *yet*! Ever and anon creeps in that fatal "and yet"! The disparity of our ages – my doubts concerning my own feelings. Do I love him? Have I ever loved any man? Am I capable of love? 'Tis sometimes a matter of doubt, in very truth.

'Now, from sundry familiar sounds below, I gather that it is time for me to "raise me from my couch". Should I not, Maid

Marian will be impatient. Strange – how we are the "servants" of our servants! Yet so it must be, it seems.

'Maid Marian? Doth *she* languish and fret and doubt, as I do, o'er some dashing "Robin Hood" of her own? No doubt she doth. However, I must to my ablutions – or, in common parlance, my bath. Oh well. So let it be! Heigh-ho!'

At this, Mrs Plumleigh-Bruce, having rather unexpectedly found herself roaming in Sherwood Forest, closed her first entry in her diary, and went to her bath.

3

Drunk men sometimes show their drunkenness with lightning suddenness. Having been quite silent for a long while, they will all at once spring from their chairs, wrap themselves in floor rugs, balance things on their heads, use a falsetto voice, put their hands on their hips and imitate women, etc.

In very much the same way certain women, stimulated by the admiration of a man, will suddenly let it go to their heads, and behave, to themselves and to the man, with totally unbalanced vanity and coquetry. The next entry in Mrs Plumleigh-Bruce's diary, made next morning, showed that she was entering this phase of intoxication.

'Another day!' was the startling and astonished opening cry of Mrs Plumleigh-Bruce's entry.

It seemed as though the regular workings of the solar system were beginning to have some peculiar effect upon her nerves.

This morning, however, the temperamental writer was out of Sherwood Forest, and in the world of commerce.

'"He" came round yesterday morning for cocktails, and we talked, for once, business – just commonplace dreary business.

'And yet "he" has the gift of making even "business" interesting, and I ended up feeling quite excited. It seems that he has been put on to "a good thing" in the City, and is anxious for me to join him in "playing the market".

'He himself is investing heavily and was anxious that I too should have a little "flutter".

'I was certainly not averse to this, but was certainly dumb-founded when I learnt that by "a little flutter" he meant no less than two hundred pounds!

'Indeed, in my all-pervading hatred of business and "specu-lation" I argued with him for a long time, but he would not hear of my investing any smaller amount. It would not, he said, be worth while, and there was no sense in doing that sort of thing unless one does it in the "proper" way.

'I still argued, however, and seeing my reluctance, he at once dropped the matter. He never "forces" matters like this – that is what is so winning about him. He seems, at times, to have an almost uncanny insight into my temperament, and to know that it is useless to attempt to "force" Joan Plumleigh-Bruce into any line of action! – that she is a "tough proposition" and cannot be persuaded into anything against her will.

'But – poor boy! – he looked so sadly crestfallen! He could not disguise it! It was obvious that he had so wanted me to take a part in his speculation and share in its success – that he wants to link his life, in every way, with mine – even "financially".

'At last my heart melted and I said that I would "reconsider" the matter. I said that I could certainly not invest the amount he had suggested, but that I might "put in" a smaller sum, if he would give me time to think about it – and that I would give him my decision in the evening, when he came to dinner.

'And sure enough, after dinner, *his* will prevailed, and the stubborn Joan meekly followed his instructions in writing out a cheque for fifty pounds!

'And in doing this I do indeed feel myself more closely linked with him than ever. So much so that I ask myself if I have done wrong!

'Is this the "thin edge of the wedge"?

'Will I, at last, find myself inextricably bound to him?

'The investment – some sordid thing to do with "Chromium" or something – I have a note of it downstairs in my desk – is, as he calls it "safer than houses". One stands nothing to lose, and a good chance of reasonable gain in what he calls a "quick return". I trust him explicitly in business matters, but all the same in my feminine soul I hope the return will indeed be "quick"!

'After all, he "made" twenty-five pounds for me over "Stucco", and so, even if the "worst came to worst", I stand to lose only twenty-five pounds. In fact, if one works it out, I stand to lose absolutely nothing!'

Here Mrs Plumleigh-Bruce had tripped up on her simple arithmetic.

'And then he looked so boyishly happy, on my acceding to his request! Indeed so much so that I could not refrain from giving him a chaste kiss on his forehead!

'After which, needless to say, business was temporarily forgotten!

'Not that he took the smallest advantage, as most men would, of my impulsive, maternal gesture. He looked at me as if merely dazed with delight – so boyish! Indeed, looking at him standing there, I could not refrain from patting his cheek and making the exclamation "Boy!"

'This seemed to both "nettle" him and yet please him at the same time, and later, as we sat on the settee (I allowed him to hold my hand, which was all he attempted) I could not help "twitting" him with the ignominious expression "Boy!"

'Then, suddenly realizing I was in fact talking to a highly experienced man, and recalling his record in the war, I changed the epithet to "Soldier Boy!"

'He then accused me of mercilessly *"vamping"* him! *Was* I?

'I have something of the devil in me, perchance.

'But still he took no advantage of my "devilment", if such it was. Once, only once, did he kiss me. This was after I had said I intended to call him "Boy", or "Soldier Boy", from henceforth.

'His kiss was strange – something unknown to me before, and indeed refreshing to one who is used to the miserable muddled maulings of men. It was reserved, reticent, reverend. It was as though, indeed, I am in very truth a "little tin god" – or should I say "goddess"? – to him.

'He does not kiss me – he has *never* yet kissed me – in what I call "that way". He seems to know instinctively that I do not like being treated in "that way" at all.

'Soldier and man of the world that he is, he is curiously ethereal in some ways. Is it possible that here his nature matches mine? Is it possible that he, like myself, does not *think* in "that way"?

'Men have called me "frigid". The accusation has been hurled at me so often that I have almost come to believe it true. It has worried me.

'And yet what if I have found one who thinks not after such manner? – one who reveres what the world so contemptuously calls "frigidity" – one who is, in that coarse sense of the word, "frigid" himself? – one who worships at the shrine of Pure Beauty and High Companionship rather than the lewd and lecherous lust of those such as whose name I shall not allow even to sully these pages.'

Here, obviously, the wretched Mr Stimpson was being lashed at by Mrs Plumleigh-Bruce's merciless pen.

Although, Mr Stimpson – now made a pale, almost colourless figure by Gorse, did not enter her thoughts very much these days, Mrs Plumleigh-Bruce, occasionally remembering what he had said to Gorse, would get into uncontrollable rages with him.

'"Hogs" indeed!' continued Mrs Plumleigh-Bruce, in her sudden angry confusion of mind most unjustly thinking of Mr Stimpson, not as one who had merely suggested going the whole hog with her, but as one who had accused her of being a hog herself. 'Is it not *they* who are the hogs? Is it not *they* who have "feet of clay"?'

Appeased by this outburst Mrs Plumleigh-Bruce became more calm and elevated.

'Did not Plato exist?' she asked. 'And Socrates, what of him? Is there no such thing as Platonic relationship? And is it not possible that I have found one who sees eye-to-eye with me on this matter most vexed?

'And, if such were the case, would I not cast a different eye on the proposal he makes – an eye even more favourable than now it is? Certes, 'twould be a blessed boon.

'And so to my ablutions.'

By 'ablutions' Mrs Plumleigh-Bruce meant her bath, and by 'Platonic relationship' and a 'blessed boon' she meant a conceivable relationship with a prosperous young man in which, though married to him, she would seldom, if ever, have to fulfil the normal sexual obligations of marriage – perhaps the highest earthly good conceivable by women diarists of this kind.

4

In Mrs Plumleigh-Bruce's next entry there were no exclamations either against or about the solar system, to whose regularity and order she seemed to have become inured; and she began, instead, on a light, Restoration note with:

'Yesterday evening to the play, where we were vastly entertained!

'"Boy" (N.B. I am calling him "Boy" quite naturally already!) took us all in his car – the five of us – D.S., L.P. and wife, "Boy" and myself.'

(D.S. and L.P. were the initials of Donald Stimpson and Leonard Parry – the Major.)

'Twas the small theatre – "The Kemble" in the Oxford Road – run by young Miles Standish – our young acquaintance of The Friar. We had the best seats in the house, and, owing to "Boy's" influence, free of charge.

'"Boy" it seems, is interested in things theatrical – about which he knows much and in which he likes to "dabble" – and he is putting money into the little "Kemble" – hitherto, I gather, running at a loss or barely making a profit. "Boy" tells me that it could be made a "property" if run in the correct way, and that all it wants is "putting on its feet" in a businesslike manner. Poor young Miles Standish is hardly businesslike (he does not look it anyway) and so luck seems to have come his way.

'Both going and returning I sat in the back with D.S. and Mrs Parry – the latter seeing to it that her husband sat in the front with "the driver" – this obviously to keep an eye on me to prevent anything "taking place" between her spouse and myself in the darkness of the car!

'She had some justification, for, as I know to my cost from a certain episode the Christmas before last, the Major is not to be trusted in the back of a car! He made, on that memorable occasion, the most crude advances to me, thinking they were undetected by the others, and Mrs Parry was not going to permit a recurrence of such a thing!

'How she hates me – that thin, spinsterish, dried-up woman! And yet what have I done? Is it my fault that I undoubtedly attract men – that they make, willy-nilly, these monstrous attacks on me when given the chance? Is it my fault that I have been compelled to learn that I have that indefinable quality – "It"? – a gift more embarrassing than flattering in most cases, as I would like to assure her – who is so insanely jealous of it. Even at the theatre she saw to it that I was as far removed from poor L.P. as possible.

'The play? Trash. The acting? Good. Young Miles Standish

should go far if given the chance, and it seems as though, if "Boy" should take him up, he may yet find his way into the "West End" – that "Mecca" of the struggling actor.

'When the curtain had fallen, owing to "Boy's" influence, we all went round "behind the scenes". A fascinating and dis-illusioning experience – the tawdry paste-board scenery, the smell of grease and glue – the thick "make-up", the powder and pomades of the play-actors in their pokey little dressing rooms!

'I have often been told that I myself was "cut out" for "the boards" – maybe with some truth, for I could certainly have acquitted myself better than the so-called "Leading *Lady*" last night – but, seeing these "merry mummers" – these puppets from the other side of the "peepshow" – I felt grateful that I never succumbed to the temptation to try my hand in this direction.

'We were all treated with the greatest deference, however – this no doubt, being again due to "Boy's" influence as a prospective "backer".

'In the car going home I was forced to sit next to D.S. – who has, by the way, a streaming cold, which I have no doubt I shall catch. I do wish people would not inflict their sniffing proximity upon others when in this condition. Faugh – the fellow was very offence!'

5

The solar system was still kept at bay in Mrs Plumleigh-Bruce's next entry, from which the Restoration spirit had also dis-appeared. Instead there was a feeling of breathless, hothouse intrigue.

'Last night, bringing roses, he came.

'I chid him for his extravagance, but knew how useless it was.

'It was after I had dined, and Mary's evening off. We were both in childish playful mood – relieved, perhaps, by the absence of Mary – and I made him help me arrange the roses – a few of which I took up to my bedroom (they lie on my dressing table as I write) – allowing him, for the first time, to enter these "hallowed precincts".

'My bedroom – intensely feminine and furnished, I flatter

myself, a little more than fairly well – is my favourite, and I wondered how it would affect him.

'How different was his attitude to that of D.S. who, needless to say, always thought it beseeming, whenever he was permitted to enter it, to smear my sanctuary with leering and lewd approach.

'He looked round him shyly, strangely, as though ardent. eager, with ethereal awe. Then, without a word, he followed me out.

'In the more "prosaic" sitting-room we resumed our playful talk over coffee. Now I always call him "Boy" (or "Soldier Boy") and he has taken in gleeful impudence, to calling me "Bunny"! This is a reference to the shape of my mouth. He once told D.S. by the way, that I had the "loveliest mouth he had ever seen on any woman".

'I fear that before long I was mercilessly "vamping" him yet again! Poor boy – he simply asks for it! And, as he never takes advantage of it, I simply cannot resist the temptation to tease and torment him.

'I know it is wrong but can woman ever flee from her own femininity? I am but human. Besides, in a way, I know he likes it!

'Then suddenly, we became very serious, and solemn, and talked about "*That*". How it happened I know not, but I suppose I led him into it. His boyish burning eyes, combined with that strange severe, solemn, self-restraint, puzzled me, and I had to find the answer. I did.

'He said that he does not really feel "that way" about me. He says (as he has said before) that it would be "sacrilege". He said that he has never really, in his heart of hearts, felt "that way" about any woman – that he has a higher ideal. He said that he has betrayed that ideal in the past, but that with me things were different – that in me he had found the "perfect blend" – what he had always sought and waited for – the blend of the spiritual, the mental, and the physical.

'He said that my "beauty" at moments "fascinated, bewildered, maddened" him, but that he was content to let it remain thus. He said, at last, that if only I should consent to marry him, I would not be bothered in "that way" unless it was my own desire.

'Then, imploring me to marry him, the poor boy almost

completely broke down. He flung his head on my lap and seemed to almost sob.

'What was I to do – what say? At last, stroking his head, I whispered to him "My Soldier Boy" and reminded him that he was, after all, a Soldier.

'At this he pulled himself together and apologized.

'He said I had "taken the spine out of him" completely. Then, trying to throw off his emotion, he assumed a forced jocular tone and said "Well – what about a good stiff brandy?" He got one for both of us, and we talked gallantly about trivial matters before he left.

'Is it true? Is he indeed one of those rare beings who, in his own words, are content to worship from a distance, from afar?

'Or is he deluding himself? Wily Daughter of Eve that I am, I fear that he is. Should I marry him would not "that way", ere long, become uppermost in his mind? We women see deeply and look ahead.

'But, whatever the outcome, Eve must bathe. And so to my bath.

'Ah, well. The future will look after itself. And if it does not, who cares? Not I, I vouch, verily. Ho-la! then, and to my bath!'

CHAPTER TWO

I

A FOOLISH journalist, writing long afterwards about Gorse, said that he 'played incessantly upon the vanity, greed, and folly of women'.

The journalist was foolish, but he was here not totally inaccurate. To have spoken a more entire and exact truth he should have said not that Gorse played upon, but that he had the supreme gift of stimulating, the vanity, greed, and folly of women. These qualities having once been fully stimulated, it was hardly necessary for Gorse to play upon them: they practically played themselves.

The journalist might also have added that one of Gorse's finest gifts lay in his quick instinctive recognition of vain, greedy, or foolish women. The wretched Esther Downes might with some justice have been called all these things, though her age and the circumstances fully excused her, as they certainly did not with Mrs Plumleigh-Bruce.

The vanity, greed, and folly of Mrs Plumleigh-Bruce 'Heighhoing' and 'Ho-laing' to her bath, had now, clearly, been stimulated to excess, were indeed violently over-active, and Gorse had, henceforth, little more to do than play a quietly encouraging and passive part.

Gorse, later, had the pleasure of reading Mrs Plumleigh-Bruce's diary. She was unaware that he had done so, but there were, in fact, hardly any documents belonging to Mrs Plumleigh-Bruce which Gorse did not somehow gain access to and read.

Gorse's pleasure in Mrs Plumleigh-Bruce's sprightly out-pourings did not derive from his sense of humour: for Gorse – though gay, debonair, and full of jokes – was, like Mrs Plumleigh-Bruce, entirely without humour.

He saw nothing particularly funny even in her style. His pleas-

ure arose, rather, from the profound satisfaction with which he
was able to retrace, step by step, the absurdly easy success of his
psychological and other devices.

She had, to begin with, simply gobbled up his premature enlistment in the Army, his Military Cross, and his Parisian sophistication. (Gorse was a little worried on reading that he spoke
French 'fluently', for he feared he might have to live up to this.)

Then she had swallowed, seemingly without any difficulty, a
rather difficult mixture to put down any patient's throat – the
mixture of a belief in his 'boyishness' and a belief in his astuteness, prosperity, and solidity as a businessman.

But he had done it. ('He has money and he obviously knows
how to handle it. Indeed this "boy" is already handling mine!')

Gorse had been rather surprised by the facility with which he
had made her remove five hundred pounds from a deposit to a
current account, and he put it down to the fact that he had not
really any formulated motive in making her do so. It was not, as
yet at any rate, any part of his major plan, and so he had not
been forced to be in the smallest way too persuasive.

He had also been surprised by the ease with which he had
made her put fifty pounds into his imaginary 'good thing' in the
City.

He had originally intended that she should refuse to invest
anything, and that he should look 'crestfallen' because of her
refusal. But when she had offered him a cheque, made out to
himself, for fifty pounds, he had thought it best to take it. He
had now recovered, he realized, the money which he had given
her on the mythical bet on *Stucco*, and was twenty-five pounds
in hand. This twenty-five pounds ought, he thought, roughly to
cover his general expenses in dealing with her.

Gorse took no self-congratulatory pleasure in her blithe
creation of him as one who 'ran' a large Vauxhall car. This had
been child's play.

The car, in fact, belonged to his friend Ronald Shooter, still
safely in Paris, and had been lent to him along with the house
and the housekeeper in Gilroy Road.

Here, however (as was not the case in making her invest
money), Gorse had a definite design in mind.

Gorse had also liked the internal evidence given of the relish
Mrs Plumleigh-Bruce had taken in his imaginary interest and

monetary speculation in the small local repertory theatre – 'The Kemble'.

Gorse, as has been said earlier, liked the theatre both for its own sake and for the curiously strong effect an assumed esoteric knowledge about it – an assumed power 'behind the scenes' – had upon human nature.

He had, therefore, gone to some trouble in cultivating the acquaintance of Miles Standish, to whom he had spoken on his first night at The Friar.

The young actor, it will be remembered, had not liked Gorse at all at this first meeting. He had, in fact, suspected that Gorse was up to no good in life generally, and that he was possibly destined to see the inside of prison bars.

Struggling young repertory actors, however, have no objection to being backed financially, and when Gorse, in subsequent talks, suggested that he might do this, Miles Standish, without exactly altering his view of Gorse, was not so foolish as not to listen to him.

Gorse talked in a big way, and was extremely plausible – and plausible, for once, not of his own volition.

For Gorse, with the slightly 'silly ass' air which his monocle bestowed upon him, did look, in fact, like a typical vain and foolish backer of plays.

Young Standish, indeed, soon began to take Gorse most seriously as a possible backer – looking upon him in the remote recesses of his mind, as a perfect example of this sort of 'sucker'.

Not that Miles Standish was being in any way dishonest or meaning to take advantage of Gorse. Struggling young repertory actors believe too fervently in themselves and their prospects ever to entertain the conscious thought that their backers can suffer – or, at any rate, the thought that their backers can suffer in anything but a noble cause.

2

But, above all, Gorse, in reading Mrs Plumleigh-Bruce's diary, was pleased by the internal evidence it gave of his success as a 'boy' – a boy being 'mercilessly vamped', 'twitted', and 'curiously ethereal in some ways'.

He had sensed, at an early stage, that Mrs Plumleigh-Bruce

was all but sexless, and as soon as he had got really to grips with her, he had set to work to achieve the paradoxical feat of stimulating – along with her greed, vanity and folly – her sexlessness. She was, he thought, quite vain, foolish and greedy enough to have this trick played upon her.

It was rather difficult, he had found at first, to be burning with subdued physical passion and curiously ethereal at the same time, but after a while, with her aid, the task had become easy.

And so he had permitted himself to be sadly crestfallen, vamped, twitted, wrongfully encouraged, maternally and impulsively kissed, dazed, nettled, allowed to hold her hand, bewildered, reserved, reticent, reverend, teased, tormented, ardent, eager and awed, to Mrs Plumleigh-Bruce's heart's content.

As he was in no way physically attracted towards the woman, and she was in no way physically attracted to him, it suited both (he reflected philosophically) down to the ground.

PART TEN

DEBATE

CHAPTER ONE

I

T HEY *are at rest, they are at rest, they are at rest*
or
    They are at rest – rest – long long ago at rest.

The Major, sitting alone in the Plumleigh-Bruce nook at The
Friar, at about six-fifteen, was again grappling with November
the Eleventh.

Of the two lines the Major fancied the latter – 'They are at
rest – rest – long long ago at rest'. As opposed to the other it
had a sort of onomatopoeic, marching lilt (Left – left – Left,
right, left) which he had been anxious to introduce for a long
time.

But one moment. *How* long, to be precise, *had* they been at
rest? The Major had to face the fact that it was hardly ten years,
taken all in all. Was that long, long ago? It wasn't. But one
mustn't fuss. It was long enough – damn it. Get on with it for
Heaven's sake.

What did you do with them now they were at rest? He had
some ideas for rhymes, but they somehow didn't get him anywhere. There was 'jest' (Fate's grim . . .) and there was 'lest' (We
shall not forget them . . .). But we shall not forget them lest *what*?
Lest something rather awful happens to us, presumably – but the
Major beat his brains in vain for any sort of majestic retribution

rhyming with 'rest'. Best? Zest? Guest? Messed? Confessed? Test? Pest? West? Crest?

The Major thought he would leave this for the moment and consider another stanza whose opening line had come to him only this morning while shaving.

They have fled – they have fled – they have fled.

Now – surely – if he could not do something, perfectly simple, with 'bled', 'dead', and 'Poppies red', then his gift had altogether deserted him.

Nevertheless the Major, after five minutes of intense concentration, and after having considered 'bed' (earthy), 'fed' (worms), 'led', 'head', 'said' ('twas or 'tis), 'wed' and 'dread' – had made no progress of any sort.

This was all very infuriating, and the Major, to console himself, re-read a stanza, probably the concluding one, which he had composed last night and which he believed definitely would do, with a little touching up.

> *Shall we, then, fail those who did not us fail*
> *Amidst the splintering tumult of War's gale –*
> *At Ypres, at Arras and at Passchendaele –*
> *And did not yield?*

There were only two little bits of trouble here. He wanted to underline the 'us'. But how could you do this without using italics? An impermissible device, surely?

And he did not like the two 'dids' – 'did not us fail', and 'And did not yield'. The last line, because of this, was a hopeless anticlimax, was it not?

The Major worked for another five minutes, this time with greater success, indeed almost with inspiration. Had he got it?

> *Shall we, then, fail, those who did deign to fail,*
> *Amidst the splintering tumult of War's gale –*
> *At Ypres, at Arras, and at Passchendaele –*
> *Nor dreamed to yield?*

This, the Major thought, was pretty well perfect, and he was particularly pleased at having at last got in Ypres and Passchendaele. He was a little worried about the order, in time, of the scenes of action – Ypres, Arras, and Passchendaele. But he could look this up – and what did it matter, anyway?

So pleased was the Major with himself that he began, foolishly, to dally with improvements on what he considered almost perfection.

What about making it *Mars*' great gale instead of War's? And what about the *screaming* tumult, the *thundering* tumult, the *moaning* tumult?

Mr Stimpson at this moment entered the bar, and greeting the Major, ordered his beer from the barmaid.

The Major, putting away pencil and paper, prepared to talk to the man, angry at being interrupted in a fine creative mood.

2

'Well, you're a stranger all right,' said the Major. 'Very nice to see you. How are we, now we're on our feet again?'

Mr Stimpson was indeed a stranger, not having entered The Friar, or seen the Major, for more than two weeks.

Two days after the night upon which all five – Mrs Plumleigh-Bruce, Major and Mrs Parry, Mr Stimpson and Gorse – had gone to the theatre, Mr Stimpson's ('Faugh – the fellow was very offence!') cold had developed into influenza, and he had been forced to take to his bed.

Very nearly three weeks, indeed, had passed since Mr Stimpson had seen either Mrs Plumleigh-Bruce or Gorse, and he had come into The Friar on this, his first evening out – with the vague hope of meeting them. He had given a lot of thought during his illness, to these two, and had imagined, correctly, that they had been into The Friar a good deal.

His impulse, on sitting down beside the Major, was at once to ask about 'Our Lady Joan' (whom he had once or twice telephoned from his sick-bed) but pride withheld him from doing so.

Instead he asked the Major, as usual, about the news generally, and before long they were, again as usual, One-abouting each other.

A man who has lain in bed for a fortnight must not only necessarily be rather weak physically (and therefore less agile mentally and vocally than usual); he has also not been in a position to have heard ones about anybody at all – certainly not the 'latest' – and, one-aboutedly speaking, he is impotent, atrophied.

The Major, sensing his late tormentor's weakness, took cruel and horrible revenge. Stocked with a fortnight's Ones About – all fresh from the oven of businessmen's lunch-time conversation over drinks – he struck mercilessly at Mr Stimpson – beginning with the One About the Page Boy and the Bishop, the One About the Shop Assistant at Selfridge's who had a Cold, the One About the Young Plumber of York (limerick), and the One About the Old Gentleman who had Climbed Mount Everest.

This Old Gentleman 'reminded' the Major of the One About the Hypnotist who went to Blackpool, who, again, reminded him of the Old Lady who went to Tussaud's, who, yet again, reminded him, firstly of The Centipede with a Wooden Leg, secondly of The Girl in the Lift, thirdly of the Old Man of Cape Peele (limerick again), and, finally, of The Chairmender who Went to Buckingham Palace.

Mr Stimpson, now totally deflated, feebly attempted to make the Chairmender who went to Buckingham Palace remind him of The Billiard-Player who saw a Ghost in Bed, but not being able fully to recall the anecdote, he fumbled at its beginning, and was smashed to pieces by the Major, who had no qualms in interrupting him, with the One About the New Chauffeur and the Duchess, and the One About the Piano-tuner who was Taken to a Night Club in Montmartre.

Mr Stimpson made no further attempt to retaliate, and the Major, seeing his complete and pathetic exhaustion, had pity on him and related no further anecdotes.

They spoke of other matters, and before long Mr Stimpson asked after 'our Lady Joan'.

'Oh – she's all right,' said the Major.

'Been in here a lot?' asked Mr Stimpson.

'Yes. Quite a lot,' said the Major. 'Mostly with young what's-his-name. They seem to be getting very thick – those two.'

'What do you mean by "thick", exactly?' Mr Stimpson could not resist asking.

'Oh – they just seem to be going about a lot together. He's still gadding about in that huge great Vauxhall of his, by the way. How he gets all his money – that boy – I don't know – but he certainly knows how to find it somewhere.'

'Yes. It beats me, too,' said Mr Stimpson, who had given

this matter much thought during his illness, and who was not as happy about the friendship between Gorse and Mrs Plumleigh-Bruce as he had been. He had not minded, indeed he had, as is known, enjoyed Gorse's worshipping Mrs Plumleigh-Bruce from afar on the old basis. But worshipping from afar in a large Vauxhall car, and in Mr Stimpson's absence, was less pleasing.

'Well – how are you?' said the Major, changing the subject. 'And what on earth did you do with yourself in bed all that time?'

'Oh – read a bit – and thought,' said Mr Stimpson. 'Thought mostly. I was pretty bad at one time, and one gets thinking, you know – thinking seriously.'

'Yes – I suppose one does. And what did *you* think about?'

'Oh, Life, and one's soul, and one's past, and one's future, and all that.'

Mr Stimpson, like most people who are seldom ill, had seriously entertained during his illness the thought that he was going to die, and had, indeed, been looking into the matters of his soul and the universe with more care and at greater length than he had for years.

'That's bad,' said the Major. 'Nobody ever got anywhere by thinking about their soul.'

'Well – one's got to think about it some time, hasn't one?'

'Has one?' said the Major. 'I never did. *Why* has one?'

'Well – one's got to meet one's Maker – or Creator, or whatever you care to call it – sooner or later, I take it – hasn't one?'

'Has one?' said the Major, heartily. 'I don't really see why.'

The Major, it may be said, was not only constitutionally unreflective and determinedly irreligious (Armistice Day poems excepted); he was, at this period, sharply anti-clerical as well – this owing to his hated wife having recently come under the influence of a popular local clergyman and having taken to going to Church at unusual and highly inconvenient hours. He was therefore in no mood for this sort of thing from Mr Stimpson, who, however, rashly persisted.

'Don't be silly,' he said. 'One's got to believe in Something – hasn't one?'

'Has one?' said the Major, rudely. 'What?'

'Well – *Something*, that's all,' said Mr Stimpson. 'There's got

to be a Reason somewhere – hasn't there? There's got to be a
First Cause, you know. You can't get away from that, at any
rate.'

'Can't you?' said the Major, more rudely still. '*I* can.'

'Well, then, you're cleverer than most people,' said Mr
Stimpson, faintly beginning to lose his temper. 'Who Caused
you, for instance?'

'My mother and father, so far as I know,' said the Major.

'Yes. And who Caused them?' asked the shrewd logician. 'May
I ask?'

'You certainly may. My grandfather and grandmother. And a
very nice old couple they were too. Though the old boy used to
drink like a fish.'

'Of course, now you're simply trying to treat serious matters
in a spirit of levity,' said Mr Stimpson.

'A spirit of what?'

'Levity was the word I used,' said Mr Stimpson, heavily.

'That's a new one on me,' said the Major. 'I've heard of Spirit
Levels, of course. In fact I've used them. But Spirits of Levity
aren't much in my line. However, you were talking about my
grandmother and grandfather. Go on.'

'I was *not* talking about your grandmother and grandfather,'
said Mr Stimpson, with great testiness, for his temper was
growing rapidly worse. 'I –'

'Then who were you talking about? That's what I thought you
were talking about.'

'I was talking about *Things*. I was talking about the First
Cause!' said Mr Stimpson, and added, more quietly and sar-
donically, 'Your grandmother and grandfather weren't the First
Cause, you know.'

'I didn't say they were. I certainly *hope* they weren't anyway,'
said the unchastened Major. 'Go on, then. What *is* the First
Cause?'

'The First Cause of *Things* – the First Cause of the *Universe*.
May I ask who you imagine First Caused the Universe?'

'Ask me another,' said the Major. 'Who?'

There was a pause.

'Look here,' said Mr Stimpson, trying to regain his composure.
'Who makes a Watch?'

'A watch-maker, I presume.'

'Very well, then,' said Mr Stimpson. 'There you are.'

'Where?' asked the Major.

'Well – if a watch-maker makes a watch – the First Cause made the Universe – that's all.'

'Why?'

'Really. This is absurd,' said Mr Stimpson. 'If you can't see –'

'I really can't see what watch-makers have got to do with the Universe,' said the Major, interrupting Mr Stimpson again. 'And even if they have, who made the watch-maker who made the watch, and who made whoever it was who made the watch-maker?'

Mr Stimpson decided to dodge this.

'And who,' he said, 'keeps the Watch Going? Can you tell me that?'

'The mainspring, I take it. Or it always did when I was a boy.'

'Precisely. The Mainspring. I'm talking about the Mainspring of the Universe. I couldn't have put it better myself. And who winds and regulates the watch? It doesn't wind and regulate itself, does it?'

'I don't know. Why shouldn't it? You haven't been reading Paley's Evidences, or anything like that, have you?'

Mr Stimpson, who had never heard of Paley's Evidences, implied that he had by replying that he didn't see what Paley's Evidences had to do with it, and that all he wanted to know was Who Started it all.

'All what?'

'The Universe!' shouted Mr Stimpson in his anger. 'Who starts a *car*? It doesn't start *itself* – does it? Even *you* couldn't make a car start by itself – could you?'

'Well – I could if I had a self-starter,' said the Major. 'And anyway I always get other people to start the cars *I* go in. That's one of the advantages of not having a car of one's own, and travelling in other people's.'

'Are we talking about Cars?' said Mr Stimpson, with an extremely deceptive air of calm. 'Or are we talking about the Universe?'

'I don't know,' said the Major. 'We were talking about my grandmother and grandfather not so long ago. So what *are* we talking about? Cars, or my grandmother and grandfather, or the Universe? Or Watches?'

'We were talking about the *Universe*,' said Mr Stimpson. 'Cars and Watches are completely irrelevant.'

'Irrelevant or Irreverent?'

'Irrelevant,' said Mr Stimpson. '*And* irreverent. Both.'

'Oh dear,' said the Major. 'I know what you're trying to talk about.'

'What?'

'God,' said the Major. 'I've seen it coming on for a long while.'

'And may I ask,' said Mr Stimpson, in his rage thinking that the longer he made his words the icier they would be. 'May I ask what Harm there may Accrue in peacefully discussing so major a topic as that of the first Creator and Originator of the Firmament in which it so *happens* that we *happen* to dwell – in other words, the Deity?'

But the Major was not frozen. He had, however, now lost his own temper too.

'No harm at all,' he said. 'But it so "happens" that I "happen" to think that it "happens" to be silly to "happen" to talk about the Deity – as you "happen" to put it – in a public house and over quiet drinks.'

At this ridiculing of his use of the word 'happen', Mr Stimpson completely lost control. Having taken another sip at his beer, he banged down his glass on the table, and said, with a livid air of resignation:

'Very well. *I* don't mind. It doesn't bother *me*. It's the old story. "The Fool hath said in his Heart" ... Yes. The Fool hath said in his heart ... I needn't go on ...'

'Meaning I'm a fool?' said the Major. 'Go on. Say it.'

'I'm neither saying nor meaning anything,' said Mr Stimpson. 'I'm merely *thinking*.'

'Well – if you're not saying or meaning anything, why go to the trouble of saying it?'

'Oh dear,' said Mr Stimpson. 'The Fool hath said. The Fool hath said ... Oh – dear. Oh dear ... Dear me ...'

The voices of both were now raised, and other people in the Saloon Bar of The Friar (which was still empty enough for the overhearing of conversations at almost any distance) realized that a terrible row about God was going on between two men. These people stopped talking and listened eagerly.

Unfortunately for these listeners, at this moment Mrs Plumleigh-Bruce and Ernest Ralph Gorse entered the bar, and gaily greeted the two angry men.

CHAPTER TWO

I

BECAUSE of Mr Stimpson's recent illness – because he had not been seen for so long, and his call at The Friar tonight was a surprise one, the greetings were much gayer and noisier than usual, and an apparently happy quartet completely took the stage previously occupied by the two dangerously angry adversaries.

The listeners to the latter soon, but with intense annoyance and disappointment, resigned themselves to what had happened – the fact that a bitter religious war had been replaced by a smiling and loquacious reunion – and, after watching and listening with faces which made no attempt to conceal their unhappiness, returned to talk, in a lifeless way, to each other once more.

Before long, however, Mrs Plumleigh-Bruce and Gorse, who were in exceptionally high spirits, began to notice that these were not shared by the two men, who, when the first necessity for superficial cordiality had passed, sank back into a condition of sullen and smouldering contemplation of their recent dispute.

So obvious did this become at last that Mrs Plumleigh-Bruce, who was in even higher spirits than Gorse, was so bold as to remark upon it.

'You two seem to be very quiet tonight,' she said. 'Is anything the matter?'

'No. Nothing's the matter,' said Mr Stimpson giving, as he always did, the show away. 'Nothing's the matter at all. Nothing.'

'Now then, Donald, I know you,' said Mrs Plumleigh-Bruce. 'Come along now. What is it? Or is it just depression after flu?'

'No. Nothing like that. My friend here and I have just been engaged in a slight argument – that's all.'

'Really. What about? Have you been quarrelling? What's the argument. Come along, Leonard,' she said, addressing the Major. '*You* tell me.'

'Oh. It wasn't anything, really,' said the Major. 'I've just been having Paley's Evidences and Watches thrown at me, that's all . . . It doesn't bother *me* . . .'

At this injustice all Mr Stimpson's anger returned. Nor was he able to subdue it in the smallest way.

'*Me* throw Paley's Evidence and Watches at *you*!' he exclaimed. 'That's a good one – I must say – from someone who threw Paley's Evidences at me.'

'*I* didn't throw Paley's Evidences,' said the Major.

'What did you do, then? *I* didn't start Paley's Evidences – did I? You started them – didn't you?'

'No – I didn't start them. I just mentioned that you might have been reading them – that's all. And you certainly started throwing Watches.'

'Really,' said Mrs Plumleigh-Bruce. 'What *is* all this about?'

'To say nothing of Cars,' added the Major.

'Look here,' said Mr Stimpson. 'If a man can't mention Watches and Cars without being accused of throwing them at people – things have come to a very strange pass.'

'What *are* you two talking about?' said Mrs Plumleigh-Bruce.

'It's all perfectly simple,' said Mr Stimpson. 'I just happened to mention that somebody has to make a watch and somebody has to start a car – but he doesn't agree with me. What do *you* think?'

'Well, of course, somebody has to. But what are you arguing about?'

'Yes. *I* know someone's got to start cars. But all I was asking,' said the Major, 'was who started the starter, and who started the starter of the starter, and who started the starter of the starter of the starter? That's simple enough, isn't it?'

'Oh – I see,' said Gorse. 'You've been getting on to first causes, I take it.'

'To *The* First Cause,' said Mr Stimpson. 'The First Great Cause – that's all. In which, odd as it may seem, it so occurs that I chance to believe in. That's all.'

'And for which I got called a fool for daring to not believe in. Yes. That's all.'

'I did *not* call you a fool,' said Mr Stimpson.

'What did you call me, then?'

'I said The Fool in his Heart,' said Mr Stimpson. 'Saying The Fool in his Heart isn't calling somebody a fool – is it? It's just saying The Fool in his Heart – isn't it?'

The two were now once more calling attention to themselves, thus renewing the hopes of the outside listeners – and Mrs Plumleigh-Bruce, noticing this, cut in.

'Well it all sounds very foolish to me,' she said. 'Let's change the subject – shall we?'

'Willingly!' said Mr Stimpson, with passionate eagerness. But it was easy to see that the man was not passionately eager to do so.

2

In about three minutes' time, Mr Stimpson, having been questioned solicitously about the details of his illness, and his present state of health, by Mrs Plumleigh-Bruce, was more or less appeased, and (the Great First Cause, Watches and Cars rapidly occupying a more distant and diminished place in his thoughts), he returned to what had been very much in the forefront of his mind during the last fortnight – Mrs Plumleigh-Bruce and Gorse.

'Well – don't let's go on about me, and my ailments,' he said. 'What have *you* been up to – the two of you? Gadding gaily about, I take it?'

At this a rather curious look (not unnoticed by Mr Stimpson) took place between Mrs Plumleigh-Bruce and Gorse, who were both silent for about two seconds longer than they might have been.

It was as though, Mr Stimpson thought, they had news of some sort to break, and that neither knew who should do the breaking.

Mr Stimpson – always more shrewd and sensitive about matters concerning Mrs Plumleigh-Bruce than about most others – was correct in his surmise, and it was Gorse who undertook the announcement of the news.

'Yes,' he said, with a joviality which did not deceive Mr Stimpson. 'Gadding gaily and giddily about. And *she* is going to gad, so far as I can gather – egad even more gaily and giddily than ever, before many moons.'

'Oh – really? In what way, and in how many moons?' said Mr Stimpson, looking intently through his thick-lensed spectacles at Mrs Plumleigh-Bruce, who was therefore obliged to speak.

'Well, before *any* moon, really,' she said, with a nervousness almost entirely foreign to her. 'In fact the day after tomorrow to be precise.'

'And whither gaddest thou, pray?' said Mr Stimpson, noticing her nervousness and trying to increase it. But here Gorse took over again.

'She gaddest to the gay city – so far as I learn,' said Gorse. 'To the Metropolis – to the very centre of gadding and gaiety. Is that not so?' He appealed to Mrs Plumleigh-Bruce.

Gorse's 'So far as I learn' and 'Is that not so?' augmented rather than removed Mr Stimpson's general suspicions, and he made up his mind to get at the truth by blunt questioning.

'Oh – really?' he said. 'And for how long?'

'Oh – about a week,' said Mrs Plumleigh-Bruce.

'And where are you staying?'

'Oh – where I always do – the good old "in-laws" at Wimbledon. Very little gadding there.'

'And what made you suddenly decide to do this?'

'Oh – one's got to make a change,' said Mrs Plumleigh-Bruce. 'And they've been asking me for so long I can't very well go on refusing.'

'And you?' said Mr Stimpson, turning ruthlessly to Gorse. 'Are you gadding at the same time?'

'Oh – dear me, no,' said Gorse. 'I'm staying more or less put."

'More?' said Mr Stimpson, most unpleasantly. 'Or less?'

'*More*, on the whole,' said Gorse, in a detached way. 'Though I'm not saying that I propose to stay absolutely put. In fact I hope to be in London myself for a night or two at least. In which case couldn't we *all* foregather? Couldn't we have another drink at The King's or something? And then do something a little more exciting afterwards than we did previously?'

At this Gorse looked Mr Stimpson in the eye in a way which Mr Stimpson did not like. The reminder of that evening in London, in fact, together with this look, had the effect Gorse desired. Mr Stimpson, knowing what Gorse could reveal, dropped his cross-examining manner at once.

'Well,' he said. 'It might not be a bad idea. But what sort of thing?'

'Oh – a show – or something like that,' said Gorse.

'Yes. Sounds all right to me,' said Mr Stimpson, meekly, and here the conversation was changed.

3

Not a word of it, *not* a WORD of it, thought Mr Stimpson, lying awake in bed just after three o'clock next morning.

He knew what they were up to. *He* knew what they were up to all right.

Those two were going gadding about London together.

He knew what they were up to all right. *They* needn't think they could try and fool *him*.

He saw the whole thing, from beginning to end, through and through.

But Mr Stimpson, even in the horrible clarity of the black fourth hour of the day, was seeing the thing neither from beginning to end nor through and through – for he was unaware that Gorse and Mrs Plumleigh-Bruce proposed to spend a week in London together at the same hotel, that Gorse had several times proposed marriage to Mrs Plumleigh-Bruce, and that Mrs Plumleigh-Bruce had finally (and less than twelve hours ago) accepted Gorse's proposal joyously.

PART ELEVEN

GORSE OF ASSANDRAVA

CHAPTER ONE

I

HAVING worked herself up to 'Ho-lahing' to her bath in that last entry, Mrs Plumleigh-Bruce seemed to have been infected by the romping, fickle, carefree spirit of her own words, and had neglected her diary altogether from that time until nearly two weeks afterwards.

But three days before she went with Gorse into The Friar and was cross-examined by the sceptical Mr Stimpson, she had felt an impulse to resume it.

The cause of this impulse revealed itself at an early stage in the entry.

The solar system was, apparently, still slightly exercising Mrs Plumleigh-Bruce's mind – but this time less because of the regularity of its motions than because of its having suddenly speeded up.

'Day follows day in maddening whirl!' she began. ''Tis – how long? – near a fortnight surely – since I last put pen to my paltry thoughts on paper!'

The day-whirled woman then sharply contradicted herself.

'Nothing has happened,' she continued. 'All goes on as before – except that D.S. has caught influenza, and has "taken" to his bed. I thought that night at the theatre that such might be his fate.

'I wish the man no ill, but must say that, in my present predicament, his "room" is somewhat preferable to his "company".

For "Boy" is ever-present and I have long been fearful of some clash between these two. "Boy" cannot bear the man after those remarks he made concerning me, and "Boy", for all his outward calm, has a fiery spirit.

'And D.S., too, had he been present to witness to what extent these days "Boy" dances daily attendance on me, might well have been spurred to jealousy. For after all the man loves me – in his brutish, boorish way.'

Now Mrs Plumleigh-Bruce revealed her real motive in resuming her diary, which was, at times, it will be remembered, also an imaginary letter to a disagreeable woman friend with whom it was necessary to hold one's own, or to snub. From this woman friend there was a piece of news too glorious to be withheld.

Mrs Plumleigh-Bruce did not disclose this news crudely. She cleverly pretended to have forgotten about it, and then, more or less by a happy chance, to have remembered it.

'What, then, has been happening since I last covered these pages with my scrawl?' she wrote. 'Let me see.

'Ah – yes! A morsel of mighty interest! And that gleaned only yesterday morn!

'"Boy", it seems, is a close relation of the famous *Gorse of Assandrava*! He is his nephew! When I say "is" I should say "was", of course, for the great soldier, alas, as all know, is no more.

'It is funny how many people have not heard of "Gorse of Assandrava". They forget so easily. I myself was somewhat "vague" about him, but as soon as "Boy" mentioned him – which he did quite casually and by accident – I remembered the Assandrava "episode" and the General's heroic firmness and decisiveness in that "gruelling" dilemma.

'"Boy" was surprised by the intense interest I showed, and brought, in the evening, sundry "cuttings" he had preserved from old newspapers, and "illustrated weeklies", recalling the story and giving pictures of the General – to whom, by the way, "Boy", if one looks closely, bears a likeness most remarkable!

'I told "Boy" that he should indeed be proud, and asked him why he had not told me before. He seemed to think there was no reason for him to have done so. "Boy" is curiously reticent in some ways. He does not believe, as I have learned time and again, in "putting his goods in the shop window".'

Here Mrs Plumleigh-Bruce, having crushed her woman friend with wonderful delicacy yet thoroughness, suddenly began to talk to herself in a manner much too candid for the eye of anyone – least of all any woman friend.

'One can be too reticent, I sometimes think, for I have to admit that this belated "disclosure" in some ways put "Boy" up in my estimation – made me see him in quite a "new light" indeed!

'Although I have often subtly "pumped" him, "Boy" has always been very reserved about his "forebears" – to such an extent that I have even sometimes thought that he has a "skeleton in the cupboard", or that he secretly felt that he might lose favour with me by being forced to reveal that he does not emerge from – well, what shall we say? – *quite* the top drawer?

'And (I must 'fess to my shame!) I have sometimes had faint, fleeting doubts concerning this myself.

'When I first met him I was in doubt about him. His bearing and voice were, of course, vastly superior to anything I have met amongst men in this town (with the exception perhaps of L.P.) – but for a long while I wondered whether he was really in any way "our sort".

'He seemed, then, as I remember, a little too "dashing" – too "fresh" as I believe they call it nowadays – too "knowing" in the wrong way – and this in spite of his brave and brilliant record in the War.

'It was, perhaps, his voice that slightly "put me off". Every now and again a slightly "common note" seemed to creep in to an otherwise perfect gentleman's accent.

'On knowing him better, though, I discerned that this was simply because he speaks in a slightly "nasal" way – that it is merely a very minor physical defect which gives him, every now and again – so seldom that I now barely, if ever, notice it at all – that rather "common" note.

'And now I have discovered out of the blue, that he is the nephew of Gorse of Assandrava! Verily, he hath put me myself to shame! We both now, it seems, have "Generals" in the family! – but, before General Sir Trevor Gorse even General Sir George Matthews-Browne, of whom I have been so proud, seems a mere nobody! Indeed, *I* shall have to take to minding *my* "p's" and "q's" in front of the "Boy".

'Yesterday evening, having extracted so much from him I deftly "pumped" him further about his "family". They have all, he said, in a vivid expression, "Followed the Drum".

'He calls again at twelve today. And so, to make myself seemly in Milord "Boy's" eyes, M'Lady "Bunny" goeth yet again to her ablutions!'

2

'A strange day yesterday,' Mrs Plumleigh-Bruce wrote next morning. 'From the moment "Boy" came for cocktails in the morning there was a curious electrical atmosphere. I could see that he was excited, and before long I as usual "dug out" of him what it was.

'It seems that he is now in a position to acquire the house in Gilroy Road for the sum of £2,500 – "lock, stock and barrel" – this meaning furniture and everything.

'He showed me a letter from Paris from his friend "Ronnie" confirming this, but making it clear, in a friendly way, that the transaction must be "speedy" or that it would fall through.

'"Ronnie", so "Boy" tells me, has been living a very "wild" life in the gay city – (apart from other things he is an inveterate gambler at "the tables" it seems) and is at the moment in "sore straits" for ready cash. Consequently he is letting the house, which he never liked, go for a "mere song".

'"Boy" asked my advice, and I, having been to tea at the house and thoroughly overlooked it more than once, could not possibly advise against the proposition. (D.S. himself – and he should certainly know if anyone did – has said that it would be a "smashing" bargain at £2,500 – then not thinking of the furniture.)

'But then "Boy's" mood changed. He became somewhat silent, and, for him, almost "sulky". But (once again) I "dug out" of him the cause of his change of mood before long!

'He said that he knew that he had a bargain, but that there were plenty of other bargains going, and he didn't particularly want a house in Reading – "Unless – well . . ."

'I knew perfectly well what he meant by that "Unless – well", but all the same this devil in me (will I ever cure it?) made me ask him what he meant by the words?

'Then "Boy" showed a mood I have never witnessed in him before. He said, not angrily, but with unusual firmness, that I knew perfectly well what he had meant. He had meant unless I was going to marry him.

'He then talked to me, very quietly, but still very firmly, like a "Dutch Uncle" for some time! He repeated that there were plenty of other bargains in house-property, in which he had speculated a lot in the past, and that although this particular one was certainly a "smashing" one, if it went through, money was not everything, money for its own sake never meant anything to him, and that he did not want to buy a house in this part of the world unless something lured him and tied him to it. He was really a London man, where all his ties were.

'Also, he said, he did not really like taking advantage of his friend Ronnie in his present low financial position.

'He then said that he was not "proposing" to me there and then, and reminded me (truthfully enough!) that for nearly a fortnight he had made no attempt to "press" me. But, he said, there had to be limits, and the limit was very nearly reached.

'At this I asked him, somewhat flippantly, how I could either reject or accept his proposal if he had made none for so long a while!

'He smiled at this, but replied that I knew perfectly well that his "proposal" had always been there, as firm as rock and that he had only been waiting for the smallest "sign" from me for him to make it again. He had given me many a chance, he said, to make this "sign", but I had not given it. (The truth!)

'He then said that I was something of a "delayer" and a "coquette" (how well he knows my character!) – but that he was not the sort of person who could put up with that sort of thing too long. He might have "taken" it from another sort of woman whom he loved lightly, but that with me, whom he loved so differently and deeply than ever before, the matter was different. I must not think that because he was able to hide his feelings under a gay exterior, they were not "burning him up" within.

'In short, he said, he had to have an answer – Yes or No – and that before the end of the week, and that *that*, he was sorry to say, was very little short of an ultimatum!

'Should the answer be "No" he knew what he would do. He

would return to London at once and never be seen in Reading again.

'He would forget that he had ever been to Reading. He would certainly give up the project of buying the house in Gilroy Road. By doing so he knew that people would think him a plain fool for "losing a chance of a lifetime", but he did not care. He said that his buying it would involve his coming to Reading constantly, and this he would not do. All the associations would be too unutterably painful, and he might run the risk of running into me.

'Besides, he said, the very house was now so closely linked, in his mind, with myself – that it would be anguish even to enter it. The house, he said, *was* me. It was I who had first advised him about it from a woman's point of view, and that while he was listening to my advice, and every time I had been there, it was me, and only me, whom he had dreamed of dwelling in it as his wife. He said I must have known this. (I *had* guessed as much!) He wanted it to be *mine* – in every *way* mine. He wanted everything he *had* to be mine, he exclaimed.

'I remained silent as he went on fervently in this strain. Then, controlling himself with an obvious effort, he suddenly became light-hearted again and gave me another drink.

'Only once did he refer again to the matter during that sitting. Then he said, lifting his glass "Well – here's to the jolly old ultimatum!" But although he spoke lightly, I could see in his eye he was in deadly earnest, and thinking his own thoughts.

'At this moment he reminded me physically more than ever of his "illustrious relation" – and made me think that there must have been much in common between General Sir Trevor and Ralph Gorse. He is not to be played with.

'Heavens! It is nigh on a quarter to twelve, and I must get up!'

Here Mrs Plumleigh-Bruce left her diary, which she resumed later in the day.

3

'Teatime,' she wrote at about five o'clock 'and here I am scribbling again! 'Tis but to beguile the burdensome hour, for "Boy" is in London today on business, not returning till late at night, and thus leaving his "Bunny" to her own resources!

'I feel strangely lost and melancholy without him – I am surprised how much – and would find, even, the company of D.S. less distasteful than usual. But not only is he still down with flu – there would indeed be "ructions" should "Boy" learn that I had met him in his absence and without leave!

'All day "Boy's" "ultimatum" of yesterday has been on my mind. "Before the end of the week", he said. Did he realize, when saying it, that I am now left with *only two days*!

'Yes – if I know his character he knows only too well! Just as, if I know his character, I know there can be no further dallying with him. He once said, talking of some business matter that "one doesn't deliver an ultimatum twice". He said that it would not be an *ulti*matum if one did.

'Is he, then, holding me up at pistol point? Is he playing upon his knowledge of what I should feel should I give him a "Nay"? Does he know – perhaps only too well – that should he return to London next week, never to see me again, I should be the wretchedest woman on earth?

'Yea – there I have admitted it! – It has come out at last!

'Let it be faced. "Boy" has given "colour and richness" to my life such as I never dreamed would come my way. Still I have doubts about the depth of my love – still I fret and fluster over the disparity of our ages – and yet I know now that life without him, in this dark and dreary town (the rain pelts down outside by the way!) would be barren, empty, a very desert.

'No. "Nay" I cannot say! Then what else but the fearful "Yea"! He has me trapped – has he not?

'Or is it "bluff"? Should I still "dilly and dally", as he has well-nigh accused me of doing, would he really depart? Would there not still be subtle means of "bringing him to heel" – of "keeping him within my web"?

'No. "Bluff" of that sort is not in his nature. It is not written on his face. Sir Trevor did not "bluff" on that famous day at Assandrava. Would Ralph, on this?

'"Pistol point", then, it seems to be. But is he not justified? 'Tis long since he first "proposed". Have I not, in fact, "dallied and dillyed" with him, dangled him, like very paper puppet, on playful string?

'And have I not, in my heart of hearts, *enjoyed* doing so? Am I *not* a "coquette" as he says? He sees deep into my nature, without ceasing, it seems, to yet worship the ground I tread on!

'Then at lunch yesterday – (taken as usual, at the little Italian Restaurant, still struggling so bravely in this mediocre town which concentrates its mind on hard cash rather than good cooking) – at "Belloto's" – where the proprietor, "Mario", ushers us always to our own corner table, and treats us already somehow (these Italians are so shrewd in matters of this sort!) as though we were newly married or betrothed! – then at lunch "Boy" sprang yet another surprise – in truth a most puzzling and perplexing proposition!

'It seems that business will keep him in London nearly all of next week, and he did no less than ask me to join him there – staying at the same hotel as his own – near Victoria Station – nothing less grand, if you please, than the Buckingham! At first I thought he was joking, but I soon saw that he was quite serious.

'He asked what harm there could possibly be? The hotel was big enough for both of us, he said; and that I, if necessary, could have a room in one wing and he in another – a mile away in a hotel like that! Thus he tactfully made it clear that he was not "suggesting" anything (the thought *had* flashed across my mind!) and that I would not be "compromised" in any way.

'Then I asked him how he thought I was going to afford to stay at a place like the Buckingham, and pointed out that I was not a millionairess.

'He replied that he knew indeed I was not – but that that didn't mean one need not "go on the spree" once in a while. Particularly, he added, meaningly, if there was something to "celebrate".

'I ignored this only too obvious hint!

'Then he said that he knew the manager at the Buckingham, and that he could assure me that I would "get out" – even if I stayed for the whole week – well under ten pounds.

'Thus again he showed his tact – in the way he took it for granted that I would, in the present circumstances, "pay my own way". (Another man – D.S. for instance – would have thought it befitting his masculine grandeur to offer royally to pay the whole bill himself. It is these subtle little "touches" which reveal the inner "gentleman".)

'And, sure enough, before long, he had me myself seriously entertaining the idea. I am still. What harm *could* there be, and would I not like a "good time" in London for a week?

'But the proviso! "*If* there was something to *celebrate?*" Sometimes I think that I am in "Boy's" web rather than he in mine — that *he* tempts *me* rather than I tempt him!

'*IF!*

'Come now, Joan Plumleigh-Bruce — let us weigh the "Pros and Cons". Which first, then?

'The "Cons". Get the worst over first — square up to them in proper style — ("steel-true and blade-straight" as he has always called me).

'Well — the first can be said in plain enough English. *Do I love him enough? Do I?* And, if I do not, would it be fair to *him*?

'Then — our ages. What would the wagging tongue of the world say to this? Would it accuse me of being a "baby-snatcher"? Would it say that I have enmeshed him — that I am "after his money"? Not that I care — or ever cared — a jot for the world's opinion, and nor does "Boy". I have posed the problem to him and he has laughed it to scorn. But what might he think *later*?

'Then — my *liberty*. I have a fierce, proud, independent spirit — it is carried to a fault in me — and should I again, at this age, submit to the "yoke" of wedlock? Would it "work"?'

Having thus frankly stated the 'Cons', Mrs Plumleigh-Bruce proceeded to undo her brave work by arguing against them in such a manner as to turn them, almost (if not entirely), into 'Pro's'.

'And yet — what *is* love?' she asked. 'Is it not *giving* rather than *taking*? If it is in my power to give "Boy" deep, deep. happiness (and this I do not doubt) is it for me to withhold it? He told me, early in our acquaintanceship, before he knew anything about me, that I naturally "radiate happiness" to all and sundry, and, if he is right, if indeed I have this gift, should I not bestow it on one who can appreciate it to the full — one who thirsts for it? Surely this would be "fair" enough to him — indeed more than fair — in fact only right and good?

'It would be different if the physical side were uppermost — either in his mind or mine. Then the matter of our respective ages would verily "loom large". But between "Boy" and myself, is it not utterly beside the point?

'And am I as "mature" and unattractive as all that? Many men think not!

'Then, my independence. I have this strain deeply, I know, but am I not really – strange contradiction – also dreadfully dependent – at times yearning to lean on another? To this day I do not know whether I am dominant or really seek dominance. Would "Boy" dominate me, or would I dominate him? He once said that "I ought to be taken in hand". Well, I might let him think he was "dominating" me, but little would he know (devilish offspring of Eve that I am!) who was "pulling the strings"!'

Having thus neatly arranged and adjusted the 'Cons', Mrs Plumleigh-Bruce began to examine the 'Pro's'.

'And now to the "Pro's".

'No one, I think, ever has, or ever could, accuse me of being commercial, but it would be absurd to say, at this stage of my life, that I am loftily "above" financial considerations of any kind. I would marry "Boy", if so I willed, were he a penniless beggar and I had to support him – but all the same I cannot help taking our respective financial positions into account, and in this case it seems that it is I who am, comparatively, the "beggar-maid"!

'An assured income – the "right" sort of house in the "right" sort of place – proper servants in place of one struggling Irish maid (not that in any event would I ever discharge my faithful Mary!) – frequent visits, if not a *pied-à-terre*, in Town – a large Vauxhall car at my disposal – what "beggar-maid" would look with haughty disdain upon the thought of such material pleasures?

'Yes – even his car seduceth me – let it be said! I should like to see the expressions on Pam and Roger's faces as I drove up in it, married to the nephew of "Gorse of Assandrava"! A slight difference, I think, to Lieutenant Roger Braithwaite, recently "invalided" (such is their story) from the Indian Army!'

Pam and Roger were a married couple, related to Mrs Plumleigh-Bruce by marriage and particularly detested by her owing to what she believed was their aloofness or disdain.

Mrs Plumleigh-Bruce, carried away by this thought, now went on to imagine the 'expressions' she might possibly observe on the faces of several other people as they saw her alight from the large Vauxhall car with the nephew of 'Gorse of Assandrava' as her husband. Indeed she became so carried away by this ravishing theme that she at last completely lost her original one – that of the 'Pro's'.

'Ah, well,' she concluded, 'who shall say? The rain still pours down outside – it is near seven o'clock, and I must scratch and scribble no more. Whatever befalls, I only know I feel drear and dead without my "Boy" (where is he, I wonder?) and I mean, believe it or not, to have a cocktail at this moment all by myself! Have I ever done this before? Am I "taking to drink"? Anyway I shall drink a solitary toast to tomorrow, and to "Boy's" return.

'Tomorrow he calls at twelve as usual, and has promised, by the way, to take me, in the afternoon, for another drive. And to where – think you? To see what he calls the "haunts of his childhood". In other words to "Gorse of Assandrava's" one-time abode, just outside Lingbourne! It is within fifteen miles of Reading, he says, and is now inhabited by his other uncle, the General's brother – his uncle George – a Brigadier-General himself.

'For "certain reasons" we are not to "call" – we are merely to "observe from a distance", "Boy" said over lunch yesterday.

'To this moment I do not know what he meant, but the drive should certainly prove interesting!'

CHAPTER TWO

I

'*INTERESTING!*' wrote Mrs Plumleigh-Bruce, alluding, two mornings later, to the final word in her diary. '*Interesting!*

'It is said, I believe, that we British are famous all over the world for our gift of "understatement"!

'Well – it is done – it is over! It has happened. One Joan Plumleigh-Bruce is the "betrothed" of one Ernest Ralph Gorse.

'There it is. That is all! Somewhat "interesting" I think!

'How did it happen? Shall I ever forget? It is stamped indelibly on my mind, and there it will remain for ever.

'And yet there was nothing "dramatic". It simply happened. Hardly any words were spoken. We simply drove on in silence.

'And yet what were our thoughts in that long silence! I could see that he was controlling his excitement only with the greatest force of will-power. And I? Well, I was strangely cool, calm, collected – uncannily so, it almost seemed.

'Perhaps this was because I had instinctively predicted so well what was coming, and in my innermost soul, had known what my answer must be.

'He called here at twelve in the morning, and we had our usual "cocktails". Yet again the atmosphere was somehow "charged" with "electricity".

'I asked him about how he had got on in London, about his business affairs – but he seemed disinterested – distracted. He kept on looking at me in a way I have never seen before, and his answers were "perfunctory" – sometimes little more than "monosyllabic".

'The "ultimatum" was coming! When would it be delivered? It was like a very thunderbolt hanging over our heads!

'In my nervousness I chatted wildly of this and that, trying desperately to "make things go". And, at last, my efforts succeeded. By the time we went off to lunch he had "rallied" and we were both talking as gaily and foolishly as a couple of children.

'Lunch at "Belloto's" – at our usual table with Mario hovering! – and then off in the car to Lingbourne to "observe from a distance" the "haunts of his childhood" – in other words the Brigadier-General's house just outside Lingbourne – "Grasswicke".

'I asked him what his mysterious "reasons" were why we should only "observe from a distance" and he replied that it simply was that I didn't know his Uncle George!

'The Brigadier-General, it seems, is well over sixty, and something of an eccentric and recluse. Also, something of a "martinet".

'"Boy" told me that, when you knew him, he was a charming and gracious old gentleman of a really old-world type – but that his "eccentricities" and "ways" had to be obeyed in every particular!

'He has, "Boy" said – a hatred of the three things – what is known in the family as Uncle George's "three C's" – Cats, Cars and Callers!

'He is *afraid* of Cats, and will either run a mile from them, or even produce an airgun and aim at them from upstairs windows! – he *detests* Cars, which he looks upon as an abominable modern invention of the Devil! – and with casual Callers he is hardly able to be *civil*! He also dislikes the Telephone, and, if one wants to visit Uncle George, "Boy" said, one has to write a formal letter about three weeks ahead! Then he is charm and hospitality itself.

'It took us about half an hour to reach "Grasswicke", which is a few miles beyond Lingbourne, and I was amazed when I found we were entering by Lodge gates! It is a very Estate!

'We passed in the car through this "right-of-way" (another of the Brigadier-General's *bêtes-noires*!) and slowly approached the house itself.

'As "Boy" drove along, at a seemly speed, he pointed out various haunts and "nooks" where he had played in as a boy, and then we stopped at the best spot from which the House and Gardens could be seen – having backed and turned the car, in order that, "Boy" said, we could "make our escape" in case the old boy was in the Gardens or on the prowl!

'And what a lovely place – Elizabethan in period, with certain slightly later "restorations", and all mellowed by time to the perfect old English Country House – the ancient yet perfectly kept lawns with cedar trees leading up to the lovely façade of the back of the house – tennis and croquet lawns at a further distance – and a glimpse of the romantic old stables and a kitchen garden further away! Though we were seeing it at the worst time of year, and it now had a "deserted" look, its peace and loveliness sank into my being. It is from such places that the very "salt of the earth" have sprung – to do their duty – and some to die – in the far-flung corners of the earth.

'I could see that "Boy" was himself moved as he quietly cast his reminiscent eye over the scene, and he was silent as we drove back towards commonplace, commercial Reading.

'Then, when we had passed through the gates again, he stopped the car, and looking back, pointed to a small church in the distance. I knew it was coming, and, sure enough it came!

'"Well," he said, resuming his usual gay air. "That's where all the Gorses's have been buried and married since time immemorial. How would you like to be married there, with Uncle George as best man and with his blessing?"

'I hardly know what I replied, and he covered my embarrassment by going on gaily.

'"To say nothing of the blessing of all his blessed relations," he said. "Although they're a very nice lot really – even if some of them are a bit too grand and stuffy for *me*."

'I was still silent, and then, without looking at me, he said, very quietly and thoughtfully –

'"Well. Which is it to be? Yes or No, Bunny? Here's the good old ultimatum, I'm afraid."

'There was a pause, and I said I did not know what to say. He said he would help me then. Let us try both. Was it "No"?

'"No," I stammered feebly, after another pause.

'At this he himself was silent. Then he said "Well, that means Yes, you know, Bunny". He put his hand on mine. "Now. Don't say any more at the moment or there may be an emotional scene in the middle of the peaceful English countryside. Let's go back to tea – shall we – or Mrs Burford'll be getting into a state."

'He took his hand away from mine, and we drove on.

'Then believe it or not, there was complete silence for something more than five minutes!

'And that was *that*!

'Only when we had passed through Lingbourne again did we begin to speak – about indifferent matters – and only when we were approaching the gloomy precincts of Reading did he say "By the way, you know you're leaving this God-forsaken town, and coming to London with me next week?"

'I was taken aback by this, and let him know that I was, but he said that I could not go back on a promise. I ventured to doubt whether it was a promise, but he swore that I had promised to "celebrate" – *IF*. I suppose I had.

'Then tea, with Mrs Burford's wonderful scones as usual, at Gilroy Road.

'A sweet old thing – Mrs Burford! Does she "guess"?

'"Boy" and I agreed that everything should be kept secret from everybody for the time being – but that perhaps Mrs Burford should be the first to know. At present she isn't even aware that the house, if all goes through, will have changed hands in a few days' time. "Boy" said that his friend "Ronnie" in Paris had insisted that it should be "broken gently" to the poor old thing. She is an old "retainer" who has "kept house" there for years, and it might come as a shock.

'"Boy" said that he would like to keep her on or "take her over". By this he meant have her somewhere else, for, he says, he does not *really* want a house in Reading *permanently*. Buying the house is only another of his "speculations" – though probably the luckiest he has ever struck, and he has other ideas.

'All this almost whispering over "cocktails" taken after Tea at No. 21 – lest Mrs Burford should overhear!

'I asked him what his ideas were, and he said a flat in town and a house in the country – somewhere, if possible, very near "Grasswicke" (he had an actual place in mind). For all his "roots" were there, and that he knew I would captivate the Brigadier-General. What did I think?

'The notion certainly seemed attractive enough to me, but then we agreed that it was absurd to discuss all that sort of thing just at present. There is my own house to be thought of, and Mary, and Mrs Burford. He said that it was quite clear that I had "captivated" *her* already.

'Then, over a *third* cocktail (I am drinking far too many cocktails these days, but has not this very upheaval and earth-quake in my life warranted it!) the spirit of mischief got into both of us, and we decided to go to the "good old" Friar where chance, mere *chance*, had brought us together!

'At The Friar we met L.P. and D.S. – the latter just up from his sick-bed. The two men had been arguing about something and were most *surly*! However, I soon "thawed them out" and then D.S. began to "cross-examine" me about my visit to London, which "Boy" had revealed.

'Knowing what we knew, "Boy" and I could hardly keep our faces straight, or from giggling or laughing outright! – particularly as D.S. obviously had some suspicions of some sort at the back of his mind and adopted quite a "bullying" manner.

'But "Boy" came to my rescue, and after a while he adopted a much milder tone.

'Talking of angels! – D.S. (if "angel" he may be called!) has this moment rung up! It seems that his "daily" is now down with "flu", obviously caught from himself, and he has asked me, if I was going away on Monday, whether my Mary could not "help him out". He said that he would pay her full wages while I was away, if she would come to him, and it seems a fair enough proposition. At any rate I told him I would think about it, and we rang off.

'Poor D.S.! I feel, at this stage, almost deeply sorry for him. If only he had an inkling of what has gone on and will go on!

'How will the news be broken to him, and how will he take it?

'Poor man. I suppose he loves me after his brutish fashion. I suppose he might have made, in his own way, a "worthy" husband.

'He will not, I fear, at all like having been "cut out" by a mere "youngster" like "Boy"! – who does not seem to think I am "long in the tooth" or that I have "feet of clay"! Well, the man must learn. The hard way, I fear.

'Heavens, Mary has knocked without, and I must up.'

2

Gorse's reflections, on reading these later entries, were of the same sluggishly satisfied and entirely humourless nature as had characterized his reading of what had preceded them.

He had enjoyed (without laughing at) the airy 'dear-me-I-almost-forgot' way in which she had introduced the General ('Let me see. Ah, yes! A morsel of mighty interest!'). And he had enjoyed his physical likeness to General Gorse ('if one looks closely').

He had not, however, liked her coy ''fessing' to having had at one time secret doubts about his having emerged from *quite* the top drawer, and he had intensely disliked reading that she had at times thought he gave forth a 'common' note.

Here Gorse was struck at what was, perhaps, his most vulnerable point, for this otherwise almost horribly realistic young man was not only bitterly ambitious socially – he was at times almost idiotically vain in this direction.

Moreover, the suggestion that he would not 'pass' in any circle whatsoever, was an assault upon him, as it were, professionally – upon the pride he took in the art of his life.

Gorse was almost as incapable of real anger as he was of real humour, but, on coming across Mrs Plumleigh-Bruce's most candid words, he stopped reading for a moment and his sluggishly satisfied expression changed into something slightly more lively and thoughtful.

In fact Gorse never forgave Mrs Plumleigh-Bruce for this passage in her diary, and he was, at the last, to be a good deal less merciful with her than he might have been had she not written it.

However, as he read on, Gorse greatly relished the success of his 'ultimatum. and her weighing of the 'Pro's' and 'Cons', and he noticed the speed and deftness with which she had turned the 'Cons' into 'Pro's', while leaving the latter intact.

The 'Pro's', he observed, were really very few in number – probably capable of being resolved into four constituents only – his promise of virtual sexlessness in the case of marriage, his money, his car, and his General.

But this almost elementary piece of psychological chemistry had flown like wildfire to the childish woman's head.

Each of the four constituents, he realized, made each of the others more potent and credible. The car, naturally, gave credibility to the money, the money gave lustre to the car, the General gave glorious colour to both, both gave substance to the General, and the promise of virtual sexlessnes in marriage undoubtedly made all even more splendidly tempting than they would have otherwise been. The grasping widow wanted absolutely everything and believed she was going to be given it.

The General, of course, had been Gorse's *coup de grâce*, and, though thrown in last, was really the base, or yeast, of his composition. Sometimes Gorse wondered whether he could have dispensed with the General.

The General, however, was a dangerous element, and Gorse, before using him, had taken considerable pains in further research in regard to his soldier-uncle. This had been done in the Reference Room of the local Library, where Gorse had alighted unexpectedly upon the General's brother – the Brigadier-General. The latter in fact lived in the house a few miles beyond Lingbourne to which Gorse had taken Mrs Plumleigh-Bruce (having himself, beforehand, made two exploratory and thoughtful journeys there in his car).

Gorse, realizing fully how dangerous an element the General was – particularly if used in combination with his brother – had held him back until practically the last moment.

The General, and his brother, he had decided, must be used only at the beginning of the final stage – indeed within two days, at the most, of the final delivery of his 'ultimatum'.

After that Mrs Plumleigh-Bruce must be swept away to London, and, under his eyes, given no time or opportunity to think or inquire about anything – least of all Generals.

Gorse (who had not then read anything of Mrs Plumleigh-Bruce's diary) had been a little nervous on that drive to 'Grasswicke', and he had therefore been more delighted than he had expected to have been at its romantic outcome.

The final stage of this Reading adventure, Gorse believed while driving Mrs Plumleigh-Bruce back from 'Grasswicke' into Reading, had now been passed. The rest was child's play, merely a matter of going through certain easy, necessary, and perhaps rather boring motions.

And, sure enough, the necessary motions were very easy indeed. They were better. They were so easy as to be amazingly exhilarating.

CHAPTER ONE

I

THE vast Buckingham Hotel – slightly modernized downstairs and in its bedrooms, but giving forth an air of a museum or mausoleum in its considerable acreage of staircases and passages above – catered mostly for birds of the briefest passage. This was because it was in the Buckingham Palace Road and so extremely close to Victoria Station.

It had, however, a regular clientele, mostly of elderly people with memories, who dined in the old-fashioned Restaurant rather than in the modern Grill, and liked its thickly carpeted, hushed, mausoleum-like quality above.

In all three of these ways – in its modernity below, its dim and dignified spaciousness above, and its countless birds of passage mingled with a sedate and faithful clientele – it bore a certain resemblance to the famous Hotel Metropole in Brighton, where Gorse had years ago robbed Esther Downes.

Here Mrs Plumleigh-Bruce and Gorse arrived on a Monday afternoon in time for tea.

Gorse had engaged a small single room for himself, and a large double-bedded room (on the same floor and at about a distance of two hundred yards) for Mrs Plumleigh-Bruce.

Gorse, having unpacked and walked from his own room – along a corridor so high and hugely silent that he was aware of the sound of the clanking of the key in his hand against the uncouthly ponderous and savagely serrated piece of metal to which it was attached – had tea in Mrs Plumleigh-Bruce's more spacious and opulent room.

Gorse and Mrs Plumleigh-Bruce made the latter's room more or less their headquarters during their stay in the hotel. On the first evening they had drinks there and, instead of going out, dined in the old-fashioned Restaurant.

2

Those two, even on their first night, made a marked impression upon the regular and for the most part elderly diners in the Restaurant, and, later, the more they ate there, the more marked, and the more displeasing, did this impression grow.

And this applied to nearly all other public places they visited in which they could be studied.

For those two were not the couple they were in Reading – either to the outside world, or in their own eyes.

In the provincial town the few people who had watched or known them together had either given them little thought, or had grown used to the slight oddity of their companionship. In London things were different.

Londoners, seeing or listening to them for the first time, found this couple not only slightly odd. They found them slightly, or even decidedly, repellent.

Mrs Plumleigh-Bruce had, as is known, become entirely used to Gorse's flamboyant and rather 'common' manner – so much so that she did not notice or think about it. The observant Londoner was not thus blinded, and found Gorse's monocle and youthful bravado highly distasteful – particularly when he was seen with the obviously much older woman. Such an observer thought of Gorse at his real age – that of twenty-five – and of Mrs Plumleigh-Bruce at her own – that of forty-one.

Mrs Plumleigh-Bruce had also become entirely used to what she called in her diary the 'disparity' of their ages (while being completely deluded as to the full extent of this disparity). She thought of 'Boy' as being in his thirties, and she also believed that she might be taken as being no more than thirty-five.

Then again, the moment they entered London, both began to behave in an entirely different and more loose and excited manner.

Gorse, though Mrs Plumleigh-Bruce did not notice it, became much more dashing and 'common' than he had ever been in Reading, and Mrs Plumleigh-Bruce became much more girlish, flirtatious, and audibly talkative. Gorse noticed this, and of course encouraged it, for the more excited and silly he could make her the more he was pleased.

Hence arose the very unpleasant impression they made upon the average observer, who could not make out which of the two was the more offensive or culpable. Was it the swaggering and foolish and slightly 'common' young man? Or was it the woman, who could not exactly be called 'common', but whose unbecomingly girlish manner and loquacity made her fully as unattractive as her escort?

And what was their relationship? Were they about to be married, married, or living together out of wedlock? And, whatever the case was, who was the seducer? Had a middle-aged woman, with money, ensnared a foolish young man? Or was a predatory young man exploiting a matured and moneyed woman?

There could, of course, be no doubt that there was something of some serious sort between them. It was revealed in their eyes, their talk, their gestures – the whole impudently intimate and self-assured aura they cast forth.

Dining in the evenings in the sedate Restaurant of the Buckingham Gorse soon developed the habit, after dinner, of holding Mrs Plumleigh-Bruce's hand over the table, and looking swimmingly into her eyes, while she looked swimmingly down her nose.

This disturbed the other diners, as well as the staff, very much indeed – elderly women residents of the hotel exclaiming 'Really!' and using such epithets as 'nasty', 'disgusting', 'horrible' or 'unhealthy'.

One such embittered woman went so far as to say that Mrs Plumleigh-Bruce 'ought to be flogged'.

'Boy' and 'Bunny', however, did not dine very often at the Buckingham.

It was Gorse's business not only to maintain but to increase Mrs Plumleigh-Bruce's general state of excitement, and this he did by taking her to theatres ('shows'), dinners and suppers at West End restaurants, and to night-clubs – all in such a way as to make her drink the greatest amount of which she was capable without realizing she was doing so.

At the theatres, restaurants, and night-clubs they made, of course, much less of an impression than at the Buckingham. All the same they succeeded in making an impression.

Indeed they succeeded in being an outstandingly distasteful couple in nearly every place to which they went.

CHAPTER TWO

Very early in this incanny sojourn in London Gorse got down to what he called to himself 'business'.

In the afternoons it was his habit to take Mrs Plumleigh-Bruce for long, circuitous drives in the car to places like Virginia Water, Hampton Court, and Maidenhead. He thus further excited and exhausted her, and so made her more readily susceptible to the drinks she took in the evenings.

On one of these evenings, having rather mysteriously absented himself from her on the pretext of 'business', Gorse returned to Mrs Plumleigh-Bruce's room at about seven o'clock in what she called in her diary 'jubilant mood indeed!'

He was now, he said excitedly, the owner of No. 21 Gilroy Road, and he flourished at her two large sealing-waxed envelopes, intimating that they contained deeds and documents.

In his haste to get a drink for both, and because of the necessity to leave her room immediately in order to lock up, in his own room, just at the moment, the precious titles to his new property, his showing her of the contents of the envelopes was finally somehow overlooked and forgotten.

On returning to her room he had further good news to break – though, according to Mrs Plumleigh-Bruce's diary, '"Boy" most mercilessly made me verily grind my teeth with vexation!'

He had, it seemed, 'sold out' and made well over a hundred pounds on the investment into which he had originally urged her to put two hundred pounds. And because she had been so timid in putting in 'only fifty' her own gain amounted to something less than ten pounds.

'Boy' insisted, however, that she should have the full ten pounds – 'a round sum if but a paltry one', as he put it, and he made her accept two five-pound notes from him then and there.

Later that evening, Mrs Plumleigh-Bruce – insisting on 'paying her way for once', went with Gorse to another night-club, where she drank so much that she had almost to be assisted home and to bed.

But the next day, over further cocktails, she had rather hysterically revived by lunch-time, and Gorse took her for another long drive in the country in the afternoon.

During this drive Gorse announced that his buying of the car now looked as though it was 'out'.

This was a pity, for he had longed to give it to her as a wedding present.

If he bought it, he said, on top of having bought the house in Gilroy Road, he would be practically penniless. His practical pennilessness would be evanescent, of course, since the house in Gilroy Road could be sold at an enormous profit in due course.

But at present it looked sadly like 'no car'.

As Gorse's methods with Mrs Plumleigh-Bruce have been so often demonstrated and illustrated before, it would be wearisome to give in detail the conversation about the car which took place between the two.

It need only be said that Gorse slowly made it clear that, if a loan of five hundred pounds were forthcoming, the car would be his – or rather Mrs Plumleigh-Bruce's – and that Mrs Plumleigh-Bruce tentatively offered to lend Gorse this sum, or part of it.

Nor need it be said that Gorse at first hotly rejected her offer. But later, over drinks in the evening, he thought better of his sterner attitude in the afternoon.

In fact he was visited by a sudden inspiration.

She would have, after all, the *car itself* as security! The moment it was bought (and she could witness its buying), she could put it (if she wanted!) into any garage of her own choice (a secret one if she wished!) and just hang on to it!

By seven o'clock that evening Mrs Plumleigh-Bruce had offered to lend Gorse the five hundred pounds now in her current account.

This offer, again, was firmly rejected.

Though there was no real harm in it, Gorse 'did not like' doing things this way. He had no intention of starting his married life in debt to his 'Bunny'. But then came another inspiration.

What if 'Bunny' put the money into a Joint Account from which they could both draw?

'Boy' would probably not have to touch it, and, if he did have to do so, for incidental expenses, Bunny would be consulted. In fact, 'Bunny' temporarily would have to 'dole out' money to the great financier – 'Boy'! A strange reversal of the situation, but perhaps it would be 'jolly good' for him!

Before midnight the matter was settled, and the next morning Gorse obtained three specimen signatures from Mrs Plumleigh-Bruce as well as her signature to a cheque for five hundred pounds. He then left her to open a Joint Account with her at his own Bank – a Joint Account from which either could draw separately, and in which there was already money of his own amounting to over two hundred pounds.

'Boy' returned shortly after midday, and, over cocktails at the new Cocktail Bar of the Buckingham, showed 'Bunny' a printed document she had to sign, and also a new chequebook from the Bank in which they were both now banking.

'Bunny' signed the document in a state of delight and bemusement caused by the newness and strangeness of the new and strange chequebook, which bore the opulent and imposing address of Cavendish Square.

Gorse was aware of the childish delight people take in new, unblemished chequebooks from new Banks. (They get a curious notion that they are in some way beginning their financial life again with a clean sheet.)

The rattled-out new cocktails in the new Cocktail Bar, taken together with the new chequebook from the new Bank, made Mrs Plumleigh-Bruce think practically nothing at all about the document she signed.

Two days later, Gorse – having enticed Mrs Plumleigh-Bruce into a delicious defiling of her new chequebook with a small sum – asked her to telephone the bank as to the exact state of their Joint Account. This she did, and was told that it stood at £723 5s 11d.

From Gorse's point of view all was over now. There were hardly any more necessary motions to go through.

He almost regretted having to do no battle of any sort with Mrs Plumleigh-Bruce about the five hundred pounds, and, brooding in his bed, it occurred to him that, had she only shown some sort of resistance, he might have done better.

She might, after all, have nearly or even completely forced him to marry her — and was marriage to her such a bad idea? Why had he limited himself to five hundred pounds?

Gorse (as yet unmarried) all his life took a very light view of this bond, and he was keenly anxious to see America, to which he had always made up his mind to go if he was forced into marrying anyone undesirable.

However, the infatuated woman had proved herself totally unable to face the idea of parting with the luxurious Vauxhall car.

Gorse, who had by now read her diary, imagined that her vision of the 'expressions' on people's 'faces' on seeing her drive up in this vehicle with the nephew of Gorse of Assandrava as her husband, had simply been too much for her.

And so, as they had come his way so absurdly easily, he thought he had better settle for the five hundred pounds, and go through the final necessary motions.

2

Even the final necessary motions, so far from being tiresome, Gorse found as exhilarating, or even more exhilarating, than those which had preceded them.

Gorse just at this period was, possibly, in the heyday of his existence. Exuberant in his youth and an assured knowledge of his gifts, he was enjoying nearly every moment of his life. And, with a zest for such things which later was lost, he was enjoying the Buckingham, the motor-driving, the theatres, and the night-clubs. Also, at this period, he had more money than he ever had later, and saw great riches coming his way.

These hopes somehow never materialized. Soon after his relationship with Mrs Plumleigh-Bruce his fortunes did not exactly decline but were only kept at the same level by serious exertions on his part. Finally, when his fortunes did decline, his confidence in himself declined also, and with his confidence his skill.

Gorse, robbing Mrs Plumleigh-Bruce, made the mistake of thinking there were countless other and richer women waiting to be defrauded in roughly the same way.

Thus Mrs Plumleigh-Bruce, by her quite exceptional silliness and credulity, almost certainly had an adverse affect upon Gorse's career.

He was never to find another Mrs Plumleigh-Bruce, and, because of this, a sense of frustration and disappointment slowly began to tarnish, and, at last, to corrode his belief in himself. And this, in its turn, caused him to take to more crude, criminal, and violent methods with women.

3

In the days that followed Gorse made Mrs Plumleigh-Bruce write out a few more small cheques, for small pleasures, on their Joint Account. He also, with her sanction, cashed two small cheques of his own on this Account – which was now seen by both in the light of a further sentimental 'bond' between them.

Gorse remorselessly kept up the drives in the country, the theatres, the night-clubs, and the drinking necessarily attendant upon such outings.

The young man, as has been said, was enjoying these things to the full; but the mature and over-excited woman slowly began to tire seriously.

Finally she reached such a stage of exhaustion and over-excitement that she could hardly be said to be in full possession of her senses, as Gorse observed from reading her diary, in which, perhaps because of her over-excitement, she still wrote either last thing at night, or first thing in the morning.

Gorse had discovered her diary on the afternoon of their third day in London. On that afternoon Mrs Plumleigh-Bruce had visited some of those relations whose 'expressions' she was so anxious later to see, and Gorse, who from the earliest possible moment had established the precedent of keeping or asking at the Reception for the keys of both of their rooms, had entered hers in order to explore it thoroughly. He had found little to interest him apart from the suede-covered *My Thoughts* – which she kept hidden beneath clothes in the lowest drawer of her chest of drawers. Thereafter, whenever other opportunities arose, he took a glance at it.

Seeing from her diary that she was tiring, and that she was secretly anxious to go home before he had achieved all he desired in the neatest way possible, Gorse, in the last few days, threw in further pleasures, excitement, and enticements to keep her going. He began to make her drive the car (she could drive a car after a manner, and soon, under his tuition, which was kind and clever, was handling the Vauxhall with great skill and pride): he took her to two places in Bond Street to choose an engagement ring, but would consider nothing cheap, and saw to it that both should indulge in heavenly deliberations before making a purchase; and he casually promised to take her, and a few evenings later did take her, to meet Leslie Rodney and Joan Farrell (the then extremely famous married actor and actress) in their dressing rooms at the Coburg Theatre, in Shaftesbury Avenue, after Gorse and Mrs Plumleigh-Bruce had seen the play.

Gorse had obtained an introduction to this couple through Miles Standish, who had all his life known and had at one time been on long tours with the now highly publicized couple. Standish had given this introduction with much reluctance, but could not risk offending his potential backer with a refusal.

Before taking Mrs Plumleigh-Bruce to the Coburg, Gorse had first visited Leslie Rodney and Joan Farrell after a matinée with his letter of introduction, and so, in front of Mrs Plumleigh-Bruce, he was able to give an impression of being on easy, if not familiar terms, with the two celebrities, who, because of this false familiarity disliked and distrusted Gorse almost as much as did Miles Standish. But they showed all the outward cordiality which their profession and distinguished position demanded. (Mrs Plumleigh-Bruce came out of the stage door entranced with delight and awe at their 'simplicity' and 'naturalness'.)

And during all this period Gorse engaged Mrs Plumleigh-Bruce in incessant discussions as to when and where they were to be married.

Although he wanted to be married at the church at 'Grass-wicke', with the Brigadier-General's blessing and all that, he chafed at the delay which such a thing would cause – the 'reading of the banns, etc.' – and favoured an immediate marriage at a Registry Office in London. After all, he was not 'religious' – or, at any rate, not religious in that way.

But here the more romantically-minded 'Bunny' restrained her impetuous 'Boy', and at last made him agree to marry her at 'Grasswicke'.

('What a tussle I have had about it all!' she wrote in her diary. 'But as usual, after adroit handling, poor "Boy" gave in! How little he knows how he is being "handled". Will this be the "pattern" of our married life? It will, methinks privately – but "mum's the word", and he will probably never know what is taking place for his own good!')

'Boy' and 'Bunny' spent, in all, twelve days at the Buckingham – 'Bunny', on the last day, returning to Reading by herself; this owing to an obligation on 'Boy's' part to attend a 'Sparktone' meeting in the City. ('Sparktone' was the name of the wireless firm in which he had much money, and of which he was a Director.)

Their parting, however, was to be of the briefest and most stimulating kind.

'Bunny' was to take her courage into both hands and drive ('little me all alone?') the Vauxhall back to Gilroy Road.

Here she should arrive at about two-thirty at the latest, and then, with the aid of Mrs Burford (who had been telephoned) she would prepare tea and await the arrival, by train, of her 'lord and master' at about four, or earlier.

This would give Mrs Plumleigh-Bruce a further chance of 'captivating' Mrs Burford, who was (both now agreed) a 'dear old soul' to whom the 'News', both about the real ownership of the house, and the impending marriage, it would only be fair to break soon.

'And by the way,' shouted Gorse – amidst the noise of the starting engine (and of an electric drill – at that period a much discussed and hated innovation – at work about fifty yards away) – as he saw Mrs Plumleigh-Bruce off in a side-street near Buckingham Palace Road, 'You know this is yours now – don't you?'

'*What's* mine?' cried the deafened Mrs Plumleigh-Bruce.

'Oh – only the car,' Gorse replied, putting his mouth near to her ear. 'I paid for it yesterday – and all's signed and sealed, and your property entirely. So take care of your own property – won't you? Off you go!'

Gorse moved away and waved, and off a slightly stunned Mrs Plumleigh-Bruce went – driving her car towards Reading with just that extra *finesse* in accuracy, timing and patience which distinguishes a new car-owner from a normal car-driver.

Gorse, who had so patiently and cleverly taught Mrs

Plumleigh-Bruce to drive the Vauxhall, forgot, for the moment, the divinely new Sunbeam two-seater, which had become his property only yesterday (and which had been immediately behind the Vauxhall while he was saying goodbye to Mrs Plumleigh-Bruce), and watched her until she was out of sight.

He thought well of his lady pupil.

PART THIRTEEN

GORSE THE ABSENT

_____

CHAPTER ONE

I

FOOLISH, vain, greedy, lethargic, affected, mouthingly arrogant, and for the most part unpleasantly dishonest in mind Mrs Plumleigh-Bruce certainly was, and all these qualities, taken together, might have been said to have added up to a species of serious evil in the whole. Nevertheless it would be hard to say that she entirely merited the evil which descended upon her that afternoon and evening.

This lady owner-driver of a Vauxhall car arrived at 21 Gilroy Road, Reading (now the property of her future husband), at about three o'clock, and was let in by Mrs Burford, the dear old soul whom Mrs Plumleigh-Bruce had so captivated, and who would almost certainly be employed by her after her marriage.

To fill in the time before 'Boy' arrived at four (or earlier), Mrs Plumleigh-Bruce further captivated Mrs Burford by going down to the kitchen for the first time, asking how the delicious scones were made, and entering into a womanly and woman-to-woman conversation about the house generally. In doing this she was unable quite to conceal a prematurely possessive, patronizing and employing manner – a manner which Mrs Burford did not fail to notice and which she thought mysterious as well as slightly insolent.

2

Mrs Burford was far from being the dear old soul romantically created in the roseate conversations of the betrothed couple.

In spite of her professional grey hairs, soothing manner, cosiness, stoutness and spectacles, the housekeeper ruthlessly took monetary advantage of her absent employer – Mr Ronald Shooter – bullied and nagged and constantly changed the young girls whom she employed to help her run the house, had countless acquaintances to tea, drank stout with them at Gilroy Road and in public hoses, gossiped, dwelt upon or predicted every sort of local misfortune or scandal, and denigrated friend and foe alike while predicting or loftily contemplating such disasters.

Gorse (to whom she had always been as sweet as honey) she disliked because he was an intruder and possible spy or reporter on behalf of her employer; and she had been even sweeter to Mrs Plumleigh-Bruce, whom she disliked even more than Gorse.

The gifted scone-maker, in brief, was not at all the sort of person to sustain, encourage, fortify or soothe Mrs Plumleigh-Bruce in the evil which fell upon her that afternoon and evening.

3

At about a quarter past four, Mrs Plumleigh-Bruce, having temporarily parted from Mrs Burford, began to look out (through the gracious bow-windows of the spacious and well-furnished sitting-room) for Gorse, who should, unless his train was late, have already appeared.

Dusk was descending, and in its grey, hazy light, Mrs Plumleigh-Bruce took great pleasure in surveying the stately outlines of the Vauxhall car.

Had she been alone in the house Mrs Plumleigh-Bruce would probably have experienced not the faintest feeling of apprehension when, at half past four, Gorse had still not appeared.

But because of the nearness of Mrs Burford a faint irrational uneasiness came over her – or rather stole up to her from the kitchen below.

There was, possibly, a logical psychological cause for this

seemingly illogical uneasiness in Mrs Plumleigh-Bruce. The woman below had, undoubtedly, a sixth sense for impending disaster.

Disasters falling upon others were, after all, the very breath of the housekeeper's being.

The late arrival of anyone would at once put the thought of disaster into her mind – the thought would rapidly develop into a distant hope, the distant hope into a yearning, and the yearning, finally, into a state of excitement in which the woman became inspired – a prophetess.

At half past four this final prophetic stage had certainly not been reached, but some of the preliminary symptoms were doing something more than mystically stirring within Mrs Burford: they were mystically being conveyed, in the hour of dusk, and with its aid, to the waiting woman upstairs – conveyed in the sound of slightly impatient footsteps, in the rather noisy opening and shutting of oven and other doors, and in the distant but peculiarly audible rattle of cutlery and crockery.

Taking a sudden dislike to the dusk and to the noises below, Mrs Plumleigh-Bruce switched on the electric light. But this only made her feel a good deal more dreary and slightly more apprehensive than before. Also she was dimly disturbed on noticing, as she drew the curtains to, that the lamps in the street were already lit – for this announced the unmistakable arrival of evening, or even of night.

Four-thirty being the time arranged for tea, Mrs Plumleigh-Bruce forced herself to wait until a quarter to five before calling to Mrs Burford from the top of the basement stairs. This she did under the pretence of being merely solicitous about the scones and in no way disturbed by the lateness of the arrival of the temporary master of the household.

But Mrs Burford, by this time almost in her yearning stage of hideous prediction, would not permit any such evasion, and treating the matter of the scones most lightly, said: 'He *is* late – isn't he?'

Mrs Plumleigh-Bruce here pretended that she herself took this lateness in as light a spirit as Mrs Burford had taken the matter of the scones, but then made the grave mistake of saying that 'he' might have missed the train, and would be on the next one. This was playing into Mrs Burford's hands.

Mrs Burford said, accurately, that even if 'he' had missed the intended train, the one after it should be in by now, and that 'he' should be here by now.

This agitated and dismayed Mrs Plumleigh-Bruce, and Mrs Burford, seeing this sign of weakness on her face in the light of the basement stairs, at once took further advantage of Mrs Plumleigh-Bruce. She dropped the vague and rather self-conscious 'he' and, having repeated that the tea and the scones were of no consequence, added, humorously, and just before turning resignedly from the bottom of the basement stairs to her kitchen: 'Yes, *your* gay young man's *certainly* got behind in his time!'

Mrs Plumleigh-Bruce naturally regarded this as being abominably familiar, and, on returning to the drearily electric-lit sitting-room, decided, as she listened to every footstep in the lamp-lit street outside, that she would almost certainly not 'take on' Mrs Burford after her marriage.

Matters were then made worse for Mrs Plumleigh-Bruce by the telephone ringing.

The telephone was just at the top of the basement stairs and Mrs Plumleigh-Bruce, certain that it was 'Boy' calling to explain his delay, cried joyously down to Mrs Burford, who was half-way up the basement stairs, 'All right, Mrs Burford, I'll take it!'

The telephone call was, however, a case of one of those wrong numbers whose wrongness takes a very long time in being argumentatively (and at last angrily) revealed, and Mrs Plumleigh-Bruce, having known all the time that Mrs Burford had been listening on the stairs, had to cry down 'All right, Mrs Burford. Only a wrong number!'

Then Mrs Plumleigh-Bruce returned to the sitting-room in a state of fierce irritation with Mrs Burford, and serious anxiety about Gorse, which, after listening to more footsteps in the lamp-lit street outside, she at last decided she must control. She went yet again to the top of the basement stairs, and told Mrs Burford to bring up the tea. There was no sense in waiting and spoiling the scones.

Mrs Burford, bringing in the tea and scones, had now very nearly reached her inspirational phase, but, fearing disappointment, she concealed her condition with further insolent humour.

'Well,' she said, putting Mrs Plumleigh-Bruce's tea in front of her. 'It looks as though your young man's gone and deserted you - doesn't it? – *good* and proper!'

'Well,' replied Mrs Plumleigh-Bruce, also affecting humour in order to conceal her emotions. 'Even if he has, he's left me a very nice car, just outside!'

'Well, he's left you Mr Shooter's car, at any rate!' was the retort of the gay, cosy, dear old soul, as she went to the door.

Mrs Plumleigh-Bruce very nearly let Mrs Burford close the door behind her without making any reply. But something made her say: 'What do you mean – "Mr *Shooter's* car", Mrs Burford?'

4

'Why, just Mr Shooter's car, madam,' said Mrs Burford, respectfully and meekly, and to this Mrs Plumleigh-Bruce replied, What do you mean – Mr Shooter's car? It was Mr Gorse's.

Well, it wasn't madam, said Mrs Burford, and Well, it *was* said Mrs Plumleigh-Bruce – because she knew for certain that it was.

Well, Mrs Burford didn't know *how* Mrs Plumleigh-Bruce knew for certain it was, as she (Mrs Burford) happened to know for certain it wasn't – unless Mr Shooter had sold it to Mr Gorse, which wasn't very likely.

And here Mrs Plumleigh-Bruce completely lost her nerve and her temper, and said that recently *other* things had been changing hands – including housekeepers, even.

And then, naturally, the storm broke.

CHAPTER TWO

I

DURING a lull in the storm, it did not take long for Mrs
Burford to prove that neither the house nor the car belonged
to Mr Gorse.

She went upstairs and showed Mrs Plumleigh-Bruce a letter
she had received from Mr Shooter from Paris only yesterday
morning. This letter, which was in a totally different handwriting
from the one Gorse had shown Mrs Plumleigh-Bruce, by a happy
coincidence covered both matters. As well as speaking of returning in a fortnight's time to 21 Gilroy Road, in a manner
which made it abundantly evident that he was not conscious of
having sold the house to Gorse, Mr Shooter mentioned both
Gorse and the car, jovially 'trusting', that 'our friend' was using
both the house and the car, 'to say nothing of the housekeeper',
in a 'fitting manner'.

Mrs Burford then supplemented this evidence firstly by telling
Mrs Plumleigh-Bruce that she could there and then ring up Mr
Shooter's solicitors in Reading, who for years had done all the
business concerning the house, and secondly by naming the garage
in Reading where Mr Shooter always kept his car. The owner of
the garage was a personal friend of Mrs Burford's, and would
explain that the car had only been lent temporarily to Gorse.

But what did it matter? Mrs Plumleigh-Bruce had not, by any
chance, lent or given any *money*, or anything like that, to Mr
Gorse – had she?

Mrs Plumleigh-Bruce then made her inevitably ghastly evening
at least three times more ghastly by admitting that she had.

The inspired prophetess at once changed into an inspired
interpreter of past history.

She had always *known*. She had known it from the *beginning*!

The moment she had clapped eyes on that young Mr Gorse
she had known!

She had never liked him. She had *never* trusted him. *She* had never been taken in by his so-called 'gentlemanly airs'.

Then, watching Mrs Plumleigh-Bruce growing whiter and whiter in the face, the inspired interpreter turned into a glorious, divine, Christ-like comforter and sustainer, taking control of the entire situation.

Almost with physical violence she compelled Mrs Plumleigh-Bruce to sustain herself with tea, while she made the necessary telephone calls to Mr Shooter's solicitors in Reading, and to the owner of the garage in which Mr Shooter kept his car.

Then, again almost using physical compulsion, she forced Mrs Plumleigh-Bruce to talk on the telephone to Mr Shooter's solicitors, and to the garage-owner.

Both confirmed Mrs Burford's assurances in a manner which left no conceivable doubt in Mrs Plumleigh-Bruce's mind as to their genuineness and accuracy.

The garage-owner – a Mr Berry – asked with some anxiety about the present whereabouts of the car, and Mrs Plumleigh-Bruce said it was outside the house. Mr Berry suggested that he should come round and call for it, and Mrs Plumleigh-Bruce agreed.

Mr Berry said that he would be round in about twenty minutes, but did not appear until about three-quarters of an hour later.

Mr Berry, though kindly, was a gloomy and tactless man, who made more inquiries and comments than he should have done with a woman in so tragic and humiliating a predicament. And, on departing – having put Mrs Plumleigh-Bruce through the black shame of removing her luggage from the car she did not own into the house Gorse did not own – he suggested that it was, surely, a matter for the Police, and that at once.

This threw the prophetess, the interpreter of history and divine consoler, into yet another sort of ecstasy – a police-ecstasy of the most violent kind. She was the personal friend of an authoritative police officer in Reading, and she insisted that he should be telephoned at once.

But here Mrs Plumleigh-Bruce just managed to restrain her, though she had first to become hysterical and almost to use physical compulsion herself with her comforter, guide and friend.

Mrs Plumleigh-Bruce did this for several reasons. She felt she could bear no further humiliation that evening: she was too feeble to undergo further questioning, and she still felt that Gorse, though he had lied about the car and the house, might not have robbed her financially. That could only be ascertained by telephoning the Bank about their Joint Account next morning.

Over and above this Mrs Plumleigh-Bruce had already an instinctive feeling that she would never apply to the police. The risk of the hideous public exposure of her folly and infatuation which such a thing might entail would (she dimly foresaw) be too great.

Instead of telephoning the police Mrs Plumleigh-Bruce telephoned Glen Alan to speak to Mary. (She had intended to do this at tea-time, probably to say that she and Mr Gorse would be in to dinner.) To her surprise there was no reply from Glen Alan.

Then Mrs Burford insisted on Mrs Plumleigh-Bruce drinking brandy, and again tried to make her telephone the police, urging that she ought, at any rate, to have the advice of a *Man* at once. Didn't Mrs Plumleigh-Bruce know a *Man* she could go to?

Slightly stimulated by the brandy, Mrs Plumleigh-Bruce realized that she did indeed want the assistance of a Man, but she could think of only one – Donald Stimpson.

Could she swallow her pride, she wondered, by going to him and telling him all? Might he not forgive her? Might he not even forgive her and marry her?

At this moment of her life the idea of marriage – as a refuge and means of restitution of her lost pride before herself and the world – was immeasurably desirable to Mrs Plumleigh-Bruce.

Over a second brandy she decided to telephone Mr Stimpson, if possible meet him, and confess all.

But there was no answer from Mr Stimpson's number. He was, Mrs Plumleigh-Bruce guessed, almost certainly round at The Friar.

Then, in order to escape from the hateful house, and the hateful housekeeper's presence, Mrs Plumleigh-Bruce said that she must go home. Her maid Mary, she said, would be getting anxious about her.

Mrs Burford asked what she was going to do about her luggage, and Mrs Plumleigh-Bruce, almost running out of the house, replied that she would send Mary or 'somebody' (she hoped Mr Stimpson) round for it 'later'.

She did not intend to return at once to Glen Alan, but to go to The Friar in the hope of meeting Mr Stimpson.

The Friar was nearly half a mile away, and on her way she was caught by a sharp shower of rain.

On arriving at The Friar she found only one friend – Major Parry.

CHAPTER THREE

I

THE Major was exceptionally drunk and exceptionally inspired.

He had got drunk in the morning on the strength of some staggering news imparted to him by Mr Stimpson (who had also taken a lot to drink) and his evening drinks had (as they had with Mr Stimpson on that night in London) flown like wild-fire to his head and rendered him practically insane.

He was inspired because he was drunk, and drunk because he was inspired. He had got his rhyme for 'fallen!' ('They are fallen, they are fallen, they are fallen.')

His miraculous solution of this long-standing problem did not look at all good to the Major next day. But tonight it was all as simple as pie!

He was suddenly going to change the rhythm, go into inverted commas, and brackets, and give a grim yet intensely exciting picture of a sort of foppish but magnificently exuberant sort of ex-public school leader in battle itself. Thus:

'(Just listen! Isn't that the Major callin' –
In accents loud – yet cool and calm and drawlin'?
"Come on now lads – just stick at it! Stone-wallin'!
No whimpering – no whining now, no crawlin'!
Nothing's too bad for *us* – *nor* too appallin'!
It's *they* – not us – that's goin' to take the maulin'!
What's wrong with death? Adventure most enthrallin'!")'

And so on and so forth. He'd work it out properly tomorrow, but the idea was simply terrific.

Perhaps he shouldn't make it a Major, because he was a Major himself and they might think he was trying to advertise Majors and being conceited. But that could be changed tomorrow, too.

As he put his pencil and paper away and sat back in a daze of delight, Mrs Plumleigh-Bruce entered.

2

In her state of distress Mrs Plumleigh-Bruce was quite unconscious of the Major's present condition.

The Major, however, even in the dizzy mist of alcohol and military realism surrounding him, at once suspected that she was in a state of distress, and somehow pulled himself together and asked her what she would drink.

On her asking for brandy, his suspicions were confirmed, and on returning with the brandy, he asked her outright if anything was the matter.

Mrs Plumleigh-Bruce replied that well, as a matter of fact there was, quite a lot really, and that she was anxious to see Donald Stimpson. Had he been into The Friar this evening? Or did the Major know whether he was likely to be in?

To this, the Major, looking at her in an odd way, and giggling, replied, Well, no, and what with all these goings-on of his it looked as though he wouldn't be quite as regular a frequenter as usual.

The odd look, the giggle, and the curious remark were not taken in by the distraught woman.

The Major then asked if *he* could help. Come along now, what was it all about?

Then Mrs Plumleigh-Bruce, having looked at the Major, had a sudden impulse to tell a 'Man' something of the truth.

She said that it was a very long and complicated story, but the point of it was that it looked as though she had been 'done out of some money' by 'our young friend'.

'What – not young Ralph Whatsisname?' asked the Major, to which Mrs Plumleigh-Bruce had to reply Yes.

The Major then asked Where, When, How? And how *much* money?

And Mrs Plumleigh-Bruce, beginning by telling him half the truth, soon found herself telling it almost in its entirety.

In her relief at finding that the Major showed no signs of being either a prophet, an interpreter of the past, or a rhapsodist of any sort, she told him about her recent trip to

London, the house in Gilroy Road, the car, and the Joint Account.

'But why on earth a *Joint* Account?' the Major exclaimed, and before long Mrs Plumleigh-Bruce had half-confessed that she had half-contemplated marrying Ernest Ralph Gorse.

The Major saw without difficulty that this was in fact a full confession, and said that something must be done at once. He mentioned the Police, and False Pretences and all that, and went to the bar to get Mrs Plumleigh-Bruce another brandy and a large whisky for himself – as if doing this was obviously the quickest and most efficient way of getting to the Police.

But, on returning to her, the silly, excitable, but kind-hearted and in many ways sensitive maker of verses saw that Mrs Plumleigh-Bruce was in no mood either for the Police or for drinking any more brandy.

He therefore told her that she had better go home at once, and, with his aid, look at things in a new light in the morning. He would escort her home.

Mrs Plumleigh-Bruce agreed to this, and the Major, having rapidly drunk his own large whisky, as well as (in a waste-not-want-not-spirit) Mrs Plumleigh-Bruce's brandy, took her out of The Friar.

On the walk back to Sispara Road in the lamp-lit darkness Mrs Plumleigh-Bruce noticed that the Major had suddenly become very inebriated. He was, in fact, staggering – at moments reeling. But the Major's staggering and reeling were so infinitely preferable to Mrs Burford's prophesying that Mrs Plumleigh-Bruce was scarcely offended by it.

Glen Alan was reached, through dense rain, at about eight-thirty.

The house was dark, and Mary, mysteriously, was not in the house.

The Major knew exactly why Mary was not in the house, but he did not reveal his knowledge to the agonized woman. Instead he put the lights on for her, 'stoked' the fire (which was nearly in ashes) and, promising help early next morning, blundered away into the darkness and rain.

3

It was not until Mrs Plumleigh-Bruce had poured out another brandy for herself and was sitting by the slowly kindling fire, that she noticed that Mary had left a letter for her in a conspicuous place on the sitting-room table.

She thought at first that this must be a brief note explaining her servant's absence. But, on opening it, she found that it was an eleven-page letter.

Mary, though an intelligent girl, spelt and wrote so badly that Mrs Plumleigh-Bruce could hardly be bothered to read it. She simply glanced at some of its phrases, weakly trying to make some sense out of its illiterate but passionate ramblings.

> '*Left everything in Apple Pie Order Madam,*' she read, and '*would never Let you down*', and '*You have alway been So Good to me*', and '*Would never let you Down and Have left everything in Apple-Pye order I trust*', and '*He says it would be unsuitable for me to Continue under such circumstances*', and '*I hardly know wear I am*', and '*surely it would be unwise for me to refuse such an offer as I am only a poor girl and it is a chance of a lifetime I know you will agree and so do all my friends*', and '*I dred to meet You it is such a strange Contradiction in all ways*', and '*there is only a little while now*', and, finally, '*I am still your humble and obedient and devoted servant in every way and only wish to serve you and will Help out whatever he says whenever you Only ask me and I remain your*
>
> > *Respectful and gratful Servant,*
> > *Mary McGinnis*'.

It was only when Mrs Plumleigh-Bruce had at last gone to bed (and was re-reading this letter, under the silk-shaded electric light and in the comforting presence of her silken Marie Antoinette doll) that she realized that her maid Mary McGinnis had left her and would be marrying her friend Mr Donald Stimpson very shortly.

CHAPTER ONE

I

NEVER, to the end of her days, could Mrs Plumleigh-Bruce in the smallest way understand the mad event which, along with her personal tragedy, made it absolutely necessary for her to leave Reading almost at once and for ever – Mr Stimpson's marriage to her maid Mary.

But Mr Stimpson's motives were really very easy to understand.

Mr Stimpson had always, even while making love to Mrs Plumleigh-Bruce, looked on Mary in a highly libidinous way, and, on her coming to work for him, his carnal desires completely overcame him.

Then, during Mrs Plumleigh-Bruce's absence in London, Mr Stimpson made some inquiries about Gorse's whereabouts. He telephoned 21 Gilroy Road, and was told by Mrs Burford that Mr Gorse was at the Buckingham Hotel in London, and would probably be there for about a fortnight.

Then, with mounting suspicions having telephoned the Buckingham Hotel and ascertained that both Gorse and Mrs Plumleigh-Bruce were staying there, the Estate Agent had not the slightest doubt that the two were living together in the large hotel in sin – sin which, he somehow felt, would almost certainly be later redeemed by marriage.

Thus, his sudden violent carnal desires towards Mary coincided with almost equally violent desires for revenge upon Mrs Plumleigh-Bruce and Gorse.

The two things together, however, might still not have made him take the spectacular move he did, had he not, one morning, accidentally run into a journalist on a local paper, and said to him, half in joke, that he was thinking of marrying his maid, who was 'by the way, the most perfect cook in Reading or anywhere'.

The journalist sensed at once that Mr Stimpson was speaking only half in joke, and spoke of the 'wonderful story' it would make, of Mr Stimpson's delightful 'originality and courage' should he take such a step, and of the enormous publicity which he would like to give it locally.

The journalist toppled Mr Stimpson over into seeking Mary's hand in marriage. The Mr Stimpsons of life are excited almost as frantically by the idea of large local publicity as by the idea of the fulfilment of their carnal desires, or the sweetness of revenge.

2

The trouble was Mary herself.

This chronically and incurably obedient girl, shocked beyond measure by the proposal, entreated Mr Stimpson, almost on her hands and knees, not to make her do such a dreadful and ridiculous thing.

But her temporary employer and master was absolutely adamant.

With sudden proletarian fervour he himself doggedly visited and entertained Mary's many friends, and made them his supporters.

The distressed, weak Mary was told that she was missing 'a chance of a lifetime', that if she married the Estate Agent she would become a 'lady', and that she need never do a 'hand's turn' ever again. Also she could support her mother in Ireland.

Under extreme pressure from Mr Stimpson and his working-class supporters, and for the sake of her mother, Mary at last gave in.

About only one thing was she herself adamant. She was a Roman Catholic, and insisted upon being married in a Roman Catholic Church.

Mr Stimpson pleaded with Mary about this matter, but was

quite unable to shake her, and so, as rapidly as possible, he embraced the Roman Catholic faith. This caused delay, as he had to go through quite a lot of tuition and examinations about the nature of, and one's earthly obligations to, the First Cause.

But he got a lovely big picture of himself and his bride in the paper, and he soon found himself very happy in his new faith (more so than Mary) and they were, on the whole, an unusually happy couple.

This curious sort of thing is constantly happening in provincial towns.

CHAPTER TWO

I

MAJOR PARRY telephoned Mrs Plumleigh-Bruce on the morning after the evening he had seen her home in the rain, and could hardly get any sense out of a stupefied voice.

He suggested coming round, and (Mrs Plumleigh-Bruce feebly agreeing) was at Glen Alan by ten-thirty.

Mrs Plumleigh-Bruce was white, not made up, and in her Kimono.

She had wretchedly been attempting to make herself, and make herself drink and eat, some coffee and toast, and the sitting-room in which she received her guest was made even more bleak and sordid than it might have been by this scrappy unfinished meal on a tray and the dust and ashes of last night's fire.

Mrs Plumleigh-Bruce had long ago lost any ability she ever had for housework of any sort, and this morning she was, of course, quite incapable of putting up any sort of decent performance in this direction.

Mrs Plumleigh-Bruce apologized for the 'state' the place was in and explained that Mary had left her. The Major then said that he knew already that this had happened, and had only not told her last night in order not to distress her further.

'It's all the funniest business *I've* ever heard of,' said the Major. 'And I only hope they'll be happy, that's all. But I doubt it – don't you?'

'Yes. I do,' said Mrs Plumleigh-Bruce, and, the Major, seeing that Mrs Plumleigh-Bruce, who had obviously been crying a great deal, might easily cry again, changed the subject, and it was not alluded to again.

The Major, then, in duty bound, had to speak of action being taken in regard to Gorse.

Mrs Plumleigh-Bruce said that she didn't see that there was

any action to take. She had opened, of her own free will, a Joint Account with Gorse – one from which they were both permitted to draw – and so she had virtually given the money to Gorse.

Nevertheless the Major argued that it must be a case of getting money by false pretences, or something like that, and urged her to apply to the police or see a solicitor (his own) at once.

Then Mrs Plumleigh-Bruce suddenly recalled that she did not as yet know for certain that Gorse had taken any money from her, and the Major, realizing that this was not utterly impossible, said that the Bank must be telephoned; and he himself undertook to do the telephoning.

But this was a long and arduous task and one which the Major was not able to complete by himself. Before giving information the Bank required details which only Mrs Plumleigh-Bruce could provide, and she had to go to the telephone.

It was finally ascertained that the rather weird sum of £8. 3s. 11d. stood to the credit of the Joint Account of Mrs Plumleigh-Bruce and Ernest Ralph Gorse.

After this telephone call Mrs Plumleigh-Bruce broke down. She began to cry, and fled from the Major in order to conceal her tears. She was heard by him sobbing in the Study, Den, Hidey-Hole or Snuggery.

When she at last recovered she rejoined the Major in the sitting-room.

Here the Major again began to talk of resorting to the law, but Mrs Plumleigh-Bruce would still not hear of it. Everything would come *out*, she kept on repeating, everything would come *out*.

Even if there were any redress on the score of 'false pretences', or anything, she would have to explain the nature of these pretences – her folly and credulity about the house and the car, her ridiculous acceptance of Gorse's proposal of marriage, her Joint Account with him, and her stay with him in London. Imagine, she argued, how it would *look*!

Gorse was nothing more nor less than a young and possibly dangerous criminal. That was all he was. And he was a criminal of whom she was *afraid*. She said, truthfully, that she had always been a little afraid of him. And how could she, Mrs Plumleigh-Bruce, ever hold her head up again in the world if she were involved in a criminal case of *that* sort?

The Major saw that there was a lot of truth in all this, and, because she was already breaking into tears again, decided to delay pressing her any further until she was more composed.

After a while, Mrs Plumleigh-Bruce, having looked around the sordid sitting-room and at the uneaten breakfast, found her misery beginning to turn more towards the loss of Mary rather than the loss of her rich young lover, her money, and her self-respect.

She had to have *someone* to help. Who was she going to get, and how was she going to set about it?

Here the Major was at a loss, and could only suggest that his wife might help. In fact why not let his wife come round now? She could tidy up, and take charge generally, while Mrs Plumleigh-Bruce went to bed. That was where Mrs Plumleigh-Bruce certainly ought to be.

Then, Mrs Plumleigh-Bruce, in a panic, asked the Major whether he had told his wife about this.

The Major swore that he had not breathed a word of the matter to his wife. But, of course, he had told her the story in full detail last night.

Then Mrs Plumleigh-Bruce made him swear, on his sacred word of honour, that he would never tell his wife, or anyone. And the Major, rather uneasily, did this.

He then continued to urge bringing in his wife to help, and Mrs Plumleigh-Bruce at last consented.

The story to Mrs Parry was to be merely that Mrs Plumleigh-Bruce was indisposed by fearful and prolonged neuralgia, and had suddenly lost her maid during this period of suffering and practical collapse.

The Major, not being on the telephone, was unable to telephone his wife, and so was compelled to leave Mrs Plumleigh-Bruce in order to fetch her.

He was glad that he was compelled to do this, as he was thus able to explain to his wife, on the way back to Glen Alan, that his wife knew nothing about the Gorse business and that Mrs Plumleigh-Bruce was merely suffering from fearful and prolonged neuralgia and had suddenly lost her maid during this period of suffering and practical collapse.

Mrs Parry, who hated Mrs Plumleigh-Bruce as much as Mrs Plumleigh-Bruce hated her, was extremely exhilarated by the task set her, and was kindness itself to Mrs Plumleigh-Bruce.

Though rather base, Mrs Parry was not as base as Mrs Burford, and, on the strength of her exhilaration, brilliantly disguised her inner happiness.

She made Mrs Plumleigh-Bruce go to bed, brought her Bovril and toast, tidied up the sitting-room and kitchen, and set about the task (over the telephone) of getting Mrs Plumleigh-Bruce a new maid or help.

She left Mrs Plumleigh-Bruce in the afternoon to sleep with the aid of Aspirin, and she called again in the evening to cook a light meal, which Mrs Plumleigh-Bruce managed to eat.

Suitable domestic help at Glen Alan was not found until two days after this – two days in which Mrs Plumleigh-Bruce's neuralgia grew slowly better (so that she came downstairs) and in which she was visited regularly by the Major and his wife.

The Major, whenever he was (with his wife's exhilarated permission) alone with Mrs Plumleigh-Bruce, still urged action being taken about Gorse, but Mrs Plumleigh-Bruce would still not consent to this.

The Major, undoubtedly, behaved remarkably well and selflessly with Mrs Plumleigh-Bruce. This was probably because she had now lost nearly all her physical attractions in his eyes, and, with this complication gone, he was able genuinely to pity her.

She had not become less physically attractive to him because he had seen her so pale, and puffy-eyed, and slatternly and miserable. He could have looked to the future and got over that.

She had become less desirable because two other men, Gorse and Stimpson, had made it plain that they had no desire for her.

This woman was not desired, in fact, at the moment, by any man – and women, in such a pass, mysteriously lose every capacity they have for creating such desire.

Unto those who have, it shall, uncannily, be given. Unto those who have not, it shall, uncannily, be taken away.

2

Mrs Plumleigh-Bruce, despite the Major's sustained but kindly pressure, never resorted to the law about the abhorrent young man who had tricked and plundered her.

All she did was to beseech the Major somehow magically to 'hush it up', and to help her leave Reading as soon as possible.

But the Major, who had already revealed everything to his wife, was unable to hush it up.

And, with the aid of the inexhaustible Mrs Burford, who was enormously powerful locally, this strange scandal somehow reached nearly every quarter of the town and became, very nearly, a legend therein.

And Mr Stimpson's astonishing marriage to Mary (with the picture of the wedded pair in the paper) of course made matters a hundred times more fascinatingly complicated, and so worse for Mrs Plumleigh-Bruce.

Sispara Road itself was on to it very soon. Mrs Plumleigh-Bruce's next-door neighbours – the Chiropodist and the Commissioner for Oaths (living respectively at 'Rossmore' and 'Deil-ma-Care') – had been closely watching Mr Stimpson, Gorse, and the Vauxhall car coming and going for a long time; and, as soon as the news filtered through, the Chiropodist and the Commissioner (with the industrious support of their wives) spread it all along the whole row of pebble-sprayed, gnomed, brass-infested houses – from 'Rossmore' and 'Deil-ma-Care' to Strathcairn, Mon Repos and Lyndhurst – and thence to Greenways, to Grass Holme, to Colombo, to Ivydene, to Montrose, to Cranford, to 'Kismet', to Belle Vue, to 'Chez-Nous', to Champneys, to 'Wee Ben', to Seafield, to Val Rosa, to 'Ourome', to St. Alban's, to Loch Corrib, to Mansfield, Sandbourne and all the rest.

Mrs Plumleigh-Bruce was fully aware of what was going on, and, with the Major's assistance (after two months of intense suffering), at last let Glen Alan and found refuge in Worthing, Sussex.

She first of all stayed at a small hotel there, and then took over a small maisonette in the upper part of a small grey house in a small grey road from which one could walk to the Worthing sea just within ten minutes.

What Gorse had done, for about six months, improved Mrs Plumleigh-Bruce's character, manners and accent wonderfully.

But the monocled young man's fine endeavour was at last lost.

For gradually Mrs Plumleigh-Bruce began to forget her humiliation and, coming out of retirement, to sit for longer and longer periods in shelters on the sea-front at Worthing.

And there she struck up acquaintances who were all, before long, acquainted with her relationship to the General – General Sir George Matthews-Browne.

And Mrs Plumleigh-Bruce's rich, regal, mouthy, throaty, fruity, haughty and objectionable voice became a recognized noise in the wind and desolation of the hopeless and helpless sea-front.

PART FIFTEEN

COLEOPTERA

CHAPTER ONE

1

THAT afternoon Gorse, having watched Mrs Plumleigh-Bruce going off in his friend Ronald Shooter's Vauxhall car, stopped to survey her gift to him, the ravishingly new Sunbeam, and then, because he was so intoxicated by the sight of this, he did an unusual thing. He returned to the Buckingham Hotel and drank a glass of port.

He lingered over the drink, happy in the thought that he had plenty of time on his hands.

But at last, having paid his bill and having gone to the Porter's desk and asked for his luggage to be brought down from his room, he returned to the Sunbeam and drove it up in front of the great hotel. His luggage was put into the car, and he drove off.

Gorse had no exact idea as to where he was going to drive, but for some reason felt that somewhere in the middle of England would be the best and safest place for him for the time being.

Gorse found himself quite inadvertently using to himself the word 'safest', and he wondered why it had come into his head. For he had, really, no feeling of being in any way unsafe.

2

Gorse, particularly with women he was defrauding, always talked at great length and with much apparent erudition about the finer points of the 'law', but in fact he knew next to nothing about it.

In this case he was quite certain that the 'law' could in no way distress or annoy him, and he had no intention of changing his name or employing any busy devices in the way of concealment or flight.

In the first place he was confident that no proceedings would be set in motion against him by Mrs Plumleigh-Bruce. He predicted that she would take precisely the horrified and hopeless attitude that she did.

In the second place, even if she did otherwise, he was not in the smallest way afraid of any action she might take.

He was not only prepared to swear black and blue that she had given him the five hundred pounds as a present: he rather relished the idea of being called upon to do so.

In such circumstances, he felt, he would be able (as he put it to himself) to 'take it out' of the 'silly bitch' in 'no uncertain manner'.

He had, he saw – with the aid, paradoxically, of his own crime – severely compromised Mrs Plumleigh-Bruce by staying so ostentatiously with her at the Buckingham. Should she 'start anything' in regard to his crime he would be willing to swear that he had lived with her there under conditions of the extremest sexual intimacy. And he knew that the world would believe it.

The five hundred pounds with which he had bought the Sunbeam car (he would swear) had been a present for 'services rendered' to a woman more than fifteen years older than himself.

In other words, Gorse was prepared to pose as what was, in the stupid, excited late 'twenties of this century, a much more publicized and talked-about type than it is now – a *gigolo*.

Great odium, of course, was then attached to this word by the public, but Gorse was not the type to fear popular odium. He also knew that much greater shame was borne by the employer of the *gigolo* than by the *gigolo* himself – and that this was a sort of shame which Mrs Plumleigh-Bruce would be less able to endure, perhaps, than any woman in England.

In fact, he 'had her every way', so far as he could see.

Even if he was sought by the police, he thought he was not at all likely to be traced.

The car was his own, bought and paid for in an entirely straightforward and honest deal (honest, that was to say, as between himself and the dealer) in Great Portland Street. He therefore had no intention of refraining from using it, henceforth, wherever and whenever he wished. He was prepared to flaunt it.

3

Gorse, musing thus, was taking a remarkably inconsequent attitude.

If the police were active the car could in fact be traced by means of the cheque written out to the dealer, who could give its description and number. And the oaths, black and blue, which he was willing to swear about his relationship with Mrs Plumleigh-Bruce might not have stood up to keen, thorough or fierce examination.

Gorse's glass of port made him feel more inconsequent than he might have been, and as soon as he was in the Sunbeam his peace of mind became, for a character normally so alert and perspicacious, almost fatuous.

He was, perhaps, stupefied by the pleasure he took in driving his new car to nowhere in particular in the unexpectedly warm and sunny February afternoon.

The fact that he was running in a new car, which had not to be injured by being driven at a speed of more than twenty-five miles an hour, added to his sense of slow, god-like calm.

4

All this inconsequence – which he had shown, really, from the very beginning to the very end in his dealings with Mrs Plumleigh-Bruce – Gorse was never to experience again.

After this Gorse slowly lost his inconsequence. He began to think – to think before, during, and after the commission of his crimes. He became, therefore, less of an artist and less successful in his art – like a painter who nags at perfection in a picture until he is distraught, or a writer who thinks about the intricacies of meaning, grammar or syntax until he nearly goes mad.

Too much thought is bad for the soul, for art, and for crime. It is also a sign of middle age, and Gorse was one who had to pay for the precocity of his youth in the most distasteful coin of premature middle age.

CHAPTER TWO

1

GORSE, driving slowly to nowhere in particular in the middle of England, thought of himself as very much the master of himself and of his car. But he was the deluded victim of both – particularly of his car.

In his attitude toward his car, though, he was not making an error in any way peculiar to himself. It was one shared by the owners of the multitudes upon multitudes of other cars which he met or which overtook him on his way.

For it was just about at this period that these vehicles, so strongly resembling beetles if seen from the air, finally took complete control of the country, the countryside, the villages, the roads, the towns and the entire lives of the human beings who dwelt or moved therein.

Gorse was, one might say, on that sunny February afternoon, driving unconsciously not into the middle of England – but into the middle of the hideous Land of Coleoptera (the rather sinister name for beetles used by serious students of insects).

2

When Gorse was born, in 1903, these machines were not distinguishable as Coleoptera. They were rare, explosive, laughably crude and high in stature, constantly breaking down, and objects resembling, on the whole, absurd and lovable grasshoppers rather than beetles.

But slowly, as they multiplied, they changed their shape and greedily clung closer to the earth which they were at first merely to infest but at last completely overrun.

By the time Gorse had reached his majority they were recognizable as beetles.

There were large, stately, black beetles – small, red, dashing (almost flying) beetles – and medium-sized grey, blue, white, brown, yellow, green, orange, cream, maroon, and black, black, black and again black-beetles.

Soon after Gorse's majority the beetles got into a great state of confusion. They began to run into and seriously obstruct each other.

Because of this there was a sort of beetle-revolution – a battle not between beetles and beetles but between beetles and men. In this rather bloody revolution the beetles demanded, and succeeded in easily obtaining, from men, what they considered justice and order for themselves.

Men, having surrendered unconditionally, set to work (not unlike the unhappy builders of the Pyramids) laboriously and carefully to satisfy the demands of their crawling yet pitilessly exacting new rulers. The beetles were not magnanimous in victory.

Vast new roads had to be made for the convenience or pleasure of the beetles; open spaces were set aside for them in the smaller towns in the country; and in the larger towns the most complicated buildings (in which the beetles, when seeking rest, could dive underground or go spirally upwards to floor upon floor) were erected.

Thus there in due course appeared a vast slave-army, spread all over the country, of harassed but sedulous attendants upon beetles.

There were beetle-physicians, beetle-hospitals, beetle-nurses, beetle-feeders (by means of tubes), beetle-washers, beetle-oilers, beetle-watchers, and beetle-guides.

The watchers and guides were sternly made to wear smart uniforms and to salute any passing beetle; and, in private houses, beetles were given private bedrooms, in which if the weather was cold, they were solicitously covered with rugs.

There were tens of thousands of men who spent many hours of the day (or night) lying supinely underneath beetles and examining their greasy intestines by the light of torches.

All this went, not inexcusably, to the heads of the conquering race. They multiplied further, took further advantage of the conquered, and went further afield.

Dizzy with success – doctored, nursed, fed, washed, oiled,

watched, guided – they entered into a mad round of dissolute pleasure. They went to race-meetings, tennis-tournaments, theatres, horse-shows, dog-races, golf-tournaments and so on and so forth.

In these open-air places (at golf-tournaments for instance) they bore an ugly resemblance to swarming bees. And in such swarms they still got into frantic muddles and obstructed each other – Ford arguing with Hillman, Alfa-Romeo with Bentley, Swift with Sunbeam, Talbot with Wolseley, Alvis with Buick, Cadillac with Fiat, Essex with Chrysler, Hispano-Suiza with Citroën, Austin with Bean, Daimler with Hupmobile, Lagonda with Lincoln, Morris-Cowley with Humber, Morris-Oxford with Studebaker, Vauxhall with Triumph, Standard with Riley, Packard with Singer, Rover with Bugatti, Star with Beardmore, Rolls Royce with Armstrong Siddeley, and Peugeot with Invicta – to say nothing of obscure conflicts between the Amilcar, Ansaldo, Arrol-Aster, Ascot, Ballot, Beverley Barnes, Brocklebank, Calthorpe, Charron, Chevrolet, Delage, Delahaye, Erskine, Excelsior, Franklin, Frazer-Nash, Gillett, Gwynne, Hotchkiss, Hudson, Imperia, Italia, Jordan, Jowett, Lanchester, Lancia, Marmon, Mercedes, Opel, Overland-Whippet, Panhard-Levassor, Peerless, Renault, Rhode, Salmson, Stutz, Trojan, Turner, Unic, Vermorel, Vulcan, Waverley and Willys-Knight.

But there their slaves were, exhausting themselves in giving them intricate but necessarily bawled instructions as to the manner in which they might extricate themselves from their difficulties. (Beetles were always and still are very bad and slow at going backwards.)

In the nightmare of Coleoptera only two sorts of beetle retained any dignity or charm. These – the lumbering Omnibus and Lorry – were very large, very helpful and for the most part smooth-tempered. Furthermore they killed men, women and children very little. (All the other beetles had begun to kill men, women and children at a furiously increasing pace – practically at random.)

3

Gorse, then, whose whole character and aspect were, really, of a very beetly kind, knew as little of what he was doing as of where he was going.

(In fact he ended up that day in a medium-sized Commercial Hotel in Nottingham.)

Other beetle-owners (that is to say, beetle-slaves) who overtook or met Gorse on his way, at least knew where they were immediately going, and had a very rough unconscious idea as to their ultimate destination on this planet. They imagined that they would one day, having worn their lives out in beetle-service, die, more or less painfully and slowly, in bed. And most of them did.

But the red-haired Gorse – the reddish, reddish-moustached, slightly freckled beetle-driver, driving slowly into the era of the all-conquering beetles, did not have even this trivial advantage in unconscious foreknowledge.

For he was to die painlessly and quickly. And he was not to do this in bed.

THE END